Advance praise for Jacqueline deMontravel and
Escape from Bridezilla

"Jacqueline deMontravel's writing shimmers and the wit
doesn't relent. Emily Briggs does it again, entertaining us with
all of her quirks, madcap adventures and trying to stay grounded
in a wedding-challenged environment."
—Darcy Miller, author of *Our Weddings* and editor of
Martha Stewart Living Weddings

And praise for *The Fabulous Emily Briggs*

"You will smile knowingly and burst out in giggles all the
way through this smart, snappy novel!"
—Melissa Senate, author of *See Jane Date* and
The Solomon Sisters Wise Up

"Jacqueline de Montravel's *The Fabulous Emily Briggs* is a beautiful book. A book that conjures up the Manhattan of our
dreams, the Manhattan of today—full of Häagen-Dazs and errant mothers, longing and call waiting, early morning runs
around the Reservoir and Manolo Blahniks. A terrific read that
explores the endless possibilities between men and women. I
loved it."
—Pamela Clarke Keogh, author of *Audrey Style*
and *Jackie Style*

"This book has an appealing mix of career ups and downs
and romantic entanglements, as well as a very likable protag-
onist and wonderful dialogue."
—*Romantic Times*

Books by Jacqueline deMontravel

THE FABULOUS EMILY BRIGGS

ESCAPE FROM BRIDEZILLA

Published by Kensington Publishing Corporation

ESCAPE FROM BRIDEZILLA

JACQUELINE deMONTRAVEL

KENSINGTON BOOKS
www.kensingtonbooks.com

KENSINGTON BOOKS are published by

Kensington Publishing Corp.
850 Third Avenue
New York, NY 10022

All Kensington titles, imprints and distributed lines are available at special quantity discounts for bulk purchases for sales promotion, fund-raising, educational or institutional use.

Special book excerpts or customized printing can also be created to fit specific needs. For details, write or phone the office of the Kensington Special Sales Manager: Kensington Publishing Corp., 850 Third Avenue, New York, NY 10022. Attn. Special Sales Department. Phone: 1-800-221-2647.

ISBN 0-7582-0841-3

First Kensington Trade Paperback Printing: February 2005
10 9 8 7 6 5 4 3 2 1

Printed in the United States of America

1

"Let's do it."

This was how Henry said it to me. Delivered from behind the screen of the *Times* travel section as we finished our Sunday morning just-used-up-my-calorie-count-for-the-month brunch at Silver Spurs diner. I wore sweats, glorified by the trendy label branded on my butt, while Henry had on the same sweater as the captain on a fish box.

This was how Henry said it to me? The most recounted story of your lifetime. Sitting, surrounded by a moat of grandchildren, the first stitch to crochet their impressions of love and romance I'd have to narrate would be this? I'd lie. Already thinking of stories to deceive my unborn progeny.

"Do what?" I asked, my tone pressuring Henry to take an alternative route.

"Get married!"

This was when it became a bit problematic.

"Is this some kind of joke? Are you asking me to marry you over frittatas and coffee with free refills at Silver Spurs? What? Were you just inspired from some godforsaken Nike ad? You did get a new pair of sneakers yesterday. Were you like 'I'll take the Air Icarus and, now that I think about it, just go ahead and ask Emily to marry me!'"

The *Times* slipped from his grasp, now jumbled in peaks and clefts from draping the used tableware. Henry's body slumped against the window; the lighting swayed from the late morning shadows punched by traffic activity outside; a curious reflection worked upon him.

Impassive. Perhaps he had a trace of curiosity. I couldn't quite tell, nor did I really care to know. The important fact being that this was standard Henry Philips to Emily Briggs freak-out behavior. His ability to remain composed when I had one of my minor outbursts, how he never found the need to scold me on these occasional overreactions, or to offer a few pointers on how to better control my soft lapses of verbalized irritation, something others have unsuccessfully attempted, may be why Henry had made it to this point.

It had proven to be a valuable skill of his, this facility to tune me out, which pleased me immensely. Gave me the license to be as ridiculous as I was able and not crucified as a result. That I never had to give some schmaltzy apology with promises of sexual favors later. (He'd get those regardless.)

Henry also had the good sense not to ask me as I took a swig from my decaf hazelnut, saving him and our neighboring diners from being pelted by my coffee-tainted spit. That would have been very rude of me, not to mention gross.

Exhaustedly, I took a ladylike sip from my decaf hazelnut.

"Sure, why not? I'll marry you."

I couldn't be happier, though I had no idea how Henry took it.

2

I made a pact with myself ages before I even had a boyfriend. That if some higher being from above did intend on my living with someone other than dogs or misfit family members and actually making this solemn in-sickness-and-in-health promise—whatever that meant—I made this internal pact that I would not become one of those "Wedding Girls." Turn into the dreaded "Bridezilla." The bride that floated past the sundial movements of flowered heads toward a groom who successfully fulfilled his given task by showing up.

I wouldn't be that girl that bought all of the bridal magazines minutes after the proposal. (Though I did buy a few, seven actually, this morning. Just a day after Henry proposed and that was only because it was a Monday, newsstand day, so naturally I just had to pick them up. Quite standard really—precisely the same thing as buying a Fodor book before a trip. Though I've never been one for travel books, as that's too touristy.)

I'd never turn into the Bridezilla that plunged her freshly ringed finger into her bag for her mobile, speed-dialing all of her friends and family, sharing the news while her future husband drummed his utensils on the linen-clothed table. (I didn't have my cell and the table was Formica.)

I wouldn't obsess over the date. (Mentally set for the weekend

after Labor Day, as I have been tracking the weather patterns for
the weekend after Labor Day for the past six years and every Saturday has been positively perfect. There was one rainy day, but it
was just for a few twilight hours where the drops fell from the most
glorious lavender sky feathered with brushes of rose. And why had I
been tracking weather patterns for the past six years for this particular weekend? Perhaps we should consider the peculiar people who
went to such extremes as installing computer chips in the back of a
bird's neck.)

I wouldn't obsess in searching for distinctive party favors and
bubbles in sterling containers with a baby blue toile ribbon. And I
absolutely would not become completely manic over my dress. My
cousin Anne Briggs-Whitten had that covered, since we were related
and I had insider intelligence for her penchant for matching poly-
ester Izod outfits and how she never swam in the deep end with excuses of delicate eardrums. Anne married for professional reasons,
and this was her area.

In some ways, I could look to her services as a comparable exchange for my introducing her to Jason, her husband most likely
chosen for his high earning factor by working in the financial sec-
tor. The added bonus, to Anne's delighted discovery, was the hidden
fortune generated from a wallpaper design Jason had created when
fulfilling his service in his father's home distribution company.

The wallpaper pattern, a pale blue ticking stripe bordered with a
beaded edging like sugar dollops on a wedding cake, used to add
flair to antiseptic rooms seen in hospital corridors and the reception
nook of a nationwide tax office. Each order of his paper earned
him the kind of royalties more associated with failed musicians who
write pull-the-trigger tunes played when a baseball player hits a
home run.

They met through me, though I would never do something as ir-
responsible as intentionally match my cousin with another human, especially someone as warm and good-natured as Jason—destined to
be the kind of man who calls boys who aren't related to him "son."
Introduced at one of New York's benefits that bring out all the professional husband hunters, their courtship progressed into marriage
with the easy process of buying presents with computerized shopping
carts.

She now lavishes expertly, a self-described sybarite. (Anne practices new words like a boy with a new golf club.) I've seen her go through caviar like sandwich spread. She puts together Botox parties with friends like it's a lunch at Pastis. Her most recent addition to this sybaritic lifestyle being the Palm Beach home, so massive you have to drop crackers to find your way around. And though they've yet to even spend a night there, *HG* already shot their gardens with a year exclusive to feature their pond brimming with human-sized lily pads that guide you over exotic fish that swim to the water's surface at the brush of your hand and suck on your finger like a baby's lips on a pacifier.

Anne had already made appointments for Vera Wang, Badgley & Mischka and Valentino—and Bergdorf's, of course. Had to remember to call Anne and make sure that we had an appointment at Bergdorf's, as they carried the most beautiful Carolina Herrera georgette silk, drop waisted, cap-sleeved gown that I found while glancing at one of my bridal magazines.

The location was the easy part—to be held at my childhood summer home in Bridgehampton.

"Bridgehampton is out," barked my mother, sticking out her cheek to interrupt me from the mental lists I had been composing while waiting in her kitchen.

Did she just say that Bridgehampton was out? Okay. *I am not one of those Wedding Girls,* I said like a mantra.

"What the hell do you mean Bridgehampton is out? It's not the Plaza for God's sake."

"Oh yes. The Plaza. I have a date secured for the second Saturday in November, which makes perfect sense. Seven months to plan a wedding is purely preposterous. And I do think it is far more elegant to have an autumn city wedding."

Why doesn't she just rent a supermodel daughter and have her perform the wedding to her specifications, as she had essentially been autopiloting her parenting of me for the past thirty years.

Mother took the seat next to mine and reached for a magazine from her stack of bridal publications and books. Flipping through the magazines with that these-pages-are-so-privileged-to-be-graced-by-her-touch manner of hers, Mom started in, "I'm afraid that the house will still be rented through the end of October."

My family—the all-American 2.4-kid kind with a father, mother, and brother who happened to be more than twenty years younger than me—had just returned to the city after spending a year in Prague, where my father had expanded his company. They kept their East Eighty-fourth Street townhouse and rented out the Bridgehampton home, which had been of no inconvenience to me since I had to spend most of last summer in L.A. working on a film Henry and I created based on our cartoon alter egos.

Henry is a cartoonist and I am an illustrator. Or, more precisely, was an illustrator. After a year working in Hollywood, I had taken an early retirement from my drawing career to focus strictly on my painting. I am more about my art than the art of furthering my career through shallow measures, now allowing for Henry—the now provider, which I think I will enjoy immensely—to maintain this high earning necessity to keep our family robust. He also works the Hollywood hustle brilliantly, his I-won't-drop-to-their-level unintentional game plan playing to his advantage. I will now be much happier as a result, my happiness being the contribution to our family.

I peered at my mother, amazed by how beautiful she could remain despite her persnickety demeanor. She was the kind of woman that would look natural sipping in smoke from a sterling cigarette holder. (Though she quit smoking in '86 for fear of yellowing her teeth.)

Her classic sense of style and devotion to exercises that come with a spiritual philosophy like it's a gift bag after a great party have prevented her from having a consultation with a surgeon who makes line drawings on your face. She had the refined bone structure of a doe without that stretched like Silly Putty skin, which had always amazed me because I didn't know if I was the little kid calling the emperor on his new, nonexistent clothes, as these women really do look like a Batman villain.

Catching something of interest to her in one of the bridal magazines, she reached for a pair of heavy rimmed circular glasses that looked like two black condoms secured with a curved piece of wire. With her crisp cotton shirt, cashmere cardigan, and gray flannel pants, she was either dressing for a Harry Potter party or recently took fashion inspiration from FDR.

"Apparently your father stands to make a substantial return just by extending the rental for the month of September. And there's another caveat you should know. The house is on the market."

She has got to be kidding me.

"You've got to be kidding me!"

"No love, I'm afraid I'm not. We don't use the house anymore, now that we spend summers in Europe."

She says this like she's fired her longtime florist because they stopped using frosted vases.

"Don't look so expired."

"This is beyond tragic. I'm devastated. What a bad day. Michael Jackson at his sentencing bad day."

"Stop being so melodramatic. We have great options, and I've already secured Maidstone, Wolffer Vineyards and, as mentioned, there's always the Plaza."

"But I don't want to get married on some herringbone parquet floor where guests get real psyched to do the electric slide or get my dress dusted from saying my vows in the middle of a grape field. I don't even like wine—I'm more of a vodka girl. I want to get married in my house. What's the point of having a childhood home if it won't be properly commemorated, sold just before I get married?"

I thought of Jackie (Jacqueline Bouvier, more specifically).

"Like Hammersmith."

"We need to hammer what?"

"Hammersmith! Where Jacqueline and John F. Kennedy were married."

"You are such the dreamer."

My mother just then patted me on the head. Like a dog. Which happened to come yapping into the kitchen. A pug with an alarming nasal infection moved toward me with the waddle of a fair-skinned tourist after their first day in the Galapagos and missed patch of sunblock behind his knees.

This pug approached me or, more precisely, my foot and fell instantly in lust.

"What the hell is this?" I asked, toeing it off me unsuccessfully.

"That's Mao, part of Oliver's package to return back to New York."

Package? Oliver, my younger brother, had the life of a GE CEO before the days of Enron.

"And don't get too attached, darling. I am just testing Mao out."

"Testing him out? He's not an espresso machine."

Just then, Mao took a break from violating my leg to give a few sneezes and a burp.

"Then again, he certainly sounds like an espresso machine," I said, watching him return to his conquest.

"Mom, can you please tell *Mao* to ease up on the PDA. What's he on? Doggie Viagra? Can't you get him some dog dildo?"

"Emily. You know fine and well that an animal of ours would never display PDA," she said, enunciating key words. She then tried shooing him with little flutters of her hand not strong enough to whisk away a dusty gnat.

"Besides," she started in with that matter-of-fact way of hers, "you're entirely not his type. Completely wrong for him."

"Right. Of course. Possibly because I've had my allergy shots this season." I extended my legs to create a slingshot, clamped Mao and centered him, deeming him a pellet that I thrust across the room, successfully splattering this blobby pug against the prewar concrete wall. His skinny legs extended from his paunchy belly like a shocked Humpty Dumpty just as he was about to fall.

This made me laugh.

"Oh, Emily!" Mom scolded. "Oh, Mao!" she cried. Mother ran over to Mao, tending to him like he was her slain war hero. The image made for an unusual picture of one of those Fabio-covered romance novels, painted by the same velvet canvas artist who brought you the dogs smoking cigars while playing pool.

She was stroking his fur and whispering soothing words into his ear, so now the dog and younger brother in this family had garnered more of my mother's maternal instinct than her firstborn. I've entertained the idea of being illegitimate, searching for the man that delivered our mail in the early seventies to seek a paternity test.

"This is ridiculous," I huffed. "And why not get a real dog, the kind that doesn't come with hidden costs from the thousand-dollar carrier cases and jeweled chokers? You're not getting all Auntie Peg on me."

Auntie Peg was the great-auntie who will never cease to exist. Darkening the festive mood of a holiday gathering with the obligatory ten-minute chitchat, trying to remain composed by her automated reply of "as long as you like it, dear." Seated in her mobile armchair, a tartan blanket draped on her lap and a swarm of pugs that nipped about the tassels of her blanket like misbehaved children.

"Please don't compare me to Auntie Peg, darling, that's extremely inconsiderate."

I found it interesting that Auntie Peg had the power to penetrate the hierarchical rungs set in my mother's self-absorption.

"I'm off to the museum," I snipped.

"The museum?"

"Yes. A public institution exhibiting paintings and other works of art."

"Why, Emily, you couldn't very well go to the museum dressed like that."

I looked down to evaluate my appearance in a chiffon blouse with a cross wrap, gray pants with camel pinstripes, and a suede coat with fur trim.

"Um?"

"Emily, just look at your shoes," she said, saying "shoes" like it was the name of the scandalous gossip target of the day.

I peered down at my just-violated toe, which had on a brown suede Puma with an orange stripe.

"I'm not going to the Costume Institute ball. I'm just getting in a bit of the arts. Since when did the museum have a dress code?"

But this was useless. I was speaking to a woman who still wore a navy blazer, ballroom gloves and Ferragamo bowed shoes every time she traveled on a commercial flight. She honored a past time when manners showed your status better than the limited edition LV bag bought after your name was crossed from a waiting list. Mom, skilled in bar car-chatter, versed in the kind of social skills where the hostess mingled with her guests while holding a tray of stuffed artichokes.

"And, Emily, we must discuss the wedding. The wedding!"

With that said, I lifted myself from my chair, gave Mao an apologetic scratch behind his ear where he returned the affection with a lick to my face (the animal was truly infatuated), a peck to my mother's cheek as she gets kissed, never kisses, and walked out of the house with no regard to her curious rumbles that trailed me.

Feeling insecure about my sneakers, I decided to forego the Met for a little window indulging. I walked along Madison, passing the display booth boutiques with storefronts peddling clothes propped on invisible silhouettes in the same positions featured in the shopping pages of the fashion magazines. I zigzagged through other walkers in congested midtown. Looked up as the buildings stretched to the sky while we clambered at their base.

I passed the imperious lions that guard the New York Public Library, walked under the shadowed gleams of the Chrysler. Chose the left breach imposed by the Flatiron and stopped to buy an apple at the farmer's market in Union Square. With the sustenance gained from chomping on a picked-from-Amish-hands piece of fruit, feeling quite wholesome and cleansed with proletarian ethics, I finished off the last leg of my city walk to Henry's apartment, which I've casually pitched as my primary residence for the past few months—living in the proverbial sin before giving my housing situation the loaded "living together" label.

Walking down East Twelfth, and if you ever assumed that a pigeon pecking in the middle of a street would be able to fly to safety from a mad city cab driver, you haven't lived in New York, where cabbies literally pencil in road kills on that chit you assumed recorded passenger fares. I had to quickly look away when I saw that this particular fatality had trampled more than a few feathers.

Slowing my pace, Tide-scented air puffed from the basement grates of an apartment complex, slapping my ankles with that unbalanced wave of humidity you feel after stepping outside an overly air-conditioned office building. As I approached my favorite townhouse, I became exhilarated, faintly making out the owner exiting the red-painted door like a diver swimming to surface. She closed the door too quickly for me to look inside. Her dog, more appropriate for the Moors with a few ducks stuffed in its mouth, poked his muzzle in sensitive areas until she snapped a few commands in Italian. He retreated, sat and looked at her obediently until she shouted the name of a pasta sauce to switch him back on. The dog clearly understood Italian. I didn't know Italian. In some ways, this dog was more intelligent than me.

Reaching the apartment, I had somehow forgotten about the

paper trail of torn magazine pages I had left in the kitchen. Henry's nose focused on the page that had been given the highest honor, fridge door placement. It was a picture of the most perfect butt, an extreme close-up shot barely clad in boy-cut Eres turquoise bottoms and a few specks of sand.

"Let me guess," mused Henry. "This is your way of telling me that you're a lesbian."

I walked over to the refrigerator door to give the picture a closer inspection. It was truly the most spectacular piece of butt I had ever seen. A woman's body, when perfect, blew away a male physique of rock star *Rolling Stone* cover proportions.

"Possibly," I said easily. "In a repressed kind of way. But the original idea was to achieve that butt, causing guilt of extreme portions every time I opened that door for an unnecessary scoop of Ben & Jerry's Chocolate Fudge Brownie. Lowfat."

Henry opened the freezer door so it gave a lip-smacking suction, pulling out the very container of ice cream I had been trying to avoid—it was frozen yogurt, to be specific, but I had my suspicions of the labeling as semantic marketing.

"I love your butt," he said, slapping my butt. "Now get two teaspoons and let's polish this thing off."

Which seemed a great idea in theory, but I was surprised that Henry had not been aware that the container was considerably light, absent in its contents aside from a teaspoonful left (a ploy one uses so you could soothe yourself by saying you were not a fully grown, oinking pig because you didn't actually finish the entire pint), having been devoured after a night of looking at magazines, feeling inadequate with myself and resorting to the comfort of Ben & Jerry's.

Henry peeled off the lid, his lips breaking into a supercilious smirk as he must have made a mental visual of my actions last night.

"Hmm." I poked my head in the container. "The maid did it."

"Maid my ass, or, truthfully, it's your ass that's in question here."

I gave Henry a wounded princess look.

"And speaking of this ass," he said, scrutinizing the picture on the fridge. "I think I know her."

"Know her? Right. Of course. People are now recognized by their butt cheeks."

"No. Really!" he laughed. "That's Carmenia's butt. You remember Carmenia, she's that Brazilian, or is it Argentinean? That model that dated Gil Stephens."

Gil Stephens was one of the FOX producers whom Henry and I, now strictly Henry, worked with.

"You see that raisin-shaped mole?" Henry pointed to a mole, indeed the size and shape of a raisin, just under the fold of her right cheek. My fiancé was touching a woman's butt—the most perfect butt on the planet. The boy was basically committing adultery before my eyes.

"Henry!" I scolded, swatting his index finger away from Carmenia's butt. "This is wrong on so many levels. First, I don't like you ass-picking Carmenia so brazenly before me, and then why? How could you identify this glorified freckle? You must have been doing some hard-core poolside scanning to pick up that blemish."

"Oh, Emily."

I've clocked in a lot of "Oh, Emilys" today.

"Carmenia's mole is to butt like Cindy's mole is to upper lip," Henry said as if reading from a legal document. "She had it surgically attached so she could 'make her mark' in the butt modeling business, so to speak."

I then swiped Carmenia's butt off the fridge and threw it into the garbage.

"She's trash," I said, feeling like the last unwanted squished cupcake at the end of a bake sale.

Henry opened up his arms. I had the vague impression that my body was meant to be folded into the vee he created. But I am completely uninterested in being all sweet and cuddly based on my current agitated state. His stare acted as beams, magnetizing me into his outstretched arms.

"Listen, Emily. We need to discuss our living arrangements."

"But. But. But."

"But what? Emily, you really must get your mind out of the trash—though Carmenia's butt does have that effect."

Oh, for God's sake—enough with Carmenia's butt, which had about as much artificial padding as my first bra (I was a late bloomer, very self-conscious back then).

"Seriously Em, now that you're painting and with us doing the big marriage thing, it's time we stopped living like VW Vanagon drifters. L.A. one month, my post-grad apartment a few months. We need to put down our roots. Get a warm, sunny place that we can grow with."

"You sound like a tour guide at the Botanical Gardens."

"I was thinking SoHo or TriBeCa—a loft perhaps. So I've made some appointments for us, tomorrow at four."

"Four?"

"Four."

I began to think of the day I had planned—buying new canvases, brushes, and supplies with no place to put them. The calls to potential wedding locations, planners, and did I want ecru invitations with a Palatino typeface or white with Caslon Open face? Should I get a personal trainer or just do an added workout from my *Buns of Steel* tape?

"Emily—no buts. And no butts!"

But?

3

Arising a few hours earlier than usual, I headed straight for my newly purchased box of Frosted Flakes. I was very excited about this, getting up a few times last night hoping it would be morning so I could have breakfast, only to notice that, while it was still dark outside and not because we were still in March, there were hours to go before I'd break open that new box.

I've been going through a sugary cereal phase, with kid-tested mother-approved choices so that my breakfast would not be completely deficient of the essential vitamins and nutrients I needed for a balanced day. Choosing cereals like Kix and Frosted Flakes over Fruit Loops and Lucky Charms. (I am also an avid reader of cereal boxes.)

As a kid, my mother had acted as Lady Capulet to my love affair with Cap'n Crunch, not allowing me to have him because she put this in the "junk" category. Now that I've broken through the bondage of eating based on parental consent, perhaps I'd reacquaint myself with this unrequited love. Do they still even make Cap'n Crunch? Panic. Could it be—Cap'n Crunch was no more? Completely tragic. Considering that I'd most likely be seen in the comedy section of a video store over tragedy, I quickly laid to rest any remorse over Cap'n Crunch's untimely demise and reminded myself how lucky I was to have Tony.

Tony the Tiger had always been in such good spirits—possibly from all of those fortified vitamins and minerals. And after all these years, he hasn't gone through the protean transformations as other noted spokespersons. He must have had the same fitness trainer as Dick Clark. Tony was the kind of cover model that I found especially welcoming in my current mood.

I poured myself a bowl, sliced up some bananas, added the milk, and began inhaling my breakfast. Twirling the box around for something to read besides another bridal magazine that would only underline how unprepared and ineffective I was in my wedding duties, I became thrilled upon finding a game of logic—promoted as an intelligence test used from the days of Mesopotamia.

The questions were written in grape over a golden pyramid with two sphinxes bordering the edges; the geometric puzzles gave it a hieroglyphic feel. Now this was why I really loved kid cereal, for the fun games that I could ace, giving me a strong dose of self-confidence before I began my day. Clever marketing from the team at Kellogg's. I should really send them a note.

My preoccupation with the game eclipsed my former bliss of eating my cereal. The first question showed numbers that clung to the sides of differently colored triangular peaks like clouds to a mountain. I had to figure the missing number on the last one. Moving to the next problem, as these games always began with a harder question to show it involved some mental exercise, this question had a few boxes with various lines crossed in them where I needed to choose the shape that didn't belong. Figuring that they were all in the same color, I picked the one with too many lines, as that did not appear to be as symmetrical and harmonious in that Mondrian way. Mondrian would have chosen box "D." The next question, I had to apply the same logic but with triangles—very simple, almost too easy, as it had the same properties as the earlier question. Lazy people, these Mesopotamians, the messy one naturally got my nix.

Then I read the answers and tallied my score so I could be reminded of how brilliant I was.

Okay. But perhaps if I just retook the exam now that I understood the questions. I mean they really weren't written all that clearly.

This game was purely ridiculous.

Okay. I am stupid and have a giant butt.

Hearing the phone, I glanced at the microwave clock illuminated in neon—8:36 AM. The caller was my mother, as warned by the brilliant invention of caller ID, ranking right below the electric toothbrush and Dustbuster. Considering that calls this early have familial latitude, I resolved to remove all bad karma at once and picked up the phone rather than have the machine be victimized by the rant of her voice-mail therapy.

"Emily, darling," she said, her tone more in sync with an alpha wife than a submissive homemaker, which caused me to fumble the phone out of nervousness until the droop of Henry's pajama sleeve skimmed my coffee, the stain creeping up the cotton fibers igniting an alternate anxiety.

"Oh, for God's sake!" I shrieked, turning on the faucet to soak the sleeve under the running water.

"Emily, you really should control your anger. Here I am, calling you in the most cheerful manner with the most divine news. Perhaps I should just catch up with you at another time after you've dealt with your repressed issues."

"Sorry, Mom. It's just that I spilled coffee on Henry's pajamas."

"My goodness, is he all right? You know about that woman who sued McDonald's because the coffee was so hot it burned her. She should be embarrassed for herself."

"McDonald's coffee? Lawsuits? What are you talking about?"

"Well, Emily, dear, it really isn't polite to spill coffee on your fiancé."

As opposed to someone else?

"Mom, I'm wearing Henry's pajamas."

"Excuse me!"

I could just picture her horrified expression—think eyes popping out of their sockets on bouncy coils, tongue sticking out, and flecks of sweat popping from her head—after imagining that Henry and I do indeed sleep together.

"And you really should attend to the stain before it sets in. There was this program on that home and garden channel with this crafty lady who used vinegar water. A Portuguese woman, from . . ." She paused, and I heard the snap of her fingers so she could jog her memory.

"From Portugal?"

"Precisely!

"And you should check out the Intimates Section at Barney's. They have the most lovely nightgowns. Proper sleepwear. Especially important now that you will be a married woman. No more pajamas. Lingerie, darling. That's how you keep your man from straying. And if he does stray, at least you'll find out from the relationships you will cultivate with the lingerie shops. That's how Mrs. Coleman found out Charles was cheating. The sales help at LaPerla ratted on him after selling him a thong that wasn't in her size. Mrs. Coleman would never wear a thong—that's an under-40 piece."

If you ever sat in on one of my mother's lunches, these were the kind of topics getting the heavy play, even during a national crisis of sending U.S. troops proportions.

"Didn't you mention you had some news to share? I believe you even said 'most divine news'?"

"Oh, right! I am giving you and Henry an early wedding present."

Present! The most divine word.

"Mom, that's really unnecessary, with all of your help in the planning," I said, lying.

"Don't be preposterous, take everything that you can get—from me and everyone, darling. Now, as you know it's been a sort of family tradition to have our wedding portraits done. Your great-grandparents on my side, both your grandparents, and your father and I have all had our wedding portraits painted. As you know, your granny even sat for Sargent."

That had been a striking mark on my mother's docket, that her mother was painted by John Singer Sargent. No matter how badly Oliver or I screwed up, at least we had lineage, and this painting secured evidence to prove the impressive bloodline.

These wedding portraits all hung in the Traditional Room, the one room in the house that had never undergone a makeover from one of my mother's decorating whims. From Hampton to Hagan, she had about as many renovation incarnations as Britney had publicity stunts. But in the Traditional Room, you experience the sort of time travel one would have when visiting Graceland, without the kitsch and with more chintz. There are hand-me-down works of art, porcelain knickknacks of fooffy dogs, and a pincushioned couch upholstered in my mother's family plaid, which has the misfortune of hues in an appalling brown, green, and yellow (though she did look into changing the pattern, apparently forbidden by the plaid people).

Really she should just will those things to Oliver, as I'd auction them off and use the cash toward one blowout year of living the rock-star life. Travel, hotels, and fun restaurants for 365 days of carefree existing that no descendant would ever be able to match with all of their maintenance of a respectable, genteel life. Collecting inanimate luxuries with curatorial discernment only so they could be passed down and remembered through some silver teapot whose only use was holding a bundle of calla lilies for that John Pawson meets Shabby Chic effect.

Mother added, clearly impressed with herself, "I found a wonderful discovery. He lives in Brooklyn, but apparently has a studio in SoHo."

The SoHo studio legitimized the Brooklyn part, I gathered.

"This Linus Heller," she continued, "he painted the Lowell sisters and is just finishing up Autumn Benson's portrait, having time to fit you and Henry in!"

"Okay. Let's slow down here. First off, you know how uncomfortable I feel when having to pose, even for getting my passport picture taken. I'm reduced to a gerbil being stared down by a python. And as sure as I am that this Linus guy is quite talented, his painting Summer and all, I just don't think Henry and I have the time right now. With his work, finding a new place—the wedding! Sitting around to have some foppish artist who gets his gigs because his mother plays bridge with women who have a day of beauty every day, it just seems an indulgent expenditure of our time."

"Oh, Emily, you're being quite the prima donna. 'Indulgent expenditure of time'? You go for one sitting. He takes a snapshot of the two of you and finishes the rest on his time. How hard can that be? And now that you're not working anymore."

And so it began. After making the declaration that I would follow my calling as an artist, Mother interpreted this as "she's seen our side." Will never earn the income to match her lifestyle, ready to start a family, and mingle with Chapin moms so her daughters will be invited to all the right birthday parties. Being an artist was just some label to a nebulous career, like her vocation: "Catherine Briggs—Not For Profit Fundraiser." She has the business cards.

Tic-tac-toe, I said to myself, which is what I do when I didn't want to become entangled in a conversation with my mother that no one would win.

"Why can't you at least meet with Linus? Or perhaps just find an artist of your choosing?"

Hmm. I walked over to the kitchen junk drawer to retrieve my Smythson business planner, which I had bought especially for organizing all my meetings with gallery owners, clients who wanted to commission pieces from me, etc. The only entry: a lunch with Daphne, my best friend, to discuss painting her children, who happened to be named Henry and Emily.

Here this Linus character received all of the profile work from being on Harrison and Shriftman's PR list, one of those boys that could wear jeans bought from Scoop.

My face began to boil with irritation.

"Here's my proposal," I commanded. "I will paint the picture. You don't have to pay me unless you have some kind of deadline, and then we can work out a fair price."

Silence. Phone-line-dead silence.

"Mother?" I shook the phone to jiggle the battery.

"Yes, Emily. I don't know about this. I feel it's sort of like using floral arrangements made with flowers from your garden."

"Huh?"

"Oh, darling, do I need to pontificate this awkward fact to you? What's the point of having a painting done by a member of the family—not showing the expense we put into it?"

I could hear her tap-tap-tap to the counter with her expertly painted nail.

"I believe it's done all the time. Even by your distinguished John Singer Sargent. Perhaps it has something to do with family believing in the gifts of their family. Preferring to patronize them over some random stranger."

"Oh, all right," she relented. "And of course I will pay you."

Relieved. I did like the idea of being paid for my work, as I had not been entirely comfortable with the concept of having Henry give me an allowance. Perhaps I wasn't entirely uncomfortable in having an allowance. I mean, I do need to maintain my looking pretty for him, the purchasing of pretty things for our home that we will both appreciate.

"Also, I do get a bit worried about your business sensibilities. Perhaps you should consider getting one of those business managers?" she said.

"But I have one. A very good and high-end one I found on Fifty-seventh Street," I said, looking at my Smythson business planner, impressed with myself in not having to lie.

"Very well then. I expect to see a sketch two weeks from today. That's April second, love."

And with the frightening realization that I was under the Queen Mother's employment, she hung up the phone. Oh, for God's sake, the woman would always find a way to have a hold on me.

I opened up my satchel, leaned against the kitchen table, and pulled out my sketchbook. Furiously drawing images that had no hope, based on the fury of a windstorm pushing ideas along the slippery coils in my brain.

Henry walked into the kitchen, rubbing one of his eyes with his knuckle like a little boy in drop-seat footsie pajamas with a blankie. A shadow crept over my face as he loomed over me, locking me into my seated position with his arms and peering over my pad.

"Whatcha doing there, Emily? Drawing two figures who are about to duel? Or is it fencing?"

He was right. The figurines were embroiled in some sort of face-off, about to have it out. Perhaps their combative poses were made because Henry was still in the doghouse.

"Just working on a commission."

"Really," he mused. "And this is all before 9:00 AM," he added, looking to the microwave clock that flashed 8:44 AM. "I must say that I'm impressed."

I tore off a sheet and added it to my pile of rejects with an attempt at another sketch, but became annoyed with the mess I kept adding to. Neatly stacking up the scraps of my work, I gathered the papers and walked over to the trash, which was burping up garbage. Lining the top of the bin with the heavy vellum paper, I pushed down the garbage like a compressor.

Feeling Henry's gaze, I turned to him, only to be under the

scrutiny of his bemused smirk, which was exhilarating in a sexual context but now just added to my annoyance.

"You know, Em. A new place will be ideal for your painting. This realtor at the Gallagher Group described to me this promising loft on Grand Street. 'Stunning! Duplex! Balcony! Sun-flooded!' " he exploded. "Sounds ideal. And enough room for a studio so you can paint properly. With a real disposal system," he laughed, right as my head was about to free-fall into our garbage.

I stood up, wiping a strand of hair behind my ear. The idea of a "sun-flooded" loft did have considerable appeal. I pictured myself with an eight-foot canvas and little brush stemming from my hand like a wand. Wearing black capris and ballet shoes in that Lee Krasner fifties artist chic sort of style. Always picturing my outfits with the setting.

Henry seated himself at the table, lifting up the box of cereal to give Tony's mug a closer inspection. I situated a bowl and spoon on his place mat, vaguely registering how our habits resembled that of an old married couple with battery-operated ears.

"Frosted Flakes?"

Henry preferred the kind of bird-feed cereal you found at a store where the tattoo-fingered cashiers have medical degrees, assuming he'd start his day off sensibly, when really the nutrition facts were almost identical to Frosted Flakes unless you had a need for fiber, low sugar, and iron (something I've already researched). Essentially, you needed about ten bowls of either cereal to get all of the vitamins and nutrients you need, and Henry wasn't that hungry in the morning, but I could eat ten bowls of cereal any time of the day (something I've been known to do). We also rarely shopped at grocery stores, preferring the charm and unprocessed foods of specialty markets.

"Since when did we start eating Frosted Flakes, Em?"

"I must have made a mistake at the store," I said without meeting his eye. Not that I was ashamed of my sugary eating habit, I just couldn't have him think that I've fallen for commercial marketing.

Pouring his bowl, Henry discovered the damn IQ test on the back of the box. The wrinkle of his brow and affected looks of pondering into the air indicated that he had found something redeemable in the kid-brand food.

Repositioning the box so he could read the answers on the side panel, I paid particular attention while he tallied up his answers. Henry then applauded to himself while reading the box.

"This stuff is a joke!"

Oh, please.

"Now how can we expect to further advance the intelligence of this country's youth and, to use Kellogg's words, 'Jump-Start Your Brain' when this is about as simple and useless as a game of tic-tac-toe!"

Good thing I didn't circle my answers on the box.

"Tic-tac-toe!" he echoed.

"Yes, tic-tac-toe. Speaking of which, the painting I'm working on is for my mother."

I broke Henry's interest from that demoralizing cereal box.

"Your mother?"

"Yes. Quite amusing, really. You see, she wants me to paint a portrait. Of us! A wedding portrait to maintain some family tradition that keeps the divorce rate down because it would depreciate the value of some expensively commissioned pieces."

"You and me? A wedding portrait? Commissioned by your mother?"

For a boy who just scored in the leading percentile of our nation's population, he appeared to be a bit of an imbecile.

"I promise not to inconvenience you in any way—your time— and we only have to hang the picture whenever my mom comes to visit. Which I promise will be infrequently."

Infrequently for certain, otherwise Henry and I will break a long-standing family tradition where I'll be the first (but not necessarily the first deserved) Briggs member to have a divorce.

"No. Of course I don't see this as an inconvenience. It's just so incredibly Edith Wharton of your mother to come up with such an idea."

Henry laughed, spooning some soggy flakes into his mouth that, I acutely observed, seemed to be giving him energy despite the fact that they weren't as smart as his regular flakes. They're all just flakes, I again assumed.

Henry looked to the microwave clock, which set him to frantic mode as he dashed from the table to take a shower, mumbling something about a godforsaken meeting that had to be scheduled for the absurd time of 10:00 AM. Henry was not a good performer in the morning, despite his high IQ as evidenced by the Frosted Flakes intelligence test. Not that I was particularly hung up on my poor score. I mean, what did the Mesopotamians know about art, color, or the fall collections? And look what happened to Mesopotamia— you don't see us driving cars or warming our homes from discoveries made by their society. Hmm. Then again? Oh, forget it.

I cleared away Henry's breakfast, washed up the dishes, and gave the counters their sixth coat of Windex for the morning. Tying the strings of the garbage, Henry gave me his departing words from the doorway, reminding me that we'd meet up with the realtor at the apartment on Grand Street and that he'd e-mail me the list of our afternoon appointments.

Seeing Henry off with an incomplete wave as he already left a miasma of dust in his hasty exit, I looked at the kitchen and then lifted my hands to inspect them. I had just cleaned up after my fiancé, and I couldn't say that I liked it.

4

The timing of Henry's proposal and my decision to focus on my art may have been sabotage. Wedding duties or paint? When you have a To Do list as long as my 1982 Christmas letter to Santa. (I stopped writing to Santa about a decade ago. Okay, last year.) The Christmas of '82 had a particularly detailed list, as scratch-and-sniff stickers, collecting animals that clipped onto your bookbag, baseball hats with horns sprouting from the cap, and anything rainbow or unicorn were all the rage.

The refrigerator seemed to be a good place to begin. I needed food for nourishment. Opening the freezer door, I felt the chill of Henry's sly sense of humor. Carmenia's butt, now wrinkled from being salvaged from the trash, had "Butt Patrol" written on it and was taped to the carton of Ben & Jerry's.

Despondent and starving, I began wedding To Dos.

Dress
Location
Registries
Invitations
Licen—

This was boring, tedious, and put me in sleep mode better than the *Charlie Rose Show* when the guests were some cabinet member and a writer for the *Atlantic Monthly*.

Reading through bridal magazines would spur my inspiration. Deciding to sift through *Vogue* (I really couldn't relate to all of those smiley girls in poofy dresses looking into the sunset), I couldn't help but study the models' figures with intense focus. If I'd had one of those loupes jewelers used to inspect a diamond, I'd be using it to assess these surgically enhanced bodies.

Thinking of diamonds, it soon occurred to me that my engagement finger did not wink and shine with the most precious of glows. How did I let days slip by without even questioning when I'd be receiving the fun present one gets from being proposed to? I love presents. How haven't I even wondered when I'd be receiving my engagement ring? I completely lost it.

Adding to my checklist: "Engagement ring!!!!????"

Back to the magazines, my annoyance further spurred by seeing one flat stomach perching below one manufactured boob after another. I made up a game, "Real or Fake," parlaying my enjoyment and extremely satisfying act of making checks, which I used to check anything fake. Defacing an issue of *Elle* with checks, I logged onto breasts.com for my answer. According to Dr. Jean Parnell, it was quite common to have two breasts not the same size; in fact the percentages favored lopsided breasts.

Returning to *Elle* to review my answers based on my research, I believed I had a perfect score. Forget cereal boxes, this was a game that I excelled at, thoroughly impressed with myself as I buffed my paint-stained nails on my sleeve. My ringless fingers. Ringless? And what the hell was that about?

In Henry's defense, perhaps he wanted me to choose my engagement ring. We'd shop at Harry Winston or Tiffany's and make the decision together. In fact, this was quite brilliant of him. Henry truly knew me! How if he proposed with a ring that I found unacceptable, it would have completely ruined the moment. Possibly even interfered with my decision process. Now we'd shop for the ring together—make a day of it. Buy the ring, register, and have a deliciously long lunch at La Goulue that included many cocktails. Henry was now out of the penalty box for Carmenia's butt (but he didn't have to know that yet, as I needed to leverage this and was in the mood for being treated tonight).

The microwave flashed 3:11 PM. 3:11 PM? Now what could that be about? For an entire day I hadn't even made one check on my wedding To Do list. So I added "Real or Fake" to the last line and checked that. I didn't quite know how "Real or Fake" applied to my wedding duties, but at least I got to make a check.

Completely opposed to taking cabs in daylight, I walked to the realtor appointment and used the time to come up with a believable excuse on my lateness. But all that came to mind were images of fake boobs and butts, imagining the blobs of silicone, Botox, and fat injections used to swell up these body parts oozing into the city's streets and crevices like a globby monster from a campy fifties flick.

If I did have implants and possibly died someday (a concept I have not yet come to terms with, as I slightly believed that I was one of the immortal ones), in my 1,400-thread-count quilted coffin would be my remains of bones and two balls of jellyfish.

I arrived at the SoHo condominium in less than an hour, my late arrival hardly noticed, considering that Henry had been under the care of a woman hired for her social-climbing skills. Entering the apartment, she matched my image of her, just slightly younger and without the newscaster blowout. Wearing the requisite realtor uniform—black, expensive labels bought at the Barney's warehouse sale—she had the urban-hint-of-sex-appeal look in stilettos, slimming pants, and cardigan with the plunging V neck.

Perhaps I should have changed from this morning. I had on my purple low-cut cargo pants in a larger size (one size above my normal size, which was a brilliant device of mine so I would feel particularly skinny on fat days), an Anna Sui knit cardigan in a blue Fair Isle pattern, and a lavender Marc Jacobs coat with oversized buttons.

Henry beamed on sight of me while I regarded the realtor, who appeared to be making the moves on my fiancé, as indicated by the claw clamped to his arm. And, though I couldn't quite make out but felt pretty certain, her index finger stroked his skin in deliberate movements in the manner of the Grinch's finger on his chin indicating he was cooking up something mischievous.

"Emily!" Henry cried, walking over to greet me with a kiss, which I reveled in, as Claw Woman was reduced to observing our bliss.

He then introduced us and I entrusted my hand into Barbara "Call me Barb" Paulson's claw, which had the smoothness of an insect after a spring rain, mentally calculating her monthly Sephora bills for the maintenance of her clammy claws.

"Hello, Emily," she purred. "Henry was just telling me how behind you feel."

Behind? Behind! Did he really tell her about my butt? I couldn't believe Henry shared my personal insecurities with this barracuda. I felt so hurt and betrayed.

"About the wedding preparation," Henry prodded, probably interpreting my Emily smirk of abhorrence.

"Oh, right," I said casually. "The wedding. I actually checked off something from my To Do list today and feel quite accomplished as a result."

"Really," he said, amusingly, "and which box received your check, may I ask?"

"Fake or Real," I blurted.

"Fake or Real?" Henry and Call me Barb questioned in unison.

"Wow! This is amazing," I said, deflecting their unnecessary inquisition to further explore the capacious room where our conversation had been echoing.

The room had all of the standard downtown features—wall of windows, floors stained with the gleam of melted butter, and sparse décor—the key pieces a kidney-shaped coffee table and purple couch in the same boucle texture as my coat. The apartment's main attraction was that it was a duplex, the addition of stairs in a New York apartment considered a phenomenon akin to elevators in country homes.

Ready to move in and Henry did the very boy thing, asking all of these tiresome questions about maintenance, square feet blah blah blah, while I envisioned putting my crystal chandelier in the mirrored bathroom and how I would fill in the awkward triangular corner with my easel and paint things.

"Okay," Henry directed. "Let's see the next place."

After seeing the Grand Street apartment, our choices became progressively worse. Too dark or not enough space—the décor in most of them stifled me. The sole furniture of a Broome Street loft was the desks and chairs where I used to keep my number 2 pencils and box of Crayolas. I wondered if the resident was an elementary school teacher and lifted things from the office.

Henry, registering my Emily smirk, pulled me to the side and away from Barracuda Barb. She seemed annoyed, which pleased me.

"Seen anything you like?"

"Only the Grand Street place. Nothing else seems to have any of the added features. That something distinguishing, special."

"I knew you'd say that!" he said, eyes laughing at me.

"But didn't you like the Grand Street place?"

"Sure I liked it, but it's an imprudent investment. Twelve hundred square feet is hardly worth over three million." He put his hand around my waist and pulled me into him, looking into my eyes the way he did before we were about to get it on. "Emily, think about it," he whispered. "The walls had about as much stability as tracing paper. They're just cashing in on the Boffi stainless kitchen, newly painted walls, and stained floors."

Henry could be so practical.

Barb interrupted us.

"Listen, I hate to interrupt."

So then why were you interrupting?

"But I do have one more place I could show you."

Coming in between us with her cashmere cleavage that a credit card could get stuck getting swiped in, I noticed that her breasts absolutely got the fake check. She then started in with her pushy peddler tone.

"It's really the most fantastic place of the lot—on Reade Street. Penthouse triplex, Val Cucine kitchen where you choose the finish," she rambled on like an airline stewardess instructing the multiple uses of your floatable seat cushion.

Having no idea what she was talking about, what even made a Val Cucine kitchen such a perk, and not that I'd ever turn on the stove—aside from lighting one of my two cigarettes I had in a year—I did appreciate the idea of having a Val Cucine kitchen.

She continued describing the brochure copy attractions. How the loft could easily be made into a fourth bedroom. "There's nothing else like it on the market!"

There's nothing else like it on the market? They all say that.

And then Henry, dropping his hands from around my waist and utterly absorbed by Barb, asked excitedly, "But why didn't you tell me about this earlier?" Referring to the apartment list that I forgot to print out because I had been too busy researching fake breasts. "I don't see a Reade Street apartment on your listing," Henry said, squinting his eyes to his FAQ sheet.

"I didn't include it because it's a bit higher than your spending price."

He looked to the crumpled piece of paper that seemed ready to double for a Kleenex.

"Look," said Barb, a bit firmly for my liking, as I then reminded myself who was working for whom. "Reade Street is just two blocks from here; we might as well go ahead and at least look at the place."

Henry and I gave why-not shrugs of our shoulders, dutifully following Barb to our impromptu appointment.

Okay, this was better than Christmas morning 1982 when I stumbled onto a floor padded not only with all of the presents I had asked Santa for but also Calvin Klein jeans, a point-and-shoot camera, and a pair of Nikes my mother had had made into roller skates. The ceiling was supported by five columns that appeared to be inspired by the Parthenon after a raw food diet, and Barb rambled something about how the architecture of the loft was based on the principles of Feng Shui, which essentially could be the same as telling me that my moon was in Gemini and how that affected my daily happiness, but the selling point seemed to hook Henry.

Above, there were rows of glass-cased rooms that looked down to the main floor in a similar setup to the boxes at Madison Square Garden that encircled the court. There was a curtain of glass walls, oak floors so slippery you needed ice skates, bathrooms with steam-heated floors, and the closets! I would actually be able to give my clothes some space for the first time in their cramped existence.

After testing out the stairs a few times, I returned to the main room, finding Henry and Barb immersed in a chat at the corner window. But I knew it wasn't anything illicit because Henry had out his list, making all sorts of scribbles that appeared more active than one of his creative-drawing moments that always seem to come at the convenient time of 2:00 AM.

"Okay then, Henry," Barb said, right as I arrived. She acted as if she had been trying to conceal something, sneaky Barb, when I very well knew she had been playing it coy and vindictive to make me feel insecure, when really Henry and I had complete trust in one another.

"And Emily, nice meeting you. I'm sure you two have a lot to discuss."

What the hell did she mean by that? Was she trying to insinuate that she and Henry were making plans to have an affair?

"Right," said Henry. "We do have a lot to go over, Emily." His voice boomed in my direction. "About our next home."

Snapping me from a mental image of myself following a trail of Barb's black designer-label clothes—bought at a reduced price at the Barney's warehouse sale—deliberately left about the loft's leading selling points like clues, finding Henry crawling on top of her on the top staircase, I paid Barb with the sweetest smile I could muster. The smile probably appeared more saccharine than the one I had anticipated.

5

We walked to no particular destination in silence. I had been preoccupied with the decorating of our new apartment—hanging my canvases, pointing to big strong men where to situate the retro furniture that I'd be purchasing from nearby SoHo shops and a basketball hoop with a basketball. (Though there would be no basketball playing allowed, they must be included for the effect—it was all about the effect. I mean no one really uses the pool boy who comes with the Palm Beach estate, unless you're . . . er . . . I started imagining a very young Antonio Banderas. Again, it was all about the fantasy.)

Henry asked if we could stop at the bookstore on Astor, knowing that I'd agree without protest. I loved bookstores the way I loved diners. How hours could slip from the mental travel spurred by pictures and words.

He consulted the floor plan and we went to the Home and Architecture section, where Henry began stacking all of the Idiot and Dummy guides to buying a home on his arms, while I preoccupied myself with a coffee-table book celebrating the works of I.M. Pei, choosing the homes that I could live in.

"Tonight we'll divide the reading—bone up on how to negotiate, apply for a mortgage, select inspectors, contractors, et cetera," Henry said, wrenching me from my fantasy state.

Was Henry asking me to intentionally read boring stuff? Perhaps he should just read everything and give me the abridged version from what he learned. Or maybe he could just handle this part of the home-buying process, letting me focus on the decorating and spending needs. But I wasn't about to share this with him, not wanting to start something. I excused myself to check out the magazine racks and selected every home décor publication without "Country" in its name, as those seemed to mandate a basket, something dried, or quilted on their covers.

Finding Henry dog-earing one of the recyclable books we now had to buy, I moved us toward the checkout before he added another breeding ground for dust mites to an already alarming pile. The line appeared to be tediously long, but moved quickly. Henry handed the cashier two hundred-dollar bills after she gave the final total. I didn't notice Henry carrying hundreds the last time I checked his wallet, wondered how one acquires bills not dealt from the slot of an ATM and why Henry would be part of this group.

Outside the store, I noticed the grayish tint to the air, which seemed inherent to downtown with the buildings' inconsistent sizes and style, like mismatched china. Henry stopped to scratch the hair out of his head, studied the store receipt, and flicked it away with a snap of his wrist. He watched me cautiously as my eyes widened, lips pursed.

"Trash receptacle?"

Henry looked from side to side.

"I haven't seen any trash receptacles."

"How can you just shamelessly add to the filth of these city streets and have the nerve to gripe about how dirty New York has become? It starts with you, Henry. You are the problem."

"You can't hold me responsible for the city's pollution because of one slip of paper."

"Oh, yes, I can. Just watch me."

I realized that, during our contretemps, Henry's piece of paper had fluttered away like a moth finding no light to singe his wings on. I became occupied by hunger, but didn't have a specific craving. Reaching Jerry's on Prince Street, we settled on the restaurant by giving one another affirmative nods. Henry intuitively opened the door, where I ducked under his arm and followed our friendly waitress to a side booth. (Anyone was friendly after spending an afternoon with Barracuda Barb.)

After giving my order, I opened my wedding planner as a distraction from the rumbles of my stomach while not giving in to the empty calories of a breadbasket probably pinched from an earlier, carb-averse table. Having no interest in the crispy peasant bread as well, Henry became enthused by my task, excited when he saw "Church?" alone on its page.

"So you want to have a religious service?" he asked.

This thought had been sliding about my brain noodles, considering a church near St. Mark's Place if we decided to get married in the city.

Henry asked what denomination the church was, and I answered somewhere in the lower eastside.

"Religion," he said gruffly. "Catholic, Presbyterian, Protestant?"

"I don't know," I said, annoyed. "Something that believes in God."

We both turned away from each other to diffuse the annoyance factor fueled by this particular subject. A Neil Young classic played from above, and I wondered if Young had been fading away rather than the preferable intention to burn out.

Returning to my original mission, I opened my planner, faintly alarmed by the sheets of whiteness, and pulled a blank page seam by seam from its hand-sewn binding where I would rewrite my notes into a new planner bought specifically for the move. I looked to another table as a way to stir my thoughts and began to write.

READE STREET LOFT
Basic Necessities:
Basketball (Google Nerf?)
Basketball net
Kidney-shaped coffee table (ask Barracuda Barb if we could
    buy the one from the people who lived in the Grand Street
    apartment)
Picasso drawing from the Blue Period

Henry scooted in closer to me, eyeing my entry. Apparently amused by my list, he pulled it toward him right as my pen was about to hit the paper, only to be left hanging in the air.

"Basketball? A Picasso! Forget our concerns about how we can afford the loft, we're in debt till our twilight years from your 'Basic Necessities.' So, Emily, does this mean what I think it means? I gather you're taken with the Reade Street place?"

Taken? Try completely infatuated. I felt the way I did when I found a dalmatian-spotted shirt I loved at Roberto Cavalli that I had to have. If I didn't buy it, I considered my wardrobe unacceptable, that I wasn't well dressed unless I had that shirt.

"I loved it too," smiled Henry. "But the pragmatics of this, Emily, is we just can't afford Reade Street right now."

Can't afford!

"Are you okay, Emily?" Henry looked frantic.

"Um, I guess so. But you were talking about my car. Right?"

I have a Ford Mustang.

"Your car?"

"Right. There's no garage at the Reade Street place."

"Emily, you're completely losing me. Now let's get to the pragmatics."

Pragmatics were meant for people that aimed to fix governmental problems. Henry pinched my chin before it free-fell into my lap.

"Unless!" he perked.

"Unless?" I asked slyly.

"I have an idea. Just excuse me for a second."

And Henry got up from the table, leaving in a flurry of his dust.

I turned back to my Reade Street Basic Necessities list, closing the book, becoming depressed by this hopeless fantasy.

Staring about the restaurant alone. Bored. I reopened the book and tore out another piece of paper, outlining tomorrow's agenda. I had to get my career on track and earn millions so I could buy the apartment for us based on my insanely successful career as an artist. I wrote:

Morning workout at gym (endorphins good for the spirit and inspiration)
Met to view collections (inspiration)
Light shopping (for high profile meetings with galleries—on budget, so only Barney's, no Bergdorf's)

While I was crossing out the "no Bergdorf's" part, Henry returned to the table with that wide grin of his covering his face.

"I have an idea!"

Well, I have thousands, but look where that gets me, I thought, sifting through my scribbled wedding planner pages.

"We may be able to pull off the Reade Street loft."

I closed the book, practically jumping into Henry's mouth.

"My first idea was to economize, do some quick budgeting based on all of our expenses and income coming in. Since you aren't bringing in as much with your new career direction as an artist."

And why didn't he just say "since you are a waste of life sapping me of every penny"?

"Henry," I interrupted cheerfully. "You're right. The wedding! Let's blow off the wedding and use the money for the loft!"

"No, no," he insisted. "That's not what I was getting at."

"Oh." After a slight pause, I again interrupted him. "Well, I could ask Mom and Dad for some money, which may be weird. I already feel the burden of being under her employment from painting this wedding portrait of us."

"Emily, can you just clam it for a second!"

I clammed up.

"When you were fluttering about the loft, I did some interesting crunching with Barb."

Did he just say crunching? What kind of sexual position was that?

"Numbers, Emily," he said firmly. "And you really could try to control your smirks when around Barb. It's noticeable when you have a 'thing' with certain people."

Thing?

"Henry. People who are afraid of clowns, clapping monkeys, or albinos have a 'thing.' I do not have a 'thing.' I mean a 'thing' with Barb."

Henry looked to me suspiciously. I did have a 'thing' with Barb.

"Anyway," he continued, "as you know, 4,000 square feet is a ridiculous amount of space—almost obscene. With three bedrooms and baths, we could easily let out a room and we'd still have to make an appointment if we wanted to meet up with our renter. Once your career gets on track—and you'll become this famous and successful artist that your husband will live off of—we will by then have our own place. Never have to give up our lifestyles—move to the burbs, consider landscaping, zoning, and the malaise of a community from the arrival of an Olive Garden."

Renter? Olive Garden? I didn't like the reality aspect of this conversation. (Though I did love reality TV.)

"Renting out a room? In our newlywed year?"

"Just for a short while," he said hopefully.

"Okay," I said. Then, shedding some pragmatic insight of my own. "But where would we find a renter? Surely it would have to be someone we know and trust."

"Good point, Emily," he said, as if I'd made an interesting observation while he taught me about the Peloponnesian War (something, for whatever reason unknown to me, he's been known to do in the past). "It so happens that I just called a friend of mine, Taz Derning, who needs to move to New York from London."

"Taz Derning? His name is Taz?"

What the hell kind of name was Taz?

"And what does he do, adapt Puccini operas into movies?"

"Well, his name is actually abbreviated," Henry trailed off, and then there was a funny silence.

"Abbreviated from what?"

"It's pretty amusing—quite hysterical actually. His real name is Tasmanian Devil, but of course that's quite a mouthful. So he just goes by Taz."

Hysterical.

"You're expecting a girl who uses five economy-sized bottles of Windex a week to live with a guy named Taz? After the Tasmanian Devil!"

Henry nodded in affirmation.

"Me? Who, to use your description, does a Navajo rain dance outside our apartment before removing my shoes so no grain of dirt will get into our home? Live with a beast that leaves crushed tin cans and fish bones in the wake of his dusty trail?"

"Emily, just picture Reade Street."

The staircase, the columns, and those glorious windows—the loft was better than a chichi downtown art gallery that held openings where Carmen Kass and Lenny Kravitz made appearances. Hmm.

Perhaps I could moonlight our home as an art gallery for my collections? As I was becoming disturbed by the idea of cigarette stubs and muddy shoes soiling the floors, Henry chimed in.

"At least think this through, Emily. He'll pay whatever we ask."

"Fine," I said, somewhat taken aback by my voice's preadolescent tone. Becoming more composed, I said softly, "I will think it over. Can we just forget about all these *pragmatics* now, I've had quite a day."

"Well, then I have just the thing for you."

Henry reached into his satchel and displayed a sapphire blue velvet box on the table, the Formica diner table of Jerry's. A high-end diner that was essentially the same as any other diner, except they had chromed coat racks at the sides of the booths and added warm mesclun salad to their menu to justify the more expensive prices.

He flicked the box across the table with a snap of his fingers, where I was expected to open it. Frozen, I reminded myself of my original hope where we would buy a ring together, considered ways of saying how I'd rather not see what was inside the box.

"Well? You really aren't quite yourself. I assumed you'd open that box quicker than a carton of Ben & Jerry's."

Paying him with a polite smile, I did as I was told.

Snapping open the box, I should have been wearing my reading glasses, as it was easier to read the fine print on not-meant-to-be-read electronic warranties than see this excuse for a diamond. Imagine dropping a glass, sweeping up the broken pieces onto a chopping block, and further smashing them with a hammer. One of those shards would be about the same size as my diamond that I would have to happily cherish, wear as a testimony of love to my husband till he passes on, which will probably be before me, as I am going to make his life miserable for presenting me with such a ring.

"It was my grandmother's," said Henry, happily doing the honor of prodding the ring from its cushioned insert and sliding it onto my finger, where it lopped to the side. And not because of the weight of the diamond. It didn't fit. Henry's grandmother must have been a big woman.

"Look at your elegant little finger. You do have gorgeous hands." He pulled my hand to him to give it a closer look. "Hmm. Looks as if you may have something to add to your To Do list."

What? You mean pawn this off and get a new one with your credit card!

"It's a bit big for you. You'll have to get it resized. Otherwise, what do you think?"

"It's. Nice," I said with extreme care and great force.

Our waitress approached the table, and I noticed she took the same fashion direction as Barracuda Barb, wearing the ubiquitous tight V-necked sweater to accentuate her cleavage. They probably sold them three to a pack. I then watched Henry watching her.

I then had the courage to ask Henry the loaded question, but had to pause while he took a bite from his fried zucchini. He didn't seem to be prepared for its degree of difficulty, as the piece of slimy vegetable slipped from its fried battered duvet. He bobbed his head as a gesture that he'd be able to attend to my incoming question once he took care of this renegade food.

Henry was completely irresistible. You couldn't help but love him, no matter how small my ring or pathetic my proposal.

"So, Henry," I started. "I was wondering if you were breast-fed."

He dropped his fried zucchini.

"Emily! So I gather we've now moved from butts to breasts? Makes sense, I suppose."

"Really, Henry. I've noticed you. How you have a tendency to stare at other women's breasts. Blatantly."

I then peered down to evaluate my own rack, which wasn't all that bad, as well as rather buxom in proportion to my body. And it also would not receive a check in the "Real or Fake" game. Henry wasn't losing out with my chest, though my wearing crew necks as opposed to more flattering cuts should be reconsidered if I wanted my fiancé's eyes to stop scanning the globes.

He then took my hands and gave them a slight squeeze. Henry looked into my eyes with such sincerity, I saw the boy that made my insides swoop and swish like a fish riding in its tank in the back of a taxi.

"Emily, I love you. Are you even aware of how beautiful you are?"

Naturally, this would be a rhetorical question. I've always been hard on myself when it came to evaluating my own looks—avoided mirrors like a vampire. People would categorize me as being pretty, as easy-to-look-at in that catalogue model kind of way, whereas I've always been more interested in being considered a natural to appear in *Italian Vogue*.

Henry was still speaking. I believe I even missed a few of his adulations.

"I don't know anyone as beautiful, passionate, talented, creative, funny, and smart as you."

Well, that was a start.

"And, no, I wasn't breast-fed."

"You weren't!"

"It was the late sixties. My mom was into that feminist thing at the time."

He then looked at my breasts and I, too, gave them a closer inspection.

"I'll just have to make up for that lack of breast-feeding tonight."

Leaving the restaurant, Henry reached into his pocket for his Tic Tacs. Spilling the last four into his palm, he looked momentarily stumped, possibly because they appeared so enormous in comparison to that diamond he recently had been inspecting.

I fingered two of the sea mist green pellets before he'd realized that those missing mints were lost from my habit of munching on them lately.

We both tilted our heads to the sky so they were perfectly positioned to sip in the air. It felt warm for March. If it were a more seasonable month, we probably would have cabbed it as it was still too cool to walk, but considering the unexpected temperature we decided to take advantage of the time outdoors.

I had an ugly engagement ring.

Arriving home exhausted, Henry went right to bed. So much for his urge to breast-feed. Completely awake with my eyes closed, I could have either spent the rest of the night in this state of wakefulness or used the alert time to do something more productive. Getting out of bed, I slipped on a pair of sweats that said "Kick Ass" on the rear. Moving to the couch, I kept staring at my newly ringed finger, pinching the tiny diamond. There was something unique and quaint about it. Perhaps I would grow into it—meaning grow to love it, not become obese and thick-fingered—the ring was getting resized the day after tomorrow, as that was the next Wedding Planning Day.

Turning on the light, I gazed about the apartment, which was all about Henry's stereo equipment. His speakers were worth more than my entire savings. I imagined that Henry pictured these speakers, hearing the concert hall sounds that pounded from their black cushioned padding, right as we entered the main room of the Reade Street loft.

Shifting my gaze to the floors, there appeared to be a layer of that cottony New York City dust. This town was absolutely filthy. I went into the kitchen to get a dishcloth, making a mental note to find a more effective dust cleaning method and log on to Restoration Hardware. Returning to the room, I knelt down and began swiping the floors. Crawling to the edge of the couch, I flickered the towel in lightning motions under the lining in an attempt to capture the dust beneath. Allergy season approached and I needed to remove unhealthy trappings.

Feeling a light kick on my butt, annoyed, I tilted my head to find Henry wearing that annoying smirk of his.

"I am just doing what I'm told," he laughed, keying me in to my "Kick Ass" pants by pointing to my butt. "And you do have a kick-ass ass. Though I may be more turned on if you substitute the dishtowel for a whip and swap the adorable yet unflattering sweats for those panties of yours with the purple fur trim."

I rewound my mind to a few years back. To a time when I used my obsessive-compulsive cleaning of places unseen to the eye but seen in my head with High Definition accuracy. When I Windexed and dusted out of angst about my single status. Telling myself that when I was in a relationship, I wouldn't squander it on frivolous arguments and unnecessary drama. Now experiencing the very moment I've always dreamed of.

6

New Yorkers must travel for the privilege of soaking their bare feet in morning grass. They cannot detect the weather by opening a window when opposing buildings manipulate the natural light and air—more privileges. With their need for convenience and fix for all things cutting edge, urbanites are considered the most modern of earth dwellers.

New Yorkers do not own toolboxes, unless used to store cotton balls and eyelash curlers. They have numbers for maintenance people who drive vans with company names painted on the doors. I will avoid modern conveniences in the same way that I am suspicious of the talents of a screenwriter who writes his work on an iBook at a Starbucks.

With my oversized ring with its undersized diamond, the toolbox became my brand of convenience, preventing me from having to travel to a jeweler, as it contained duct tape. Use #127 to pad rings the size of a baby's bracelet.

My day was already under siege by the rumblings of a possible Bridezilla attack, a day strictly devoted to my career. I would not even glance at a bridal magazine. I would make a trip to the Met to be inspired. Even though I would be in the general vicinity of Vera Wang, I would not go in. Just, perhaps, walk past it.

I dressed in haste, forewent my walk to take a cab, and justified the saved time for a quick peruse in Vera Wang. I froze outside the boutique, watching the stick figures in their new season's purchases, fantasy brides that had the kind of unattainable qualities I put to paper, as they shushed in and out of the glass entrance, looking more like a casting call for a Jackie O biopic. Did I have the right place? Was this one of those excursions that you needed to dress for? Vera Wang was painted in gold on the window; the doors were trimmed in coordinating 24-karat. This was the place where girls were made into princesses.

And here I stood outside Vera Wang in my Pumas and cargo pants. I imagined trying to enter the doors only to be rejected and spit out in the same nifty effect as a children's book with spells and witches, where inanimate objects took on nasty human characteristics, the Vera Wang door taking the form of a very belligerent bouncer.

And my Pumas? Since Mom did say that I couldn't possibly go to the museum dressed in sneakers, never one to rebel against dress codes, I walked north a few blocks to Theory and bought a fitted jean jacket. At Searle, I found a pair of white low-cut denim pants, feeling very Back to School circa 1985 by asking the salesgirl if I could wear my purchase out of the store. She gave a haughty giggle and then a once-over, showing the fangs of a slobbering jackal as if I had never bought clothes before, a small-town girl new to the city and completely overcome by my first New York shopping experience.

Surveying the store one last time to see if I had missed any merchandise, I found a selection of Pumas in the far corner under a row of headless mannequins. Securing a salesperson that didn't appear to have vampire marks on the side of her neck, I added a pair of navy Pumas with a turquoise stripe to the mix, quickly changing into them a few blocks away from the store in a courtyard of a private townhouse.

And, in case I thought I wasn't paying attention to the mission of this small spree, I was in complete control. I couldn't possibly justify spending money on a new pair of throwaway shoes just to go to the museum, considering that there were no quality shoe stores in the area. And, since I had to stick to a budget so I could move into the Reade Street loft, I needed to economize. A new pair of Pumas bought just for an outing to the Met had been a perfectly justifiable expense.

* * *

I started my museum visit by showing support to the Met's curators in viewing the current DaVinci exhibition that focused on his
journals. Leo and I had a great deal in common, as I am also an avid
journal keeper. Perhaps my own journals would someday be marveled at beneath the glass of climate-controlled displays.

I eschewed the headsets to avoid the burden of following the exhibition in a controlled time, along with possibly being trailed by
foreigners with different hygiene habits than mine. And, regardless
of my not wearing a headset, an Italian, or perhaps he was Spanish—
a man who wore his short-sleeved gingham shirt tucked into his
pulled-too-high jeans, who either used too much hair gel or proved
my theory that some foreigners were on a different wash cycle—approached me.

"Vu vike DaVinci?" he asked in some Franco-Italian-Anglaise,
which was either a really Euro come-on or he knew very little English.

"Leonardo? He seems very nice, though I never did meet him."

Euro laughed at me, adding to the oily wetness of him with his
flecks of spit that shot from the wide front gap of his cigarette-stained
teeth.

I was quite impressed with myself. If Euro had made the moves
on me pre-Henry proposal, he would have certainly been the recipient of an Emily smirk. But now, feeling more mature and perhaps a
bit forlorn for the attention, I felt quite charitable.

"Vy vont vu join me?" he said, to my breasts.

Just then I remembered my ring, feeling as if I had just been
given extraordinary superpowers. Drunk with this control, I lifted
up my hand, which looked like I took the Mayor's recommendation
to be armed with duct tape with the city on red alert to neurotic extremes.

"Thanks. Real enticing offer. Real sweet with you being from out
of town and all. Checking out the sites, getting in a little culture,
taking in Leonardo—and not in the ninja turtle or the Hollywood
heartthrob way! Very well then, I really should be off, working. Off
to work. And I do need to meet someone."

I bolted, hoping that he really didn't know how to speak the
language, otherwise I had just added to his impression of the

dumb dizzy American blonde without having the excuse of being a blonde.

In the next room, I was pulled to Leo's sketches of aqueducts like a magnet to a fridge. Feeling smart and interesting, learning—getting the culture in—perhaps I should retake the IQ test on the cereal box when I returned home.

In the main room of the exhibition, DaVinci's pages of notes were pulled from the Leicester Codex, rolled out like ancient scrolls (selling for over $15 million at Sotheby's—almost four Reade Street lofts, not that I had been particularly obsessing over its price). Interesting, these scribbled notes on handmade paper with no fun doodles that one would see in one of my journals. For the man who stretched the beauty of a smile to century-endured marketing, he did have scribbly handwriting.

Having learning enough, I eschewed the last room and went to the reason for my visit, the portrait galleries. I always began with Francois Boucher's *The Toilet of Venus,* to be reminded that in 1751 men found women who didn't skimp on their carbs to have the ideal body type. The model was portrayed as being so beautiful that pudgy winged cherubs dressed her, a trend that should be brought back.

Feeling that late-afternoon pinch of drowsiness, all of the condensed culture and antique incensed air began to tire me. Before I had a turn-of-the-century-corseted collapse, I cut to the room with the Sargents.

While his portrait of Madame Gautreau had been the number-one-selling postcard from visitors who wore cameras around their necks, I always preferred Sargent's *Mr. and Mrs. I.N. Phelps Stokes.*

In many ways, Sargent reminded me of Henry James. They both had an appreciation of the new American woman and celebrated her spirit, strength, and independence. Sargent's depiction of Mrs. Stokes established that. In his painting of her, she is the one prominently featured. Her stance is proud and confident, while her husband looks on, slightly shadowed in the background. She asserts herself, shown from her hands firmly planted on her hips and that great grosgrain-banded straw hat.

I also loved what she wore—very Ralph Lauren his early years, with a dark coat nipped at the waist, crisp white shirt with a dark bow tied at the collar, and that wonderful elegant skirt, probably linen as this was more of a spring outfit, which cascades down in an avalanche of white. She has a soft, pretty face with dark hair, rosy cheeks, and blue eyes—the kind of girl I would have shared a thermos of peach schnapps mixed with orange juice in the back of a wood-paneled station wagon.

What I found most intriguing, considering my current occupation, were her knuckled hands clasped at her waist. The gold wedding band nestled with the engagement ring like stuck-together pasta. The diamond was emerald cut. Classic, simple, large—I'd gather four carats—very much in the mode of the Fairfield County ladies. The rings stood out, and Mrs. Stokes showed no shame in having them notably pictured.

Mr. Stokes's hands are folded in a manner that shows he is not the spineless husband that plays to the demands of a bossy wife. Quite attractive, also wearing white linen, he has a trim beard and angular face, and I felt somehow drawn to him even though he's just a figure in a portrait. But this was incredibly immoral of me, considering that his wife and I had a bond, that I was engaged even if my ring finger may not prove so.

"Emily?"

Startled, shaken from a mental zone similar to the one I get from running, I turned to face the source of my interruption, and was greeted by J3 Hopper. J3, a friend and business relation of Henry's and mine who we knew from L.A., was largely responsible for the financing of our film, *Combining Art Forms*, based on the coming together of our cartoon strip's alter egos. A project I had no longer been involved with, due to that slimy way I felt, the way you needed to cleanse yourself after a day of commercial flight travel.

J3 was my unusual acquaintance who I could get the tab on if I read *Forbes*. He ran an electronics company, specializing in computer games. His success never seemed to be mentioned when we met up, as there always seemed to be other, more important things to cover.

J3 was assured, confident, and today, looked quite attractive—similar to Mr. Stokes, with the chiseled cheekbones you could roll a marble down, dark hair, and rugged good looks. His deep blue eyes, gleaming under a thicket of dark brows, struck me as mysterious—intense and sparkling. I hadn't recalled how handsome he was. It may have been the distinctive brows, which I never really took to, considering he wore sunglasses a lot—though never indoors.

"J3!" I beamed, kissing him on the cheek. I noticed a slight flush of red to his cheeks.

"I was afraid to approach you. Honestly, I've never seen you so absorbed."

"Right," I said, embarrassed from being noticed. "It's just that this portrait gets me every time. I always see something different when I come to visit."

Both J3 and I looked at Mr. and Mrs. Stokes.

"It really is something," he said. "Sargent said that, when he painted, he was most interested in uncovering the personality of the sitter. With this particular couple, you can tell that he was impressed by them, how Mr. Stokes truly respected and admired his wife."

"That's exactly it!" I said too loudly, so the entire room looked in my direction. I became nervous from the security guard's sudden approach toward me, but was saved by a kid who appeared to be more of a liability by humming loudly from tunes that filtered into his ears from an iPod.

"Sorry," I said, considerably lower. "But there is this confidence about him that I'm completely drawn to, an intelligence, really. I'm sure he could be quite prickly, as shown by his quiet male authoritative stance, but he has no problems if his wife asserts her character. Again, that takes an admirable bit of security."

"Apparently they were expats," J3 added. "I believe he was studying medicine in Paris."

"Architecture, really. But you were probably thinking of Sargent's own parents. Expats themselves, Sargent's father was a doctor in Florence."

"Right. Of course. And most of Sargent's portraits were of Americans. He loved Americans. His paintings captured his sitters in a simple refinement, signifying the vitality of a new nation."

"And then we have Madame Gautreau. *Madame X,* rather."

J3 and I walked over to *Madame X,* where I allowed him to pontificate, interested to hear his opinions.

"Of course, I don't have to fill you in on the scandal this painting created, as you are up on your Sargent, with her sexy gown that has nothing on today's dresses that make me wonder if these girls would save money by not having to buy couture and just go out in their expensive lingerie."

I knew exactly what he meant! Something I've often fumed about.

"Sargent even retitled the painting from *Madame Gautreau* to *Madame X*," he continued. "I think he did that because he was less impressed with her. It was his favorite painting, as he did achieve this dramatic quality—her tense elegance—but I think that Madame X could be any woman, the idea of a woman with a predatory sensuality.

"Apparently she was American, quite a social climber in the Parisian circles. Whereas, back to your Stokes friends, they were probably just in Paris to have a good time, not overly concerned with the whole 'do we fit in being Americans' and all. Confident."

Right. My words exactly.

"And," I said, "I know with you being a boy and all."

J3 looked down at himself, as if making sure that he was indeed a boy.

"While her dress is undeniably sexy—the low cut, jeweled straps—I just find it ostentatious. The little tiara on her head pretending to be some huntress," I paused. She really had a great deal in common with every other husband hunter striving for the Saturday morning Grace's Market Place to Gracious Home walk.

"She is predatory in a sensual way," I continued. "But it's too easy. Sure. Show some cleavage, wear obscenely expensive items—quite materialistic really," I said, as if speaking for Madame Gautreau. "But if you were to remove these inanimate symbols of wealth, she loses her power."

I pointed to her hand, not too close to the painting, as I seemed to be under the security guard's surveillance from my earlier blurts.

"Look at how she's holding down that hardwood table, practically making a Hulk-impressed dent. She needs the support to show herself truly. She needs the material goods. She asserts yet also retreats, not quite complete, certainly not at one with herself."

"So I take it you two wouldn't be meeting up at Pastis later?"

"No!" I laughed. "I'd be much happier taking in a morning run with Mrs. Stokes over there."

While he glanced back to the other painting, I noticed J3's build. Strong, he was also taller than I had remembered. Perhaps he just looked better because I'd only been with him a few times. And the first time we met was at a pool, where no one really looks the way they normally do under a haze of sun and through the tint of glasses. In fact, I'm almost fearful to imagine what I must have looked like. I panicked. I really needed to make more of an effort lounging poolside.

Stealing a peak at J3's watch, I saw the time was just after 3:00 PM. I had to start wearing a watch, but anything other than Cartier would be unacceptable.

"Oh, jeez!"

"Emily? What is it?"

J3 looked concerned. I needed to calm down more. Perhaps take yoga. But I really didn't like yoga.

"It's just that I am supposed to meet my best friend—new client actually—but it is Daphne. She has two kids, a catering company, and a kitchen to renovate, so my being a bit late won't really matter."

Was this too much information? But J3 just smiled. He even appeared amused.

"Oh, well, I was hoping that I could take you to lunch."

Really? Lunch! Hmm. Well, I could just blow off Daphne, she wouldn't care, but then again today was career day, and the only thing marked in my Smythson business planner was this appointment, so it would be in poor favor to skip my one confirmed meeting for a friendly lunch—the hardship that came with ambition.

J3 led me in the direction of the room's exit. We walked in a comfortable silence.

"Do you know what amazes me?" he asked.

I responded with a curious smile.

"Here I am in the business of interactive, cutting edge computers—noise, novelty, and annihilating your opponent in the most entertaining fashion. And here we are, looking at pictures, sculptures, created from very simple mediums, and yet they have the power to move. You can see more, learn more, and never tire of a painting. There is always something curious and new to be discovered. And, again, all created from very simple mediums."

"Exactly," I said, not understanding my response. "Then again, can you get to the level where you find the missing terrorist? Or whatever your best-selling game is that's ripped off from the latest world crisis."

Outside the museum we both looked at each other. I began to feel saddened by our coming departure.

"So?" he asked cautiously. "How's Henry?"

"Yes, well. Henry." I mumbled, looking down to my hand and then lifted up my engagement ring. "We're engaged!"

J3 directed his gaze to my hand.

"Wow. Congratulations," he said, sounding surprised.

"Thanks."

"Your ring, it's—" J3 made a sudden pause. "Nice."

I looked to him amazed.

"That's exactly how I said it, right after Henry gave it to me! Not that I'm materialistic or anything, but it just took me a minute to find the ring. Not that I'm a big diamond person. Working with my hands, I need to keep my hands free," I mumbled in my insecure rant. "But it is rather small in diamond standards."

"It looks like you have it properly safeguarded with all that tape."

"Right," I said, putting my hand back down. "It's a bit big. The ring, not the diamond. So I need to get it resized."

J3 took my hand, giving my fingers a thorough examination.

"And I see that you're not one of those girls who goes for the picketed fingernail look."

I forgot about the appearance of my nails, splotched with paint, my cuticles sanded down from work and packing.

"No. You know, considering that it's difficult to maintain with my profession and all."

"Of course!" he said in that "duh" way. "Your illustrating."

"Painting, really. I've decided to focus on my art. That's actually why I came here. I've been commissioned to do a few portraits and am curious about Sargent, using his career as a model for my own. You know, aim high!"

"Sargent," he pondered to no one in particular. "Interesting choice. Most appropriate."

"Well, then," I leaned in awkwardly to give J3 another friendly kiss to the cheek, but this time his face did not warm with a blush.

"So great seeing you. How funny that we bumped into one another? At the museum."

Hello—of course at the museum.

I began to walk away, thinking about my dreaded cell phone that I'd have to use to call Daphne so I could apologize for my lateness.

"Hey, Emily," called J3, running to my side. "I'm in the city for a few days before returning to L.A."

"Gosh, you must think I'm such a Madame X, I haven't even asked you what you were up to in the city."

"Working, as always. Perhaps I can take you and Henry out for a celebratory engagement evening."

"That would be great! It's just that we're a bit occupied right now."

"Oh, right. Of course, with the wedding."

J3 kept my pace, walking with me in the direction of Daphne's.

"Well, actually we're in the middle of a move. Or trying to be in the middle of a move. You see, there's this great loft on Reade Street, but it's so big and a bit out of our price range. But I so want for us to live there, as it's now hard to imagine living somewhere less impressive, not that I am materialistic or anything," I took a moment to remind myself that I wasn't materialistic. "But we have to think unconventionally if we really want it. And here I am giving serious consideration to letting a fraternity brother of Henry's named after the Tasmanian Devil move in with us."

Did J3 have any clue how to interpret my language?

"Tasmanian Devil?"

"Taz, for short."

J3 watched a couple as they pushed a canopied baby carriage past us, but I gathered he used them as a distraction so he could gather his thoughts.

"You know, Emily, I've basically made the Four Seasons my permanent New York address. I mean, they accept packages for me even when I'm not registered, plus the whole 'Will you be having your freshly squeezed grapefruit and Frosted Flakes served to you at 6:00 AM?'"

"Frosted Flakes?"

"My livelihood comes from video games. Have to start my morning like a kid."

"Love Frosted Flakes, especially the games. Except not my box's current game."

"The IQ test of the great Mesopotamians?" he said with a curious smile.

I nodded, somewhat astounded.

"That one was ridiculous. I felt so inadequate after basically being told that I was stupid," he said.

"Me too!" I blurted for the eighteen-thousandth time this afternoon.

"So, considering we eat the same breakfast food, perhaps I could be your renter. I mean I'd hardly ever be there, with my life in L.A. and traveling. I'll pay full price."

"J3, what a fantastic idea. But, really? I mean I don't want you to feel obligated."

"Obligated? Emily, I live in homes that come with room service and toiletries wrapped with hotel signage."

And this was bad why?

"Aside from my place in L.A., essentially a locker, I have no place to put my bag down and stay for a while. This would be ideal for me."

"But wouldn't you at least want to see the place? Though it really is quite amazing—three floors, terrace, these vapors with therapeutic properties that shoot from the bathroom. Excellent for your pores. The windows and space—I mean it really is fabulous."

"Of course, I wouldn't have thought otherwise. Considering that you are Emily Briggs."

Feeling embarrassed.

"Soon to be Philips," I said, wiggling my taped finger. "And, speaking of which, I just need to clear it with Henry, but I'm sure he'll be thrilled."

At the corner of Seventy-ninth, the WALK sign blinked its warning to hurry it on up unless you wanted to suck in exhaust fumes for a few useless seconds. I began to step from the curb when J3 pulled on the back of my sweater lightly, not enough to stretch its shape, saving me from a renegade Chinese food delivery man. I would have been part of the one-out-of-ten-million statistics to make it on the local news for being rammed by the wire basket hood of a bicycle. Had I renewed my health insurance?

"Thanks," I said in a trembling voice.

He smiled.

"No problem, just watching your back."

"I'll say."

"So I'll be at the Four Seasons till next Thursday, and hopefully I can get you two out to celebrate more than your engagement, considering that we all may be living together. You can just reach me there. And you? Are you at the same number?"

"Not really. And I'd give you my cell number, but I don't give anyone that number. I never use it."

"Of course, how could I forget, you find them to be very rude and discourteous. How John Singer Sargent of you. A fine correlation, as I know you will be this century's answer to portraiture and then some."

Smiling, completely reddened from all of this excitement and humility, I just spoke to conceal my discomfort.

"Okay. Right, then. I'll be calling you."

I straightened my pose, not because I had just been viewing Sargents and felt particularly self-conscious about my posture, but rather from feeling quite exhilarated. My shoulder blades went to places they've never been to before. I believe I appeared to be an exclamation point.

7

The kind of bliss you have when you get a check in the mail, having no idea where it came from but quickly cashing it anyway— this is how I felt while walking to Daphne's. I needed this moment. And my time was due. I could also use a big check made out to me that I had no idea where it had come from. Aside from Henry asking me to marry him, J3 agreeing to move into the Reade Street loft had been the first bit of good news in some time.

A protester screamed her issues at the corner of Madison, her causes unknown with all of the counter-productive yelling. These protesters really should reassess their tactics if they wanted to utilize their time effectively. I tried to calculate how I could cut across the street without being accosted by scary protester person, but the traffic did not flow in my favor. As I approached her, she smiled, targeting me the way the man with the thankless job of giving out flyers to a gentleman's club spots the pedestrian with the greased hair and gold chain.

"Hello!" I said, as friendly as possible to the activist who gets her haircut at a dog groomer's.

The fact that I even acknowledged her so favorably appeared to have propelled her into a state of disbelief, as the corner of Seventieth and Madison just received the MUTE switch.

Taking the moment to scan her billboard and signage, the reason for her not getting a real job and spending her afternoons to take out some frustrations that may be better serviced in a therapist's office, I saw she had been protesting about a woman's right to choose.

And here she tried to target me, when back in one particularly promiscuous summer I bought pregnancy kits that came two to a pack—a staunch one-issue voter—a poor utilization of one's time indeed. She needed to implement a Smythson business planner system. But, from the look of her, she may have been more of the Filofax type.

Once I moved away from the radius of her pitched space, it was as if my safety barrier had been broken. Her yelling resumed.

"You have a choice!" she called, to my back.

Punching in Daphne's number on my cell, I spoke quietly, as I found it discourteous to chatter about in public. Then the world's loudest bus approached. The world's loudest bus then stopped, directly in front of me.

"Hello?" said a barely audible voice on the other end of the receiver.

"Hey. Emily?" I screeched, not to myself but my goddaughter. "Is your mom there?" I yelled over rude bus noise and waved about the air of exhaust that would need about a week's worth of facials before clearing the grime to get back to my natural skin tone.

"Yeah, she's here. Hold on. Hey, where are you? Mommy said you were coming over, and I wanted to show you my blue dress. I have shoes and gloves that match with a little bag because I am a real lady."

The girl had become her godmother in training.

"Soon, love. I'm just approaching your building."

"Yeah!" she wailed. I could picture her engulfing the receiver like a lion swallowing his trainer's head.

Now that I was hearing-impaired, Daphne came on the phone.

"Emily? I thought you were coming by at two?"

"Sorry," I whispered. "A little held up, but I'm outside your building right now."

"Oh dear lord, speak up! No one is listening to your conversation. Speaking on cell phones is quite common these days, you know. See you soon," she said, hanging up.

I walked into a small Frenchwoman, knocking her over actually. She scrambled to the ground somewhat melodramatically. I offered my cell phone hand, but she started swatting at me, yelling *"Merde! Imbecile! Dans la lune!"*

Using my high school level French to interpret, I knew this was bad. I tossed my phone in one of my bags to quickly rid myself of the evidence and dashed into Daphne's building, because lawsuits didn't fit into my budget right about now.

I loved Daphne's house. I dubbed it my "Safe Place." No harm could happen to you here, aside from a child swinging from the shower curtain after watching *Tarzan* (which is now banned from their household) or a tricycle slamming into a falling Christmas tree (caught on video but erased by a distraught Emily). Now that I think of it, it seemed quite surprising how few visits Daphne's children had to Lenox Hill Hospital. But Daphne, dubbed the Madonna of Moms, had the kind of knowledge of whether Cheerios is better than Chex and can rattle on about glycemic and fiber indexes like traders following the yen.

The living room was painted in a shade of dove gray that sprouted from parquet herringbone floors and covered with art bid on from auction sales you read about in the next day's papers. Recently coming into some money from a wealthy aunt with no children of her own—the best kind—Daphne used some of her inheritance to buy a few incredible works of art, complemented by a smattering of scooters, toys, and stuffed animals gobbled by the couch's crease.

Always undergoing a constant state of transformation (not counting Emily and Henry's growth spurts), the kitchen usually had large tarpaulins draped around like backdrops in a photographer's studio. Since Daphne ran her own catering company, she had to keep up with the latest kitchen accessories the way I keep up with boots.

Daphne even rivaled my mother in the number of renovations she gave her kitchen. Whenever they met, they shared this secret language of contractors, architects, and new stoves the way a *W* accessories editor sought to discover a burgeoning jewelry designer. Daphne always appreciated Mom's recommendations for her experienced eye, while Mom loved Daphne's young, modern approach.

She greeted me at the entrance with her expensive hair, dressed in white denim pants, a charcoal sweater, and fitted jean jacket. Either she just came from Vera Wang or this was the Upper East Side uniform. Her long blond hair was brushed back, delicately balancing on the tips of her ear lobes before it naturally cascaded past her shoulders. Not even a jog in the park would undo her natural style. I've asked her many times in the past how she could keep her hair so perfectly, but she'd respond rather evasively, guarding her secret as would a director of CIA military operatives.

I always felt disheveled, inadequate next to Daphne. Her clothes came from the tissue wrapping of roped shopping bags and slipped onto her tiny frame. Her delicate features were prim, her profile simple and perfect like the cutout from an old-fashioned silhouette.

In that Sixty-ninth and Park tone, she said, "So? Let's see it."

See what?

"Emily? The ring! I'm surprised you haven't smacked me in the face with it."

I raised my hand languorously. Daphne took a firm grasp; her eyes widened, but not from trying to spot the diamond.

"Lord of the rings!"

"Yes, I thought the movie was too hyped as well."

"What the hell is this?" she said, dropping my hand. "It looks like Emily's missing tooth covered in silver magic marker!"

"Emily's missing a tooth?"

But from the anger in Daphne's voice, I could tell we weren't about to discuss her daughter's missing tooth.

"Emily, this is completely unacceptable. You have to get rid of it."

I regressed back to when I used to steal neighborhood pets, pawn them off as strays to my mom, and ask if we could keep them.

"I can't just return it like some sweater that I got in the wrong size."

"Why not? It clearly doesn't fit, so you have the perfect out."

As I was about to give my rebuttal, Daphne interrupted, "Don't give me the sentimental value line, which went out with drafty old castles."

I wanted to write an anonymous letter to Daphne's editor at

Gourmet, saying her recipes made my guests suffer from salmonella, do things that placed me in a school therapist's deviant file.

"But it was Henry's grandmother's," I said in a final effort.

"Did she make pies for a living?"

"Apparently a German woman, big boned."

"Though who am I to talk," she moaned, patting her stomach. "I can't seem to fit into any of my pants. It looks like I have to pay Oz a visit."

Daphne wasn't making any trips over the rainbow—no easy feat— she referred to her nutrition expert.

"It's not too bad," I said, feigning admiration to my silver-baby-tooth diamond. "In fact, the ring is growing on me."

"You'd need to gain another two hundred pounds before it grows on you!"

"Come on, Daphne," I snapped, now fully riled. So my fiancé wasn't chosen because he knew when to put his name on Louis Vuitton's waiting list, giving his wife the right gift come Christmas. Henry and I weren't that kind of couple. And I wasn't materialistic.

I had to figure how to subtly key Henry into getting his name on Vuitton's waiting list.

"This ring is much more appropriate for me, my lifestyle. With my painting," a heated pause. "And you know how I can't justify having a Cartier tank with all of the Wonder Woman Timexes I've lost."

I really wanted a Cartier.

"Imagine losing a four-carat engagement ring and how bad a day that would be."

Daphne, not looking satisfied, led me into the kitchen, where I became the target of two children with waving hands and barnyard screams until they settled in the vee of my arms.

"What a gorgeous dress, Emily."

She pulled away to give a curtsey, aptly showing her French blue velvet pinafore Florence Eisemann with a satin bow.

"And how about showing me that missing tooth of yours?"

Emily proudly opened her mouth, poking her upper lip.

"But the tooth fairy said she'd still give me a treat even though it's missing."

"How much do teeth go for now?" I asked Daphne.

"Twenty. But if we put that diamond from your ring under his pillow, she'd get considerably lower."

"Twenty? Whatever happened to a silver dollar and one of those tooth fairy certificates you used to get from Penny Whistle Toys?"

Daphne placed some cookies and bite-sized brownies onto a square celadon plate, arranging and rearranging them in different patterns.

"Mommy," said Emily, tugging on her sweater. "I'm dehydrated."

"You're not dehydrated. You're seven."

I asked Daphne if I could help, her wave saying if-I-had-a-second-I'd-need-it-for-my-used-up-seconds.

"So I'm thinking of having my tubes tied."

"Tubes tide?" I wasn't versed on contractor terminology.

"A hysterectomy. I've been getting so fat, and the idea of being pregnant again . . ."

I looked to Daphne's size 4 figure. She was not fat.

"Don't go there, Daphne."

She put the plate in front of me, arranged in a heart. I held a brownie and asked if it was fat-free. Daphne nodded longingly as she opened the fridge door, unsealed a salmon-colored Tupperware container with cut carrots and celery marinating in lemon slices and water, and arranged a few stalks in a shrunken flower vase. She bit into a piece of celery, which sounded like boots crashing on ice. I really enjoyed my brownie, but had my suspicions of its fat content. Two little hands slammed on the plate, followed by some giggles. Emily then darted to the fridge to take a bottled water.

"Andy and I had to attend this dinner the other night, and I couldn't even zip my red Zac Posen dress. This is my safety dress."

"Safety dress?"

"Dress that makes me feel thin even on fat days."

I nodded, thinking of my beaded Celine.

"So you just add another fifteen minutes on the Versaclimber."

"Fifteen minutes? Who has fifteen minutes?" she moaned.

"I believe half of Hollywood, now that reality television is such a success."

"Emily. I just can't be pregnant again. I just had Emily and Henry. Henry was born, like, a day ago."

It did seem that Daphne was always pregnant. Pregnant and making low-fat pastries, but I wasn't about to share that with her.

"Well, forget about me and my problems. You're getting married!"

"Indeed I am, though I may not have the ring to prove it," I said, looking down at my hand.

"That's for sure."

"But we are moving. In fact, Henry and I found the most fantastic loft on Reade Street. Without getting into the whole rigmarole of how out of our budget it is."

"Let me guess. Your realtor named Bunny said she had just one more apartment to show you but it was a bit out of your range. That you just needed to take a look?"

"Barb. Her name is Barb. And that sounds pretty accurate."

"They are cunning, those realtors. Good old bait and switch."

Daphne then lifted up a canvas tarp dusted with plaster to reveal a coffeemaker. Opening the aluminum lid of a glass jar, she poured in the beans. The kitchen began to sound like Starbucks without the overly produced jazz tunes.

"But Henry and I rationalized that we could still get the place if we find a roommate."

"Rent out a room? When you're newlyweds? Why on God's earth would you want to do that?"

Because it would be really fun and I'd dry off from my shower in a mist of eucalyptus.

"Emily, you couldn't possible consider this as a viable option—that's so artist SoHo 1974."

"But it really is great. Four bedrooms, walls of views—I've never seen anything like it. With all of the space and bedrooms, you'd have to make an appointment to see the person you are living with. And, the best news, I just bumped into J3 Hopper in the museum, and he said he'd take the room."

"J3 Hopper?"

"You remember him—J3 Hopper of Moon Chip."

"Right, the boy who plays video games for a living," she said sarcastically.

"He really is amazing. You should check out his domain—very impressive."

"You mean J3 is a prince?"

"No, dopey. The Web site for his company. And there are lots of zeros when Googling him."

"I don't know about this."

"Well, better J3 than the Tasmanian Devil."

Daphne looked confused.

"Trust me, Daphne, when you see this place. Just listen to Cold Play and buy expensive things online."

"No, I'm sure it's fantastic—very Emily free spirit, the early nineties. So," she continued, sliding a mug smelling of hazelnut under my nose. I loved being under Daphne's care. "How are we on the wedding planning?"

"Well, considering that today is a professional day."

She looked to me, probing for more details.

"I alternate days, one day strictly for wedding planning, the other to work on my art and business."

"And how far are we on the wedding side?"

"Well, I did finish the Real or Fake assignment," I quickly said, not willing to go any further than that.

"How about the location? Date set?"

"Actually, that is a bit of a problem. Had to nix Bridgehampton. On the market."

"Well, if that's not completely unfortunate."

"No kidding. And now Catherine wants to have it at the Plaza, which is a bit too Husband Number One and counting for me."

Daphne then pulled a black leather-bound folder from a stack of cookbooks, re-covering the area with a sheet from the impending remodel. Taking a seat next to me, she took out photos of Henry and Emily with instructions on the portrait she'd like to have me paint of them.

Giving her direction some thoughtful consideration, I pulled out my sketchbook from one of my Searle shopping bags. Flipping through the preliminary drawings I had sketched of Henry and me for our wedding portrait, it dawned on me that I'd be making two pictures of Henrys and Emilys.

"Let me see that," said Daphne, slipping my book from under my pen where it made a flatline.

"Emily, these are fantastic!" Her eyes lit up, mouth widened—the

kind of reaction I would have preferred when she saw my engagement ring.

"I'm actually really excited about doing these portraits. At the
museum, I became so inspired from seeing the Sargents. How his
paintings were more than pictures of society people—really expos-
ing the character—that's what I want to do. Rather than trace an
image seated before me, I want to learn about my subjects, spend
some time with them, see them at their homes and learn how they
exist."

Daphne watched me as if she were under a spell. Shaking her
head, she said, "Well, you can certainly spend as much time as you
want with those two terrors." And then Emily and Henry ran in on a
Lenny and Squiggy cue.

Emily was naked, her dress flowing from the top of Henry's head,
and they howled like Indians. In fact, Henry and I had done something similar to that the night we came home from the Botanical
Garden benefit, but under entirely different circumstances.

"I see that Emily still hasn't passed her nude phase."

"Yes," moaned Daphne. "Though I'd prefer it if you steer away
from any nudes of those two. I always found that photographer who
took pictures of her kids naked to be a bit weird."

"Will do," I said, taking my sketchbook back from her to draw a
few ideas. As I scribbled Henry in one of Emily's protective locks,
Daphne looked on.

"Momm-meee!" wailed Emily from the other room.

"What in God's earth," Daphne grumbled to herself.

Then Emily and Henry returned to the kitchen panting like
dogs.

"Henry won't give me back my sticker book," said Emily. Henry's
face was tattooed with stickers.

"I want you both to stop it."

"Mommy," said Emily, more calm. "Why is it that you always take
Henry's side?"

Daphne looked to me distressed, and I lifted my hands in a sur-
render position, not about to touch that one. Considering that I was
practically an only child, I would be of no help here.

"I'm the parent!" settled Daphne.

"But," said Emily.

"No buts. You're grounded. Time out. No Disney videos. Boarding school. Military school. Just behave! Pizza or Chinese?" she then asked more calmly of her children, receiving cheers for pizza and all the jumps and excitement of a Jack Russell after spotting a life-sized salami.

Even viewing parenting at its most challenging, I still had that occasional longing where my final word could soothe these tiny voices through a bribe or video-watching privileges of a singing sponge.

"But Mommy, what about my sticker book!" Emily wailed.

"Be an older sister and take care of your brother. We have guests."

Then Emily did her toe stomping bit.

"Emily. I will not tolerate this—you know I'm getting paid whether you act this way or not. Why did teachers say this?" Daphne asked me, and I shrugged. "As if we cared whether they would be paid or not. Em, am I losing it?"

She then breathed out her last threat to her children.

"Go into the den and watch the wedding video."

They both slipped into line. I found it strange how Daphne's kids loved watching her wedding video.

"So behave," ordering her last threat, "otherwise you'll be locked in the broom closet." Mumbling to me, she added, "The broom closet we don't have. And I will give you a dose of castor oil!" Then Daphne, again, said to me as an aside, "What is castor oil anyway? Where does one buy castor oil?"

I supposed a dose of castor oil would be as unlikely a punishment as swallowing a bundle of dynamite or a head flattened by an anvil.

"And what's an anvil?" I asked.

Daphne shook her head, returning to reprimanding her offspring.

"I will give you castor oil and lock you in the broom closet if you both don't behave. Then you'll have an overcoming-all-odds life story for the college essay. You know, I don't really care anymore." She then yelled to her children. "Go ahead, run around with scissors, give up the piano, take drugs."

She then took a gulp of air. Her face was so distraught, then changed, like cutting a smooth papaya. I wiggled my finger to Henry and Emily, where they leaned on the side of my leg.

"Henry," I said, "what I'm about to say may not apply to you the way it will your big sister, but just humor me and listen up. Now, Emily." Emily nodded. "These are very crucial years for you, and there are different ways of handling them. You can act up as much as you want or be the kind of little girl that goes along with the program."

Emily began to crouch, not taking her eyes off of me. She seemed drawn by my shoes, noted by her stroking my laces like a pet bunny.

"Now if you do go with the program, I have a pretty good suspicion that in your later years this will mean less bickering input from your mother. This is invaluable advice. Major. What first begins as her unnecessary involvement in selecting the girls you have play dates with to choosing your extracurricular activities, later becomes more involved. From the colleges you will apply to, even the boys you date, she will have an opinion. But if you show at this early age that you can assert some responsibility, she will give you some more latitude. You want that latitude."

I looked to her sharply.

"Emily?" she asked me. I nodded. "I like your shoes."

"Thank you. And I'm glad we had this little chat."

And from this they both, remarkably, retreated from the kitchen quietly.

"You know, Em," Daphne said to me, apparently using the mini-break from supervising her children to pull her hair into a chignon. "I worry about those college essays. I mean how will Emily and Henry be able to truly distinguish themselves from all the other Ivy applicants? At least I know Emily will have the grades—she's already showing such progress in class—but Henry? Perhaps I should just stage a high-profile kidnapping, get him on that Amber Alert thing. Is that hard to do? Have his picture on the cover of the *Post* and then, come college application time, he will be that kid who outwitted his kidnapper. What an essay!"

Daphne searched my eyes for feedback. I became more focused on my drawing.

"So?" she prodded.

"I don't know. Maybe you should just have him spend a summer on a kibbutz or something."

She seemed to take this under consideration, then shuddered and waved her hand.

"Or maybe I can have him do one of those wilderness adventures in Alaska. You know, where he has to make his bed out of leaves and such."

She then gave a ferocious look of worry.

"Or perhaps have him spend a summer on a ranch in Montana. Or an August in France!"

Her face now brightened.

"We have some time, not worth stressing over now."

As I put my pen down to evaluate what I drew, Daphne peered over my shoulder to assess my progress—memorializing a stickered Henry with Emily pounding her foot to the ground, hands on waist.

"Your talent has always amazed me," Daphne said, her tone considerably more calm than before.

I had a feeling she wasn't just smoothing me over. The painting I made for her a few years back of a modern-day take on the *Alice in Wonderland* tea scene had placement next to the Brice Marden in the living room.

"Have you ever considered changing agents?"

"Sure. I suppose I need to give Joanna the boot now that I am moving away from my illustrating, though it's a bit tricky. I mean, this is the woman that introduced Henry and me."

"Oh, stop being so emotional. You know it's all about management."

I supposed this wasn't a good time to share with Daphne my Smythson business planner. She expected a plan, something laser printed with graphs and pie charts.

"In fact, you should meet with Daniel West Galleries."

"Daniel West Galleries!" I cried.

Daniel West Galleries was perhaps the most prestigious art gallery in the city. He repped all of the great expressionists and nurtured the up-and-coming talent that made cameos in Gwyneth Paltrow movies.

She took a card from a stack of writing paper, wrote a number and slid it in my direction.

"Daniel West. On Fifty-seventh Street," she said, repeating what she wrote.

"Sure," I nodded spastically. "Gigi Jones is showing there right now. One of my favorite artists."

Daphne nodded.

"Okay then. Daniel is the right place to begin, and I have a good feeling about this, especially considering that my acquisitions from his gallery have essentially been subsidizing his Montauk manse. I will give him a call this afternoon and make sure he takes you on."

I shook my head in vehement protest.

"Daph! You know how I feel about handouts."

"Oh, please. Don't pull the self-righteous Emily bit on me. I'm not some furry-chested, gap-toothed, smarmy guy patroning you à la *Flashdance*—one of the best films ever even though I will never understand the casting of Michael Nouri—so I will get you the meeting, then it's up to you."

"But what if I'm not good enough? If he doesn't like me?"

"You really are getting all Jennifer Beals on me. Emily, sometimes it amazes me how you have no clue as to how fabulous you are. Now, you still have the Polaroids from your first collection?"

I nodded. Daphne had been referring to my first body of work, which included her *Alice in Wonderland* painting and a series of pictures based on fairy tales in modern settings, which showed at a local gallery in the Hamptons. It had been a success. Every work in the show sold for its asking price, where I had been grateful to just have the show and a really fun party afterward.

"Okay then, you're right. And hopefully you can mention to Daniel that I'm available on consecutive days after the day after tomorrow."

A thought wandered into my head from my post-graduate year. Days playing Ultimate Frisbee in the park, coming home to a machine blinking madly from a tape filled with messages, where I would choose the best option and make it home sometime in the dawning hours of the next day, maybe later if I didn't have brunch plans.

"Oh, just forget it. I'm available whenever."

The buzzer rang, delivering a pizza for Emily and Henry and signaling Daphne's need to get ready before the sitter came.

I organized my things while Daphne slid the dish of cookies into the mouth of a Glad plastic bag. Sealing its rim, she handed it to me as a goody bag from my visit, saying there was a hidden surprise.

We walked by the nursery where Emily quietly read to Henry, his head resting on her shoulder. Momentarily suspended from our intended mission, we saw this pair that had transformed from total chaos to tranquility like the motions of a crackling fire to the disintegrated log fuming slithers of smoke.

Daphne attended to the delivery while I made myself useful, collecting Emily and Henry and giving them tasks in the kitchen. They seated themselves when Daphne made her entrance holding the box of pizza at her stomach like a skirt filled with apples. Emily opened the carton, maneuvering the slices onto their plates, giving the piece with the cheese that clung to the rest of the pie to Henry.

Emily asked if they could have ice cream for dessert. Daphne saying they'd have Jell-O, avoiding their imploring eyes. She took out two plastic cups of red Jell-O, adding a third after I made an Emily look, and shot squirts of whipped cream onto the rubbery surface while filling me in on the pertinent details of her evening engagement with "my husband."

They were invited to a dinner party held by friends they knew from Vail. Our topics veered into a dramatic direction when they centered on her obligatory social life, which I found difficult not to be too judgmental about, especially after hearing an excessive amount of information on the pressure to be a stay-at-home mom by choice. Now that her notoriety as a caterer and entertainer veered into the potential of seeing her name on a stock ticker, Daphne had lost the ambition.

She then asked me if I felt cold. I felt fine.

Daphne punched in more codes on a device that sounded like a drunken canary than it took for me to type out my senior thesis.

"We just got this air temperature control system," she said proudly. "I can actually coordinate temperature with the movements of different people."

Ever consider adjusting the vents?

"Mommy's always cold," said Emily, adeptly scooping up Henry's Jell-O while he used his spoon to make airplanes.

I gave my kiss good-bye, and Daphne expressed her disappointment that I'd be missing Andy's puppet show. Over Henry and Emily's squeals of excitement over this show that had more fanfare than Yul Brynner's last *King and I* performance, I asked if he could be persuaded to do an encore the next time I visited.

*   *   *

During my ride home, my mind spun quicker than my thoughts could effectively register. Overwhelmed by the abundance of good tidings I had received, what I was most excited about at that moment was my bag of treats. I ate another brownie and opened my sketchbook to a clean page with images of Henry and Emily still fresh in my head.

I drew them side by side, Emily in her French blue pinafore dress and Henry in a striped button-down. Their blue eyes were large and magnificent, too big for their bodies the way a newborn's eyes look in an ultrasound. Henry's head tilted on Emily's shoulder while hers locked onto his cheek.

8

Next to the bed, a tall glass of milk and two Godiva chocolates were laid out for me like medication. I looked at the folded stationery. Henry had sketched a drawing of the two of us in the form of a plastic couple on top of a wedding cake made from containers of low-fat pints of Ben & Jerry's.

"Hi, Em," the note read.

I know you wanted to make s'mores tonight but had to go out with some people from FOX on the Upper East Side, where I'd just as soon head for suburbia and get some fresher air out of the meeting. Tried calling you but didn't leave a message knowing how you are with etiquette on mobiles.

Unless I get lost coming home, hope to be back early but no need to wait up. Enjoy the sweet, my sweet.

Love, Henry.

Not certain if the note had a hidden message about whether both the chocolates were for me or meant to be shared, I reread the note comprehensively and then popped a Godiva in my mouth. Yummy but too quick, very similar to an orgasm, but this way I get the calories.

Sitting at the edge of the bed, I realized this was not the first time Henry had avoided a plan with me. In fact it had become a regular pattern. Staring at the note, my eye kept wandering to the other chocolate. That turmoil didn't last long. Essentially validating that my day consisted of Frosted Flakes, Jell-O, chocolate brownies, and now Godiva, I would be a little girl forever, albeit a fat little girl with a bad complexion as a result of this kind of diet—a prime subject for a Dr. Perricone "Before" picture—and I would have to eat organic food that needed to be weighed on a scale.

I stretched on the bed and began to draw our wedding portrait. Now that I had the image in my head, which was based on the pose of the Sargent portrait of the Stokeses, it was only a matter of putting the picture to paper.

Beginning with a long clean line to create the skirt of my dress, I then added the bodice, my arms, and head. Drawing Henry proved to be more difficult. I lost control of my artistic ability with a picture that started to resemble the alphabet of a dead language. Hoping that my efforts would evolve into something magnificent, like a tangled network of city grids that came into focus when viewed from above—such wishful thinking—I broke from my miserable attempt by collapsing back on the bed, drifting in and out of sleep.

I dreamt that I walked down an aisle, or I assumed it was me walking down an aisle, because it really resembled one of my yet-to-be-filled-in cartoon faces dressed in a wedding gown—a mix of animation and reality in an homage to *Mary Poppins*.

I walked toward the altar and Henry, who was also an incomplete drawing and just a faceless cartoon dressed in a tux. The closer I approached the altar, the greener my face turned. Suddenly a snout began to grow, reptilian scales popped from my skin—a transformation of Incredible Hulk proportions where I evolved into a green lizard on steroids. My clawed hands ripped from my duchess satin—the damage to the dress—I wondered about refunds.

As I opened my mouth to breath a torrent of fire, I heard a cell phone. Someone had their cell phone on in the church? How rude. Probably one of Henry's guests. Perhaps this was why I had been turning into something that stomps on train sets in campy Japanese films, for fear that an ill-mannered person would have their cell phone turned on. But it kept ringing until I made myself wake up from this sweat-inducing nightmare, realizing that it had been my cell phone ringing from one of my shopping bags.

I answered the phone. "Emily?" said Daphne. "How odd. I was deliberately calling to leave a message on your mobile because it's so late."

Looking at the bedside clock, I saw it was after one in the morning.

"What are you doing up? And why do you have your phone on?"

Rubbing my eyes, trying to make out what had been happening, I started rambling.

"Have I been a monster?"

"Not too bad," chirped Daphne. "Not as obsessive as most of us, but I do detect that you haven't quite been yourself."

I steered away from this direction. "I must have never turned my mobile off," I said, filling in the pieces—notably the injured petite French lady who currently spent the night in Lenox Hill Hospital.

"Well, I'm glad I got you because I have some amazing news to share—you're meeting with Daniel West. Tomorrow!"

"Tomorrow?" I said in a panic, running around the room to try and find my Polaroids. "Why for God's sake so soon?"

"Don't fret," she commanded. "He has to go to Paris for a few weeks, maybe even a month, but Daniel really wants to meet with you. He loved your film, *Combining Art Forms,* and has always made comments on your talent, always admiring your *Alice in Wonderland* painting whenever he's over. Now I got you the meeting, all you have to do is dance. Tomorrow, four PM, at West Galleries on Fifty-seventh.

"Listen, I have to run. Andy had too much to drink tonight, petrifying the nanny with stories about his days bumping into Robert Chambers at Dorian's and the Mad Hatter."

Robert Chambers, the Literal Bad Boy.

I took my sketchpad and headed the page "Literal Bad Boys," drawing thumbprint faces as icons—Robert Chambers, Mark Bundy—but I quickly lost interest in Literal Bad Boys, as it became difficult to imagine lustful thoughts with men that looked at women's heads as dandelions.

The next page I entitled "Bad Boys—Greatest Hits." Steve McQueen, Marlon Brando before he got fat, JFK Junior and Senior, Paul Newman in *Cat on a Hot Tin Roof.* After Paul Newman, I became depressed; the likelihood of meeting my Bad Boy would either take a Oujia board or just be unlikely, as they were dead or aged. On a fresh page, I wrote "Bad Boys Who Want Emily Briggs." Michael Schoeffling/a.k.a. *Sixteen Candles'* Jake Ryan, George Clooney, Jude Law, Johnny Depp.

Madly scribbling, ink bleeding through the page, I loved this exercise. Found it more arousing than a night cloaked in steamy air, moving to the effects of drinks with tequila, dressed in something Cavalli. There's sultry music played by a rock star who can pull off wearing leather pants. I dance with hands stretched to the air, chin lobbing shoulder to shoulder and Henry looking like a Bad Boy who wants Emily Briggs. I bolted upright. Looked to Henry's side of the bed and discovered he wasn't home. I leaned back into my pillow, deflated for not having my wanton lusts realized with a blink of an eye, wiggle of my nose—sketch to my pad.

Feeling a tickly sensation to the side of my cheek, I began rubbing my face furiously, afraid that the effects of turning into a Bridezilla were returning. Awakened from another bout of sleep, I found Henry shielding himself from my pattering hands.

"Whoa there, Emily!"

I really have turned into a monster.

"Oh, Henry!" I cried.

"You're always thinking of chocolate," he said, giving a wicked glance to the empty plate. His hair was a relief of undulated peaks, like the top of a baked Alaska. I wondered if he went for the deliberate disheveled look where product is needed, like distressed designer jeans or, considering it was Henry, that he had no time to use a hairbrush.

"I can see you've enjoyed your Godivas?"

"Right. Sorry about that—eating both the chocolates, hitting you and all."

He smiled and I pretended not to notice, returning my focus to Henry who appeared to be the end result of the Fab Five, dressed in Seven jeans, a suede blazer, and the long striped scarf I'd bought for him for Christmas, given to him with hopes he'd wear it to impress me, though I'd anticipated it would become a nesting ground for dust mites, curled up in a ball in the corner of our closet.

Giving him the once-over, I said, "You don't look anything like that guy who opposes offshore drilling in Alaska."

"Yeah," he laughed, leaning toward me to kiss my cheek, smelling like George Hamilton. He wore cologne, which struck me as odd. I never was one for cologne.

"You smell," I said, wiggling my nose like a distraught bunny. "You just smell," was all that I could say.

"I actually have some news." Henry said, avoiding the issue of his smelliness.

"Me too!" I yelled, Henry wiping his cheek from my speck of spit. "But you first. I need to brush my teeth while I listen. Okay?"

He nodded uncertainly, probably because he really knew I needed to brush my teeth, which I found somewhat embarrassing. So I raced into the bathroom, squeezed a strip of toothpaste onto my electric toothbrush, and ran back into the room cleaning quietly so the buzzing noise wouldn't interfere with what Henry had to say, as I always had been extremely courteous and respectful.

I turned off my electric toothbrush, because Henry waited to talk the way you waited for traffic to pass when speaking on your mobile.

"Well, it's official," he announced.

I tilted my head confused, mildly panicked, dropping my arm holding the toothbrush. I knew I've been in a bit of a sleepwalk, but never remembered us getting married.

"So I've gotten the go. *Duncantics* will be a regular series on FOX. Sunday nights. Pencil it in."

Sunday nights weren't good for me. Always viewed them as a weekly New Year's Eve, how you spent your New Year's being the same as how you spend your Sundays. Thus I tried to do something intelligent and healthy—read, avoided sugary cereal, and chilled, or did something really crazy like honor the request of my imaginary publicist so I could be seen at a fabulous party, picking shrunken Bernadin entrées from a teepee of pebbled ice. Generally, I ordered sushi, finished reading the *Times* Style section and the captions in the magazine.

"Aren't you excited? And I'd love it if you could contribute. Have Lily make a few appearances perhaps?"

Combining Art Forms had been the first time that our strip characters were ever featured together. Henry wanted a more regular venue for Duncan—his character's alter ego who was a politician turned rock star—while FOX waited to see if they could still hire the same people along with getting the assured backing before giving Henry any commitment.

"Of course! Not everything has to be about the wedding."

Now Henry looked confused.

"I mean. Just excellent."

"And it looks like George Clooney will sign on again to do Duncan's voiceover. He loves going to the office unshaven, lunching on burgers and shakes. But for some reason I can't imagine George Clooney eating a burger."

George Clooney!

"George Clooney! George Clooney!"

"Whoa there, Emily—when I say 'George Clooney' you have the same reaction as when you're told 'Private Chanel Sample Sale.'"

"But I never got to meet him when he worked on *Combining Art Forms.*"

As a matter of fact, the producers were rather evasive when making the film, noticeably vague whenever I asked about George and how it should be essential that he meet the creator behind his leading lady, albeit a cartoon one. It actually seemed rather suspect, how I'd make a few inquiries as to when I would be able to have that promised chat, but always got the runaround.

I also became agitated at their choice of Kate Hudson to be the voice behind Lily, my character. I saw myself as more of the Christy Turlington type. Even though she couldn't act, it was only a matter of reading a script, being a cartoon and all. First I thought that Kate Hudson was a bit young for George—despite their being cartoon characters—but then I found myself strangely jealous of her, even though she and George rarely read their lines together.

"Hey?" I asked, pulling closer to him. "Does this mean there will be a Duncan/Henry doll/action figure in the works?"

"I don't know about a doll, but they do intend on marketing this thing—videos, T-shirts, cards. And why do you ask?" he said, smoothing the wrinkles of the bedsheet.

"Well, it would be great to hammer its face in every time we have a tiff, a healthy way to take out the aggression. Don't you think?"

Henry shook his head in that way of his.

"What's even better," he said excitedly, diverting the topic, "the Reade Street loft, though still a bit of a pinch to the funds . . . well, let's just say we don't have to entertain the idea of living with a Tasmanian Devil."

"Oh," I whimpered.

"You want to live with the Tasmanian Devil?" Henry then clenched my chin so tight he unlocked my jaw.

"No, of course not," I said, getting up from the bed to return to the bathroom. Filling a glass with water, I rinsed my teeth. After spitting into the sink, I looked into the mirror, where Henry's reflection watched me.

"My news," I started. Henry followed me back to the bedroom, and we both began to undress. I slipped on Henry's pajama top, and he changed into the bottoms. We were good that way, buying one pair of pajamas that we both got simultaneous use from. And here we thought we'd have financial woes.

"It's just that part of my news was that I found a renter."

"You did?"

"Yes, actually. J3 Hopper, as a matter of fact. I bumped into him today at the Met. He's always traveling—based in L.A., having recently bought a home there—but said how he would love to have a place to stay when he's in New York that doesn't come with room service."

"How curious."

"I know. Exactly my reaction."

But I think Henry was interested for a different reason. I loved hotel living for the punch-in-the-extension conveniences, blanketing your body within a plushy white bathrobe. I have told a number of people that I should be buried in a hotel robe, which would expedite my entry through the gates of heaven by already being in dress code. The heaven I envisioned is a sort of eternal stay at the Amandari in Bali. There were also rivers of chocolate and Oompa Loompas.

No Oompa Loompas.

Henry sat on his side of the bed, distressing the sheet he had made such a point to straighten earlier. He gave it a studied look before peeling back the layers. Propping his pillow, he shifted toward me.

"You know Em, Reade Street *is* bit of a pinch to our budget."

Our budget? Did not like the sound of that at all.

"And, from the sound of it, J3 does fit the ideal renter composite. The idea of living with a guy who recently mugged for the cover of *Wired* . . ."

"Really? He was on the cover of *Wired?*" I said, sounding quite impressed. Not that I'd ever read *Wired*.

I then thought of J3 at the museum—his height, presence, and intellect. His looks became more absorbing the more times you see him, like an Ingmar Bergman film (or the one Bergman film I had to see for a film class). At first study, you question the meaning of significant elements and, after seeing it a few times, features become more prominent and interesting. You begin to dwell on images you quickly wrote off at the first, cursory glance.

"I really like this idea. And you know what the best part is?" said Henry, lifting up the blanket for me to slide in next to him.

"Aside from having someone to share all of our bridal registries with?"

"Free video games! But not only that," Henry said like an excited little kid who just broke his score. He propped his head on his hand to look down on me, while I imagined what he'd look like if I magic-markered a Mike Tyson tattoo on his face.

"Early previews of his video games!"

"So you mean to tell me that you're basing the person who will live with us, in our new home, on receiving early copies of video games?"

Henry seemed a bit dumbfounded.

"Uh, yeah!"

I thought about living with a designer for Chanel and getting early collection pieces.

"Okay then. So J3 will be our renter? We're going to put a bid on Reade Street?"

"Absolutely!" said Henry, extending his hand up in the air for a high five, something I haven't done since I played college sports, but I supposed it was appropriate, considering the momentous occasion, so I high-fived my fiancé in our bed, agreeing to take in a roommate.

9

"What are you wearing?" asked Daphne over the phone as I dressed for my interview with Daniel West.

"My black Michael Kors pants, fitted Chanel sweater, and"—I paused, holding in my breath to accentuate my calf with the same motion as tucking in your tummy for too-tight jeans—"my sexy suede Dior boots."

"Change."

"Change?"

"Change!" she ordered.

"Excuse me, Ms. Wintour, but I do recall these being recent runway items."

"Daniel is expecting a creative personality, someone with a touch of the exotic. You must show your openness to experimentation. Your love of color!"

Was she talking about my meeting or having an affair with a Masai tribesman?

I was waiting in the reception area of Daniel West Gallery, which I knew was the right place with "Daniel West Gallery" painted outside the door in dripping red paint, probably brought to you by the people behind the latest teen slasher movies.

In my head I kept calling him "Daniel West." Daniel West was a brand, one that I knew on a commercial level. Just as I wouldn't call Orville Redenbacher "Orville" or Frank Perdue "Frank" from the many times I met with these two men, it would be inappropriate to refer to Daniel West simply as "Daniel."

Turning the knob to go into the gallery, you went from red and white to black and white. I began to think of the "what's black, white, and red all over" jokes, supplementing the uninspired interiors with skunks in blenders. The walls were so bare they were blinding, with one black canvas for which I couldn't identify the painter, and considering it was really just a black canvas, that made it a bit more difficult to attribute.

I was feeling pleased with myself for not taking Daphne's advice on what I'd wear, as I fit right in with the black and white composite without even doing a scout.

The receptionist pointed to a seat and I sank into a high-backed couch that had an uncomfortable scratchy texture. Overcome by tiredness, I considered nodding off, until the receptionist awakened me, informing me that I would meet with "Mr. Daniel West" in about fifteen minutes. He then offered me a water, which I declined because I wasn't sure if I was being graded on this and didn't want to appear as the high-maintenance type.

He smiled, returning his attention to his Smythson planner and wrote something, which I figured to be a mark that passed in my favor. I then took out my Smythson to show that we were indeed of the same tribe. Having my book also gave me security, something that preoccupied me, with no coffee table displaying magazines to read or other attractions for awaiting guests unless you elected to stare at the black canvas that took all of two seconds to commit to memory.

Scribbling nonsensical notes also distinguished me from the yappy cell phone type, which was an important quality I wanted to distinguish myself as. Luckily, the view onto Fifty-seventh Street had some clever animation with its bustle and color of New York street energy. I must have been nervous, going to such efforts to impress a receptionist, whose job was to answer a phone, an easy enough skill that required no prior training.

Suddenly, a bird made a terrifying splat into the window, its wings frayed into every direction before it slid from our view. I turned to

the receptionist and he met my gaze, his face contorted to hysterical directions, and then we both burst into laughter at the expense
of this bird—this bird now probably squatting somewhere in a halo
of stars. My relationship with the receptionist shifted to a new, more
intimate role.

"Miss Briggs?" asked Daniel West from the side of the reception
desk.

"Oh, hi," I said waving, trying to act composed, but that would be
like hitting the brakes after driving over 90 mph, not that I would
drive over 90 mph (unless it was very late and the highways were
free of traffic).

"What's so funny?" asked Daniel West.

"Well. You see, there was this bird," but I stopped, realizing that
Daniel West may be some animal rights fanatic and not find the humor in a bird that would soon be swept into the dustbin of a worker
in a gas station jumpsuit.

"Have you been to the new gallery before?"

His last gallery had been located on Prince Street, which I'd
frequented many times, drawn by the great parties where you discussed art with celebrities in a mist of champagne.

"No, but I rarely missed your exhibitions on Prince," I said, as we
both stared at his name dripped in blood. Daniel West Gallery—very
clear.

He laughed at me with his eyes. Daniel West was quite handsome.
His butt most certainly was, thoroughly analyzed as he showed me
to a conference room adjacent to the gallery's main viewing room.

Presenting a seat at the end of a long steel mesh table that seemed
to be created from the underwear of armor, I shimmied onto it with
flirtation in mind. The chair felt rather uncomfortable. It could
have benefited from a cushion, but that would have disrupted the
style of the unfurnished room.

Breathing in his $100-an-ounce cologne, I thought that, while
cologne topped my list of dislikes on men, worn on Daniel West—
with the dark shoulder-length hair tucked behind his ears, a black
cashmere sweater, and Prada loafers—the style worked.

I leaned down to give him my portfolio, an aluminum box that
encased eight and a quarter-inch images of my paintings glued onto

thick pieces of black poster board and a few Polaroids of my most recent works. He thumbed through the pictures delicately, giving each frame significant thought. This lasted about eighteen hours.

"Very Lucian Freud, yet you have this classic training—like the great portraitists if they were on something. Manet, Velasquez," he finally said. "There's even a hint of Picasso—his early works. But I also see some Jenny Saville from the realism. And then there's the Claude Belcham appeal—whom I represent, as I am sure you know."

Daniel West dropped the names of varied artists the way the fifth floor of Barney's tested out the brands of new designers. Usually I'd be weary of such overt namedropping, though considering this man had the power to direct my future, I'd play along.

"Listen, Emily," Daniel West said, shimmying the metal lid on top of my portfolio. He then shot his dark eyes at me. If he kissed me, I wouldn't be offended. "You're good, young, and I like this little pixie thing going on."

Pixie thing?

"So, by the time I return from Paris, I want to have another meeting to see if you have enough sketches to base an exhibition. A portrait—or two. Possibly three paintings—shoot for an entire body of work."

Was it just me or was his list of demands increasing as he spoke? I should really have used that Smythson planner of mine to take some serious notes, especially considering that there was no one else in the room to copy from. Did he really call me a pixie?

"If I like what I see, I will be giving you the go-ahead to produce enough paintings for an exhibition. We want to shoot for before the summer. Everything stops during the summer months, so you need to work fast and brilliantly."

"Sure," I said happily, apparently agreeing to produce more pieces than I had ever created, unless we counted the paintings I made in the particularly rainy summer of '84 that focused on my friends' belly buttons (really an excuse to ogle my tennis instructor's abs). Suddenly I had an image of all of my Smythson planner sections—the wedding, the move, and now a major exhibition. And then there was that wedding portrait of Henry and me. Well, that would just have to be part of the exhibition, along with the picture of Daphne's Emily and Henry. Daniel will just not be privy to such minor details right now. I started making notes in my head.

"Okay then." Daniel West gave me his hand, for me to shake, and I offered him my hand with the duct-taped finger. He seemed perplexed by this.

"Too big!" I laughed, and he just looked inquisitively. Why did he call me a pixie? I hoped that wouldn't stick.

"Jean Paul, outside in reception, will take your information and go over the deadlines with you and set up our next meeting."

"Sure, Jean Paul."

"You know Jean Paul?"

Of course I knew Jean Paul. We watched a kamikaze pigeon slam into your window but, again, Daniel West may have been some animal rights activist, so I just gave him a nod.

10

Arriving home, my body gelled with exhaustion, though the excitement from another day's promising events gave me some artificial buoyancy. I found Henry in the kitchen reading one of my bridal magazines. He looked up from what appeared to be an absorbed read.

"Ah, Emily. Just the girl I want to see. Come here," he said, tapping his knees for me to sit on. Settling onto his lap, I flipped my legs over the side of the chair.

"Now, you know why these 'Wedding Girls' become, to use your term, 'Bridezillas'?"

I shook my head to say that I had no idea.

"It's because they've gone about this wedding process completely the wrong way. The hors d'oeuvres, for example, are mini-masterpieces."

Henry flipped to a page with lush photography of bite-sized edibles that were more appetizing than a fashion spread of Chanel paired with Levi's. He began reciting the captions.

" 'Ceviche served in a martini glass combines tuna, mango, pineapple and spicy wasabi caviar, grilled baby corn wrapped in nasturtium leaves.' And look how tiny and beautiful these things are—I wouldn't be able to eat them feeling all guilty for that underpaid, overworked amigo who had to wrap all 150 baby corns in nasturtium leaves like it was some special rite in a religious ceremony. Which, by the way, is completely downplayed in all these weddings. I mean, they completely overlook the momentous celebration of it all—seeing that it involves God and so forth—and just go right to the mini Waldorf salad."

Henry was fully involved, bouncing his knees up and down to the beat of his excitement, and I almost fell from his lap.

"And this leads me to my most important point—the alcohol. Also completely underplayed, if mentioned at all in these magazines. I mean, if you get the guests blitzed right at the get-go, they won't notice the harp player in the gazebo woven with vines of clematis. Alcohol, my dear Emily," he said with a quick peck to my cheek. "Focus on the drinks, not the little things, and then we've got ourselves a wedding that may not be remembered because of all of the blackouts. The important thing is that everyone will be guaranteed a good time. Even if it's at the expense of a few cases of tequila."

Henry's ability to take something abstract and make it simple always impressed me. He had cleverness—a skill that funneled his irreverence and drawing ability into a cartoon—made omelets from pouring them out of a shrunken milk container, and used spackling for uses other than spackling. (Or what I assumed were uses other than spackling.) We could live in the expensive loft just by generating more money from it. How an overly hyped wedding was basically just a big party.

"Hold on," I said, jumping from his lap to retrieve my wedding planning book. Scribbling notes, I ran back to Henry's lap. "These are really good ideas."

Henry glanced at the first page with the Fake or Real check.

"And what did you mean by this? Fake or Real?" he asked, considerably more somber in tone. "Does this have anything to do with the ring?"

"Er, no!"

He looked into my eyes, hurt. I did not enjoy this look and couldn't bear to hold his gaze. Pulling me in closer, he gave a tight squeeze and then released me so I could breathe.

"It *is* the ring," he said, lifting up my fingered hand. "I was wondering where all the duct tape went, as I have been starting with the moving boxes."

"Henry, it's not the ring," I blurted. "Just this game I played about fake breasts and real breasts."

Henry stared at me, confused.

"I know this may sound like it has nothing to do with planning our wedding, but I desperately wanted to make a check, as I've been feeling quite inadequate lately."

He waved his hand along with some *sshhs.*

"No need, Emily. I've been the one who should be exploding with apologies. First I give you some feeble proposal and then a ring that I'm sure your little friends have had some definite opinions on."

I shot him an Emily smirk.

"There are two things I need to make clear. First off, one of the reasons I love us, as a couple, is that we move along to our rhythm. No pageantry, no circus—we're real. I never intended to give you some schmaltzy insincere proposal. And, secondly, as you know, I barely speak of my family, or my father, to be more precise. The guy treated my mother horribly. They were divorced when I was six, and my mother then went on the *Sally Jesse Raphael Show* to complain about him."

I always looked away from Henry when he told me about his mother, how she vented her trials on tabloid television. He seemed to take this rather seriously, typically discussing his mother's livelihood as a frequent guest on the talk-show circuit in intimate moments. She even won their dining room set on *The Price Is Right.* They ate their holiday dinners off of a table won on *The Price Is Right.* I had to sniff the side of my finger and mentally play upsetting Discovery Channel footage to contain my laughter.

"The only couple in my family that I can base a real marriage on is my grandparents. My grandfather was a history professor at Stanford, my grandmother a homemaker. The ginger-snap-baking kind."

My eyes lit up. I loved ginger snaps.

"I just remember them sitting, silently communicating while they shifted letters on a Scrabble board. It wasn't much, like that ring, but who said the size of a diamond had to measure the love?"

Never being one for tears, I threw my hand to my face because I truly had been moved to a deeper place. We were like one of those couples that communicated and expressed their feelings like the too-good-to-be-true parents that wouldn't split up because of contractual obligations on a WB show.

"Now, back to the wedding," he said, opening the book. "No to frozen soufflés made with five kinds of berries, yes to Big Gulp–sized drinks with eight kinds of alcohol. So what we need to do is go to a Seven-Eleven, buy a supply of Big Gulp containers," Henry directed, while I jotted it all down on a fresh To Do page. "And, while we're at the Seven-Eleven, we'll just check to see if they cater so we can do the whole late-night munchies theme. Our guests are going to love us!"

I studied the page. Happier that the blank pages were being filled with ideas, I still had concerns.

"Henry, while I love your creativity and involvement in all of this, I do have one big question."

"Shoot."

"Where should we have it?"

He looked in the air, seeming to give my question some thoughtful consideration.

"I wanted a wedding in Bridgehampton—not happening. Mom has this idea of a big society wedding in the city. The woman is infatuated with the Plaza. And then there's the whole sentimentality issue—finding a place that expresses the both of us."

"I got it!" he said, again almost knocking me from his lap. "The Riga Royal!"

That was the stupidest idea I'd ever heard.

"You love going there for their retro drinks, the kitschy décor. Or how about the Howard Johnson's in Times Square!"

No, *that* was the stupidest idea I'd ever heard, which Henry must have gathered by my Emily smirk (they came involuntarily). Looking up to the air in that pondering way of his, his face brightened.

"I know—the Stanhope Hotel!" he cried.

I shared a lascivious smile with Henry. The Stanhope was the setting of one of our unforgettable trysts, where an impromptu check-in and elevator were involved—all under the influence.

"You are so right. So here we'll please all the parties that count, and you and I can reenact our steamy affair," I said.

"And the party favors—forget these custom-made wrapped chocolate bars, silver picture frames, scallop-topped boxes filled with pistachio dragées and bamboo woven fans. Condoms! We will be giving away condoms! And, in respect to the whole 'custom-made' trend, we'll go with custom-made condoms!"

I snatched the book back from Henry's clutch, taking all of this down in a fury. Looking at what I wrote, I felt a tingle more associated with yuletide cheer under the guise of an eggnog buzz (or, more likely, vodka, as who really drank the eggnog?). Many checks were being made.

"And we haven't even gotten into the fun stuff."

Fun stuff? I began to swerve back into panic mode.

"The honeymoon! Any ideas where you want to go?"

I had to think of something quickly before Henry would suggest some spiritual wilderness adventure with many chanting bald men and the need to pack a hand shovel for toilet purposes.

"Well, naturally, none of those $799 seven-night packages where the honeymoon suite has a two-story champagne glass whirlpool."

Henry's brows swiveled into a question mark. I supposed I underestimated my fiancé—who would never go for a champagne glass whirlpool.

"Henry Philips, I've accomplished more with you in this past hour than I have this entire wedding-planning time."

"Two minds, in the colorful creative package, are better than one."

I looked at my ring, Henry watching me momentously. The story of his grandparents, picturing them playing Scrabble, was all very warm and touching. I still hated the ring, not that I was materialistic or anything.

"So? Are you excited?" he asked.

I was excited. And then I began thinking of what I'd have for dinner.

11

"Do I look reality television thin?"

"You want to look reality television thin? You'd go on reality TV?" Henry questioned me mockingly.

"Er, no!"

Of course I would never do something as cheesy as go on reality television. But, then again, if I were asked? Maybe, perhaps.

I pulled on my black embroidered Gucci pants, Marni parka created at the expense of a family of foxes, and Manolo boots whose heels have been whittled down about a quarter of an inch due to their being scraped and sanded from being over-worn.

Henry watched as I got ready.

"Why on God's earth are you dressed for a movie premiere?"

We were getting ready to go to the closing for our Reade Street loft. We were the successful bidders, and now owners, of our first home, and I felt very grown up and now a legitimate lady who could wear sunglasses on top of my head and be taken seriously when shopping at Oscar de la Renta.

After some heated bidding done over Henry's cell phone, to which I had to relent and agree that they had some advantages, we were embroiled in a bidding war that Henry won over coffee and frittatas at Silver Spurs. Many momentous acts have happened over coffee and frittatas at Silver Spurs. I wondered if we should have our wedding at Silver Spurs, but that idea lasted about two seconds.

So I dressed for our closing the way a starlet would dress for her first premiere because it wasn't every day that you bought a loft. This outfit would be memorialized, always remembered as the clothes I wore to the closing, right down to the La Perla thong (baby blue with a creamy lace).

Giving Henry a huff, not justifying with an answer his ineptitude about why one would dress for a closing, we set off to the bank and had to pay a great deal of money just to get a certified check. Sitting in the lawyer's office on chairs bought in the furniture section of Staples, we made out more checks to people I didn't know or hadn't heard of.

I looked wistfully as Henry slid one check after another to a very large man with a dandruffed mustache. His shoulders were dandruff free, which may have been attributed to his having less hair on his head than inside his ears. At least he had the good sense not to do a comb-over, though I thought he could afford plugs after seeing Henry's and my savings disappear in a matter of minutes, and we came away with nothing to show for it. No fun toy, a trip requiring two planes, or putting a lone hanger in my closet to use with something pulled from tissue scented of designer fragrance.

Barracuda Barb arrived as Henry scribbled his signature on the last document, after signing his name more times than Justin Timberlake greeting fans down an unguarded red carpet. After a few congratulatory handshakes and discussions on how brilliantly Barb handled the bidding, Henry and I shared a glance and fell into the sight of one another until Barb intercepted the moment, offering to take us out for a drink at the inappropriate time of 3:45 in the afternoon. Barb hatched another one of her plans where she could insert herself into the front and center slot, and I needed to intercept her machination. I excused myself to call J3, telling him that it had been made official and we'd be living with one another.

Considering that J3 had to return that night to L.A., he asked if we could all meet up for a drink, at 4:00 PM at Thom, which I immediately agreed to.

"Henry," I barked, directed more to the bitch sniffing my property.

"We have to go soon. Meet up with J3, since he's leaving tonight."

They both turned to me, Henry with an expression of acquiescence, whereas Barb started to show her Barracuda fangs.

"Okay then, Barb," said Henry, shaking her hand from her shoulder socket. "We'll have you over soon. For a drink," he said, completely justifying the Emily smirk on my face.

Once we exited the office, I repeatedly said, "We'll have you over soon. For a drink," until I extinguished the mileage from such a dim comment.

With some time to pass before J3 arrived, Henry ordered me a gimlet while he asked for a Heineken. Sure enough, one of those synthetic girls marketed and produced in the same procedure as a knockoff Prada bag walked past us with the blond hair, boobs and skinny V-necked tee with FCUK decaled across the chest, which basically said "read me and stare at my chest." And Henry read and stared, responding to the subliminal messaging.

"Can I ask you something?" I said, ready to ask whether or not Henry prevented me from doing so. He took a sip from his beer, using the drink as a means to sulk away from his impending punishment.

"Now that we've demonstrated how effective we are as communicators, making me ever more confident with what we have, your taking the time and showing the interest to discuss with me the wedding, your proposal, and the ring"—I held up my hand to wiggle my duct-taped finger—"I need you to clarify one thing for me. You seem to show a very keen interest," I paused, and Henry shifted his shoulders back, shimmying in his seat toward me, possibly feeling that he was in the clear. "What's up with the blatant stares at girls who have the three Bs?"

He looked to me for further direction, and I enunciated, "Blonde. Big bosomed. Brainless."

"Oh!" he laughed, his first words in what seemed hours. "Was trying to fill in the brainless part."

"Henry. I could easily dye my hair, which would look completely wrong with my coloring. I could get a boob job, but you know my policy on unnecessary surgery for cosmetic reasons. And then there's always a lobotomy."

"You're referring to FCUK girl? Right?"

"Is there another BBB that just seductively traipsed under your nose that I should be making an example of?"

"You may not realize this, but after FCUK made her presence known, while you looked at her, I looked at you."

Huh? This was not the response from Henry I expected.

"Yes, Emily. You were gawking at FCUK, and I know it's not because you're a closeted lesbian. Because of the things you did after I told you we'd be bidding on Reade Street." Henry shook his head, unable to vocalize our night as if his speech were programmed to block such debauched things like kid locks on a cable box.

And, not that I'm materialistic and enticed to have sex through material gain, I then employed Henry's method of avoiding the gravity of hot-button issues by taking a sip from my gimlet.

"Oh, look, it's J3!"

J3 approached us with the confident stride of a lawyer defending a celebrity in a sex scandal. He and Henry made a round of cool guy handshakes and slaps to the back, then J3 leaned over to give me a kiss on the cheek that I took Mom-style.

"So, J3," began Henry, "if a girl walks into your frame of vision wearing an improperly fitted tee that deems a bra useless, isn't the girl that ogles her just as impertinent as the guy?"

"Well, that all depends."

"Depends?" I asked saucily; this would be interesting.

"Sure," said J3, taking the seat next to mine. "If the girl doing the ogling is a lesbian then, yes, she is being impertinent because her mind is on sex, something illicit, just like the guy. Otherwise, though I have been told that I am in touch with my feminine side, it is hard for me to speak on behalf of the opposite sex, but the girl that is not a lesbian is staring probably because of the inappropriateness of her attire."

I never thought of that argument. Living with J3 would be like having my personal counselor.

Henry turned back to his finished Heineken and then ordered a round of Thom's most requested martini, which was a basic martini. We all moved into a booth.

"Well, you'll be happy to know we just finished the closing, and Emily and I are prepared to move in just a few weeks from now." I smiled as Henry said this, partly because I took a big swig from my martini thinking it was the water glass.

"Yes, Emily filled me in. And congratulations on the purchase of your new home, the engagement—lots of big news."

We all clinked our glasses and drank to J3's congratulatory words. We spoke of the excitement we'd have like an upcoming trip. We promised to entertain, a sort of Warhol's Factory without all of the weird sexual proclivities and vintage clothes, pushing a revolving door that commingled all of our friends—from artists to authors and the occasional actor who chose the indie film that cost less to make than Colin Farrell's asking rate to play the latest comic book hero.

We spoke of our future, how our gatherings would develop relationships, forge interesting partnerships, where ideas would be shared and possibly propel the arts into a new form—break ground.

We'd host an annual party, the first one slated for April 30 with the theme "Six Months to Halloween." (My idea, as it gave me a legitimate reason to wear my Tyrolean Snow Vixen outfit—a Balenciaga shearling I bought especially for a canceled trip to Gstaad for a funeral of an important relative that involved inheritance money.)

After some nostalgic chatter about television before it turned into a venue for product placement, rehashing of *Saturday Night Live* skits from the original cast, Henry and J3 decided that they would dress as Two Wild and Crazy Guys. Or maybe the Duke boys and I'd be Daisy. I liked this idea—cutoffs were always a sexy look—before I figured in the incestuous implications. They then moved to the high-priority situation of our electronics. Stereos, flat screens, amps, and things with Rs and Ms. An entire language based on products you spent Bergdorf fifth-floor prices for at warehouse-styled stores on West Fourteenth Street. Where shopping happens from need, like groceries without the obscene expenditure.

I enjoyed watching the two of them, the quick brotherhood they developed the way girls do when the topics are beauty treatments and low-calorie dessert food. Henry led the discussion, and J3's input boomed in like a kettledrum, having impact and presence.

"And what specific needs do you have?" I directed to J3, as a way to reenter the conversation.

"Just do what you would naturally do, and I can contribute to your needs when realized."

I really liked J3.

"The space is so impressive, we thought it would be best to keep it sparse. The authentic warehouse fixtures, the beams, and incredible light are amazing on their own—drowning it with unnecessary pieces is kind of like adding strings of necklaces to a Valentino."

"And acoustically, the place throbs," added Henry. J3 nodded along with a passive expression. The two were completely in sync.

"The previous owners were a fashion designer and an art director, so any interference would disrupt this artfully styled place," I added. "Although if you do happen to have a Picasso, something from the Blue Period, or perhaps a Gerhard Richter—I'm not that particular.

"Then there's the matter of the cleaners for those windows, which is a demanding job that needs to be attended to by a true professional—a skill that's almost a craft. A dying art really, now that there are these new windows that rotate for easy cleaning."

Henry and I have had this conversation before. He glared at me, knowing how I said these things kiddingly, but really took the issue of household maintenance quite seriously. He then reached into his pocket and gave J3 an extra set of keys, probably to ensure the deal before J3 ran out of the lounge and we never saw him again like an East Hampton contractor.

"When will you be able to move in so we can christen the place?" Henry asked.

"Actually it would be great if I could do it in three weeks." J3 pulled out his Smythson date book.

"You? Mr. Moon Chip does not have a Palm?" I chided.

"With my schedule, I can't chance a meltdown." Returning to his planner, he said, "April 15, how does that sound?"

"Great," said Henry.

"Perfect," said J3. "I just finished a deal of my own, a new business I am beginning here in the city, and this living arrangement couldn't have happened at a more opportune time. Timing is every-thing."

We all shook our heads in agreement.

"New business?" I said as a question, but more like a delicate probe in my Barbara Walters kind of way without the crazy blowout and black sheer panty hose.

"Yes. Though it is a bit early to discuss, it has something to do with children, new technology, and art. Synergizing all of our tech-nological advancements with very simple and classic interests that will entertain while enlighten."

Henry and I looked to him, absorbed.

"Wow," I blurted.

When J3 spoke so passionately, I got the kind of tingles you felt from liking a boy when Duran Duran's "Hungry Like a Wolf" ranked on the Top 40 list.

"So, will it be hard spending time away from L.A.?" said Henry, shooting me what appeared to be an annoyed expression when J3's glance became obstructed as he took a sip from his glass.

"Not really," said J3, putting his drink down. He caught me giving a condescending smirk to Henry, but made a point to look away so as not to give off that he registered his observation. "I definitely have more of a New York sensibility than a southern Californian one. Though it will be a strain on Amanda and me."

"Amanda?" Henry and I hollered in unison, but his tone was more gleeful. I may have sounded shocked.

"Amanda Green. She's an architect. Amazingly gifted and has re-cently been designing the new photography and motion picture museum. Trent Mueller's vanity project."

I've been following the building of this museum for years. Trent Mueller, a Hollywood director "with integrity," has been trying to build this museum for over a decade but always faced opposition, everything from protesters without a cause to zoning restrictions. Eventually getting the approval, and parlaying a more artistic ele-ment by incorporating the first-ever museum that devoted an entire pavilion to photography—heralding an annual grant to an up-and-comer with some splashy party attached to it—Mueller got the go-ahead.

After an exhausting competition of architects that ranged from

Frank Gehry and I.M. Pei to a few dark horses, Amanda Green became the unknown talent that won the job based on her design that combined the cleanness of Grecian symmetry with the whimsy of a Gaudi.

Amanda Green, who dated J3. I would have preferred it if he said he was seeing a BBB starlet who just finished a film with Ben Affleck.

"Amanda Green is your girlfriend!" Henry said, nudging my chest with his elbow, breaking a rib.

J3 nodded, looking at me. I believe he expected me to respond.

"Do you have a picture?"

Meaning, I need to check her out and see if she's prettier than me.

J3's hands shifted to below the table.

"You know, I do have a write-up of her from the *L.A. Times* that has a picture."

He slid the clipping across the table. Grainy, but clear enough to reveal her beauty. She was very pretty.

"Good-looking woman," Henry said, again, nudging my chest and breaking another rib.

"Ow," I groaned, rubbing my chest where Henry just beat me. Wife beater.

"Stop it, Emily," he said, watching me give myself a feel. "You're turning me on!"

"Okay, you two," said J3, laughing. "I guess we should have some ground rules, with your privacy and all of that."

"The ground rules are," Henry said brusquely, as J3 and I looked to him with expectant eyes, "there are no ground rules!" And we all cheered, taking giant gulps from our drinks.

"But," I squeaked in, "if you don't mind making sure you leave enough milk for my breakfast, and if we could all become familiar with a Windex container. I buy them by the case."

"Emily, don't freak J3 out before he's even moved in. We'll have a maid—regularly."

I gave an Emily smirk, volleyed back by a Henry smirk.

"You see, J3, Emily won't even consider having the service that cleans the W Hotels, because no one can keep to her standards."

"They're not effectively trained in the cleaning of private homes."

"And with the milk, whatever happened to the milkman? What? They went out of business from all of the palimony suits due to straying wives?"

Henry and J3 shared an unnecessarily enthusiastic laugh at my expense, and our communion showed some curious insight as to what could come.

When we arrived home, Henry went about his evening routine, flipping through the mail, changing light bulbs, fixing leaking faucets, caulking the shower tiles, and then prepared for bed. He seemed miffed by my pensiveness, saying, "Why so pensive?"

I excused myself and turned on the computer, Googling "Amanda Green, architect." Assuming I'd receive her promotional site, my results were the equivalent of boy-you-like-likes-someone-else-news disappointing. Many, many Amanda Green architect sites came up. After about 1,800 hours and many moans from Henry on why on God's earth I couldn't shop online during normal business hours, Amanda Fabulous Green had the kind of praise given to saving-babies-from-brain-tumors medical professionals. I felt buoyed by the discovery of a site where an architectural committee rewarded the winning recipient a hefty cash prize. Beneath the renderings, you could rate the submissions of Amanda's and the other nominees' work. Opening ten false Yahoo accounts, I began writing my reviews.

12

There are many advantages to packing and unpacking Henry's things, notably the given permission to snoop. In fact, now that we were going to be a legitimate Mr. and Mrs., I supposed that meant I had free range to openly snoop. It's sort of not as exciting when you are actually allowed to snoop, no risk involved, extinguishing the so-bad-it's-good fumes of my errant pleasure.

Henry went to the liquor store to get about 1,800 boxes, pontificating that books should not be packed in anything larger than a Jack Daniel's box (he held the box up to illustrate his point, which I found patronizing), saying that if you were to pack in larger boxes, they would have the weight of an obese elephant. I asked Henry when he had ever lifted or even knew how to detect the weight of an obese elephant, to which he responded with an annoyed grunt.

He seemed to have become further agitated by discovering that we had no duct tape. The duct tape, of course, had been entirely used up to secure my ring, but Henry didn't appear to be in the mood for me to point this out.

Looking over an orchestra of Henry's bachelor accrual, popping up and down in various forms with Ikea shelving systems, mismatched pieces of furniture brought purely for function with no aesthetic value, and an entire wall of electronics more intimidating than a car with its hood open, I made the point that the Salvation

Army would be receiving a sizable donation and how lucky he would be come tax day, as donations could be written off. Henry again grunted.

"You can't just strip me of my belongings," he said.

Why not?

"Emily!" he shouted. I must have had on an Emily face.

"Obviously, we'll have use for your stereo things and books and stuff. Oh!" I cheered, thinking of something else. "And your mattress and box spring."

I then thought of his lumpy mattress and box spring.

"Do they happen to be Simmons?"

Henry added something to his list. I felt proud that he had learned from me, adopted my habit of making lists.

"We'll dump the mattress and box spring," he said, somewhat irritably.

I returned to my acceptable snoop-finding mission, beginning with the crooked stacks of Henry's books, scanning their pages to see what sentences he found worthy to demarcate with ink-blue underlines. He owned many weathered paperbacks of authors such as Jack Kerouac, Milan Kundera, Herman Hesse, and Nabokov. Probably read during those spiritual Himalayan find-yourself backpack adventures taken in the pre-Emily years, booking the trip through a chichi travel operator he found in the back of an *Outside* magazine.

Henry had been greatly influenced by Taoism, though I could never quite figure how this came into practice in his life. He never went to Taoist sermons, celebrated any special holidays where you had to eat weird food, light votives, and make guttural chants. He did, however, have a Buddha carved out of teak that he bought at Zen & Paper, a spirituality and stationery chain store he found in Brentwood. The Buddha was the Holy Cross for Buddhists, even though Henry was supposedly Taoist. It all became rather suspect. All I knew was that this Buddha would be designated for the outdoor terrace once we moved, as opposed to its current prime above-the-mantle placement.

I've never been one for the spirituality as accessory type. If an actor is quoted in their *Vanity Fair* profile as saying "I read the Kabala. I am very spiritual person," they assume the comment will distinguish them as a serious and intelligent person, their image separated from any affectations typically associated with their industry because they have the same spiritual guide as Madonna.

So perhaps the last time I went to church was Christmas Eve the year I returned home from Dartmouth so I could legitimately stalk Scott Bankstrom, but that's not to say I didn't listen to the sermon. The structure and time involved in attending a service had the same principles as why I didn't take yoga classes, all inconvenient to my freelance time. (And a bit yawn inducing.) I found my spirituality. Perhaps not under a high-beamed house of worship with music and lovely stained-glass windows, but communicating with a higher being had a place in my life—when I painted, ran, doing good deeds, charity work involving the purchasing of tickets to Anne's fundraisers— Oh, Henry's yearbooks!

Taking apart a mosaic of Ayn Rand paperbacks, I became giddy after locating the complete volumes of Henry's Carmel High yearbooks. Opening up the 1986 book, I turned to his senior picture. So completely adorable with his dark hair grown out and tucked beneath his ears, wearing a L.L. Bean Norwegian sweater, as I imagined him the type as being too cool for the dark blazer and tie look. But reading his quote became a bit disappointing. Disturbing, actually. "Ladies, stop ogling."

This disturbed me. Henry was one of those guys that told me how beautiful I was at the tapped-out keg, that I always had been the subject of his dreams. How he could picture us road-tripping to each other's colleges and, once he slept with me . . . well, we all know how that one ends. Not that this ever happened to me, as I was one of the smarter girls who knew how to screen such lines proposed to me at a keg.

I looked up upon having that feeling of being observed. Henry indeed had been watching me as he folded the flaps of cardboard into a box.

"Shouldn't you weave the bigger flaps into the smaller ones?"

"Whatcha looking at there, Emily?"

"You completely disregarded my question."

"Found my picture, didn't you?"

"I suppose you caught me. Ogling. I'm actually surprised that you were quite the player. At what? Age seventeen? Age seventeen! That's so WB bad boy of you."

"What's with you and WB?"

I loved WB.

"And what's with you abusing love-struck high school girls? That's so cruel. I mean, you should know better. Seventeen is a very impressionable and insecure time in one's sexuality, nothing to trifle with."

"Emily," he said curtly, "I was also seventeen at the time. You're making me out like I committed statutory rape."

"So your being seventeen made it all right?"

"Where's your yearbook?" he asked, cleverly diverting my interrogation.

I walked over to the desk and pulled out a box of memorabilia stored beneath. My mother recently gave this to me, which I kept at her place until she returned it now that I'd be having my own place with enough storage facility.

The cover of my yearbook had an image of my school seen through the frames of Ray-Ban sunglasses.

"Here," I said to Henry, holding out the book.

Henry turned to what I gathered was the page with my senior picture. Like a passport or professional family portrait, it was another one of those photographs I had committed to memory. Daphne and I went to the beach the Saturday before our photo sessions to soak our faces with sun. Daphne, who now avoided sunlight to club trawler extremes, employed my double-album-cover-wrapped-in-tinfoil reflector tanning system—a former habit I had no intention of sharing with Dr. Perricone.

The school photographer, this seedy little man you'd find in the crossed-off section in the video store, had skin the texture of a grapefruit with Abe Lincoln chops. He wore a cotton-poly blend button-down, its armpits soaked in sweat. He kept complimenting me on my healthy and shiny hair, saying that I should model—but only for hair, because it wasn't a business to get involved with.

I asked in my sarcastic seventeen-year-old way how he would know about the modeling industry considering his busy schedule, photographing for high school yearbooks and everything, to which he gave an unctuous laugh and said he could connect me with one of his friends in the business. I imagined some studio on the Upper West Side with a Fortuny lamp, coffeemaker, and Canon 35mm propped on a stand. I politely declined. Said how it had been a very sweet offer, but I really should stick with my original plan and attend Dartmouth, considering they had accepted me early admission and there may have been some contractual obligations.

Henry studied the page. My hair obviously shiny and healthy with overly tanned skin, I had on a blue mohair sweater and strand of pearls—the requisite senior yearbook girl's picture style, unless you were one of those very proud and excited graduates who wore their cap and gown. I wondered where they were able to obtain the cap and gown, considering that they had their picture taken before graduation.

"Looks like you were one of the girls I'd try to pick up by the keg."

I tried to throw something at Henry, but anything worth throwing seemed to be packed.

"And you quoted advertising copy?" he said, reading from my quote, " 'Sometimes I feel like a nut?—Almond Joy.' "

"Better quoting Almond Joy than Thoreau or some sappy line from a Simon and Garfunkel song, which the person probably found by reading past yearbooks."

There was a deadly pause.

"Originality," I said.

"A candy bar," Henry replied, still speaking with a curious inflection.

"Oh, Henry! Don't change the subject on hand."

I went back to looking through Henry's box, one eye on my task, the other on Henry to see if he minded that I had been overtly rummaging through his things. When he seemed to take no notice, I came across a crumpled envelope with a Hilton Hotel logo. There were a few old snapshots of Henry. Sifting through the pile, I settled on one of him fishing, standing at the rear of the boat. From the bend of the rod it appeared he caught something. Another photo seemed to have been taken in a parking lot. He wore jeans, Reef flipflops, and a rainbow-colored tee tie-dyed in a spiral swirl. I never knew Henry to be a follower of The Boys.

"Aiko, Aiko," I said, holding up the picture in question, waiting for Henry to elaborate.

He squinted his eyes, which I found unnecessary, from the blinding colors from the tie-dyed shirt.

"Right. That was taken in Ventura."

Ventura, I said to myself in a Dead Head brain-cell-deficient drawl.

"You followed the Dead?" I laughed, a bit sarcastically.

"Of course I did. Didn't everyone?"

No. Then again I did date a Dead Head for a few months in Dartmouth. Ate 'shrooms in the men's room of Lindy's before the Madison Square Garden Dead show, was continually called "pseudo" because, in my theory, I refused to conform in one of those gypsy smocks and wore a designer peasant dress. That boyfriend went on to become a commodities trader, drives a Lexus SUV with Connecticut plates, has four girls, two golf club memberships, and a wife that hosts book clubs.

In the next picture, Henry had on frayed-at-the-knee Levi's and a long-sleeved thermal undershirt worn under a T-shirt that promoted some save-a-sea-animal cause.

"Let me guess," I said, having Henry's full attention. "Your grunge period. Kurt Cobain's suicide and you lit a candle?"

"Sure, I like those bands. Pearl Jam, Sound Garden—great period in music history."

"But Henry, with all of your CDs, I have not seen one Grateful Dead or Pearl Jam disc."

"And do you still keep your Whitney Houston CDs?"

I gave him an Emily smirk.

"First off, I was more into the Sex Pistols, Talking Heads, the Clash, and such. And you would never have seen me sporting a mohawk just because I had a thing for the band."

"You never experimented with trends?" he asked dubiously.

I thought back to my high school years and the trends they came with. Unless you counted the one time I went to school and had a run in my stockings, attributed it to a punk thing, and tugged at the fuzzy seam throughout the day, I really did maintain a consistent style. I didn't even use Dippity Do or wear leg warmers with parachute skirts when Madonna claimed to be "Like a Virgin." Basically, I remained faithful to plaid kilts, Tretorns and double-layered pique shirts—styles inspired from a field hockey uniform or tennis court.

13

Moving to a new zip code, you spend hours walking the streets of a once-familiar neighborhood with an archaeologist's eye, the way a new car is thoroughly explored over a rental, discovering the hidden pockets and functions, relishing every new discovery.

It took me almost an hour and a half to find my new coffee place. The one I settled on was conveniently located three blocks from where I lived. Naturally, it was one of the first places that I found, but I needed to investigate and approve of the other local establishments. I was annoyed that they didn't offer Dixie cup samples of their decaf hazelnut, so I essentially bought eight different cups of decaf hazelnut, my bladder spilling over its allotted capacity till I squirmed about like a child in the backseat of a car before returning back to Jumpin' Joe, the newly anointed place.

I asked for a key to the restroom (even though they did have a no-public-restroom sign) from a very nice young man (who was not named Joe, there was no Joe—unless you counted the cup with two legs extended from the rim of its mug painted on a wooden board that hung outside the door like a pub sign). The very nice young man, named Pete, sported intricate facial hair in a style I had not been familiar with, which made me speculate on how many types of razors he needed in order to achieve such an intricate mosaic. He seemed the type that would have a tattoo, probably a yin-yang sign or something earthy and spiritual, branded on his upper forearm beneath that bulky olive sweater with canvas elbow patches probably bought from an Army-Navy store.

He had that distinctive accent one gets from years of taking bong hits. "Surfer Speak," where every word is dragged out, a language based on the repetitive use of "dude," "hassling," "stoked," and all breathed under glossed-over eyes.

I asked Pete if he surfed, and indeed he did. During the winter months he snowboarded, disappointed in having to spend this past season driving to Vermont from the city because of the latest geographical stipulations of the current girlfriend. Overusing the word "crud" in his description of Vermont's snow conditions, Pete's chill composure became unnaturally addled. I commented on the things one does for love, and he bounced his head uncertainly, which made me speculate on the future of this relationship, but found it inappropriate to pry and, really, I needed to relieve myself.

He then directed me to the private restroom, which was very considerate of him to defy store policy set forth by the handwritten flyer prominently taped to the rim of the counter. Though Pete did not seem to be the type that cared for "Authority."

Giving the sign more thoughtful inspection, since I no longer had to pretend not to see it now granted bathroom access, it read "No Pubic Restrooms." I became slightly embarrassed by the spelling error, "pubic," wondering what type of establishment I had deemed my decaf hazelnut coffee place, but did not feel it necessary to point out the error due to my current priority.

Pete would soon become an active participant in my life. We would be on familiar terms, versed in each other's character from the subtleties given away by our daily habits, as this would be the place I came to start my morning—Pete would be the first human contact I had with the outside world. He proved to be an excellent choice in this new role in my life, allowing me to use this not meant for "pubic"-use restroom, but I'm sure he also took pity upon noticing the tears in my eyes, burn to my face. And I would make a note of the "pubic" error at a more opportune time. Really no need to reveal too much so early on, and I really had to go.

Pushing through the shuttered saloon-style doors, politely smiling to a few workers wearing Jumpin' Joe caps, further branding that hackneyed image of a cup with two bent legs, Pete gave excellent directions to where I knocked open the bathroom door with the kind of fury I had when running into the apartment when hearing the phone ring.

Squatted in soothing relief, I flushed the beet red from my cheeks in a long deposit of decaf hazelnut. The bathroom was wallpapered in past *New Yorker* covers dating as far back as 1991. Over ten years of *New Yorker* cartooned covers were studied and saved by this anonymous collector so someday they would possibly be given placement in this literal hole-in-a-wall resting stop.

Thanking Pete for his act of kindness, I bought a Jumpin' Joe baseball hat with promises to support and market this character, commenting on how I appreciated the irreverent wink of his eye and tongue to the upper lip, how the puritan teapot from *Beauty and the Beast* could use a jolt with properties higher then caffeine.

The morning had been productive, despite the lack of checks made (none) in my business planner. I also had the good fortune to find a potter's studio en route home. I've always toyed with the potter's life—loved the short hair and overall look of Demi Moore in *Ghost*—but the getting-soiled part was the throw-off. Particularly appealing in this studio was their supply of simple white dishes, plus the added bonus of printing my own illustrations onto the dishware like those cakes with superimposed pictures on the frosting (that are quite bland tasting, better served at parties with heavy drinking, impairing taste).

I asked if they could implement my illustrations onto champagne flutes, but the pottery woman, by no means fitting the potter earthy type I expected (she wore a Prada tweed shift that struck me as not being the most practical of materials, as clay could easily set in), apologized as if she'd just doused my new Mendel jacket with red paint, saying how they really focused on ceramics.

Returning home to another morning of no painting, I became distressed upon finding an intimidating package in the size and shape of a miniature pony. Nick, whom I referred to as "Mr. Fed Ex Guy" until we formally introduced ourselves after finding a common interest in kid cereal, also fell into the grouping of new acquaintances that were like office employees, thrown into your life under a professional context, spent considerable quality time with, and had insight into particular nuances otherwise designated to family members and close friends.

Nick also had a taste for lollipops, preferably Dum Dums in a tropical flavor, and was always seen with a stick sprouting from his mouth the way an unlit cigarette is permanently clenched in a smoker's lips. Apparently Dum Dums were difficult to find. I'd never considered that a Dum Dum would be hard to find. Nick resorted to buying his in bulk from a family grocer near where he lived— Brooklyn by way of Indiana—which made me wonder why he'd come to Brooklyn by way of Indiana so he could work as a Fed Ex deliverer, something I would ask him once our relationship deepened.

He had dark hair cut in the same trimmed fuzz as his chest hair. Short with the muscle tone of a cougar, his olive skin with ice-blue eyes could give sleeping with the man who delivers your mail an updated comeback. The constant twitch to his head and blink of his left eye was the deterrent (and that he delivered Fed Ex packages for a living, not that I was materialistic). He could also benefit from not wearing the two strands of gold chains around his neck.

A bit disappointed by missing Nick's delivery, as I would have offered him a bowl of Frosted Flakes and used my girlish charm to have him assist me with this disturbing package from, I looked at the mailing bill—Kelton Design. This excited me, realizing that my new desk/filing cabinet system that would change my life had arrived.

I took out my Smythson planner bought specifically for "The Move" and turned to the page with the information on the Kelton people, a small design firm based in San Francisco who had sent me this titanium industrial steel rolling desk/filing system with wheels that would delineate my studio space and keep my business in order while also protecting important documents in case of a fire or, for New York City purposes as stated in the irreverent brochure underlining that the designers had a cheeky sense of humor, a terrorist attack.

Opening the package with an X-acto knife not intended for such a job, I found a square box of drawers, a large metal tabletop, four poles, and a cellophane bag of—I moaned—nuts and bolts, truly intensifying the fear factor. Assembly required where tools would be involved did not work with me.

Washing my paint-stained hands of residual color from this morning's attempt at work, I punched the new Bang & Oluffson receiver, realizing that the paint-splattered phone may be a look we'd have to go for.

"Hello," I snipped to the customer service guy, who I learned was named Billy. "Billy, though I realize that you only work in customer service, you should know that your salespeople promised me that there would be no assembly required. And here I am, sent a box that is a day late from the overnight delivery I had asked for, with various pieces, a few scary-looking bolts, and a slip of directions."

Billy, being the young buckaroo he was, probably just wanted to put "Kelton Design" on his resume before he pursued his career as a promising architect to outshine Amanda Fabulous Green of Mueller Museum notoriety (so I should try to be as encouraging and supportive of Billy as I could). But Billy quickly began to irritate me by pointing out that no delivery service could send my desk overnight considering I ordered it after 8:00 PM Pacific Time unless he flew it to New York himself.

Feeling a bit humbled, but also annoyed that he forgot the "service" in customer service, I pointed out that whoever wrote the directions should understand that "pole" is not written as "poll" and that you could not depend on spell check to catch such errors. (I had become especially disturbed by our country's professionals and their spelling abilities, especially on such important documents.)

So in between our volleys of who was more clever than whom, not resting too long on the fact that this boy's job would be better performed by punching numbers prompted by an automated phone system, I managed to put together my terrorist-attack-proof desk/ sliding filing system courtesy of my more uses and counting toolbox. I then had the very last and immature word, which was "Okay. Bye!" and hung up.

But that didn't make me feel any better. I attributed this to my becoming more mature, now entering the wife phase of my life, and that sometimes you needed to take the higher road, avoiding petty arguments with people in customer service named Billy.

Wheeling the desk into different positions, a dizzying process, I

did a little jump and scoot to seat myself and take a moment to reassess. An almond colored mohair sofa that I had designed in the
Bridgewater style dominated the room. The couch came to be
more expensive than I originally budgeted as a result of asking
them to deliver it six weeks earlier than the original time, so Henry
and I would need to solicit another roommate. The only other additions were a matching ottoman and my six-foot canvas of a grinning Jack cutting down the beanstalk over a Manhattan backdrop.
At the toe of his hiking boot spilled a pouch of beans with a "$"
sign.

A tremor waved through me upon hearing the phone make its
first ring in this cavernous room. I answered it curiously. My first
caller was a loud click, probably Billy from Kelton Design wanting
to get the last say.

Pushing the desk back to the first place I had situated it, I returned to my work. A blank canvas had been the cause of over three
hours of procrastination, though useful procrastination now that I
had a new coffee place and new desk. I decided that I was hungry,
even though I ate my lunch about twenty minutes ago (at 10:45 AM),
which I validated as another excuse to go into my fabulous new
kitchen. We had the two-hip-artists-living-with-a-Dalmatian image
from the industrial steel cabinets and smoked glass, but my touch
of the kelly green Francis Francis espresso maker made the entire
kitchen.

Henry had been opposed to my decision to buy the Calvin Klein
everyday tabletop, considering that we registered for the same setting (registering online, the only check I made in my wedding book—
plus Real or Fake).

His ineptitude with household priorities stifled me. He had been
brilliant with the bidding, handling the negotiations and, most impressive, when presented with the final price, Henry agreed to accept the offer only if the sellers added the teak outdoor bed on the
terrace, an expense we wouldn't have been able to afford this year
(if we ever got around to making the decision to justify an outdoor
teak bed that I anticipated would have great use once the tempera-
tures rose above 60 degrees—another thing Henry and I were not
in complete agreement on).

My housing priorities were to buy those things we needed, save those receipts (in the special filing system I would be implementing—a tomorrow project), and when we were given the identical items as gifts, they'd be returned. Henry did have to point out that we might not get those items we registered for, but I had to brush this off by saying he apparently was not well versed on my family and friends—we are very direct and polite people with an ability to communicate our wants and needs.

Opening my sketchpad, I began to draw the wedding portrait of Henry and me. Actually, I began to stare at the white page, then became inspired by the new plates I would design especially for parties. I drew a small factory shaded in silver with yarn in various neon colors exploding from its doors as an homage to the Knitting Factory idea.

Henry assertively came in, saying, "Honey, I'm home!" which made him feel very Mike Brady. He also loved the echoed effect his voice made.

"Hey, Henry," I said, puckering my lips into the air so he'd give me a kiss.

He inspected my face by pinching my chin, rotating it from side to side as if my head were a display of sunglasses.

"You have charcoal smudged on your face." He then licked his thumb and used his moist finger to rub the charcoal from my cheek.

Now this I could not understand. My father used to do the spit and clean, dabbing my candy-stained face with his saliva. Now that the years have passed, no longer under the care of paternal guidance, I could assuredly say that this was gross, not to mention the bacteria he smoothed onto my skin. And here my fiancé felt the need to cleanse my face with his spit.

Looking over my shoulder, Henry studied my Knitting Factory sketch.

"And what do we have here?" he asked, taking the book from my hands so he could give it a more thorough look.

"Well, I found this adorable little place that can customize plates."

"More plates?" He sounded suspect.

"For our parties!"

"Okay, this is curious on many levels. Firstly, why would we want customized plates of a foghorn burping up cotton-candy-colored pasta? The only thing you should be getting customized are the condoms for the wedding's party favors."

Was he really serious about that?

"And shouldn't you be working on your painting? Planning the wedding?"

My head free-fell into my lap and I made a loud humming sound—a new sound for me, but meant to indicate my distress from the overwhelming pressure.

"Emily, what about your mother? I thought her whole purpose in life after you were born was to plan your wedding."

"Let's talk about our bedroom!"

"Bedroom?" Henry questioned playfully. "You really have to stop using sex as a way to get out of things."

"No, I mean in regard to how I want to style it."

"Actually, I retract my last comment. You really should use sex as a way to get out of things."

I brushed off his counter-productive comments since we had so much to cover.

"So I imagine the bedroom to be like the inside of a cloud—all white and floaty. Henry? What are you doing?" I asked when he picked up the phone and began to dial. He then stopped mid-punch.

"Is your mother's number 8417 or 8418?"

"8418," I said apprehensively. "Why are you calling her? Don't call her!"

"It's for your own good, Emily," he said, passing over the ringing phone like it was a form to enroll myself in an institution where patients drew swirls in the air with their fingers in awestruck bewilderment.

"Hello! Hello!" the phone yelped.

"Hi."

"And who is this?"

"Mary Jo Buttafucco. Who the hell do you think it is?"

"Phone etiquette," Mom sang. "And, Emily, I can't understand why you haven't bothered to return my numerous calls. There are a couple of pressing matters we need to attend to. First, your dress. You will be meeting Anne and me next Tuesday at all of the bridal places where she has made appointments, all outlined in her e-mail."

"Yes. I shot her back my confirmation and cc'ed you."

No response.

"Mom?"

"I really wish you'd stop it with this cute chatter to try and flummox me."

"What are you talking about? Didn't you get my e-mail?"

I suddenly realized that Oliver had been away on a school overnight trip. Picturing my mother using e-mail without his assistance was like picturing Helen Keller eating a bowl of soup without Annie Sullivan. I also permanently deleted the e-mail with the appointments my cousin Anne set up. Asking her to do something like resend an e-mail struck me with panic. It would deeply inconvenience her.

Henry, listening in, motioned his hands like a wizard conjuring up a spell to prod me along.

"I'm actually calling you for a reason. Mom, I do realize that with the recent move, this series of paintings I'm working on, and the wedding that your assistance will be greatly needed."

Henry smiled, disappearing across the room like a squirrel shooting across a telephone wire.

"And all this time I thought you were covertly planning the wedding with Daphne."

Though Mom loved Daphne, she felt threatened by my relationship with her.

"You know it's not healthy—to entice your lesbianism this way, with your best friend."

"I'm not a lesbian, Mom."

Of course, Henry had to reenter the room at this moment. Raising an eyebrow, he had on a look I did not find humorous.

"And don't tell me it's because she is married." Mom blabbered, her voice piercing my head like an electric drill. "Or how you have a fiancé. Apparently it's quite common, these sham marriages lesbians have. They say that's what Hillary is doing."

I would have defended Hillary Clinton, but I had my own case to worry about. Tic-tac-toe, I then reminded myself, and I wouldn't play.

"So, back to the reason I called," I said.

"Yes, of course. And this is an unprecedented event—the Emily Briggs coming to her mother for assistance, actually seeing the benefits in family help—which brings me to Katrina and Anja."

Oh, for the life of me. Not the Katrina and Anja discussion.

"I saw Anja with Katrina the other day at Doubles, thinking how lovely it was for them to keep up their mother-daughter lunches. Come to think of it, I even saw them at Oasis for a mother-daughter spa day. Everything is always so hunky-dory with those two."

Hunky-dory?

"And Katrina gave you her congratulations."

Katrina, her maiden name something European, married to my once-best-friend Dash, and one-time love interest until the idea of having an Aspen condo with bedrooms named after ski runs began to frighten me. Katrina's quite sweet, pretty and smart, but not enough of a threat to make me jealous—the kind of girl that probably dotted her i's with hearts in grade school.

"She also made this curious little comment about you."

I wasn't about to get suckered into my mother's game of trying to skew something that Katrina had said innocently and interpret it to her advantage.

"What *curious* little comment?"

"Something about your being so independent, breaking out on your own. But only said after she congratulated you on your engagement, so she probably meant how you're painting now—or do you think she has doubts about Henry?" Mother had no intentions of my posing an answer. "Did you know she's trying to have a child? Well, she didn't actually tell me this, but I could tell from what she read while having her pedicure—*Architectural Digest,* you know."

Correlation?

"She does have a remarkable maternal quality about her. She reminds me of the late Princess Diana."

Whom my mom met once, for about twenty seconds at a luncheon, which she had been invited to by strong-arming a friend of a friend who vaguely knew the princess, all so she could now claim her as one of her old and greatly missed friends.

"You really should give Katrina a call. I've always liked her for you."

And then she veered into discussions about the friends of mine she didn't approve of (all of them), and living like a "Bohemian barefoot downtown hippie type" with the kind of career one normally associates with "druggies and people that need to take lithium so they don't take their aggressions out on walls."

Now, listening to what she had been saying on a tertiary level as I inspected my barefoot French pedicured toes, with so much to take in, what had been made clear was that my mother did not approve of my life choices. I wondered if she wanted me to take notes, actually implement her unsolicited advice and try to be the person she had intended for me to be.

As she began to say something about how she couldn't tell her friends that Henry and I lived together, and what story I needed to corroborate if approached on the *situation*, I started to wonder if she thought I was a virgin, and then extinguished the entire scenario from my thoughts.

"Did you even consider calling me, as I could easily put this wedding together with all of my contacts and social know-how?" I heard her say when I tuned in as if I had been scanning through stations.

Wasn't that why I—Henry, really—just called? I felt like bringing this to her attention, along with a mention of how she had been too busy criticizing my life choices with my being a "Bohemian barefoot downtown hippie type" and possible lesbian, but realized that this would just take the conversation to another heated level. My intentions would not be understood, and I'd just be ill-prepared for her outrage that such a comment would generate.

As she turned to the issue of my inevitable screw-up—the guest list and seating placement—I heard the other phone ring.

"Oh, other line. Got to go!"

Click.

I sat Indian-style and stared at the ceiling until Henry breezed back in, lacing up the shoes he took off only moments ago. We kept a shoeless household, something I never felt the need to go into great detail about.

"Emily, I have to run out. Something came up. Maybe we can hook up tomorrow evening."

"You know that 'hooking up' works well for prostitutes. I am not a prostitute."

"Oh, really?" said Henry, looking at me, clearly delighted, studying my reaction to his humorless joke.

14

J3 would be moving in this evening, and Henry wanted to take me to Jumpin' Joe, pitched as private "us time" the way an expectant mother took her son on a special outing before his baby sister would arrive. It would be the first time I'd share my new coffee place with Henry, so I dressed in my Carolina Herrera pinstriped skirt with my Dior boots.

Walking with my head down, making an effort not to deliberately send my mother to the hospital by avoiding sidewalk cracks, Henry asked me why I seemed so glum. I had been feeling pressure, despondent with concerns that the apartment needed more preparation and that J3 might be disappointed by his living arrangement.

Yesterday, I fell for a pair of vintage photographer lamps at Moss, but could not justify the cost until I sold a painting. Feeling the strain of Henry eyeing me, I didn't know if it would be more upsetting to share my financial distress with him. He persisted, saying how I didn't seem myself, until I relented and expressed my concerns about the importance of proper lighting. I mentioned things about depth and mood in loft spaces, how it had been difficult to share my worries, as being financially inadequate took me to the time I worked out with celebrity trainers from their exercise videos.

Henry then explained the fabulous system of a joint checking account. I've been told stories about this by married friends, didn't know if it truly existed, like exotic destinations you had difficulty in picturing and yearned to sample on your own. He went over the fundamentals of this process, saying "my money is your money— yours, mine, ours." I shook the belief into my head and made Henry review the procedure more clearly, with key details such as ATM numbers and who questioned the bills, until we spotted the Jumpin' Joe sign.

As we entered the café, the newest release by Train played in the background, revving my mood even more, until I saw a cat scamper to the corner. As my focus shifted to this hobbling cat, I noticed that she had three legs, which took me by surprise. After registering the shock of this handicap, I looked at her with a mix of freakish cur- iosity and pity. This three-legged cat, sharing our connection, mus- tered across the room in wounded war hero ceremony.

Henry, coming into this enactment as he sighted the handi- capped cat, did not share my compassion. His face crumpled in fear and disgust.

The cat now reached me, in what had been an extraordinary feat. I reached down to give her the affections she had traveled so long and hard for, only to receive a slap to my hand that almost caused my ring to slip off my finger, not a hard thing to do despite half a roll of duct tape.

"Don't touch that circus reject; you might catch something!"

"For God's sake, Henry, she's not foaming at the mouth. The poor thing just has a missing leg."

Giving Henry's warning a few moments of consideration, I scooped up the pitiful animal and brushed my cheek against hers, which ig- nited a loud purring sound.

"Emily! That's completely nasty. At least wear some surgical gloves or something."

"Sure, I'll just get them from inside my doctor's bag," I said, lift- ing up my red Birkin.

"Well, just use condoms."

Henry reached into his jacket for his wallet and, in the inside pocket, he indeed had two condoms.

"Why, for God's sake, do you have condoms?" The cat and I stared Henry down, and his eyes widened. "I've been on the pill for over a year."

"And I've had this wallet since I bought it in Florence the summer after I graduated from Stanford."

"And that answers my question how?"

I started to stroke the cat's head to soothe her from my agitated state, recalling a program on the Discovery Channel about animals sensing human emotions.

"Hey, Emily, I see you met my best friend," said Pete from behind the counter. Since the last I saw him, he'd shaved off that weird beard in the design of an English garden, showing the profile of his face. Pete was quite handsome.

I wasn't in the mood to introduce Henry to Pete, and Henry used his interruption as a way to move from our condom squabble, patting the once-repellent cat on the head.

"That there is the owner's cat. Heroine," said Pete.

Heroine? Or named after the drug her deadbeat owner used while he wasn't attending to his pet, the cat then nicked by a cab?

I gently put Heroine down, closer to her original starting point to save me from watching her make the struggle back to her resting place. The hardwood floor was imprecise, bulging in certain areas, but amazingly clean for such a high traffic area, probably because they used one of those abrasive heavy-duty detergents that establishments bought by the gallons. The cat reached its designated spot—a small pillow so covered in cat hair that the tartan print was barely distinguishable. A funnel of light shot through the front window, giving the pillow the focus of an above the mantle painting illuminated by a strobe.

"That's the saddest thing I've ever seen," I said to no one in particular, finding that I was overcome with sadness. Heroine would now be in my thoughts whenever I thought that life had mistreated me.

"Emily? Are you okay?" asked Henry.

"Isn't that the saddest thing you ever saw?"

"You look a lot sadder," he said. His head nodded toward Heroine as she happily gave herself a bath with her tongue.

"In fact," he whispered into my ear. "You seem to have some feline qualities that happily remind me of last night."

Henry had oral sex last night. After dinner and a few drinks at a nearby Tuscan bistro. Grappa.

Then Heroine began to trouble me again, making disturbing hacking sounds.

"Don't worry," soothed Pete, handing a customer a blueberry scone and mug emitting its vapors. "Just choking on some fur balls. The cat will never know her limit."

I began to think of how I had almost gagged last night.

After deciding to introduce Henry and Pete because I didn't want to appear rude, we ordered our coffees and cereal treats, which weren't actually Rice Krispies Treats as they were made with Frosted Flakes (far more preferable), and then we chose a small table with two spun-wire chairs with backrests shaped as hearts.

Sipping my coffee, I was smiling at Heroine when Henry waved me to his attention.

"Emily, move on from *Born on the Fourth of July* over there."

"I mean, it's so sad. Even those little dogs wearing cones around their heads have it better than poor Heroine."

Henry shook his head, raked his hand through his hair and pulled an issue of *Variety* from a satchel with a hole patched by duct tape. I assumed a look inspired by my ring and used the magazine as a screen from further discussion about legless animals.

Folding my arms, I stared at Henry until the beams from my eyes burned through his magazine and snapped him with laser-sharp burns.

Henry put down the magazine.

"Sorry," I said. "Didn't want to keep you from your reading."

I returned to Pete for a refill, which he gave me with compliments as an apology for having to observe Heroine's condition. I did find it odd that an establishment would flaunt such an unwelcoming attraction, but then felt ashamed by my thoughts—comparing myself to a corseted Brontë heroine who made an overdue charity call to a poor relation suffering from rheumatism.

Pete assured me that Heroine lived a happy life, that the owner spoiled her more than a cosmetic mogul's wife. I asked Pete if he found wanting a bit of spoiling to be an attractive quality in a woman, to which he replied only if she was as cute as me.

Feeling uplifted, I turned around, only to be sprayed in the face with the pushed contents of my newly refilled coffee.

"Excuse me," I said apologetically to a pair of purple cashmere-viscose blended breasts—what Versace would come up with if the Department of Defense asked fashion designers to create torpedo covers. This blonde, an Eva Herzigova with implants, glared at me, or at least what I assumed would be a glare, as her eyes were hidden behind a pair of blue-tinted aviators.

Henry had been the one most affected by the scene, sprinting from the table and calling my name like a parent to the ocean where his child bobbed up and down on a red raft in shark-infested waters. His hollering subsided; the blonde who bumped me disappeared. I surveyed the damage. Naturally, I had to be wearing a new white Gaultier shirt.

Henry darted to a counter with spices in salt and pepper shakers, tins with sugar packets, and Thermoses of different grades of milk. Pouring a jug of water onto a napkin the color of cardboard, he wiped my shirt, wetting it so it revealed the lace of my bra. Pete politely looked away and poured a new refill.

"I saw the whole episode happen," said Pete, putting a security lid on this cup. Henry stopped wiping to take this in. "Like watching an egg teeter off the counter, but you were too far away to make the save."

"I'm sure it was just an accident," snapped Henry.

"I don't know. That woman seemed to be watching Emily. I noticed her from before. She was sitting at that table hours before you two arrived," he said, pointing to the alleged table.

"Really?" I asked proudly. "Blondes do have a thing for me."

Leaving Pete's, I considered going immediately to the dry cleaners so they could attend to the stain before it fully set in. Henry asked if I always flirted with Pete.

15

J3 arrived late. We all gathered in the kitchen, and I made a pot of chamomile tea. J3 asked for cinnamon and shook the jar over his cup like fish food into a neglected tank. I excused myself for the bedroom, intentionally leaving them alone so they could continue their discussions about some new BMW XYZ car, Korean barbecue restaurants, and football trades.

While I washed my face and prepared for bed, I could hear their mumbles and the occasional crack of laughter. Henry came into bed almost two hours later, his breath smelling of whiskey. It made me wonder if he broke in the Baccarat without me.

I pretended to be asleep. Every turn I made, stretch of my hand, and soporific movement I felt could be heard by J3 even though his room was a floor below and across the hall. Uncomfortably conscious of trying to remain as still and quiet as possible, I wondered if J3 thought of me that way, if he tried to figure what stage of sleep I had yet reached.

Henry started acting frisky, which annoyed me. I interpreted his advances as an assertion of his alpha role in his home. Perhaps we should have twin beds, like Lucy and Ricky, and that thought led me to a stream of unrelated disturbing questions. Suddenly, all sensitivity to my previous silence escaped me with the thrust of my hand, which offset Henry's groping arm.

"Ow!" Henry screamed, his words slipped beneath the window and floated across the flat tops of downtown Manhattan. I *sshed* him, annoyed that my hours of trying to be a mime in bed were now futile.

"Emily, don't tell me that we're never going to have sex when J3 is here."

The thought did occur to me.

"Now come here," he said, pulling my body into him like an extra pillow.

"Henry," I commanded. "Do not even try or else I'll make a visit to the local precinct and file a report. I need some Ben & Jerry's."

Walking into the kitchen, I mumbled what Henry had said to me just as I escaped his clutches, "Priorities, Miss Briggs. Priorities," repeating the words as if I were a halfwit.

J3 watched me enter as he sprinkled cinnamon on his ice cream. I'd have to make sure we were always stocked with cinnamon.

He said his devotion to cinnamon had a madeleine-cookie effect, probably because he loved his grandmother's cinnamon raisin cake, but the exact moment could not be placed. I nodded, saying I had the same relationship with Equal. J3 spoke of his college girlfriend and how they got a dog together, an Irish setter, naming her Cinnamon. After the breakup, the girlfriend received custody of the dog.

I wanted more details about the girlfriend, but he went on about cinnamon's health benefits and its vast uses, putting it on everything from eggs to soda, and naturally enhancing the flavor of coffee and ice cream. I looked into his bowl at the melted ice cream with a dusting of brown and considered replacing my Redi-Whip with cinnamon, but that idea was as fleeting as shopping off-season for the better prices.

He then started on his second helping, perhaps even more, since I had just come in. I became annoyed that boys could have late-night splurges without the morning hangover pouch to show for it. From his wishbone shape, I assumed J3 was the swimming-laps type.

J3 went to the cutlery drawer and got an extra spoon, which I declined with an explanation on how I preferred a teaspoon as it prolonged the happy consumptive process. J3 didn't seem miffed by this. He motioned to his container of Chubby Hubby for us to share. As I no longer ate full-fat flavors the way I no longer wore tights with skirts, I explained to J3 that I preferred low-fat, which he also seemed to accept as completely normal. I also didn't consider pint-sized containers of Ben & Jerry's large enough to share.

"So do you always talk to yourself about 'priorities'?"

Apparently, he didn't see my talking to myself as completely normal, but one out of three wasn't bad.

In the freezer, the few Chubby Hubbys appeared on the verge of a hostile takeover by the majority of Low Fat Fudge Brownies. Always a supporter for the little guy over the impersonal conglomerate, I wondered if I should reconsider my habits, how it would be better to eat a small bowl of the more caloric flavor as opposed to an entire pint of the low-fat, but then no fun could be had from that.

Opening the fridge, I placed the jar of Wonder Butter on the cabinet and then reached for the chocolate Redi-Whip, shook the can, tilted my head back, and foamed up my mouth to the sound of balloons being filled with helium. Sucking the tip of the Redi-Whip can of its residual cream, I thought it could have used some more shaking. I then extended the can to J3, as I had always been a gracious host.

"No, thanks," he said. "I'm good."

"You sure? It's all about the Redi-Whip," I said, wiggling the can to further entice him.

"I like my Redi-Whip other ways."

"You boys and that damn whipped cream fantasy. So unoriginal."

"Actually, I had more of the whip-it use in mind."

I began to think of Dash, the once-best-friend/one-time love interest who now had become the literal stud machine, trying for a family with the perfect wife/baby producer Katrina. I knew his fridge from his bachelorhood days as well as I knew my own. Always stocked with Redi-Whip, but he had no chance of enacting a sexual conquest more suited to a boy who had just cleaned out his wallet space of trading cards to make room for a condom.

"Hey, whatever happened to that friend of yours? Flash?"

"No way! I was just thinking of him," I laughed, releasing a bomb of peanut butter onto its target of chocolate. I then shook the Redi-

Whip like I was a caged dancer. "You haven't invented some kind of mind reader device, have you? And his name is Dash."

J3 suspended his spoon midair. "Unless you consider mind reading the same as remembering." Now he laughed. "You've told me the Redi-Whip story. I remember stories, not names."

"I told you the Redi-Whip story?"

"Yeah. But you seemed to have been sloshed on margaritas at the time."

"Oh," I mumbled.

"And whatever happened to Dash?" he asked.

"Married to Katrina von Blah Blah. Waiting for some rich uncle to die. Trying for a kid. Moved to Fairfield County."

"Fairfield County?"

"Connecticut. I believe they live in one of the earlier Connecticut town stops on Metro North. I see my friends in L.A. more than the ones who live in places like Greenwich or Darien. Have you ever been?"

"No. And I can't say that I have a real desire to go."

"But how could you not want to visit a land where the L.L. Bean moccasin and Jeep Wagoneer still reign?" I said.

"If I want to time travel, I'm more of a mid-seventies guy. I'd just as soon make a trip to Graceland."

"Right. Perfect sense."

The container of Ben & Jerry's seemed to have disappeared. I became a bit concerned by this disappearing ice cream act—the third container this week, unless you consider Monday as the start of the week rather than Sunday; otherwise it would be four.

I supposed my theory about a haunted loft with ghosts that had a taste for Ben & Jerry's could no longer hold substance, as this pint disappeared in front of J3. I thought of just putting the empty pint in the freezer so as to not divulge my gluttonous behavior, then realized that this would be too much effort as I may forget about it later, as well as it being an indulgent use of freezer space, and tossed it in the garbage.

As I moved toward the sink to wash off my spoon, J3 complimented me on my pajamas, which I explained weren't really my pajamas but actually Henry's pajama top. Regardless, he liked the look.

J3 opened a magazine with business people on the cover, allowing me a free moment to scratch out a sandy granule from the corner of my eye that had gathered from lack of sleep. I caught him stealing a look, which pulled me from my unconsciousness like the climax of a nightmare. I then crunched my hands into fists and began rubbing my eyes, hoping this would cover up my act of removing something insalubrious from my body.

As I was about to make my exit, the phone's ring frightened J3 and me as if we were attacked by helmeted flying monkeys. As we became acclimated to the sound not appropriate for this time of night, I asked J3 if he expected a call and should we just have the machine take care of it. He nodded at my suggestion.

"Hi, Emily," boomed Daphne from the little black box mounted on the wall. "Just wondered when your threesome candidate—"

I raced to the phone.

"Daphne!" I breathed into the receiver.

"So. You're screening?"

"Right. Yes. He arrived today."

"Oops! My bad! Catch up tomorrow then?" she rambled like a child trying to get out of her punishment. "And I promise to only leave the more interesting messages on your mobile. Sorry for acting all blonde."

Daphne could be the most irresistible flake.

"Okay, Daphne. Not to worry," I shouted into the receiver, really meant for J3 to overhear. I wondered if my screaming didn't give me away. "I'm sure he'll catch on to your sense of humor quickly enough."

I hung up the phone, now intent on smoothing down the wily smile that took over J3's face.

"That was my friend Daphne. She does have a wicked sense of humor."

"So did you two make plans to arrange a better message system now that I'll be living here?"

"Yeah, pretty much," I said.

"Smart girl."

I felt wobbly from the unexpected adrenaline rush and the effects of artificial sweetener.

"Why were waterbeds so popular?" I asked.

"Why is any unsubstantiated trend popular?" he said.

"But waterbeds? I mean are they even comfortable? Or good for the back?" I blankly stated.

J3 had a look in his eyes, some kind of curious interest. I then pictured a man with a lot of hair, black briefs, and a gold chain with an Italian horn gleaming through his thicket of chest hair. He's lounging on a waterbed, one leg bent, posing for something. Cologne. Having sex on a waterbed would be another skill entirely, like downhill skiing with telemarkers.

16

The phone rang, obscenely early for a Tuesday, at 8:30 AM. And I hadn't had my decaf yet. With less than twenty seconds to take the call or have the answering machine attend to it, I picked up the phone, especially considering last night's blunder with Daphne. Now that J3 lived here, old patterns had to be readjusted.

"I can't believe you. You just completely blew us off—typical!"

I should have let the answering machine take the call.

"It's one thing to blow me off, but your mother?" said Anne, shooting out a list of injustices I had been guilty of, in between mentions that she was in the middle of a session with her private trainer. "And your explanation?" she barked.

"Oops!"

Scary breathing.

"But you see—"

I thought Anne would start in on the next string of my injustices, but she seemed to wait for a reply.

"Oops!"

Indeed, I did miss my appointment to look at dresses with my mother and cousin yesterday, but had no intention of owning up to this. I had been busy (assembling my new terrorist-attack-proof filing system/desk), but the thought of them having enthusiastic discussions over wedding topics, my every input repulsed, and an afternoon being the target of veiled insults that cut into my taste and choices held no appeal to me.

My irresponsibility in not properly addressing Anne and not braving her admonishment probably added a few extra unfavorable adjectives that bounced from her Park Avenue silk-lined walls once she became aware of my abandonment of these wedding duties.

Cousin Anne and I were quite different, a point I always ask shared acquaintances to verify. She only spoke to people who were useful to her needs—if they had a Ivy connection for her twin boys (age two), shared one of her zip codes, or had names suitable enough to emboss on a party invitation. I did not go to Harvard, I lived downtown, Palm Beach never interested me, and I avoided the social scene the way the scrawny kid hides in the corner of the dodgeball court. But Anne must amend her rules for family, something that undoubtedly caused her grief.

"You know that your mother was quite hurt," she snapped. I could see her repressed scowl on the other side of the phone line. (Anne did not give full-impact scowl as a result of the warning of her dermatologist that facial expressions deepen lines.)

"I called."

"Calling forty-five minutes before an appointment is not acceptable," she instructed.

"What is this, some cancellation policy for a room at the Ritz?"

"No. Emily."

I really did not like the way she just said "Emily."

"It's just proper etiquette. Your mother has been looking forward to this for weeks. It's all she talks about."

I thought of my mother holding the commanding post at a social gathering with news of how she and I would be looking for dresses. Essentially, the period from when I popped from her belly till the day I wore that wedding dress held no purpose.

"You should have seen your mother's face when she got your message that you weren't coming."

This mental picture was hard to imagine, considering that my mother had more faces than there were matches after Googling "California" and "plastic surgeons."

"And not that you ever cared about my time or involvement."

Anne had that part right.

"We had all the appointments lined up, this entire day planned," she prattled as I nuzzled the receiver between my shoulder and cheek, only listening for the parts I'd need to give some grunt of acknowledgment to, and then focused on my sketchbook. I drew a series of wedding dresses and alligators along the gutter. I then drew an alligator on a dress and considered sending it to Lacoste.

"A lack of respect to another's time is one thing, Emily, but the real issue is how your actions affect others. You've been completely selfish, inconsiderate, and disrespectful, Emily. A sham to do-gooders everywhere."

This was coming from a woman who drained her flooded Southampton basement into the ocean, resulting in the killing of baby ducks and endangered birds and the destruction of dunes, just so her annual Memorial Day garden fundraiser would not be compromised. The word delusional popped into my head.

"Why are you crucifying me for missing a few dress appointments? It's not like I blew off my mother's birthday so I could go to a sample sale."

"You wouldn't!" she said, aghast.

Actually, I could see myself doing something like that, but considering that sample sales were a daytime event and a birthday party for my mother would more likely be in the evening, the likelihood was improbable.

"Do you know how hard it is to get a designer to give you a private consultation?"

"You made appointments with the designers?"

"No. But I would have. Not now, of course. This is not all as simple as you make it out to be."

Life could be quite burdensome for Anne.

"It's a dress. Just a dress. No need to sound the trumpets and announce the gazette."

I could feel Anne's scary breathing through the perforated holes on the receiver.

"Well, I might have mentioned your dress shopping to Michelle Revson at the *Standard*," she said.

"Why the hell would the *Standard* want to know about my looking at dresses!"

"It was your mother's idea."

Anne didn't need to say any more. My mother had been handling my publicity since she alerted the local paper about me breaking my school's fifty-yard dash record in the fourth grade, resulting in a page three item including photo. That was the first clip she rubber-cemented in a leather-bound scrapbook that preserved all of my press mentions.

"Look, enough with making something out of nothing. I will find a dress. It's better to downplay such things, which will take out the scary factor."

"You really don't get it, Emily. This. Is not. About. You!"

Okay?

"Um, the last I remembered, it was my turn to waltz down the carpet."

"You really think that getting married is just about you and Henry?"

Interesting that Anne said Henry's name. I didn't think she thought of him as a person with a name, background, and social security number, just as the lobotomized specimen that had the questionable character to choose me for his spouse.

"It's an occasion, Emily. Something bigger than you, and it's time you owned up to this and confronted your responsibilities. You need my assistance, my sensibilities, especially with my European upbringing. Let's not forget that I'm French."

Anne's Belgian grandmother moved to America at the age of six. Her mother gave birth to Anne the summer they spent in France.

"You hurt your mother. She's even considering making an appointment to see—" Anne's dramatic pause showed she had said too much.

"Spill it, Anne."

"Dr. Berger!"

"Dr. Berger? The plastic surgeon?"

"Is there another Dr. Berger?"

It was a common name.

"You know that too much plastic surgery is a sort of disease, like anorexia or drug abuse. It's a cry for help. Your mother is crying for help."

I wondered which month's *Vogue* was the basis for Anne's point.

"I'll handle my mother."

"That's not good enough."

Heated pause.

"And my charity amazes me."

Anne really said this.

"A true embarrassment. I actually had an assistant reschedule a few of the appointments."

I wondered what requirements you needed to be one of Anne's assistants.

"And don't think I did this for you."

Of course not.

"So we will meet next Friday at the bridal salon at Bergdorf's, eleven AM. Are you writing this down?"

I didn't write this down.

"So what time will we meet?"

"Next Friday. Eleven AM."

"Where?"

"Bergdorf's. The bridal salon."

"Say it again, all together now," like Julie Goddamn Andrews.

"Next Friday at eleven AM. The Bergdorf's bridal salon."

Henry walked in, sat next to me on the couch, and I motioned for him to say something by twirling my hands in front of my mouth, but he looked confused. We really needed to develop a system.

"What are you doing?" he asked, which would suffice.

"Anne, Henry needs me, got to go."

Click.

Putting the receiver on my lap, I forgot the time of the bridal salon appointment. I turned to Henry.

"You know I really could have used your assistance from the wedding dress Gestapo there."

"It looked like you wanted soup."

"I didn't want soup," I huffed.

"Your mother, I assume?" he asked coyly. I was annoyed by his playful tone.

"No. Anne."

"Oh," he said, considerably more somber. Anne had that effect.

"They are making this complete fuss over a ball of duchess satin. Imagine what they will be like when I'm pregnant."

Henry looked to me with something like befuddlement, a new expression of his that I couldn't quite figure.

"Pregnant? Well, that's a strange correlation."

"Um. Not really."

"But your nipples, they're so sensitive. You know how you get when I'm all playful over there. Breast-feeding not being an option, I didn't think you wanted kids."

"Flash. Women can have children and not breast-feed. How did you ever go from my having sensitive breasts to my not wanting children? What's gotten into you?"

I began to wonder if it was me or were all the players in my life being corrupted by a below-average-sized man with a synthesized voice from behind a shower curtain.

"We want kids?" he prodded.

"Of course we want kids. We've discussed this."

We've discussed kid's names—the same thing, really. (Finn if it was a boy, Astrid if a girl.)

"But did you ever consider my unavailability, traveling so much for work? That following fatherly hours doesn't work with me? I want flexibility."

I was uncharacteristically silent.

"And there's this image I can't get out of my head—a bunch of little hands always pulling at me, like seaweed waving on the ocean floor."

I remained uncharacteristically silent.

"And don't you think families today are so middle-class bourgeois?" Henry made a point to say bourgeois with an accent.

I sat up from the couch in search of a Windex container (each room had one hidden within accessible reach). Settling on a duster with a bushel of pink feathers, which Henry always liked as it gave in to his banal French maid fantasy, I began to dust my work area, humming "Cat's in the Cradle."

He walked over to the credenza, becoming absorbed by the contents of his messenger bag. I started to sing "Cat's in the Cradle," and Henry's rested smile disintegrated into a scowl.

"You know," he said, matter-of-factly, "I just remembered that I need to transfer my gym membership. If I don't do it today, I'll lose my initiation fee. They have these ridiculous policies where if you don't transfer it, you'll lose everything. This is extremely annoying, Emily."

He glared at me.

"What do you want me to do? Make a sign and petition outside Equinox?"

"I just need to deal with my membership."

And after that feeble excuse from Henry's "cannot deal" episode, he hoisted his bag over his shoulder and left the room, the slam of the door causing me to twitch backward.

I began to wonder whether I really knew Henry. Transferring a gym membership? For all I knew, he could work out in wifebeater tees with hiking boots and have guys named Fritz spot him.

Anne had clearly made her point that she wasn't happy with me. (But Anne never was happy with me.) Henry clearly made his point that he wasn't happy with me.

I stared at the fresh indentation he just made on the couch, the soft proof that he sat next to me moments ago. I couldn't quite tell if the lines were darkened from being dirty or just the shadows made from that angle. I thought of spraying Woolite upholstery cleaner on the couch, but such an effort would be a twenty-minute ordeal and I felt emotionally exhausted.

Now alone, my mind rewound the episodes of what had been happening. How I had put myself on starvation mode so I could be presentable in girth-exaggerating dresses, which completely justified an all-I-could-eat binge. I bought chocolate sprinkles yesterday. First I needed to spray the couch with Woolite upholstery cleaner.

17

I would never understand how stepping into a puff of silk would have the same significance as being handed a diploma or crossing a finish line. But today I would be the dutiful daughter and fashion myself in dresses that should be accessorized with wands and crowns made from tinfoil.

I even showed my dedication to the event by arriving at Vera Wang half an hour earlier than our appointment. My mother would arrive in fifteen minutes. She always came to her appointments fifteen minutes early. Considering that being fifteen minutes late was unspoken standard New York time, I started to calculate all the hours my mother lost just from waiting. Never good at math, I began to wonder how many spa treatments that would add up to, which was something like 18,000. No wonder my mother had been so uptight from all the wasted time she could have used toward massages and facials.

I sat on a pin-cushioned loveseat in the peach room and opened up my sketchbook, as my time would not be indulgently squandered by analyzing wallpaper textures. An elderly lady with a hunchback and all of the warts and frown lines that would make her an effective sage in one of the Tolkein books inched her way in my direction. She took momentary breaks to make Darth Vader breathing noises, which made me wonder if these steps would be her last. I wasn't particularly in the mood to perform CPR, and the idea of suctioning her mouth rimmed with more funky tubers than an old potato did not appeal to me. I feverishly occupied myself with my sketches. I became so absorbed in trying to look distracted that I had no focus at all.

And, with the same luck as when the fattest, sweatiest man fits himself into the available seat next to you, she balanced herself on the cramped chaise beside me. So obviously annoyed, I tried not to show my annoyance. However, this one-breath-away-from-bug-meat woman stared at me so cavalierly that I found her either truly evil or just in need of some attention. I looked from my drawing pad and gave her a wide, artificial smile that seemed to surprise her. I believed she just wanted to stare me down, thinking I'd take her abuse.

"Oh, Emily," my mother called, sautéing the elderly woman with her eyes.

She then gave me her cheek to kiss.

"Nana!" snapped a young girl, sliding into my view as I kissed my mom. She wore an unfastened wedding dress that appeared to have another fifty minutes of assembly required. I assumed these things came with instructions.

"You shouldn't wander off like that," she scolded her nana as if she were a lost child found by a department store security guard. The girl was definitely a Bridezilla. Her hair styled in a chignon, her makeup looked professionally done—all for her fitting. I felt a bit better about myself in witnessing the other breed of wedding monsters. While I fell into the careless, callous type, this one was the "it's all about me" kind.

"I just need to get a pair of shoes, and then we'll meet back in the fitting area," Bridezilla further directed her nana. I thought if my grandmother had been given the nana title how I'd probably call her "banana."

This backless-dressed Bridezilla fascinated both Mother and me with the shame-on-you pointing of her finger. While I felt appalled, slightly embarrassed by her histrionics, Mom smiled, overtly amused.

Pulling back, I noticed that she appeared to have lost weight and, for my mother, whose dinner consisted of two rye Wasa crackers spread with shrimp pate and lemon sorbet from a bowl the size of an eggcup, losing weight was not the look she should be going for. I made a point not to comment on her emaciation because, in her twisted way, she would either interpret this as a compliment or my being jealous.

"Oh!" I said, returning to my seat. I noticed that the nana had been watching Mother and me, our exchanges a performance used strictly for her entertainment. The woman could use a magazine, or at least feign that she had been occupied with something else even though she had a voyeuristic interest in others. That's what I always did.

Shuffling about the detritus of my bag—my turned-off mobile, wallet, sketch materials, and container of Tic Tacs that I had gotten into the habit of swiping from Henry—I tried to locate the gift I had brought for my father. His birthday was tomorrow, and I bought him Dempsey & Carroll note cards monogrammed with his initials, JNB (Jed Nelson Briggs), blazing like wet ink in Garamond type. No address, since Mother had been rather discerning about who obtained such information, as if she were some reclusive celebrity or wife of a politician who received the occasional death threat.

Presents for Dad rotated among three things: Dempsey & Carroll note cards, Hermes ties, and the latest presidential autobiography on the *Times* bestseller list. I believed an entire storage room existed somewhere on the lower west side devoted to these unused belongings. My father was not a person encumbered by possessions, always telling friends and family that he could never have enough of these three things.

I'd be receiving a call from my father later today. He will thank me for the gift and offer an explanation on how he will wait till tomorrow, his actual birthday, to open the present. I never understood this about him, as if the gift giver really cared that he opened his present on his given birthday. Personally, I could never wait to open a present after I received it, peeling off the wrapping the way Mom would scrape the butter off an incorrect lunch order.

"You will be at the party, darling?" she commanded in the form of a question.

"Of course," I said, getting up from my seat. The shift of my body acted as a weight removed from the lower end of a seesaw, springing old nana into the air. Mother smiled at this, apparently more annoyed by the elderly woman's presence than I was. If she were under the woman's impertinent stare, I believe nana would have become an added foe to my mother's endless list of people who treated her unjustly.

My mother seemed to find herself in many situations where she'd been "unjustly treated," typically in the form of salespeople who appeared more interested in assisting other customers, or high-maintenance women that she always managed to get caught in an elevator with. I've even speculated that my family lived in a townhouse just to lessen my mother's amount of elevator riding shared with such rude women.

After being told the details for the 1,800th time of Dad's party (the same party he has had every birthday at The Club), as if I had been one of those preschoolers that hammered the square peg in the round hole, we were under the care of Veronica.

Veronica started her duties by complimenting us as a mother/ daughter couple, obsequiously remarking on the resemblance I had to my mother while she probably tried to determine whether she was being ravished by a cell-eating disease or was just another one of those aged Park Avenue socialites with a pug just back from a spa week at the Ashram.

"And should I call you 'Miss Briggs'?" said Veronica, which caused Mother to scrunch up her face. She then looked at me and began to laugh.

"I've completely forgotten how you will soon be changing your name. 'Emily Philips,' " she said, vocalizing the name in what sounded like an English accent.

While I would be keeping my name for professional reasons, by the look of her utter elation I felt that perhaps now would not be the right time to tell her this.

"And I have just the dresses in mind for you, Emily," said Veronica, giving me the once-over. "My, you do have the figure that couture absolutely loves."

"Thank you," I said, slightly flushed from the compliment and how Veronica could blatantly check me out with the same consent as a doctor.

"Right, then," said Mother trying to shift the conversation from a woman overtly admiring another's figure. "I think Emily had something classic in mind, perhaps with cap sleeves."

I did?

"Wonderful," said Veronica.

"You know," I interjected. "It could be fun to look at a few of the slip dresses—perhaps backless. Something with more statement."

I intentionally avoided the magnetic pull of Mom's unwelcoming gaze.

"Well, I have a few options, all dresses that are simply made for you." Veronica again gave my breasts a good stare. Perhaps she was the lesbian here. "You are rather petite," she said discerningly.

At least she didn't call me a pixie.

Even though I'd be undressing and dressing more times than Paris Hilton before she set off on a Klinstar, I naturally wore my Chanel suit for the occasion. An afternoon with my mother coupled with a dress fitting at Vera Wang required the kind of attire that would also work at a garden party for one of Anne's fundraisers.

Typically my mother makes a point to tell me how unpresentable my appearance is, but today she noticeably refrained from such comments. Passing her inspection, I supposed that my effort had been made out of the guilt I felt about missing our last dress expedition appointment.

Being shown into a room thick with wedding dresses, Mom did not radiate as I imagined she would. In fact, she looked peaked.

"Are you okay?" I asked in an endearing tone not normally used when conversing with my mother.

"Of course." Firmly grasping the edge of a chair, she then said to Veronica, "Do you have any champagne?"

Champagne?

"Sure thing," chirped Veronica. "And would you like some as well?" she directed to me.

I knew better than to fall for that routine—buying a $5,000 wedding dress under the influence. Struck by the impossibility of buying a dress for less than five grand, acting as if these prices were completely justifiable, how any girl who thought otherwise would receive the scowl of shame, how couldn't I be miffed about laying down this absurd amount of money for the dress? Now, being a responsible and practical homeowner who knew what it cost to gut a bathroom in TriBeCa, I felt uncomfortable about the idea of spending more money than Julia Roberts did on the dress she wore the night she won her Oscar.

Veronica, who had the title of something to the effect of Executive Attendant, went to secure the assistance of one of her assistants to get Mom that flute of champagne.

I used the unattended moment to thoroughly scrutinize her appearance unobserved and became worried. Her skin was loosely draped on a frame of connected toothpicks. Though you could slice a tomato on her cheekbones, her most prominent feature to skeletal proportions, she now made skeletons look obese.

"How is everything?" I said cheerfully, which caused her to tilt her head cheesy-mall-professional-picture style. "You seem a bit drawn out—lacking color."

"You know, it's all that city air. I've told your father that I am through with New York winters. Unless it's a place like Chamonix or Jackson Hole, I don't function well in colder climates."

Or you could try eating a burger.

"Why don't we go to that little diner a block up the avenue afterward? They have great hamburgers. Permissible on Atkins!" I threw in as a lure.

This made her laugh hysterically, and I didn't get the joke.

"Emily! I don't do diners."

Right, of course.

"And the only burger I care for is Dr. Berger."

"You're not serious," I said. "Anne mentioned something, but I couldn't believe it. You're gorgeous, Mom—plastic surgery is not the way to go. You said so yourself that those woman look like those models with the blown-up faces like those shoe ads you see in the subway."

"Subway?"

Of course, in the fifty-some-odd years my mother has lived in New York, the furthest underground she's been were parties held in Grand Central Station. Though it was easy to share her dislike of the subways—how they screeched to a halt that sounded like tortured monkeys, being exposed to a myriad of germs from sharing cramped space with subway people. Walking was a preferable means of city transport.

"You know, you should read *The Wrinkle Cure*," I suggested gently. Daphne had turned me on to Dr. Perricone and how he fights aging naturally, emphasizing diet, various vitamins, and creams. Though I haven't actually read the entire book, because Dr. Perricone kept referring to specific patients and I didn't really see how their miraculous treatments affected my concerns, I did like the idea of being very herbal and natural without subscribing to legions of followers who actually wore hemp by choice.

"Dr. Perricone says that any type of sugary food will leave a noticeable residual effect. Just by eating certain foods with low glycemic levels and various vitamins, the years vanish!"

Mother raised an Eliza-plucked eyebrow, looking unconvinced.

Veronica broke up our beauty exchanges to become my chambermaid, her chewed-up nails—or nails deliberately cut short as stipulated in her employment agreement—buttoned, tied, and assisted in my dress-trying activity, the dresses harder to assemble than one of those "Do Not Sit" beds displayed at Gracious Home. Every gown was just infinitesimally different from the others, like a casting of actresses for a *Baywatch* revival. After trying on about 1,800 of them, if I had to put on another dress it would have been like taking a shot of tequila when you were well past your limit—the consequences would be ugly. I felt my teeth begin to snarl.

"Mom," I said, intentionally disregarding Veronica. "I need a break."

"That's all right," said Veronica.

Damn right it would be all right.

"You know, Emily," Mom said, specifically not including Veronica. "I better call it a day. You know, with your father's party planning and everything."

Her face drained even more of its color, like she had lost thought and needed to be reprogrammed.

18

My body lumbered to the curb. I wished I'd awoken earlier that morning so I could have gotten in the run I promised myself. Even though I would have been tired by waking at an unseemly time of day (8:00 AM), it would have been worth that momentary fit of exhaustion, as the exercise would have sustained the energy needed for the demands of this day. Filled with exhaustion, lifting my hand to hail a cab an effort, the yellow blur of a taxi slid into my space when some nondescript blonde (they all look the same to me) poked in front of me and into my cab.

What a bitch! But she did have on the most adorable coral collarless wool jacket with a pencil skirt trimmed with a ruffle. As good karmic thoughts came to me—my not wishing this evil blonde ill will and mentally complimenting her on her good taste—another cab slid into the departing cab's place. I became a believer in karma.

I directed the driver back home to Reade Street, where the delight of saying my new address sparked happy energy that was almost as effective as a sugar-free chocolate chewie. I looked in my bag for a sugar-free chocolate chewie, lost some of my former happy energy, and considered getting a prescription for Zoloft. I started to hum Monkees' "I'm a Believer," possibly even breaking out a few bars.

Falling back into the slippery vinyl, thinking about home, the eucalyptus steam room, and acting very Elizabeth Taylor pre-husband-number-three made me feel quite prim and girly. If I closed my eyes, I knew I'd never wake, which would be a bizarre predicament for this cab driver, whose name appeared to be Usi Sha—something not American.

Fifth Avenue went by in flip-book pace. The sky became less visible, lost beyond trees that were beginning to fill in. After making a stream of green lights, the cab had the misfortune of trailing a traffic-abiding driver, just across from Bergdorf's. I loved Bergdorf's. Admiring the second-best store windows in Manhattan (Barney's being the first), I saw a replica of the mannerless blonde gazing at me, wearing the identical coral outfit. A greater force did exist, telling me that I should have this ensemble. An electric current shot through me. I sat up as straight as I did when having lunch at The Club with Auntie Peg.

"Driver, I'll get out here."

Reaching for my wallet, I pulled out a five and then had to dodge an entering couple padded with shopping bags. Trying to avoid mannerless people in this city was like one of J3's game targets set at its most challenging level. I should do my part in improving the city by carrying around pocket etiquette books that I'd hand to such people. Channel 4 would do a segment, the *Today* show would then have me on regularly as an expert, and the mayor would award me some honor—the Manhattan version of being knighted.

I sprinted to the window, nudging through shoppers ogling my outfit, and read the suit's designer and floor number silhouetted on the glass. I hurried inside, as if this would be my sole opportunity to secure it.

A saleslady in a fitted gray dress with an exaggerated boat neck read my expression and offered her assistance.

"Coral," I said with a gasp. "Jacket," another gasp. "Pencil skirt with ruffle."

"Of course," she said politely. "What sizes would you like and I'll start a fitting room?"

Fitting room? If I tried on another thing I'd transform into something inhuman.

"Just a size four. And there's no need for me to try it on. Here's my card," I said, reaching into my bag for the baton exchange of my AmEx and merchandise.

19

It took me forty-five minutes to find a ride home. Of course, I had to go home during that phantom cab shift when the drivers illuminated the off-duty signs. That "fooled-ya" scenario when you spot what appears to be a vacant cab, only to be in the crossfire of a disturbed driver as they flash you a supercilious smile, elated from completing a sentence to shuttle rude passengers all day. I supposed I could see their point of view, but I didn't fall into the rude passenger category. I thought of how I ended my earlier cab ride short just so I could have the lavender bag currently in hand, then thought about the facial steam I'd soon be in a treat for.

I considered taking the subway, which really outlined my desire to get home, as I rarely traveled below ground due to a troubling incident that resulted in a ruined fur jacket cut in a bomber style.

Walking toward home, home that was at the other end of the city, I noticed a limo decelerate and follow me along the curb. I tried to look through the tinted windows to see if I could make out a celebrity. The passenger window rolled down, the driver asked where I'd be headed and offered to take me for twenty dollars. Tumbling into the backseat, I drifted in and out of sleep, the driver's presence signaled by a few adjustments to AM stations and shifting the directionals.

* * *

For an apartment that Henry and I had signed our entire future earnings to, the elevator could have used a spruce. You had to pull a perforated metal door open, which didn't seem to be the safest of holding devices in a time of terrorist attacks. The floor was haphazardly arranged with five different kinds of wood, which, in this case, "five different kinds" did not mean this to be the chicest blend, as the strips appeared to be Elmer glued onto a linoleum base.

I used the weight of my body to open the elevator door. Rifling through my bag, I chipped my key at the lock, where its shrunken fit denied me access.

Just great, Henry no longer wanted to live with me and changing the locks was his feeble way to say it was over. How incredibly mature of him. I felt hurt but too exhausted to get into my emotions at the moment, just annoyed that I couldn't take my eucalyptus steam.

The door flew open, presenting the love child of Doris Day and Steve Buscemi in her retirement years. Her hair jutted divergently in rad skateboarder spikes, evidently using the wrong product. The folds of her skin were curved and rubbery like a bowl of spaghetti— evidently not a follower of Dr. Perricone's program. I gathered her to have a poor diet, be dehydrated, should ease up on those Southsides, avoid the tanning oil, and get in the habit of using sunblock. I should work for Dr. Perricone.

Wearing a pink and green reversible terrycloth robe that you slipped over your head—the kind of robe the ladies wore over their first edition Lily Pulitzer suits at the Sunny Acres Condo in Naples, Florida—its V neck zippered with a green lanyard tassel showing ample cleavage blemished with the protoplasm speckles found on an exotic bird egg.

"Fuck you! Fuck you! Fuck you!" she screamed.

Oh my God! Oh my God! Oh my God!

"I fucking hate you! I hate your bag! I hate pixies!"

What was it with me and pixies?

"Fuck you! Fucking little whore! Fuck the two-timing sneak with the smarmy grin and dark hair!"

Wait a minute here, was she trying to insinuate that I was a whore? If so, I needed to defend myself.

"Fuck George Bush the pinhead! Fuck George Bush the prickhead!"

Then again, maybe this would be one of those situations where I refrained from defending my beliefs to a belligerent stranger.

"Fuck digital cable! Fuck rectangular tissue boxes!"

Apparently, I had the wrong apartment.

I closed her door (slammed) and then noted the hall sign, indicating the sixth floor. I lived on the seventh floor and never again would be making that mistake. Taking the stairs, I bolted up the last flight. The barking watermelon seemed to have summoned my energy back. My keys worked. Henry loved me! He would never have changed the locks without notifying me first.

My legs were thick with pain. I felt lightheaded from tiredness and could feel the strain under my eyes, hoping that the fatigued strain wouldn't be visible in the form of dark circles. Plunging onto the couch, I watched the dust fairies do their dance, illuminated in a stream of light, wondering where they came from and if there was some spray that could eradicate them.

I then deliberated between a visit to the medicine cabinet for an application of DDF wrinkle cream, a trip to the kitchen for something indulgent yet healthy, or that eucalyptus steam I'd been fantasizing about all day. Option number four presented itself in the form of an adorable Henry bearing gifts of Ben & Jerry's Low-fat Cherry Garcia, two teaspoons, and a can of chocolate Redi-Whip.

Peeling off the lid, he added a cyclone in the shape of a kid's party hat to the untapped frozen yogurt. I pointed inside my open mouth so Henry could shoot me up, twisting the can above my tilted head. We were two addicts sharing their fix in a ritual enacted with no words.

"So," I said, as the saliva in my mouth slowly dissolved this yummy artificial flavoring. "I'd start referring to you by your new name, 'Fuck the two-timing sneak with the smarmy grin and dark hair!' but that's a bit of a mouthful," I said, through a mouthful of dissolving whipped cream. I couldn't believe I just said the F-word out loud.

"Emily!" Henry looked confused, even a bit scared.

"I'm referring to the barking overcooked hotdog in watermelon wrapping downstairs," I said with a lazy smile.

Reaching for the teaspoon, I dug into the carton before Henry ate it all. He had this rude habit of hogging the goods. Then again, he probably did that because I was known to polish a pint off in less time than it took to down a tequila shot.

Henry waved his spoon in the air to the tune of his words. "Oh, I understand now. You've met Mrs. Hallingby!"

"Mrs. Hallingby could use a lesson in proper diction."

"Mrs. Hallingby has Tourette's syndrome."

"So you've met Mrs. Hallingby?"

Henry seemed to find this amusing, slapping his hands over his lap, his entire body levitated.

"Mrs. Hallingby is the resident attraction. You didn't see her leave the building, by the way?"

I shook my head.

"Apparently she just haunts the place. I hear she hasn't left the complex since 1994, for someone's funeral or something. And what a place she has—did you happen to catch a glimpse inside her doorway?" he said, while I jabbed my spoon into the container.

"Honestly," I paused, effectively gulping my food as it slid down my throat, "she didn't seem to be in the mood for a guest."

"You've got to check out her space. It looks like it's in the middle of the goddamn Everglades. Wallpapered in that faux bamboo. She has this whole frog motif thing going on—these leapfrog sculptures she probably lifted from a kid's park, frog artwork, needlepoint pillows with frogs. There's even a crazy fountain with frogs in it. Live ones," he said, seeming bewildered by the notion. Haven't you heard all of those 'rig-ups' at night?"

"I thought that was you burping."

"And then there are her regular walks around the building, where she terrorizes the neighbors, cursing them out. Good thing we live on the seventh floor, because I don't think she ever ventures upward. You know, frogs are more a sea-level kind of creature."

I didn't like this idea of being cursed out by an abusive preppy frog woman.

"Isn't there some kind of safety measure about this in our buyer's agreement? We have to get out of this."

"Don't make such a big deal out of it, Emily."

My face was about to burst open with rage and shoot out a confetti of exploded brain goo.

"She called me a 'fucking pixie'!"

Henry laughed, but I didn't want him to gloss over this.

"Why do we have to lay down our entire future earnings to live above an irreverent X-rated movie watched by the same freaks who get off on nude photos of fat women on the Internet? She's the nightmare on Reade Street. This is a nightmare!"

Johnny Depp starred in the original *Nightmare on Elm Street*. Absolutely gorgeous. His slashing outcome saddened me.

"And now I'm having these awful, fucked-up thoughts where good, beautiful people get slashed to bite-sized pieces. Like dated Halloween candy served in a bowl with some green ceramic hand popping up from the bottom that you buy at a store with marked-down prices."

I thought of how vulgar I must have sounded, and it disturbed me.

"You see. It's contagious. Fucking Tourette's syndrome is contagious."

"Tourette's syndrome is not contagious," said Henry, somewhat patronizingly.

"Then why have years of being disciplined not to say a swear word for fear of God rooming me with a Lizzie Grubman type in the apartment complex of hell just lead me to say fuck?"

Fuck! I'm going to be rooming in hell with Lizzie Grubman.

"Oh, fuck!" I moaned.

"Emily, watch it. What's wrong with you?"

"You try spending the rest of eternity with girls who deliberately try to be blond and run over people because they didn't get quick enough valet service."

Fuck, I said to myself. Sometimes just saying the naughty word caused a rush with pill-popping effectiveness.

I looked down at my little Chanel coat and spectator pumps. The dual tones of black and white probably complimenting my complexion, the simplicity of my shoe began to calm me. I began to feel as if I had been admitted to the in-patient ward, my mental illness being with simple colors and procedures, rooming with a girl who always had oatmeal stains on her face—possibly a step up from living with Lizzie Grubman, but I didn't want to be an in-patient in a mental hospital.

"I did have quite a day," I said, noticeably more collected. "Mom is now Exhibit A from being exposed to the wrath of yours truly—Bridezilla Wearing Chanel."

Henry's expression pressed for more information.

"The woman looks like she's on the Dean Ornish diet and realized she couldn't eat any of the food for religious reasons."

"Your mother's always been a fussy eater." Henry took a moment. "She's just fussy in general."

"Well, soon she'll be fussy in heaven, or wherever she'll end up, but I believe her sizable donations to Saint Bartholomew will grant her a corner room in the Heaven Seven Hotel or wherever it is her type registers. And now I'll never see her in the afterlife, considering that heaven doesn't accept my kind from all of my bad behavior in handling our resident freak attraction."

Henry pursed his lips and nodded his head as a way to deflect my comments so as not to value them with words.

"And how are we with wedding planning?" he said, the tips of his mouth raised in a sort of smirk.

"Enough with the interrogation!" I barked.

Who was I and what did they do with my body?

"Chill, Emily. I thought you at least accomplished something with that big purple Bergdorf's bag that your toe keeps tapping."

I stopped tapping my toe, which apparently had been set to a nervous twitch that annoyed Henry.

"So, did you buy your dress?" he asked. I began to twitch my toe to the bag again.

"Yes, I finished all of my peas and carrots and even asked for an extra helping of brussels sprouts."

"Come on, Emily. Give me the bag?"

"Is this a hold-up?" I said, kicking over the bag where he started to prod it open. "You know that it's bad luck for the groom to see the bride's dress before the big day."

Re-stuffing the vapor of tissue into the bag, he said, "And why are you encouraging bad luck?"

"Because," I said, pinching the handles of the bag to take it away from Henry. I then pulled out the suit from the bag, modeling it against my chest. "Though this is quite lovely, I am not about to wear it down an aisle."

Henry looked to the coral suit like it was the head of his mother.

"What's wrong? Don't you like coral?"

I then evaluated the outfit. Surely a Marc Jacobs could only lift one's emotions. Though it did have that brash peachy color resembling the best-selling Nars nail polish back in the prep revival summer of '99.

"Where did you get that?"

I nodded to the direction of the Bergdorf's bag with an "isn't this part obvious" look.

"I mean, I've seen it before. Can't quite place it right now."

"Well, you either saw it in the window of Bergdorf's or on some rude blonde stealing people's cabs in midtown." I thought about the percentage of cab-stealing rude blondes in midtown as being analogous to Chinese villagers eating rice.

"And you will be seeing it at my father's birthday party at The Club," I said, enunciating The Club. "So save your appetite for lots of bad meat stuffed in pastry dough. Artichoke will be the main representative vegetable group."

Henry's face returned to its rosy color.

"Right, your father called. Thanking you for the gift, but he said he'd wait till tomorrow before opening it. What is it with your father and time? We were talking about their trip abroad next week, and he said how he always arrives for international flights four hours before the departure."

I was too tired to go there with Henry.

"He worries about Customs."

"Okay," Henry mumbled.

"And bring deposit slips from your checkbook. We'll want to cash in those fresh checks guests will be slipping to us because of our big news!"

I sat on the edge of my desk chair, opening and closing drawers because I had completely forgotten where I'd put my checkbook.

"So you've sent out invitations without my knowing?" Henry asked worriedly.

"Don't be ridiculous. How could I send out invitations when we haven't even picked a date and a place?"

Oops.

"Emily," he said, in that scary voice that said "Authority." I never responded well to "Authority." "You still haven't called the Stanhope? What have you been on these days?"

"The strongest thing I've ever put into my system are birth control pills. But after our last family planning chat, I've decided to stop taking them."

Henry's face went into a thousand different directions before it burst with red like an exploding thermometer.

"You what!" he shouted, a few thousand specks of spit visible from across the room. If my face had been in precise striking distance from his shooting point, it would have gotten ugly.

"Relax. Joke."

"Hysterical," he said, back in his patronizing tone.

Henry then patted his hand on the space next to him, I believed intended for me, considering no one else was in the room. He looked considerably more composed, so I figured I'd be safe. Though an Emily action-figure doll could be good for Henry during such heated exchanges.

"I only ask you these things because I am in love with you. I want to marry you, spend the rest of my life with you, and am well aware that this dream of mine cannot happen unless we have a proper ceremony."

"Have you been drinking?"

"Would you be serious for a moment, Emily?"

I've really been a monster.

"I know I've been a bit of a challenge lately," I said with a pout, giving him snuggles for the entire vixen effect, which I have never been particularly skilled at.

"Challenge? Battling a drug problem is a challenge. You make reformed addicts want to start using again."

I looked to him uneasily. What was with the drug references all of a sudden? I had noticed a curled-up dollar bill on Henry's bureau and wondered if he'd been sniffing coke, which would be a complete waste of all of our money.

"So I've been a bit cuckoo lately."

"Grown people who find entertainment in building igloos with their mashed potatoes are cuckoo. You've been the leader of the nest who has no reason to be there and then gets half their brain removed."

That sounded painful. And I've never liked the idea of unnecessary surgery.

"Henry, now you're the one being mean."

20

Henry and I overslept as a result of having one too many Mojitos at Casba. I raced to the shower, squirted various cleansers over my body, and quickly rinsed off the suds. Still slightly wet, hoping that my bathrobe would sop up the excess moisture to save time, I drew pencils on my face in different shapes but all in the tawny family, which I compulsively bought for the love of hearing them clink together in my Sephora basket. Wrapping the bathrobe a bit closer around my body and tightening the belt, I went downstairs to look for my missing sling-backs from last night, finding J3 making his way up the staircase, calling off my search as he had the missing shoes in hand.

"Found these in between the orange juice and milk. Thought they might be yours, as they're not quite my size and Henry doesn't seem the sling-back type."

Taking the shoes from him, I felt my face flush infinitesimally. Had no idea why they were in the fridge. But seeing J3, my carefree nature felt restored, wishing that the old Emily had just been temporarily missing and would be found somewhere behind the pints of ice cream and frozen edamame in the freezer.

"J3!" I said, a bit overenthusiastically. I strapped on one of my shoes, which felt a bit chilled, soothing actually, like a cool compress to the head.

"Emily!" he said, matching my enthusiasm. "It's been so long. What? Two weeks now."

"And what perfect timing. You"—I then put on my other shoe and stopped making amputee wobbles—"You will be accompanying Henry and me to my father's sixty-seventh birthday party. Think bowties and gingham, lots of talks about sports that aren't really sports and the next great vacation land to invest in for the prune-juice-buying crowd."

"Uh!" he mumbled.

"We have no time. Now go. Go! Go! Go!" I said, shooing him off like he was my reluctant midget neophyte about to conquer evil.

About thirty minutes later (which was about two hours later than our prearranged departure time), and after a few dozen face-overs because I decided that the smoky eye look didn't quite work on me, I relished the idea of being entertained.

In the kitchen, I gathered some Snapples, fruit, and Clif bars and packed them in a recyclable Prada bag.

Henry looked very sexy-preppy in khakis he reserved for such occasions, a suede blazer, and his long rugby-striped scarf, while J3 wore a gingham broadcloth shirt tucked into straight-leg cords and a dark blue blazer.

While Henry looped his scarf, he asked me why I was making such an effort to take snacks when we were en route to a party revolving around food and drinks. Presumably I had on one of my involuntary smirks, as he quickly veered to what the day's weather called for, which struck me as just as absurd as his last comment, since how would I have any more knowledge on this matter than him, having spent the past three minutes conversing with muted glances.

Preppy frog granny curse woman was in the lobby.

"Oh, for fuck's sake," I whispered to Henry. "It's preppy granny frog curse woman."

"Mrs. Hallingby," Henry said, having to remind me in a tone too loud, which set her off like one of those belligerent car alarms.

"Fuck you! Fuck you! Fuck you!" she screamed, to the entire world. "Fuck you and that pink dress!"

Coral.

"Fuck you for no longer being a blonde. Fucking hate blondes."

Perhaps this one time Mrs. Hallingby and I were in agreement on something. Though I wondered about the blonde reference.

J3 looked shell-shocked from the Mrs. Hallingby introduction. She did have that effect.

"J3," I nodded my head to J3 and then turned to Mrs. Hallingby. "J3, this is Mrs. Hallingby. Mrs. Hallingby, J3. And I am Miss Emily Briggs, currently living in sin with my fiancé Henry Philips, while J3 is here to make those tiresome evenings a bit more interesting. Now if you will excuse us, we have my father's sixty-seventh birthday to attend, and I don't want to miss the Carvel ice cream cake lit with sparklers."

Our family reserved Carvel only for special occasions; we were very traditional that way.

Both Henry and J3 looked to me in what seemed to be reverence.

"By George, J3, I think she calmed the barking hag down."

I looked at my watch.

"Oh fuck! Oh fuck! Oh fuck!" I've turned into Mrs. Hallingby. Tourette's syndrome was contagious.

"Henry, get a cab. Now!"

Riding in the taxi uptown, we'd have been better off getting onto the highway and heading for a Vermont ski weekend with all of this lost travel time. Then again, the snow conditions had been "rather cruddy" lately, as reported by coffeehouse Pete.

Before we headed to The Club in Westchester, we had to pick up my car, which I parked in an outdoor lot on the west side of midtown for the cheaper monthly rates. My parents were still members of the sailing club we went to when I was a child, the time we gave regimented suburban life a go for the sake of a backyard, before realizing that a regimented suburban life meant more time in cars, the storage facilities for those cars, obsessing over neighbors' cars, obsessing over lawns, the neighbors' lawns, the mowing methods of the neighbors' lawns, and all to trim that illustrious patch of backyard space we used maybe five times a year. Backyard culture fulfilled its place in Briggs history.

Mom and Dad kept their membership to The Club, because my

father would not be cheated from losing the initiation fee, now only being put out ten grand each collecting year for a space to hold his annual birthday party.

Driving along the West Side Highway, I shifted my Mustang in and out of cars like a video game. Henry rode shotgun, his hand pressing the life out of the dash, which began to annoy me because he seemed to be leaving a permanent imprint.

"Maybe you should try slowing down," he grumbled.

"We had to be there, oh, about three hours ago!" I said, slamming on the brakes before the nose of my car almost pressed into the rear of the newest Jeep model.

"You see," I said, slightly shifting my head to Henry before I realized that my gaze would be better directed to driving, "you almost got me into an accident." I threw up my hands in annoyance, and then checked on our backseat passenger. Looking in the rearview, J3 appeared remarkably composed. He even seemed to be enjoying himself. I then drove more reasonably.

I began to fiddle with the stereo system I recently had installed, tuning to a station playing eighties flashbacks. Yaz came on. You could never tire of Yaz. It amazed me how effectively a song could transport you back to another place.

Henry started adjusting every individual button and knob, testing out the treble, giving an excessive amount of attention to the levels of treble. We seemed to have a lot more treble than needed.

Now fully reeling me back from my mental sing-along with Allison Moyet, I gave him a sneer that broke him from his important task of sound adjustment in our temporary capsule. We settled on a station that played the best of the eighties, nineties, and today, Tracy Chapman complaining about something. Maybe she had stood on a welfare line at one time, but you'd think she'd be over it by now.

Henry then spoke quickly, suggesting that we switch off the Hutch and onto I-95. I managed to swerve the wheel and control the quickened flutter of my heart, all so we could hit a patch of traffic that took ten minutes to creep ten feet.

I rested my head on my hand, where I formed it into a gun and continually pulled the trigger. I had one of those moments where I tried to calculate the time it would take to abandon the car and walk to my father's party, which then channeled into rage and visions of me driving onto the shoulder while thinking of excuses I'd give to the police officer if pulled over.

This was Henry's fault. This was Henry's fault. This was Henry's fault.

What would have happened if Henry didn't have enough treble, perhaps moved on to the bass? Why couldn't he have contributed something? Programming my favorite stations would have been useful. It took every disciplinary trick I've learned to control myself and not add to the disruptive atmosphere circulating inside me.

"Why don't you program my stations?" I directed. Henry seemed overjoyed to be given a task.

For the remainder of the ride, Henry filled J3 in on Mrs. Hallingby. I enjoyed listening to him tell his version of Hallingby tales, sharing her likes and dislikes, which became increasingly embellished the harder J3 laughed. He went into great detail about her fetish for all things frog and the tall drinks woozily held in her clutches with a paper umbrella bobbing from the ice like a dinghy in stormy waters.

J3 knew there was an idea there somewhere, but couldn't quite figure it out. I thought of an irreverent cartoon, her muumuus in Pulitzer patterns a distinctive design, but the need for excessive profanity was more suited for HBO at night. Perhaps a Hallingby video game, where she and a battalion of frogs shoot down Reade Street loft residences with bubbled expletives. I became excited by my brilliant idea, considered sharing it with J3, thinking how impressed he and Henry would be at my cleverness.

"Don't we have to get off soon?" said Henry.

"No."

I passed our exit.

Turning into the next town, I felt relieved and strange at the succession of square houses with triangular roofs, and I wondered why I had such urgency to rush here. At The Club's front security post, basically an old-fashioned telephone booth in white clapboard, I gave the person with the most boring job the Briggs name for access. We then passed a ship's mast that hailed the American flag and two sailing ropes streaming from its side studded with The Club's blue and yellow sailing flag.

We wound our way down a cobblestoned path that followed

points of attractions like desirable squares on a game board—the pool where I had sex with Scott Bankstrom (the first love), an outdoor pavilion used for club dances, rainy-day clambakes, and the occasional wedding where, I believe, Scott Bankstrom married a girl he taught sailing to back when he was an instructor. Westchester and Fairfield counties were as inbred as Appalachia.

Inching our way up the hill to the main clubhouse, our incoming arrival caused the valet to lift himself from his folded aluminum chair. Braking to a stop that caused Henry's head to crash forward and then plunge to the back of his seat, I noticed that this made the valet smile, revealing a dried green speck of tobacco that stuck to his front tooth that I sensed had stronger properties than the Marlboro poking from the side of his mouth.

Keeping my hands firm on the wheel as I thoughtfully considered my '65 Mustang, with value beyond a scientific price given in a blue book, I wondered if entrusting it to the hands of this valet, burned out in every sense, would have disastrous ramifications. Henry and J3 ejected from the car to stretch their legs, starting a process that did not take into account my agitated state.

The valet took one last drag from his cigarette, the fused butt having an uncanny resemblance to his spiky salt and pepper hair. He then darted in front of the car. I watched the movement of his khaki pants secured with a navy ribbon belt decorated with icons of The Club's blue and yellow sailing flag—the Nike swoosh for the yachting set. I gave the wheel one final squeeze before relinquishing my seat to his care, watching the Mustang wind its way down the hill to be parked.

J3 held his empty Snapple bottle, briefly leaving Henry's and my sides to throw it in the hole of a receptacle topped with sand used to extinguish cigarettes. Henry also drank a Snapple during the ride. The bottle was probably currently rolling about on the car's floor. When J3 returned from depositing his drink, Henry looked at me with intense focus, a prod so I could lead us into The Club.

21

The roar of swing music and nasal laughter burst from the double-door entranceway. On its upper half, that blue and yellow striped club flag now made its appearance in stained glass. I began composing excuses for our early departure.

After all of these years, I was disappointed that The Club couldn't treat itself to a day of beauty. Certainly they had enough extra cash from dues collected by ghost members like my father. The inside of the Tudor style mansion, which formerly belonged to a prominent beer family, still smelled like the basement of a church used to hold bazaars and ballet lessons.

The interiors were inspired by the cabin of an old luxury cruise ship—impressive high beams in glazed walnut, submarine-style windows that shut with a suctioning metal clasp like the lever of an old fridge—but the columns and railings barely held their paint, eggshell flecks peeling like scabs of skin.

I noticed the absence of the Turkish carpet that had adorned the main entrance, its various pathways worn into the design from heels of shoes in lipstick shades and docksiders with lives stretched by one of the myriad uses of duct tape. Apparently, Marilyn Monroe stayed as a guest once, presumably back when The Club had been a private residence, something members repeatedly made a point to discuss.

In the main banquet room called "Starbird," Henry and J3 were remarkably poised in an assembly of tight-faced women and their tight-fisted spouses, who were not so forthcoming with their congratulatory wedding checks. Perhaps Henry had been right regarding those invitations. They needed proof before making deductions from their accounts, and this was an incentive to send out those invites, a sort of notice elegantly addressing that bills needed to be collected.

I went to the bar and thought about ordering a Long Island Iced Tea, as that was the drink you had at The Club. The cocktail could fuel a Rover with its alcoholic potency, a hazardous combination of every kind of alcohol to make those members forget about their 2.4-kid life for a while. Still a bit wobbly from last night, I ordered a seltzer that came with a sliver of lime served on a cocktail napkin with that blue and yellow flag—regurgitation marketing.

Patches of brightly dressed ladies spoke in hushed screaming, relishing the idea of having an event that gave them another opportunity to wear their Easter purchases bought during a day of shopping on Madison and Fifty-seventh, outings where they parked the car in a garage that charged $20 an hour and made reservations for lunch at Le Charlot. I watched a lot of clutching to the breasts and waved hands in front of their faces as if something reeked sour.

From their soft, handsome features, you could tell that this generation of women had been hunted in their day, all part of the rich husbands/good-looking wives equation. But from years of saying yes to the dessert menu and having their stylists follow the trends of their favorite morning-show host, this part of their lives had begun to dim.

The bartender made his presence known by shaking a martini to life. He gave a wicked smirk intended for mature audiences only, or else my seltzer had been laced with the latest drug that increases the percentage of a college's date-rape statistic.

"Just look at how overly trained his biceps are," said a woman wearing peach lipstick, whispering softly into my ear. She poked her fork into a pie shell where the fruity innards oozed onto her plate. "What does a man need with all of that physical strength? Surely the effort and time used to maintain such a body is wasted on wiping a few cocktail glasses, just to lift the occasional box of scotch."

She referred to the predatory bartender, who had an uncanny

resemblance to the guy who installed the stereo system in my car. Thinking back, that auto mechanic did have a leading role in one of my more lascivious dreams, spawned by watching the Romance Channel before bed. The Romance Channel was becoming a key addition to my life.

"He seems to like you," she said, again stealthily into my ear. I watched her sparkly drop earrings dangle as she moved, like a chandelier shaking on a cruise ship.

"I'd rather become a lesbian than be with someone like him," I said, pressing out puffs of laughter.

"You know, I happen to be gay," said peach lipstick lady.

"You're not gay! My mother doesn't know any gay people!" I took a sip of my drink to contain the balls of laughter churning in my stomach.

She had better not be gay.

Peach lipstick lady pointed to a woman across the room.

The woman she pointed to was definitely gay.

Her hair two-toned, black shooting from a strip of white roots, she probably gave her colorist a picture of a skunk. Dressed in a caterpillar green pantsuit, she seemed to share lipstick with her "partner," which I believed to be the correct terminology.

"I'm Sadie Becker and that over there is Ellen Sherman, my partner. We're breeders, the ones who gave your parents Mao."

At least I got the "partner" part right.

"Listen," I said lightheartedly to Sadie Becker, "seeming as there's no way out of this little gaffe of mine, why don't we just have sex, or whatever it is your kind does, and laugh this one off?"

Sadie Becker did laugh me off, leaving her post to move in the direction of her partner. I decided that now would be the good time to trade up from a seltzer to something stronger. A Bloody Mary. The best drink to diffuse my hangover from last night and forget my previous blunder.

I walked across the room and gave faint smiles to people who know me as Catherine and Jed's girl, making it to the corner bar without having to tire someone with the happenings of my past year. The bend of the bar's countertop was partitioned by glass where it extended outside to cater to thirsty drinkers who preferred to have their alcoholic intake outdoors. Securing the attention of

the bartender, I went into great detail about the amount of horseradish and parts of juice to Grey Goose to make my drink. This bartender was evidently accustomed to such extreme ordering, as I
recognized him as having worked for my mother before.

Turning around, I saw the sandy strands of my ten-year-old
brother's head, his Chamonix tan a handsome contrast to his light
hair. The bob of his blond head Pac-Manned through an electric
Easter egg patch. Looking down at the blinding coral of my suit, I illuminated Oliver's strip, becoming the prized pellet.

"Emily!" he wailed. His boyhood chubbiness had vanished, putting into greater focus a mouth full of tin. Mother never prepared
me that Oliver had gotten braces. Then again, she never made
mention of family issues she found potentially disagreeable.

The protuberance of scrappy metal on each of his front teeth
surprised me, small with a lackluster dimness, as big and dull as my
engagement diamond. I never had orthodontia and wondered who
Oliver had inherited the overbite from, putting back into question
my suspicions that I had been the product of the postman.

"Oliver!" I cried. Normally I would lean down a few notches to
hug him, but he seemed to have grown about three feet since I last
saw him. "Nice braces," I said. I would have made a comment like
"Brace Face," but didn't want to add to the drama and insecurity of
it all. Then again, considering Oliver's technologically obsessed
generation, anything metal would be considered the Calvin Klein
jeans of his peer group.

"J3 Hopper is here. I love J3 Hopper!" Oliver spoke of J3 like he
was Bono. It was hard to picture J3 as the Bono of anything.

J3 approached us with confidence. The broad smile under his
thicket of dark brows gave him a potential Bono-of-his-industry air.
J3 should have his picture taken with Bono. Important people who
had their picture taken with Bono rise in the cool factor.

"Quite a brother you have here. I'd offer him a job, but he said
that he should really complete the sixth grade and then we'd talk. I
think he's just holding out for a better package."

"That's Oliver for you," I said, and we all laughed until Oliver disappeared, trailing the server with the tray of pigs in blankets. "It's
sort of humiliating when your ten-year-old brother is smarter than
you," I said, turning my head back to J3 once I lost sight of Oliver.

"And your dad," said J3, sipping his beer from a frosted mug. "He seems like a really nice guy."

Nice guy?

"You make him sound like he should be on the cover of a popcorn package."

"You mean like Paul Newman?" J3 asked.

"Orville Redenbacher is more who I had in mind, but go with whatever image your mind conjures, because I barely know the guy."

"Orville Redenbacher?" he then asked.

"No. My father."

The bartender dangled the cold drink in front of my face as a way of securing my attention. I appreciated bartenders who had a sense of when to interrupt a sensitive topic.

"And what's your father like?" I asked, intentionally shifting the conversation, and then took a sip from my drink. Damn horseradish. He put in too much horseradish, which I went into great effort and detail for him not to do. The guy must have had something against me. Oh, no—I couldn't possibly be turning into my mother, where random people were conspiring against me, preventing me from having my daily doses of happiness. I decided that the preferable manner to handle such a confrontation would be to learn to tolerate drinks with too much horseradish.

"Are you all right, Emily? Your face just flared with red," said J3.

"Oh, no. Perfectly fine. Loving this horseradish, very invigorating," I said in earshot of another bartender trying to poison me.

"My dad, returning to your question, was in the Air Force. We traveled around a lot till they settled in Palo Alto. That's why I'm always on the move. It's what I was brought up on."

"Wow. You must have seen some interesting places."

"Army bases aren't the most exciting of locations, but we did live all over the world. Amsterdam, Copenhagen, Oslo, Sydney, Malaysia."

He namedropped cities the way my cousin Anne namedropped society brand-name friends she strong-armed into hosting her charity events.

"Did your father ever serve?" J3 asked.

"Serve?" I queried with an amused brow. "Unless you consider his serves every summer Sunday at the beach. He has a nice slice that he attacks Mr. Weston with when they play tennis. Otherwise, my father looks at military endeavors as the two opponents with different colored uniforms."

J3 laughed, but I was becoming unnerved by talking at this club located twenty minutes outside the city, a membership that came with a mooring and clapboard closet referred to as a "changing cabana."

"My father and I were quite close when I was younger, a relationship based on an entire language of athletics and family pets. But when I entered my teenage years, I'm afraid there were many casualties. I don't believe my father ever fully recovered from that period."

"Ah, yes," said J3, shaking his head. " 'Emily Briggs. The Teenage Years.' I feel there's an idea in there somewhere."

"Trust me," I said, firmly grasping J3's free hand, perhaps a bit too strongly, as he looked at me with surprise. "No one wants to relive that again. Ever. Especially not me."

He laughed. "Okay, then, no 'Emily Briggs. The Teenage Years.' "

"I thank you. My father thanks you. And anyone who had the misfortune of knowing me during that period thanks you."

J3 paused for a moment, his head posed in thinking-cap position. "But how about 'Emily. The Childhood Years'? I can only imagine you being quite the kid, in a mischievous kind of way."

He gave me a dark look.

"I guess I did do the typical mischievous childhood kind of things. You know, pulling the legs off of daddy longlegs spiders, terrorizing puppies over banisters. The tame stuff."

"You terrorized puppies by holding them over banisters?"

Yes.

"No-o-o!" I said, dragging out the "o."

The side of J3's mouth nudged upward so that the crease in his lip's edge looked like an open umbrella. This was J3's version of the Emily smirk. He looked quite distinguished when making it.

"So we can easily agree that you had a fortunate childhood," he said.

I supposed I did. And I had to stop feeling so ashamed of this, because a fortunate childhood only meant being crushed by the realities of adult life.

"There were lots of popcorn snacks mushrooming in foil that

had more excitement in the making of them than eating, but being blessed with a good childhood," I said as if giving a speech to a mosaic of black-tasseled graduation caps, "is a fortunate gift, because you begin your life happily, with nothing to rehash to a therapist about, probably saving many hours and a fortune in shrink time. However, a happy childhood is also an onus, because you spend the rest of your life in search of what you once had."

Lured by my prompting, we moved away from the party and toward the dock. I secretly wanted to avoid the dimming of lights and the sounds of my mother banging her fork on the edge of her glass. I've never enjoyed the part of a festivity when you had to dampen the genuine fun by having to hear all the quips made about the jolly good fellow, politely smiling, forcing out a controlled laugh at designated breaks while secretly disputing the accuracy of the sentiment.

The day cleared where the mossy green outline of Long Island across the Sound tuned in crisp focus. I looked to the bobbing boats, remembering boys recounted to friends as "fooling around with," back when fooling around on boats had been a convenient place to gather with no parental intrusions.

The water adjacent to the boat moorings had been sealed off from the Sound, a chlorinated beach that members seemed to find innovative, while I found it to be a shoddy way of not springing for a legitimate pool.

The Club's grounds were sexually charged for me. A significant piece of my carnal history could be mapped out on the various attractions. All that was needed were the granite slates that memorialized the occasions: "Summer of '85, first kiss with Alec Braddock." "Summer of '88, sex with Scott Bankstrom," which happened underneath the high diving board, opposed to on top, due to the high degree of difficulty from the disconcerting bounce in the night air.

If I dusted off the part of my brain that contained such information, I'm sure I could have thought up some more past sexual encounters, but didn't think the timing was appropriate for me to drift off into this mental tabulation while I had an escort.

J3 guzzled his beer. All that remained were a few splotches of white froth that clung to the inside of his mug, looking like the washed-up sea foam splashing beneath our view. He then put the

used glass on the wide planked armrest of an Adirondack chair.
Giving this chair some thoughtful notice, he folded his body into it.
The chair next to him looked dry, so I decided to take the seat, and
we just gazed out to the ripples and listened to sounds of the water.
A few boats were already moored for those zealous sailors who
couldn't wait for the season to officially begin.

The wind imitated the elegant tune of bustling couture; the
chimes that boats make and the movement of water added to the
nautical mood. I tilted my head sleepily, thinking how big the chair
was, almost uncomfortable with the large fit, and how it would better serve two.

J3 reached for my drink, which was a good thing considering I
was about to tip it over from my hand that went limp. He took a sip
from my glass without asking. I liked that he felt this comfortable
with me. I began to wonder why I had made such a point for J3 to
join us today.

"So," said J3 with a smile, "is this the place where you spent your
childhood summers?"

More like the place I trained to become a complete slut but,
again, I thought it would be better not to discuss such sordid details.

"A few seasons, around the college years, but most of my summers were spent in Bridgehampton."

"Ah," he said drolly. "Bridgehampton."

"Please. It's not like I grew up as some Park Avenue princess with
summers at the beach manse."

"So your parents now live off of Park?"

I nodded to the waterscape.

"You've lived in Europe. Summers were spent between sailing in
Westchester and the Hamptons. You're dressed"—J3 gave my coral
suit an up-and-down—"wearing Louis Vuitton, I believe. I see."

This made me sound quite materialistic. And I wore Marc Jacobs.

"I think you're missing the point. We ate Oscar Mayer wieners
and potato salad! But don't let my mother ever know that I told you
that."

Startled by a crashing sound, our vision snapped to the scene of
the action. It appeared that Auntie Peg had fallen out of her wheelchair. Her feathered hat, which looked like a goose nested on her
head, became a pillow fight of feathers, as if a fox had his way in the

henhouse. J3 and I shared the immediate reaction of a tragic outcome before finding the amusement in such a spectacle.

"Oops. Auntie Peg has fallen," I said, trying very hard to express concern for my elderly relation.

"But can she get up?" he said.

Without disrupting the momentum of our laughter, we figured there were enough people to help Auntie Peg get up, and we remained in our seats.

"You seem to love the summer," J3 said once our eyes were dry and the laughter had subsided.

"Love the seasons, except for those absurd below-zero days. What's that about? The ozone thing?"

"Erratic weather patterns." J3 could have added more, but didn't seem interested in directing the conversation to global warming.

"And summers were spent simply," I said, twisting my head back to the water. I wondered why I felt so committed to absolving myself with J3. Squeezing my eyes shut, I thought back to those summers at the beach, realizing that facts were not being compromised.

Days were spent collecting bugs, nesting them in mayo jars with tops sealed with punched-in squares of Saran Wrap. We organized scavenger hunts, made candles by melting crayons into Dixie paper cups, caught fish and then released them.

I now turned to J3. He watched me with a meaningful gaze.

"We entertained ourselves creatively, spent time with nature. There was no room for electronics in our summer existence. You'd be at a very different place right now if your target consumer spent their free play the way I did."

J3 raised his bushy brows, looking impressed.

"You seem to really have a connection to that place—your childhood summer home."

I gave a concentrated stare across the Long Island Sound, where further down that strip and across the bubbly topography stood that grand house. Being in Bridgehampton was like pressing the pause button on a Disney video—nothing bad ever happens, you're just stuck on something completely happy and magical. And the magical kingdom was a home that has a few years on the oaks guarding it, slightly dilapidated but still standing proud. That house, in which I would soon no longer have a rightful place, I yearned for, missing it like a long-distance boyfriend.

I then pictured myself becoming one of those loony ladies wearing geriatric glasses as big as truck windows, making drive-bys in front of my former home till the new owners would have to get a restraining order to protect a piece of property.

"I need to keep those memories intact. Catherine and Jed are selling it—something about never using it and it's not the same place—all at the convenient time of my wedding planning. Looks like I won't be having the wedding I always pictured."

"That sucks."

"Tell me about it."

"So where will you have it?"

"Hey," announced Henry from behind. I peered over the picketed rim of my seat and found him quickly approaching.

"I've been looking for you guys," he said, now standing in front of J3 and me. He held an amber-colored drink that I assumed to be a Jack and ginger.

"Shall we blow this popsicle joint?"

And by all of the popsicle-colored corduroy pants and ladies' shifts at the party, Henry was pretty accurate in his assessment.

I gave Henry a once-over. He seemed a bit out of breath; the cuffs of his pants were moistened from dew and held shards of grass. I then noticed that J3 had returned my drink to my armrest, and I took a sip. The glass was slippery, the ice cubes melted, making the Bloody Mary taste like watered-down tomatoes.

"Ready to leave?" I said, turning my head to J3. He nodded.

"Okay," I said to Henry.

We returned to the banquet hall. The Lester Lanin Band was the focus of attention, so our impending departure would hardly be noticed. Napkins crumpled like roses, toppled glasses in formless shapes like figures in a chemistry book, plates with puddles of ice cream, and the omission of servers signaled that the party approached its end.

The ladies—rosy complexions muted, their lipstick a few wipes lost from their original application—had successfully persuaded their liquored spouses to join them on the dance floor. The songs and bodies mellowed to a romantic swing tune. A mismatched couple remained at a vacant table, stragglers like items lost beneath seats from being spilled by impractical cocktail bags. I never became saddened by a party's end, always satisfied by the time I had and ready for the next thing.

We gave selected good-byes, farewells I chose carefully for those whom I noticed giving tips to the hired help even though The Club frowned upon this. These were the people who would send sizable checks rather than those small registry items given by acquaintances who would be unable to make the wedding.

We were tracked down by my mother. Perched in her palm, she had a gingham paper plate with a red plastic fork pierced into a wedge of uneaten ice cream cake rising from its melted pool. She was always about the effect.

"And where are we off to?" she snapped, apparently not having taken her medication yet. I felt as if we were sneaking out of our Christmas kiss given to scary Great Auntie Peg's fuzzy cheek.

"We already kissed Auntie Peg," I said, my tone regressing to the Scary Emily Years.

"Oh, icky."

Icky?

"I won't even do that," she said with a laugh. "Who knows what kind of hormones you could catch?"

Henry looked at us strangely, probably annoyed by witnessing our shared belief in aging skin and diseases that overuse curse words as being contagious.

"And I see you have two escorts—how deb ball of you."

Henry and J3 looked at each other, wondering if the other had insight into what had been said.

"Also, please don't tell your father; Aunt Peg invited us to Palm Beach over Memorial Day. I want to go, but you know your father and Palm Beach."

I didn't know about my father and Palm Beach.

"And was that Sadie Becker I saw you speaking with earlier?" she then said in a disapproving tone masked as approving. "What did you two discuss?"

Only the sexual favors I promised based on my gaffe.

"You know," she continued in her "You Know" kind of way, "I find Mao to be a bit deviant, lustful really."

That must have been difficult for her to share. I don't believe I had ever heard my mother use "deviant" and "lustful" in the same sentence.

"I did have my doubts about his being raised by a gay couple. So I'm thinking of returning him."

"Mom! I told you he's not an espresso maker; you can't return him just because he's a bit of an addict of the sexual sort. Just enroll him in yuppy puppy training or wherever they discipline such things. It will be a gift from me, for Dad's birthday," I said, as a hurried excuse so she'd end this embarrassing topic.

"And the next birthday we'll be celebrating will be yours, Miss Emily Briggs—soon to be Mrs. Henry Philips."

I'm sure she'd been reciting my future title to her lunching friends with the pill-inducing repetition of a spinning instructor barking out orders, "Mrs. Henry Philips" having more speaking play than "None for me, thank you, I'm quite full."

"November twenty-fifth," said Mom.

"The twenty-fifth? Mom, my birthday is the twenty-sixth."

"No, it's not darling. You were born on the twenty-fifth, but that would have meant that your first birthday would have fallen on Thanksgiving. It was quite inconvenient of you, you know, to have your first birthday fall on a national holiday."

"Sorry, I have a thing for turkey."

"So we decided to just shift the day so as not to leverage two parties, which would have made us look rather chintzy. You can't very well serve leftover pie at a birthday party."

Dad then flitted by us, shoveling a mound of ice cream cake into his mouth.

"Catherine, this is delicious. And we can even freeze the leftovers and have it for the Fourth!"

She kept looking above my head as if I wore a flowery Queen Mother hat.

"What's wrong?"

"Your father has been acting strangely, excessively happy in a social environment."

"So when's my birthday?" I said, magnetically redirecting her gaze. Feeling annoyed, I folded my hands into a frustrated rapper stance.

"Your birthday, love," she said with an unprecedented kiss to my cheek, "is whenever you want it to be."

"For God's sake, Mom, I'm not two! I won't throw a fit if I don't get the Malibu Barbie Dream House for my birthday—whenever that may be—because I know I can always ask Santa for it." (True story.)

"Actually, Mrs. Briggs," interrupted Henry.

Oh, for the love of God, here I had been acting with the manners of someone being born after 1984, totally forgetting that J3 and Henry had front-row viewing privileges for Dysfunction Junction. And, judging from their comatose-still looks, they seemed to be enjoying the show.

Mother made her affected declaration that they should call her Catherine, steering away from the "mother" label for Henry, which would be a contractual entitlement.

I felt my bra strap slipping from beneath my jacket. Momentarily suspending myself from my surroundings, I picked at it through the clenched wool in an attempt to shimmy the strap back into place. My boobs must have become smaller, something else that probably annoyed Henry about me, so I stuck my finger under the side of my collar to better fidget with the strap.

"Emily!" shrieked my mother, as if I just said a stream of curse words Mrs. Hallingby-style.

"What are you doing in the wide open?"

I imagined her reaction if I had a child that needed to be breast-fed in public.

She then said through the clench of Chanel plum lips, "Though I was happy to see that you got that smart little suit."

"When did you see my new suit?" I asked incredulously.

"From that girl who must have borrowed it from you—the one trailing us at Vera Wang. Some blond common type who is trying to make the most of herself by stealing your sense of style."

"You saw her? I didn't remember her inside Vera Wang."

"Saw her? She practically took measurements of your figure in the dressing room. It was all quite uncomfortable for me, Emily dear. I even thought she had unnatural designs on you. That she was a"—there was a hushed pause—"lesbian!"

"So, Catherine," said Henry rather authoritatively. I loved when he softly bullied my mother, quite sexy actually. "If we could return to that correct birthday of Emily's, which may become rather useful come the time when we get our marriage license, legal requirements and all."

"Silly red tape is what it is. Just the other day I received a notice for jury duty. Jury duty? Me? Perhaps I can just send some donation and be rid of it."

"It doesn't work that way, Mom," I said dryly.

"But isn't jury duty where you have to sit in some courtroom located in an inconvenient part of the city, listening to stories of women being slapped around by boyfriends? Not even husbands! And there are all of these illegitimate children in the mix."

"Okay, time to go!"

"But your birth certificate," moaned Henry.

"So? Are we having a party for you this year?" she shouted, her voice thankfully drowned in background chatter.

As we moved toward the exit, my father grabbed my shoulder, so I became missing from our crime-trailing Scooby pact. We were in the alcove of a gardening shed with a shuttered door and wheelbarrow filled with torn-up weeds.

"Emily. Hi," he said uncomfortably. "Your Aunt Peg has invited your mother and me to Palm Beach for Labor Day. You know how your mother is about Palm Beach."

No, I didn't know how my mother was about Palm Beach.

"Well don't mention anything to her, because I already agreed that we'd go."

This worried me on many levels.

"Dad. I'd rather remain out of this."

He pulled a face, surprised from my insubordination.

"Happy birthday," I said, tiptoeing so I could reach his cheek and give him a peck. "I have a feeling you'll be getting what you want. Just talk to Mom."

For a world controlled by communications, we were terrible communicators. My spirits lifted when I spotted Henry and J3. They moved up the drive toward the valet, chatting about something not centered on my parents. When I jogged to catch up to them, they didn't seem to notice I had been missing. I then circled my forehead in hypnotic migraine rhythms while I used my other hand to wave the valet out of his napping position. I turned to Henry and J3.

"I am so, so sorry you both had to witness that malnourished android in there."

"You mean your mother?" asserted Henry.

"And what other malnourished android could I be referring to?"

"Actually," said J3 for a change, "there were quite a few in there. Did you see the picked-through platter of asparagus wrapped in bacon? One little dog is going to be, literally, in hog heaven tonight."

"And that would hopefully be Mao, Mom's pug, if she doesn't get rid of him."

"Well, Mao should really pace himself," said J3. "I've seen what can happen to little dogs after an overdose of bacon. Not a pretty sight. At all."

I envisioned a little Mao stiff with rigor mortis, turned over like a toppled milk stool.

"And don't worry about your family members," said Henry. "All quite amusing. Explains a lot."

This was exactly what I didn't want to hear.

"Henry, you could be a bit more gentle to someone who's missed their birthday for the past thirty some years. Hey!"

"Oh, no," said Henry as a warning to J3. "The leverage."

"Well, why shouldn't they pony up for all of my missed real birthdays? Pony! I want a pony!"

Why did little girls always want a pony when pretty outfits picked from spreads in *W* were surely more practical?

"You're not six, Emily."

"I can be whatever age I want to be. Just ask my mom."

"Right, the woman has a real grasp on reality and aging—her two strongest suits."

Henry reached into his coat pocket for his container of Tic Tacs, wiggling the container onto his palm till four candies came out.

"Here, take these," he said, cupping half onto my palm.

"So now you're trying to shut me up with pills."

"These are Tic Tacs, Emily. Not Xanax. Which may not be a bad idea."

"Sure, you start me on Tic Tacs till my dosages become progressively stronger."

"Right, I can see the headline—'Husband leads his wife to overdose on spearmint Life Savers.'"

"Well, Dr. Perricone said that Life Savers are high in glycemic sugars."

"Who's Dr. Perrricone? What doctors have you been seeing?" Henry asked, somewhat frantic.

I became annoyed. Henry still hadn't a clue on my devotion to Dr. Perricone, despite our medicine cabinet basically being an advert for his products.

I then gave a different stoner from the earlier valet the ticket for my keys. He kept opening and closing his mouth as if testing its capabilities. Eventually realizing that my giving him the stub had something to do with his job responsibilities, he pulled my keys from a pegboard and set about the task of retrieving my car. I began to worry that the other valet had abandoned his duties because he had totaled my Mustang and gone on the lam.

We waited in silence, my arms crossed, Henry's hands in his pockets, while J3 took in the surroundings, until the Mustang pulled up to our attention. I didn't like how it looked when driven by a valet.

"Are you okay to drive?" asked Henry.

Though I had only a few sips of my Bloody Mary, I decided to toss Henry my keys, finding the idea of napping appealing. We all entered the car methodically.

After riding in silence through another commuter town just twenty minutes from the city, I rolled down my window to fully take in suburbia. Just another identical stop on the Metro-North that catered to working couples who wanted that illustrious patch of backyard. I thought of a repeat performance of an existence I once had, the new players just driving in different cars. There were many SUVs and Coopers, as opposed to the mix of wood-paneled station wagons and Crayola-colored Rabbits—the automotive fashions from my mom and dad's driving days.

The Cooper Mini middle-fingered the SUV as an environmental

hazard, while the SUV could steamroll the just-a-step-up-from-a-Coke-can with its touted safety standards. And then there were the SUVs that distinguished themselves from the other SUVs by having The Club membership sticker proudly mounted above the inspection ticket. Some fanatic members even had a stream of stickers from past seasons on the family car to show their years as dues-paying honorees. The difference between an SUV with a sticker and one without could be compared to the 10021 resident with a daughter wearing a Chapin sweatshirt to the daughter with sweats advertising Nightingale. Those nuances determine who effectively plays to the social emblems imposed by their primary residences.

"Your mother is quite a woman." J3's voice broke the quiet driving hum from the backseat.

Was he trying to make some kind of humorless joke?

"She's a character," I blithely stated.

"I had great fun spending time with them. Your whole family is very interesting. Colorful."

I didn't know if J3 was comparing my family to a remote, third-world village—a fun place to visit, but you'd never want to stay.

He then muttered something about my mother. Apparently she told him stories about me as a youngster. Youngster? The idea of her telling stories about me from my days as a youngster without my censoring caused a rush of insecurity to shoot through me.

"The one perk is that I never have to entertain that 'What If' scenario. You know, how to rub her out by hiring some hit man. Just by saying 'Mom, I'm moving to Tulsa with my lesbian girlfriend to raise hogs,' she'd have instant heart failure. No trail of evidence, no interaction with thugs that drink Courvoisier with P. Diddy. And the amount I'd save from not having to pay anyone!"

I intentionally avoided looking into the side mirror so as not to gauge J3's reaction.

Momentary silence. Henry broke the silence.

"But your father," he said, as if making a pivotal point on a courtroom floor. "I really gained insight into his character today."

Insight? My father? Henry now had more insight into my father than I did.

"I was speaking with him and your Uncle Ted."

Uncle Ted wasn't really an uncle, just a close family friend and client of my father's. The client association entitled him to uncle status.

"So here I am speaking with Ted. And Jed. Ted and Jed."

Right. Got it. Rhyming names, how irreverent.

"And they start pinning me on the subject of infidelity. It was a kind of hazing-slash-will-I-treat-their-Emily-respectfully kind of initiation. So Ted asks Jed if he's ever cheated on his wife."

"You mean my mother," I barked.

"I believe that's correct, Emily. So Jed tells Ted that Catherine can tell if he comes home having three martinis over the allowed two, having an affair would never pass the detector of your mother."

I returned to making hypnotic migraine rhythms to my temples, singing "tra la la la, tra la la la."

"Okay, things I didn't need to know about my parents. No, thank you for sharing this with me."

"But don't you think that's admirable?"

War heroes are admirable. Law enforcement officers that don't dawdle but spend their time capturing drug dealers are admirable. Taking a single carry-on for a flight to Paris is admirable. My father honoring his vows to my mother?

I twisted my head to the backseat. J3 looked as perplexed as me.

"Do you have any idea what marriage is? Not just gold bands and checking different boxes on your tax forms."

"I think you're missing my point."

Okay? Point? Henry didn't return my I'm-waiting-for-you-to-make-your-point look.

"And. Really. About that mother of yours—" he said, slowing down at a yellow traffic light though he typically ran those.

"I've known my mother for a very long time. She has her good moments."

Henry's eyes shimmered with suspicion, the traffic light reflected in his eyes. We all seemed to be absorbed by the red light before it went down to green, each of us caught in our own thoughts. I focused on my mother in various outfits and scenarios, like Oprah on the cover of her magazine—Mother cutting her image into the flesh of pumpkin, miniature mother cocktail stirrers shooting from drinks at her poolside party, trimming a tree with mother Christmas tree ornaments—all "Mother" products can be purchased from her catalogue or by logging onto her Web site.

J3 made a slight sound, about to enter the conversation, but Henry whisked in.

"You really do take after her," said Henry, shifting the car into a higher gear.

"Take after who?" I asked.

"Your mother," he said, as if it were obvious.

I stared out the window. Henry knew that comparing me to my mother was the worst insult.

22

I awoke with the memory of Mom and me making cupcakes to take to Mrs. Hirsh's class for my eighth birthday. After I ate most of the batter with a wooden mixing spoon, because that seemed the better option than licking a few strips that clung to the bowl, she didn't feel the need to lecture me on my irresponsibility and gluttonous behavior, which I anticipated, considering this had been a premeditated act.

Drumming aloud a few scenarios to resolve the problem, the idea of baking never appealed to Mom. She resolved the incident by making a trip to Terranova's Bakery on Arthur Avenue, an outing typically reserved for buying pies, cheesecakes, and other desserts for the holidays. (But, since my mystery birth date did fall near Thanksgiving, Mother placed an order for two apples, a mince, and a pumpkin pie.)

She showed a trace of distress in not being able to deal with Mr. Terranova directly, the baker she normally worked with who had gone on a hunting trip that particular Sunday. In the care of the baker's wife, she explained the eaten batter incident, the challenge of time, and how the cupcakes had to be unforgettable because Howard Nelson also had a birthday that same week and mine must outdo his.

With the back of her Popeye arm, the baker's wife swiped the beaded sweat from her brow and then blinked cautiously through thick eyeglasses. She instructed us to return in four hours, saying that she'd see what she could do under such short notice.

We then embarked on another adventure—the Met to see the Sargents—and afterward Mother bought me a Doris Kindersley sailor dress that appeared copied from the portrait of the Sitwell children at a nearby Madison boutique.

Returning to Terranova's, the baker's wife smiled at the sight of us, which I took as a good sign. Pulling the candy-cane-striped string from one of three stacked boxes, she tilted it for better viewing. There were half a dozen cupcakes in dark chocolate, vanilla, strawberry, and marbled swirl, all sprinkled with pastel confetti sugar in the shapes of hearts and stars. The Keebler elves had nothing next to these creations that were spun from fairy sugar and magical hands.

I reached for one of the cupcakes, a dark chocolate one, and Mother gave my wrist a wispy swat, explaining that there were nineteen kids in the class along with Mrs. Hirsh. I started to catalogue the members of my class and rationalized that Leah Hargrave didn't need one because she kicked me in gym class. Mother became distressed that Leah Hargrave kicked me in gym class, making empty threats in the sugar scented air, but said that was no reason to deprive her of a cupcake, and I was acting uncharitable.

The baker's wife waved for our attention, saying she had just the solution, and reached for two cupcakes that slid from a metal sheet stacked in an industrial rack that reminded me of the dentist's table that stored his more frightening instruments. She presented us with two chocolate cupcakes with a coating of crumbled Oreo cookies and drizzled with caramel. I practically dove over the counter and tumbled onto the pastry.

Mother paid the baker's wife, said she would save her cupcake for later, while mine was smeared all over my face. Those cupcakes were the talk of Mrs. Hirsh's class till Christmas break.

I called my mother to share the memory, and she said she didn't recall. Deciding I wanted a cupcake, I wondered if Magnolia delivered and had to get her off the line. Once I hung up the cordless, as it was still wobbling in its headrest, the phone screamed its startling signal.

"Who was that boy again? The one you and Henry are living with from the party? What's his name—C3PO?"

It was Mother.

"J3," I said exhaustedly. "And you've been introduced."

"Right. OB. And what kind of name is that? Well, your father was quite taken with him. They spoke about something with sound waves and the environment—one of those tiring discussions men have if they had time to fit in the Science *Times* that week. Anyway, it was all rather distracting, this R2 person. Many of our friends commented on how they thought he was the one you are engaged to. I did like him. And it doesn't appear as if he will lose his hair the way Henry will."

"Mother. Henry and I are engaged."

"Well, then let me see the ring. Oh, right, it's hidden underneath all that duct tape. And then there is the matter of not even having a wedding scheduled yet. So?" she said wickedly. "Do you like J2?"

Was this an attempt to match me with another boy?

"J3!" I snapped.

"So you do like him!"

"His name is J3, and I am engaged to Henry. Henry loves me!"

I took a gulp from my water bottle. Mother was frantic from all of the silence.

"Sorry. Just getting in my eight glasses."

"Glasses, right, something needed if you want to see that ring of yours."

I pressed the Play Message button on the answering machine to activate Henry's voice, the live one being of no use, considering he remained asleep in bed.

"Mom, it's Henry. Got to go."

Click.

I went into the kitchen. With no cupcakes, I resorted to having a kid-cereal breakfast. Pouring two bowls of Frosted Flakes, my plastic racecar prize did not come out, which struck me as odd considering it typically took two bowls before it appeared and I had more than half that amount yesterday. I dug my fingers along the sides of the box, the flakes feeling like sandy pebbles. Swishing my hand to all four sides, I then redirected my way through the middle and poked the bottom, further crunching the flakes in the process.

"What are you doing?" asked Henry, rubbing his eyes from sleep.

"Can't find the damn prize. Can't I contact the Better Business Bureau about that or something?"

Henry poured some milk into one of the two bowls, which I guessed was okay even though I had intended to eat both, rationalizing that I really didn't have an appetite as the cereal had been more about finding the prize.

Looking into the opening of the carton with one eye shut, I shook the box in a final attempt for the prize to reveal itself before I'd have to write Kellogg's a letter requesting a year's supply of free Frosted Flakes rather than sue for damages based on my mental distress.

"Give it up, Emily," Henry said in between spoonfuls of soggy flakes.

"But I was so looking forward to the toy racecar—the whole reason I bought the cereal! I feel so sad and let down. I'm going back to Cinnamon Life," I said, tossing the carton into the garbage. "Could you imagine if I was a six-year-old and the kind of tantrum this would have caused!"

"Right. As opposed to the one you're having now?"

I gave this some thought.

"So was that your mother I heard you weaseling your way out of another wedding planning conversation with?" he then asked.

"Yes and no."

Henry gave me his "I'm perplexed" look.

"It was my mother. I was weaseling out of a conversation with her, but not about the wedding. Not everything has to be about this wedding, you know."

Henry dumped the rest of his cereal down the disposal and left it in the sink, where it would mysteriously find its way onto a rack in the dishwasher. He looked concerned, and I couldn't figure if it had been because of me, or my inefficiency in organizing this wedding.

"Emily, you can't avoid this wedding issue."

My brain started to go fuzzy like the UF channel.

"Do you need to get your green card or something? I mean, you seem to be in a complete rush about this. I need to prioritize," I said, organizing my bag to begin my day. "Putting together a series of paintings for perhaps my first and only show is where my attention needs to be focused."

He seemed to be in shock. In fact, my defensiveness startled even me. This was the first time I'd spoken about the wedding planning, or really the lack thereof, and surprisingly it felt good. I had not shown any symptoms of being a Bridezilla. In fact, I may have shaken it like a cold in flu season because of some homeopathic foresight.

"If you can please be understanding, I am entering a creative streak and don't want to waste it on ideas for cake fillings and sugar flowers that no one ever eats anyway."

Silence.

I continued, "Well, the frosting is important. Have you ever seen a wedding cake with chocolate frosting?"

Henry didn't look pleased, and I had an uncontrollable frosting craving. I left him so I could attend to the finished work of little Emily and Henry, their shiny marsupial eyes staring at me. I added a stroke of French blue to Emily's dress, rubbed it in with my index finger, and smeared the paint against my chef's coat that I bought in a cookery shop in Paris. I then made the call to Daphne.

"Coming over," I announced. "Will you be ready for me in about thirty? And do you have cupcakes or should I make a stop en route?"

"Yes, come over," Daphne replied weakly. "I actually have some news to share."

She sounded upset. Williams-Sonoma probably stopped carrying the pastel Warings she had been deliberating about and now she had lost her chance for a citron-colored mixer.

Dressed in my floral printed skirt and a tight bateau sweater, I had foregone a bra when I changed this morning, as going braless felt so liberating and sexy. I then thought about the future of my boobs, wilting like three-day-old grapes. I would berate myself later in life for not wearing a bra in that early 2000 period, the way I do now about slathering my face with Bain de Soleil tanning oil back in the late '80s.

I changed into a bra. My boobs shifted in salute and faced the sun like poppies. I wondered why feminists made such a fuss about burning their bras when really they were worn in the best interest for your breasts. If those feminists only knew that society would become a place where women would have unnecessary surgery just to augment these peculiar symbols of womanhood.

What was my obsession with boobs lately? I made a mental note to self-treat my breast fixation by doing a Google.

Returning to the canvas of Emily and Henry, I covered it with a scrap of canvas and hung up my chef/painter's coat, which had fallen from being draped over the easel. Lifting the painting, I wobbled out of the room, tripping a few times, and kicked off my stilettos for a pair of ballet flats at the doorway, Mr. Rogers-slipping-into-his-tennis-sneakers style.

The elevator then made the dreaded stop at Floor 6. Please, please, please—I mentally summoned every courtesy to a holier being, only to be delivered with a Pucci-printed Mrs. Hallingby holding a straw bag with Christmas green streamers that filled in the palms of a tree painted in brown. I knew that there were only a handful of seconds before the ride would end, but time would stretch out like a hostess saying you'll be seated in minutes and you were absolutely starving.

Mrs. Hallingby greeted me in her customary fashion.

"Fuck. Fuck. Fuck! No fucking room. Think you own the fucking elevator! Can't fucking move with your fucking billboard."

"Good morning, Mrs. Hallingby," I peeped.

"And did God give you a good fuck today?"

Now she was being blasphemous.

23

At the next elevator door to open, I was greeted by another disturbed woman, though somewhat different in her degree of disturbance than Mrs. Hallingby.

"I'm pregnant."

Daphne was not at all happy.

"You're always pregnant."

"That's not funny."

"Okay." I paused for a moment. "You're always pregnant and remodeling your kitchen."

"Come on, Emily. Be serious!"

"At least you can have kids," I said, leaning the draped canvas against her Tiffany-blue wall, the ornate white wainscoting reminding me of a piece of Wedgwood.

"Oh, my God. Emily, is there something wrong?"

"No, no. It's not what you think. Well, not quite. I'm healthy, but I can't have kids."

Daphne looked to me, confused.

"Henry doesn't want to have kids. The man who loves me, the man I will marry, does not want to bear children with his wife. Wasn't that the whole point of having a marriage? To have a legitimate child? No more of those baby scares that cost me a limited edition croc Birkin by now from buying all of those pregnancy tests? Anyway. Enough about me—you're pregnant. This is great!"

"Great. I'm like Ethel Kennedy over here."

"You are so not Ethel Kennedy. Didn't she have about a dozen children? She was a goddamn Labrador retriever."

"Exactly. Three is on par to a dozen in twenty-first century standards. But you're right, I need to put things in perspective. The fact that Henry doesn't want kids is an outrage. Almost subhuman. Being against procreation is a bit selfish. But don't worry about the baby thing."

"And what if Henry and I don't make it? I will never be able to have kids on my own because my eggs will dry up or something."

She arranged her face into an expression that said she didn't buy it.

"Right. There are always kids in China."

"Stop it, Emily. You'll have children. The wide-eyed kind."

"And I really don't feel that I've pressured Henry into the entire family-package life. I have no interest in this *'middle-class bourgeois'* he so fears. And it's not as if I want to be that type of couple with an answering machine recording with our child's gurgling sounds."

Daphne walked over to the answering machine and pressed delete.

"Stop apologizing," she murmured, more as an aside as she discovered a loose thread on the cuff of her shirt.

I became tranquilized by the crafty maneuvering of her fingers while she secured the runaway thread by looping it into a knot with two clamped fingers, a skill I gathered one learns, like knowing how to use those different diaper creams that appeared to have a compensatory bonus of keeping Daphne's hands youthful. Noticing my absorbed study of her fingers, she gave me a hug, and I took in a suffocating whiff of Creed. In our embrace, she whispered in my ear, "Just trick him."

I pulled from her embrace to stare into her eyes.

"What the hell are you talking about?"

"Try for a kid without him. He doesn't have to know until you're pregnant. It's done all the time."

"That's horrible. Completely deceitful. I am not one of those types."

Could it work?

"Yeah," Daphne huffed. "I know—part of the reason you're the last of our group to get married. You can't be so by-the-book all the time, Em."

I didn't want to go there.

"Do you think of yourself as a feminist?" she asked.

God, no. Those women wanted their hair to turn gray.

"Isn't that term a bit dated? What do I have to be all feminist about? Voting? I only vote absentee, as if I had the time to wait on line in the rec room of a Jewish Center. Career? And what's so bad about having a joint checking account? Then again, I do like my freedom. The independence I have from being single."

"You see, I think you are a sort of feminist. Perhaps it's you who doesn't want to commit."

"Or maybe I just pick the wrong type."

"I've been telling you that all the time."

"Daphne! You're not supposed to agree with me."

We were having another one of our moments that illuminate our differences in approach. The trouble with having a best friend from your childhood that had opposing life perspectives was that you couldn't take stock in their analyses. How you shared a history of learning how to give a blow job on the neck of a Moosehead could stretch your bond only so far.

Daphne chose a husband for professional reasons, like my cousin Anne but without the need to select a song from a band list before their wedding dance. Daphne and Andy had a life. He was good to her and pleasant enough to me, so I never had to vent my dislikes by drawing icons of his face and making x's over them, not that I did this often. Though I did find his recent habit of quoting British poets pretentious.

"Don't listen to me, anyway," she said, the glimmer from her jeweled fingers catching the afternoon light. "I'm hormonal."

Her face crumpled like an ashen vase.

"Hormonal? The craving cupcakes kind of hormonal?"

"Oh, sorry. I didn't know you were serious about that."

"I wasn't."

I was.

"I'm hormonal and an ineffective host. Can this be any worse?

But I really have to be more optimistic. I mean, we do have good lives. Right? We should appreciate what we have. Be thankful."

Yeah. Whatever.

"Well, I have just the thing to cheer you up," I said, removing the sheet from the canvas. We both turned our focus to the portrait. Emily looked like she's asking Santa why he's ramming the Christmas tree up the chimney. Her eyes wide, glorious, and filled with bewilderment. I styled her in a linen sailor dress, the tie edged in heavy navy stitching, which had been my favorite dress as a little girl and was passed down to her. I deliberately styled Henry in a jewel-toned shirt and navy blazer for the composition; the clothes painted magnificently.

Daphne's eyelids evaporated, sliding into wide-open position.

"I'm overcome. They are the most beautiful, extraordinary children. And they're mine! Oh, sorry," she muttered.

I nodded with a smile.

Daphne sucked in her lips till they were lost from her face, her eyes becoming the dominating feature, so she had a brief moment of looking like a space alien or having had too many face-lifts.

"You know," she then cheered, "you've captured more than their appearances, Emily." Her eyes began to swell.

"Don't cry!"

I laughed as Daphne controlled her tears by swiping her forefinger against her bottom lid.

"Goddamn hormones. It's uncanny," she said with a sniffle. "Little Henry actually reminds me of a young Tobey Maguire."

I've thought the same thing.

"Exactly. Love him. Every time I squash a spider, I think I'm harming one of his people."

"You have spiders?" She sounded appalled.

"Er, no! Well, sometimes in the back corner of the hall closet."

Daphne looked concerned until the picture regained our attention. We focused on the image for the same amount of time it took to watch the *Lord of the Rings* trilogy. For fear of a toe-stomping breakdown, I left the painting in her care since she promised to have it delivered to the Daniel West Gallery by tomorrow as he'd be arriving from Paris by the end of the week. She wrote the names and contacts of other acquaintances who were interested in having their portraits done on a page of Hello Kitty notepaper. I stared at the pad in awe. She gave me the pad. Waving off my protests, Daphne said Emily was over Hello Kitty and going through a Dora phase.

"How could anyone be over Hello Kitty? This is a sorry state of today's youth."

"I know. I'll never understand this generation."

"Thanks to you and Emily for the pad. I'll be extra generous come Emily's birthday."

I stopped to think for a moment. Emily's birthday was soon.

"Hey. Isn't Emily due for a birthday? Where's my invite?"

"Yes. Well."

"What is it?"

"Well, last year you licked the frosting off most of the cupcakes."

24

Needing more time than allotted, I suddenly found myself caught in the panicked swell of lateness. Dialing Daphne's friend—there really is a woman named Mopsy Mullen—I apologized for my impending tardiness. Mopsy put me at ease, saying she could easily shift her Reiki instruction to later and could use the extra hour, as she would prefer to have her nails done in a more neutral color for her portrait, grateful for having the time to get a manicure. I mentioned that nails did not have to be painted "literally as is" like a photograph, the magic of art being that you always had a thin day and could even add a few inches after a disastrous haircut.

The silence from the line became so hushed I thought my phone had a zoning moment, until she insisted that she needed to look as close to perfection as possible; otherwise her weekend at Doral was a complete waste. She quickly added she would supply photos from her more accommodating years as reference. Mopsy also prepared me for the presence of her makeup and styling people, how they'd be on hand while I painted her as if this were some Annie Leibovitz cover shoot. I wondered about these women, planning their days with appointments made with specialists you found in the pages of *Allure*.

With the padding of extra time, I detoured my route toward Jumpin' Joe before heading uptown. Two boys with complexions that could benefit from Dr. Perricone's twenty-eight day program, wearing the oversized jeans look and jackets made out of a parachute, stopped their chattering on sight of me.

The too-big-jeans boys seemed to be approaching me, and I didn't think they wanted directions. The taller one slipped his elbow through mine, shifting my direction, while his friend lifted his American flag poly-cotton bandana up over his mouth and then linked his arm into mine. Our locking of arms had the appearance of bygone staging, where we'd sing our dialogue as the streets flooded like water chutes.

Maneuvering me into the nook of an alley, the smaller of the two spoke.

"Give me your wallet!"

Oh, for God's sake.

"Are you holding me up?" I said blithely. There was no time for this. "This is so the Dinkins years."

"Dude," said the taller one into the vigilant one's ear. "Let's just blow out."

I interpreted this as a fortunate turn of events. (I once watched an episode of *Law & Order* where a self-defense expert instructed the show's victim to make personal contact with her assailant.) The doubtful one seemed as nervous as I, noted by the nervous tap of his hand to the side of his knee, which reassured me that this would be one of those moments you shared over dinner party conversation where the discussion revolved around dodgy city scenarios.

"If I were you," I said confidently, trying to fully take in their faces, "I'd reconsider this whole thing—the blemish you will have on your permanent record. You'll never be able to run for office. And, if you're anything like me, I get upset when I discover that I have points on my license just from running a stop sign. Not that I've ever deliberately run a stop sign."

"Lady, don't make me use this."

The shorter of the two attackers reached into his back pocket for a switchblade knife. I lost my ability to laugh, a trait of mine that eased stressful situations but would be completely inappropriate in the current circumstance.

"Fine," I said hastily, reaching into my bag and refraining from acting like a girl with professional headshots.

Standard being-robbed procedure had become an ATM transaction to me, as I've been assaulted in the past. The worst experience was when I had the misfortune of riding on a crowded subway with a man who thrust up against me, finding some obscene thrill in the offence of public masturbation. I truly became an animal preyed upon in the wilds of the city's underbelly. But the most violating consequence was that he ruined my Polesi sable, which I really had no right to wear on the downtown number 6 train. Once he finished doing his thing on my coat, it looked like the pelt of a feverish animal. That was when I made my vow never to take New York City public transportation again.

"Hurry it up, bitch!" the short alpha attacker said.

I wondered why he didn't just nab my entire bag, entirely happy about that considering I had less than fifty dollars and my Louis Vuitton was worth more than $500.

"But may I please keep my driver's license?" I asked politely. "I just recently got it renewed. And seeing that you both don't appear to be old enough to drive, you wouldn't understand the process, the hassle it is to go to the DMV, deal with DMV people."

The taller one said, "Lady, are you kidding me? This is not negotiable." He pointed the knife to his crime associate. "Now give Bruce your wallet."

"Bruce?"

Then I see Bruce's head getting slammed by a Burberry umbrella wielded by my caped crusader in the form of Coffeehouse Pete without the cape. Dropping the umbrella, he did a few moves that went perfectly with Japanese accented *hi-yas* and squeezed Bruce's wrist so hard his vein-bulging fingers slowly opened till the knife fell to the ground.

I hurried over to grab it, because I had always been more of the Princess Leah type rather than the ineffectual squealy blonde. Bruce escaped while his stupid sidekick jolted toward the knife, just beating me, but then stumbled to the pavement because Pete gave him a kick in his ribs that came with hi-def audio. He managed to reach for the knife and then sprinted out of sight. Pete stood and watched him escape, as his chest pumped from exerted breathing. He looked me over with mothering eyes and approached my side.

"The police are on their way," he said in Batman delivery (as played by George Clooney). "Are you okay?"

"Yes and wow! Thanks for saving me. So superhero of you."

Pete blushed.

"I went to school in the South. Had to do something productive with those winters away from mountain activity, so I became a black belt in karate."

He put his hands on my shoulders, looking into my eyes like an ophthalmologist.

"Are the police really on their way?" I asked, fidgeting with my wallet.

"Ah. No. But we should really call them. Let's go back to the shop. Right now Heroine is holding the fort, and with two degenerate hoodlums on the loose, I don't think a three-legged cat would be much good defending the place."

We walked back to Jumpin' Joe, and I took out my phone to call 911. I had never called 911 before and always thought how suspect it was that it had the same numbers as 9/11. I wondered if that had something to do with the terrorists' deliberate use of fear in choosing that date to undermine the safety symbolized in 911.

Speaking with a well-mannered lady whom I pictured with the short coarse hair of a broom and harlequin glasses, I asked Pete the exact address of Jumpin' Joe. Edith, my 911 dispatcher, said she knew of it. I told Pete how popular his place was, attracting the right kind of consumer. He smiled and it made me feel safe.

I tried to give Pete the cash in my wallet—what you did when someone returned your missing wallet (and I've only lost my wallet a few times). He refused my gesture. I began to think of ways of how I could repay him.

"Pete, how did you know I was being mugged?"

He unlocked the door and turned over the sign so it read "Open." Heroine waddled over to greet us; her playful look pulled me from my self-absorption.

"You may not like what I am about to say," he said, tapping his head to settle an uncharacteristic trace of outrage. "Your assailants were outside the shop earlier, as well as that blonde, the one who spilled coffee on you a few weeks ago. I don't know if you've even noticed, but she's around here a lot, usually around the time you come by, and she's struck me as being sort of off. Then she started asking a few questions about you."

"Really!" I sounded like I just found out that a boy I had a crush on really liked me.

Pete looked at me suspiciously.

"I mean, how peculiar," I said, in my serious Emily voice.

Heroine nudged my knee and I scratched her head, turning on her surround-sound purring. It made me happy to know how easily comforted this handicapped creature was.

He continued, "Anyway, she looked a bit addled earlier. Then when she saw those two boys, she flew out of here. I watched her talking to them outside. She seemed quite demanding, raised her voice a lot, and then handed them a big wad of cash. Right in front of my place of employment."

He did appear to be the dedicated employee type.

"I thought it may have been a drug deal or something, until I heard her say, 'Nick her face.' "

I didn't have to let it be known that I had tried not to give up my license.

"So when she took off in the opposite direction of those two boys, I asked the lounging customers if they could take their coffee to go, gave them a few muffins on the house—"

"That was very considerate of you," I made a point to say.

"No problem. And then I went searching for them and, well, you know the rest."

I sat down at a table. Pete took the seat across from me. My heart raced and my knees kept clanking into one another. I lost all control of my nervous system. He then got up from his chair and squeezed my shoulder.

"Let me get you some tea," he said, as if this was a goddamn British novel and everything was resolved with a cup of tea.

"Emily, you really need to be calm, think straight while this is clear," he said from behind the counter, a slab of Lucite that showcased a map covered with pins in pastel colored balls like the tablets in a Tylenol capsule, stuck in places I presumed someone had traveled to. As he poured hot water over a teabag, I missed my chance to ask for a decaf hazelnut.

My phone then made its startling electronic jingle. I had forgot-

ten to turn it off when I called 911. Leaving my cell phone on
showed that I was not in my normal frame of mind.

"Emily, are you okay?"

It was J3.

"Yes, yes. I'm all right. Pete was amazing. But how do you know
what happened?"

"I don't really know. The police called to verify where you are.
Where are you? Jumpin' Joe?"

"Yes. I'm here right now. Are they on their way?"

"They said they were, after reading the wrong address. What happened?"

"Two kids tried to mug me. Apparently they had more serious intentions, who's to know, but, again, Pete saved the day."

Then two officers walked in, and I had the suspicion they were
here for me. I've always been savvy that way. One had a medium
build, chestnut hair, and a bloated face. The other also had brown
hair, but his features were prominent and his blue eyes were in dramatic contrast to his olive skin. He was handsome, especially in
comparison to his partner. They had contrasting physiques in that
Abbot and Costello/Ernie and Bert way.

I told J3 I had to attend to the police. He offered to be there as
soon as he could, which I dismissed, as I wanted to attend to the
matter swiftly.

Pete then gave me a cup of Darjeeling tea, an odd choice, and I
wondered what health benefits Darjeeling had. He then asked the
officers if they wanted anything. The handsome one asked to try
the special coconut-flavored coffee, and I became envious.

Officers Hamilton and Castiglione, names made clear from the
shrunken desk plates worn below their shiny badges, took the seats
next to mine and looked at me kindly, saying things about how
lucky I was and not to worry. They asked if I had been hurt; perhaps
I needed to be taken to the hospital. Though I felt that little-kid
thrill by the idea of riding in an NYPD squad car, I said I felt fine
and really had to keep to my schedule with an appointment uptown. Being self-employed, I had no time to get mugged. They both
smiled at one another as if I just cracked a joke that wasn't really a
joke, which really wasn't a joke.

I excused myself to call Mopsy, explaining that I had been the victim of a mugging incident and couldn't make it uptown. She suggested quicker routes for me to direct my driver. I told Mopsy how it would be unlikely that I could keep our appointment and I'd fax her the police report. Mopsy told me of her friends, all with Beatrix Potter bunny names, who had been in compromising situations yet still managed to keep their appointments, and said she could not excuse my behavior.

Returning to my seat, I didn't know if my heightened disorientation came from the assault or the fact that a former client found my excuse to have the validity of a missing homework assignment due to a paper-eating canine.

I recapped the crime to the officers as they looked around the coffee shop aimlessly, seeming to search for clues. Or possibly they were bored. I never had been an effective storyteller. They then said they'd take me over to the precinct so I could file a report. I became thrilled at now getting that chance to ride in the squad car.

Officer Hamilton asked why I was in such good spirits, considering the trauma I had just experienced, which I brushed off by saying I had an unhealthy familiarity with the city's dark side. They both grunted their acknowledgments as they tuned out to the traffic.

After spending the entire day in a cinder-block room seated on a metal-legged chair that could not support an overweight criminal, I felt the kind of sadness I had when whispering flatteries into a carriage horse's felted ear before its behind got whipped into order and shuttled unimaginative tourists on the conveyor belt tour of the park's lower loop. I wished I had never been given this depressing image of where New York's finest spent their days that made purgatory, an airport terminal, or chatting with a guest at one of Anne's tiring benefit parties seem exciting by comparison.

They should put up some pictures, or perhaps some bamboo shades over the windows that have never felt a spray of Windex. Even a car garage kept the eyes wandering with shameful glances of Playmate calendars and beer posters of blond twins in shirts cut just below the double D implants.

But the true activity was found in the animation of the people. A man in his fifties who did not fit the criminal composite was being printed for jumping a turnstile. I watched the officer carefully scroll his hands on the scan. It looked fun. I wanted to have my prints taken, a sort of souvenir, and knew Officer Hamilton would oblige my request.

We went over the details of the attack for about the eighteen-thousandth time, and I recapitulated the images of the two boys with an artist's detail. I fingered their coiled steno pad and slim Papermate to draw a few sketches so they had a more effective image to go by. They looked at the drawing with admiring smiles, complimenting me on my skills as an artist. I thwarted the rise of my ego by offering to have them sit for me, the remark prompting a shared, askew glance, as if the other could offer some understanding of what I meant by this.

They took down all of my numbers including birthday, ID codes, and I think I even gave them my mother's maiden name out of habit. They asked me if I had any enemies, who I had been in con-tact with recently, what I had done leading up to the attack. I re-membered what Pete said about the blonde and told the officers to follow this lead, which seemed to excite them, inspiring an inves-tigative element.

Tired from the long hours and feeling the effects of inhaling too much Renuzit, I had the urge to forget the whole episode. I wanted to time-travel back to the comfort of my pink budded Laura Ashley walls.

Officer Hamilton fumbled in his delivery of a paternal kiss, hav-ing to leave since his shift was ending. Officer Castiglione needed to make Xeroxes. I sat. I tried to entertain myself by making sketches of my wedding portrait on the back of a recycling manual and became more interested in watching the fraternization of offi-cers who had no crimes to solve in the presumably most dangerous city in the world. A man—I assumed a detective considering he wasn't in uniform—ate a Power Bar. Another officer peeled a banana. I could not find a box of donuts. No pizza box or bags of chips. In fact, it appeared that the NYPD was quite healthy. With all of their time in the squad car and accessibility to fast-food conveniences, I became impressed by their healthy habits, thinking a magazine should do a "Cities with the Healthiest Police" story and New York would be the surprising number-one rank. The officer with the Power Bar offered me a bite. I shook my head, thanking him, saying that I had already had lunch.

A fly lazily swooped in front of my nose, showing remarkable acceleration each time I raised my hand in an attempt to end his pestering dance. Changing my method by not dropping my hand back on the table, to the complete surprise of the fly and myself, I caught him with the motor skills of a superhero. His hind leg was pinched between my fingers. I looked about the room to see if anyone witnessed this once-in-a-lifetime feat. There was no one in the room. Having not completely killed the fly, I tried to recall whether it was the Hindus or Taoists who believed your treatment to animals corresponded with how you would be treated in the afterlife.

Walking with my captive into the main lobby, I saw Henry speaking with a dispatcher in an effort to locate me. I freed the fly and ran into Henry's arms. His parka smelled of cold—felt synthetic, almost liquid. I felt a tear stream down my face, but had not mentally summoned its release.

Officer Castiglione presented me with papers, pointing to lines I needed to sign, and instructed me to check in with him, tapping a phone number beneath an emblem of a shield. Henry led me out of the station, where I turned one last time before we made our exit, sad that I was never asked to have my prints taken.

25

I ripped a page from my business planner and scribbled a list of things that would make me as healthy as possible and quell the impending shock of tucking my winter flesh into a bikini moment. I would treat Dr. Perricone as more than bedside reading and actually follow his recommendations, right to the obsessive ounce, without measuring my food on a scale. I would take all of the vitamins, minerals, and nutrients I needed that didn't come from being poured out of a cardboard box (aside from Frosted Flakes that no one had to know about).

Writing a list that I cross-referenced with Dr. Perricone's book, I called Healthy Pleasures. I was reciting my list as Henry stumbled into the kitchen. He took a Clif bar from a box stowed in the cabinet that had more of the Henry/J3 types of foods, watching me as he unwrapped its silver foil. My Healthy Pleasures order was his breakfast entertainment.

"Yes," I said when recalled back to the other end of the line. I had spaced out from my annoyance at Henry's impertinent staring. "Oh, and five jars of Soy Wonder. What color terrorist alert are we at this week? Okay, four, make it four. And a bag of grapes. What's that about? A pound?" I then covered the receiver to speak to Henry, "I forgot how much I love grapes. Great frozen as well."

Returning to the phone, I said, "Make that three pounds of grapes and then deliver it to Reade Street. You have my exact address? Great!" I said, hanging up the phone.

Henry filled the open mouth of the trash can with a D'Agostino grocery bag. He saved his shopping bags, stuffing them all into one bag, and then stowed them in the bottom of the can beneath the garbage.

"You could just use one of the Glad bags. They're kept beneath the sink," I said, in the form of an order.

"An unnecessary expenditure of time, resources, and money."

I had to take a moment to give this some thought.

"All right, you lost me on this one."

"Consider the time involved in purchasing those garbage bags. The time then used to dispose of your grocery bags, not to mention that they add garbage to the garbage. And then you're actually paying for those bags. Kind of like eating a store-bought apple under an apple tree."

My face scrunched into something disagreeable.

"So now I completely get how we were able to afford this place. From your frugal expenditure of time—working harder, enjoying life—and the money you've saved from years of not having to buy garbage bags."

His eyes made a slow motion blink like the movement of one of those slimy Discovery Channel amphibians.

"Not quite, considering the chunk of time and expense to fund my smoking habit. What a waste. And it was you who helped me to quit."

"Helped" was a courteous way of putting it. He had to quit or there would be an impending breakup. But then Henry broke up with me before that could ever happen. So perhaps he had been correct on that assessment.

I wondered how much he saved from quitting smoking. I did have my eye on the baby blue Kelly bag and should be given a cut from his savings.

Henry looked to me with that smirk of his.

"So I have a surprise for you."

Henry's surprises began to terrify me.

"Yes?"

"Tonight. Dress up. I'm taking you out."

"You know, Henry, I'd rather not. Tonight's not good for me."

"What? You have some other date planned? I'm jealous. If this is your way of getting me to propose to you . . . oh, right. I've already done that."

Henry then opened up his arms, which I easily fell into. His hold on me felt safe. He then let go to look at me.

"So no Le Bernadin at 8:00 PM? I've already made the reservation."

I loved Le Bernadin, which he could have considered when he proposed to me. Though there was something endearing and familiar about Silver Spurs.

"Sorry, love," I said, kissing Henry's cheek. "I really need to work."

I really hoped he wouldn't get Oprah on me with a "no one says on their deathbed that they should have worked more" reminder. Thankfully, Henry wasn't that type. He then pulled the strap of his satchel further up his shoulder and reached for a green banana from the fruit bowl. (It used to have Granny Smith apples for the color accent until Henry and J3 mentioned that they liked bananas. I relented by only buying green ones.)

"See you later then," he said, exiting the kitchen.

26

I'd entered a phase of not leaving the apartment. The great thing about Manhattan was that you never had to leave home. House arrest was hardly a punishment. In fact, it could even be considered a holiday from the ornery reality of everyday living.

My painting had been all that I remained focused on. Every morning, my night's thoughts spilled onto the canvas. I'd been doing some of my best work and needed to be close to my paintings. What would happen if, say, I had been out doing an errand, perhaps buying Q-Tips at Duane Reade, and suddenly my most creative moment struck? It would be like a married couple trying to have kids for ten years and missing their one fertile chance because they didn't want to miss *Wheel of Fortune.*

I could also get around the issue of exercise—*Buns of Steel*—I did miss my runs, however, and decided to go online and buy a treadmill. The obtrusive triangular third floor window, currently the site of Henry's surfboard, would be the perfect setting—another statement piece that also provided a function.

Doing a search, there were too many treadmills with only slight differences. I felt ill-equipped to make an effective decision. J3 walked in my direction and I waved to get his attention, welcoming any input before I typed in my AmEx number.

"It's now a treadmill, Emily?" J3 asked.

I didn't quite know what he meant by this. His tone insinuated that my patterns were predictable.

"And here I thought you were such an obsessive runner because it became this outlet from urban existence."

If I hadn't recently been through this trauma where pieces of me were meant to be chopped and subdivided into different sections like pop star franchises, J3's assessment would have some accuracy. I went into some detail about the dangers of sucking in exhaust fumes, cab drivers looking at runners as targets on a video game, the elite running clubs with their special shirts, and the penalty fines given to you in the park if you ran in the wrong direction.

"You haven't run in the park?" I asked in a slight panic.

Silence.

"You mean for exercise?" J3 asked.

I nodded.

"Sure. I've run before," he said, smirking.

Tilting my head upward, I said, "Well, you do know about big electronic stuff. I'd love it if you could coach me on what I should buy."

"I'd go for a pair of grid Sauconys and hit the West Side Highway. It would save you about"—J3 paused to look at the site that showed the Star Trek Pro Elite treadmill I had been deliberating about—"so it would save you about $7,895 and get you some fresher air."

I looked at him, unconvinced.

"Well? Better getting in some exhaust fumes than cabin fever. I don't want to see you turn into some freak of Mrs. Hallingby proportions."

"J3! Of course that could never happen. I am just entering a particularly creative mode and can't be far away from my work," I said like a telemarketer.

He looked at me suspiciously and then gathered his things. I figured J3 would be going to work soon.

I closed all the windows on my computer, but a renegade ad remained on my screen saying "What Would Your Family Do If You Died?"

Nice.

Luckily the ad didn't target me, as it depicted the image of a nice Shaker Heights styled couple with the requisite boy and girl.

* * *

The intercom sounded, and I jumped up to let the packages from Healthy Pleasures in, signing the chit for a smiley deliveryman probably compensating for not speaking English. I gave him the cash I had set on the hall table for his tip and brought the bags to the kitchen.

J3 took a banana out of the microwave, which I found odd.

"Green bananas are a bit tart for me. By zapping them, they ripen. Like adding a little bleach to a new pair of Levi's."

"O-kay," I said somewhat sarcastically. "You're so scientific. I bet you were great with a Bunsen burner!"

He seemed unfazed by my prattling.

"Come on, you were the boy all the girls wanted to partner up with in lab."

He smiled.

I smiled back.

I thought back to science class, the hours imprisoned with funky lab smells and lectures from professors that made inappropriate remarks to you over their instant-coffee-stained breaths. I would use the class sentence to my benefit, asking questions such as the chemical properties of nail polish and its effects on the cuticle, or why did soap take the bubble away from a bubble bath. Then there were the boys of my teenage years only seen through the scuffed up plastic of protective goggles.

J3 smoothed the plastic coating that protected the numbers on the microwave.

He laughed. "Forgot to take the sealing off the microwave?"

"I suppose I did."

(Sealing coatings were left on all appliances to preserve their newness.)

J3 raised a brow suspiciously and then pressed his finger firmly against the sealing, which moved me, but I found his effort futile considering I've tried everything but rubber cement. He then peeled his banana, watching me. I seemed to be living under surveillance without being on reality TV, the camera's lenses in the form of J3's and Henry's eyes.

Stacking up row after row of vitamins, I unpacked alpha lipoic acid, Ester-C, Omega 3, DMAE, DHEA, vitamin E, calcium, pan-

thenol, biotin, and about a dozen more recommended by Dr. Perricone including the vitamins I had already been taking.

"Do you get any kind of residual high from taking all these pills?"
J3 asked.

I took a break from unloading the bags and gave his question
some consideration.

"You know, niacin does give your body this tingly sensation. Your
skin kind of feels like it does after a day in the sun—a bit of a burn-
scratchy-itchy thing going on."

Looking at the bottles, I noticed a jar of zinc and wondered if I
should reshelf alphabetically, then realized that this could be considered a bit extreme now that I lived with others.

"Did you know that zinc blocks rhinoceroses?"

"You mean rhinoviruses?"

"Exactly! Rhinoviruses. Very important."

J3 shook his head, depositing his peel in the disposal. I loved that
about him.

"We don't want any Elmer Fudd characters slipping on them," he
said after noticing my attention to his tidiness.

Pulling the bottle of my calcium pills out, the last jar in the bag, I
became deeply distressed. They delivered the calcium caltrate without vitamin D.

"Emily! What's wrong? Are you okay?"

I turned to J3, tears piercing the insides of my eyes. They burned
with that tired sensation. It'd been so long since I'd cried and I'd
forgotten how to control such emotions. I shut my lids and mentally
summoned my tears to stop by thinking of yellow marshmallow
chickadees and the people who ate them. The result: wetter eyes,
but the moistness more dispersed, preventing an onset of pouring
tears. Far more preferable.

"It's just that they gave me the wrong calcium pills. You need the
vitamin D to absorb them," I said, studying the bottle to see if I might
have experienced a reading comprehension error. "Without vitamin
D" it said, cheerfully promoted in an azure bubble.

"Why do they do that? Surely you need that vitamin D. I mean,
better to have it than not. Do you think if I called Healthy Pleasures
back they'd make another delivery? Just for the vitamin D pills? Just
another thing that needs to be added on my To Do list."

J3 walked over to me. He peeled my fingers from the bottle as if it were a weapon wielded by someone who forgot to take their lithium pills. He had long fingers, which I watched while he put the bottle in the cabinet, as opposed to on the table, and then looked at me.

"Emily, this has got to stop."

He then took my hand and led me to my bedroom. Hmm?

"Now go in there. Take a shower. Get dressed—no pajama bottoms and oversized cableknit sweaters—and report back to me downstairs. I'm taking you out. How about that mindless Adam Sandler movie?"

I believe I pulled a face.

"Go," he said, flickering his hands. "Get ready. I have a plan."

"A plan? I'm kind of busy," I said, thinking of the day I really intended—readjusting couch pillows into campground formation with a pile of magazines while watching canceled WB shows.

"Yeah, right. No excuses, and do as I say."

I had been acting agoraphobic. As I never associated myself with people that had phobias or wore surgical gloves at an ATM machine, it came time to board the plane away from my self-pity vacation. A few kids cavalierly waving a knife would not carve into my control, independence, and freedoms upheld by countries that distribute cargo pants for their intended use. I also feared that questionable odor you smell when walking by an elderly person's apartment, the cancerous stench that seeps its way into the fibers of your clothes and furniture and slips under the door.

I did as J3 said.

27

I found J3 in the kitchen, standing in landline phone position assuming his important mode while speaking on his mobile. His California office would just be arriving at work. After seeing me, he made his good-byes, saying that he would not be going to the office and could be reached on his cell if needed.

He complimented me on how I looked. I shifted my eyes curiously, wondering if he said this politely. I had on my black wrap dress with a turquoise necklace that I bought from an acquaintance of mine who designed jewelry before she got her real estate license.

J3 asked if I was ready, and I nodded, saying I just needed to put on shoes. I searched for my blue satin Christian Louboutin ballet flats. They were the last pair to be thrown from the closet, padding the hall floor with a troubling mess. I then considered my metallic LV bag as being more appropriate for the outfit, but opted against it since I haven't used it since the incident and just took my black patent Chanel bag I stole from my mother, considering she'd never notice buying this bag. She bought bags the way I bought grapes.

J3 stuffed his wallet in his jacket pocket, and I followed him quietly to the elevator. We walked in silence uptown toward the West Village. The brightness of the day turned the figures around us into black silhouettes. I luckily had a pair of sunglasses that I had kept in this bag. They weren't my favorites, but the bug-eyed tortoiseshell was always a good look if you wanted to dodge paparazzi, or stalkers, depending on where your planets were aligned.

Approaching a specialty boutique, the window displayed a mannequin dressed in a tux posed with a wand that he waved over a black top hat with a stuffed rabbit popping from it. We both decelerated our pace. Stopping at the window, we took in the detailed styling of the display—a deck of cards scattered about, a taffeta cape draped on a leather wingbacked chair.

"I love top hats," I said, looking through my reflection.

"Me too," said J3, turning away from the window to me. "I always chose the top hat when playing Monopoly."

"So did I! For me, it's based on nostalgia. My grandfather always wore his top hat to dinner, even during summer's hottest weeks. We'd be dressed in scrappy old sundresses and flip-flops, and my granddad would be in his seersucker Bermudas, a white tee and that old top hat.

"Come in with me," I said, leading J3 into the shop.

The store had a riotous layout, a floor plan encumbered with nooks and awkward curves stuffed with retro cocktail outfits, dresses with labels of Lanvin and Gres, along with an entire rack of vintage fur stoles. Though I could have spent some time furnishing my own needs, I had an agenda.

The crevice in the rear appeared to have once been a changing room, now serving the purpose of a shelving system with two rows of hats—fedoras, pillboxes, and one beret that had a peacock feather pinned to its side with a slip of veil dangling in the front. I stood up on my toes and knocked one of the top hats the way I did when reaching for a cereal box on an out-of-reach shelf so that it fell and cradled in my arms. Propping the hat on J3, we both stared at one another as I tilted it into place. I felt aroused and embarrassed, and returned to my job as a stylist.

"It fits."

He pinched the rim and looked into a floor mirror that swiveled within its walnut stand.

"Indeed it does," he said.

The saleslady approached us. She had on too much kohl eyeliner, florescent red lipstick, and wore a schoolgirl kilt with a fitted boucle jacket. Think Vivienne Westwood goes to Palm Beach.

"Very handsome," approved the saleslady.

J3 slipped off the hat and returned it to its perch, while I asked the saleslady the amount and gave her four twenties to quickly make the transaction without J3's noticing.

We began to walk out of the store, and the saleslady tossed me the hat like a Frisbee. I gave her a sailor's salute and then looked in J3's eyes.

"You must," I said, putting the hat on J3's head, "wear this all day. It wards off all evil."

"Well thank you, Emily, for my magic hat," he said, flicking the rim.

I studied him. He wore jeans with a cornflower blue shirt, its boxy cut unable to be tucked in, and leather sandals, with that top hat. He did dress well in that California kind of way. No one seemed to take notice of J3 in his hat, another New York perk, a city where sharing a sidewalk with a man who has a boa constrictor coiled around his neck as if it were the latest fashion statement looked mainstream.

We walked with no discussion of our route, just slight shifts in our movement as prods to the direction, mostly in silence with the occasional discussion of work and impending project deadlines. J3 had a slight bounce to his gait, which struck me as a combination of assertiveness and his boyish character.

We explored areas we knew but had never properly investigated, admiring the façades of buildings and brownstones that were more creative with their flowerbox presentations. Parks, we discovered, were our shared passion, and the city didn't have enough of them. I told him how I missed my view from Gramercy and, after saying this, realized that I preferred my former apartment's location over Reade Street. Our pace decelerated at the corner of Greenwich and Charles because of a man pulling his shih tzu on its leash, the dog's bottom giving one of the city's few cobblestone streets a scrub that could render the mayor's controversial new cleaning trucks useless. Watching this vignette play before us caused J3 and me to erupt into a giggle. When our laughter subsided into ebullience, we held each other's gaze. From the color of the dog's collar to the man's coarse hair that could scrape off burnt food, I knew that this would be one of those moments that would never lose its clarity.

My babbling went in sync with our nomadic wandering. Saying "and this is what you get from spilling paint in the garage" may not have deserved the hysterics this line produced, but it felt good, and J3 seemed open to this form of self-entertainment. When we reached the meatpacking district, we came across a charming French bistro that hosted IMG/MGM types after hours. It appeared carved from Montmartre and transplanted to this slummy-cum-trendy alley.

We moved through the undulations of the narrow restaurant, had backstage access through a scruffy little kitchen, and discovered a backyard with a pebbled floor and strings of Christmas lights woven through the beams of the open roof. The warmth generated from the sun and sporadically placed outdoor heaters that looked like the extras from a *Star Wars* film made it comfortable enough to eat outdoors.

Asking a looking-for-work model if we could seat ourselves, her artfully crafted brows and dramatic clutch to her breast gave the impression that her alternative life was more superior than the stressful demands of her hostess job. Choosing the nearest table, J3 waited till I seated myself and then pulled out his chair, removed his hat and placed it on the vacant seat that I also used to rest my bag. I had forgotten about J3's hat, having become accustomed to it the way you go topless on a European beach (applying lots of sunblock), wondering if the questionable looks we'd received were a result of his wearing it.

Reading the specials on a folding chalkboard, J3 became enthused by the possibility that one of us should order the steak au poivre. I shook my head, reminding him that dead animals were for external use only.

"If you don't eat your meat, you can't have any pudding! How can you have any pudding if you don't eat your meat?" he crooned.

I do love instant pudding, though not enough to eat an entire steak. We both ordered the special fish of the day, a bottle of rosé, and started with oysters. J3 returned to his little boy excitement upon realizing that this was the best time of year to order them. I suspected he had a bad oyster episode once, but didn't want to encourage the bad memory. Our fish was served whole, all bones, eyes, and fin. You had to be particularly skilled to not eat any bones.

I reminded J3 of the signal for choking, but the seasoning was so distinctive, rosemary I gathered, that it was worth the dissection.

We talked about places we'd like to travel to, places we could live in. We discussed our childhoods, past romances, and the ones whom we had gladly let slip away.

J3 looked to his lap. He then took out his phone, fiddled with a few switches, and put on his professional face as he answered it.

"Listen, Emily, if you don't mind excusing me for a minute, I have to take this. It's my office, and there is something that requires my immediate attention."

"Sure," I waved. "Not a problem." After saying this, I realized I'd caught a buzz.

He smiled and took a sip from his wine before leaving the table. J3's manners impressed me. Having his phone's vibrator turned on and taking a day from work to attend to me was an extravagant gesture, especially considering our diametrically opposed days. Where I found a challenge in negotiating the right hue of purple within a pastel sketch, J3 could lose or gain millions with one misguided choice.

A loud whisper floated from behind me, immediately sensitizing me to the fact that more fish was to be had now that my plate had been cleared. I gathered the hushed secrecy came from two women, and I tuned my listening to glass-to-the-wall levels. The girl directing the conversation spoke of her discovery that her brother had been seeing a family acquaintance, someone she thought highly of, but his cheating on his wife was inexcusable. Her conundrum in alliances was that the wife, socially ambitious and from a suburb outside Chicago I recognized from being widely represented in my *Freshman Faces* book from college, was interested in her brother because of who he was. I needed names.

J3 returned to his seat, his face flushed from his earlier pleasantries, and mumbling something about taking care of things that caused me to miss key points. I pressed my forefinger against the tip of my nose and puckered my lips in "ssh" position.

"Give me a second," I whispered, lifting my bottom from my cushioned seat to lean in closer to J3. "Some serious gossip happening at the table behind me."

J3 nodded and smiled as if this were completely normal. I then realized he could be useful in my fact-finding mission.

Subtly tilting my head so my chin awkwardly scratched my shoulder, I peeked at the two girls. Naturally, I had to have the luck of positioning—facing the sister of the straying husband, her flat-ironed blond hair could tickle my nose with a faint breeze. She wore a black lambskin coat over a man's tailored shirt, while the other girl had on a gray nylon turtleneck with a gray fox snippet. The two were dressed impeccably, giving my blatant snoop some justification, as I could very well have been studying them for fashion purposes. Returning my head back to its mannered position, I said to J3, "Do you recognize any of those girls?"

He propped his head to peer above mine and shook his head to say he didn't.

"Hmm." I drummed two fingers against my lips.

The waiter cleared our plates. I considered asking him for information, but now the detective sloppily trailed off.

"Would you like any dessert?" he asked.

"None for me, thank you," I said. "I have a sex scene tomorrow." Both the waiter and J3 looked at me amused.

"I've always wanted to say that."

J3 then asked for the check. He studied my face.

"And you're so curious why?"

"Because it's comforting to know that other people breathing in the same restaurant air have problems as well."

He drank from his glass with a smile, sharing my communion.

"Perhaps the drama will come up in Page 6. Not that I ever read Page 6."

He laughed and tapped out the bottle of wine.

Outside the restaurant, J3 raised his hand to cab-hailing position, but I quickly asked if we could walk home. I felt the painting pinch, wanted to make it a long work night, and hoped to walk off my drunkenness.

Approaching Jumpin' Joe, I suggested making a quick stop. I needed a decaf. J3 asked if Jumpin' Joe would become our Peach

Pit or Central Perk. I said that this would be unlikely, because friends didn't typically have such indulgent time to sit around and drink coffee while chirping about their lives.

J3 then gave his personal history of the establishments he frequented—his boyhood Baskin Robbins that kept the same hours as the neighboring movie theater, his college bar, as dark and questionably scented as a stable, how he was due for a new place. I asked what his favorite Baskin Robbins flavor was. He loved eggnog, but possibly from its being a special featured flavor. I liked Caramel Chocolate Crunch and asked if he ever had one of the clown cones displayed in the ice cream cake freezer.

Leaving Jumpin' Joe, the day slipped into night with the speed of a computer's screensaver. The street lamps clicked on, the florescent lighting changing J3's appearance. Vainly, I thought that my looks had been compromised. I would certainly have come across better under a glow of moonbeams.

When we arrived home, I fully felt the exhaustion from the day and drink. J3 excused himself to his office, while I took a moment on the couch before I went upstairs to change, finding myself dressing into my painting clothes.

Returning to my canvas, I turned on the radio, listening to NPR discuss North Korea and how they were basically brainwashed to hate Americans. I wondered if Americans were victims of such propaganda as well. My head started to hurt.

"What's wrong?" asked J3, walking to the couch with a stack of papers. I turned off the radio and started to mix paint.

"Kind of annoyed with North Korea right now."

"Oh really?" he said, clearly amused. "Ranked above or below your Cousin Anne?"

"Below, naturally."

"And the people that keep up their Christmas decorations till March?"

"I suppose above."

We both slipped into our isolated worlds, the demands of our jobs temporarily separating us.

28

I went into the kitchen, looking for something. A diversion. The kitchen, though incredible, appeared sterile, almost too perfect in its newness. It could benefit from good cooking smells—the cupcakes and frosting kind—and perhaps a bowl of limes for the accent color. I opened the stove, trying to figure out its meaning.

"You're not considering pulling a Sylvia Plath on me?" I heard J3 say, his steps approaching me until his face peered into the stove, sharing my view of looking-down-a-mining-shaft darkness. We did this for a while until I realized there would be no developments. His head was the first to retract, prompting me to do the same.

"I suppose you're right. Sleeping pills are far more preferable than cooking."

J3 took a green banana and put it in the microwave. As he unpeeled it, I walked over and gave him a whimpery look until he offered me a bite. I swallowed it in one gulp and then excused myself to return to my work.

Consulting my business planner on the endless priorities I was behind on, the crisp image of Coffeehouse Pete was more compelling than starting a commissioned piece.

Dropping the Smythson, I kicked it across the floor where it swished like a hockey puck and I returned to the blank canvas. Outlining my creation in charcoal, my arms couldn't keep up with

the vision inside my head. I filled in the outline with paint in a consumed fury. Hours went by. I stopped to take a break and noticed
that J3 had been watching me from the couch. For how long I
couldn't be certain.

Walking to the kitchen in silence, registering the work I just produced, I then grazed on a bit of everything premade. Returning to my
portrait, J3 no longer at his seat, I fell back into my painting mode.
Analyzing the few strokes of deep purple I dappled to Pete's eyes, deliberating whether the tone worked or not, I looked to the couch to
find J3 back at his seat, drink in hand, as if he were pacing himself
during an all-day conference. I became self-conscious at his presence, but quickly forgot about playing to an audience once I stroked
my brush to the canvas.

I painted for four straight hours with brief intervals of bathroom
and food breaks, my wrists paralyzed. The quietness and shift in
darkness liberated me from the day's deadlines. J3, now resting on
his back, read some papers that he looked at in his outstretched
hands.

I spoke to him while keeping my eyes fixed on the portrait.

"Do you know those private pockets inside your head that sometimes you get to? That amazing place where you feel like this is why
you're meant to be?" I asked, swishing my brush into a peachy color
I created, stroking it onto Pete's forehead. "When you have that
crystallized moment where you suddenly get what you're meant to
be? It's so fleeting. Everything becomes simplified—the most ultimately clarified and brilliant moment."

I heard papers collapsing to the ground. Turning to the source, I
watched J3 twist himself around and prop his chin in the palm of
his hand so he could look at me like a customized dress displayed
for a fashion editor's eyes. He did not tremble a brow or waver his
stare.

"Does this Dalai-Lama-and-green-tea moment of yours have
something to do with turning down that meeting for the art director position?"

A few weeks ago, J3 overheard a conversation I had with a contact
of mine from Condé Nast, who invited me for a meeting so we could
discuss the launch of a celebrity-society-gossip magazine. She'd
practically offered me the art director position over the phone. I

didn't even take the Condé Nast lunch. The idea of turning into someone who collected photographs of themselves with random celebrities in corporate frames, glanced and sneered at by one of your five assistants while you made Sharpie marks on their work, held no appeal.

"You know that I've never been good at that game. The language, dressing up in clothes that don't fit my style, how you suddenly have a taste for jellyfish salad."

"Jellyfish salad? You've had jellyfish salad?" J3 gave an amused expression.

"Ewww, no way. I don't even know if such a food thing exists. But if you happen to mumble it while riding on the Condé Nast elevator with a writer for *Gourmet*, I can assure you jellyfish salad will be bigger than sashimi."

I smoothed my coated fingers over my face, probably adding a shade of purple to my forehead.

J3's voice shifted into a chipper key. "Who did they get to edit the magazine?" He shuffled his position, asserting his interest in the gossipy turn the conversation had taken.

"Richard Bluestone."

J3 nodded.

"I never got the whole Richard Bluestone phenomenon," I said, curling my fingers like shrimp on a martini glass so I could study the accrual of paint beneath my cuticles.

"Apparently he saved a lot of children from drowning in a Hampton undertow or something, one of the kids being the son of that Condé Nast exec who looks like Groucho Marx. Gave him the entertainment editor job at *GQ* once he discovered he ghostwrote the snarky gossip section for one of those give-away magazines they dump in the lobbies of apartment buildings and health clubs in the 10021 zip."

Timing, I thought to myself. How Bluestone was situated at a wrong place at the right time now gave him the power to deem a restaurant hot and skinny ties fashionable, all by his edit notes scribbled on the column of a galley.

"Don't mention that art director thing to anyone. If you don't mind?"

I avoided making eye contact with J3, not wanting to get into the details of why Henry had not been privy to my invitation to join the Condé Nast life. As chic as the offices were, the stability of having a regular paycheck, choosing a doctor from an encyclopedic manual, and retirement plans with numbers and letters, I'd rather contend with the backstabbing than infiltrate back into corporate life. Breaking from your office responsibilities to investigate a communal refrigerator with leftover jams from a client breakfast and fancily packaged condiments not worthy to be kept by the food editor. Politely chatting with the receptionist who keeps the leather Coach tag with a rabbit foot chain on the bag's zipper, having to make an insincere compliment on her screensaver with a picture of her baby daughter who has a garter belt around her head. And a good day's work was cleverly arranging photos of an Italian designer's Jell-O colored ski lodge with the headline "Cabin Fever" that took an editor with the underhandedness of a Medici to get approved.

"You know, there is this part of me that I can barely understand. I think I should talk this out with someone I'm close with, but find that I'm incapable. And then I rationalize this as being normal, because some things about myself are meant to be private."

The sound of J3 putting his glass on a coaster reminded me that I had been speaking to someone. Now seated upright, his unrelenting gaze switched on, he was a study of controlled focus.

"Sharing your most private thoughts makes you vulnerable. When you do that, you tell the person that this is who I am. They have a choice to hurt you with this information or become closer. And that's when you are taken to a greater level provided by the collective benefits of human contact. It's called intimacy and it is key."

I looked at the painting of Pete. It was beginning to come to life, but something lacked. I needed to actually see my subject, spend time with him, before his vision came into full focus. The Pete I knew also needed a makeover, becoming especially stooped by the moss green sweater with that vintage Baghdad '03 look. I had just the idea of how to repay him for his act of heroism. Pete would have a Queer Eye makeover.

I twisted my head so quickly I momentarily saw lava lamp molecules. When my sight restored, I focused on J3. He had returned to his work, looking perplexed by the papers he read.

29

Henry bounded into the room holding a bag with pieces of wood sprouting from it. His entrance shifted J3's and my attention to his arrival. He apologized for not being home earlier, looked at my painting and then at the two of us with an expression that said he wanted to be filled in on all that he missed. I didn't know where to begin. His presence was the removal of your dessert plate when you still hadn't finished.

Shifting on my feet to keep my legs from numbing, I turned back to the portrait and added another stroke to Pete's cheek before my painterly flow washed away like footprints in the sand. Dropping the brush into its glass of water, I then directed my body to Henry.

"Hey, handsome," I said, cocking my head to kiss his cheek, then scanned his bundle.

"Presents!"

Henry, becoming excited, pulled from the package various bits of sanded wood that seemed to be glorified scraps from a pile of kindling. He walked over to one of the windows with a few pieces and began shifting them into assorted positions on the glass. With two hands pressing a longer piece, he contorted his body around so he wouldn't disrupt the placement.

"What do you think?" he huffed.

Um?

"Giving our windows a casement effect—don't you like it?"

"A bit Home Depot."

Henry's cheapening our windows struck me with fear. I suddenly thought of Henry before our time, in a room postered with St. Paulie girls while Whitesnake shouted from a boom box.

"You know," I said lightheartedly, "grant the princess her request and she may not banish you."

"From the castle I pay the taxes on?" Henry said under his breath, stuffing the pieces back in the bag. He then diverted the disagreement by turning to my portrait.

"Emily, this is amazing. You've really captured Pete, but the style is so colorful, exciting. There's this trueness to your depiction but you know when to accentuate the features that deserve to be addressed. Like a poetic caricature."

"Exactly. Precisely what I was aiming for," I said, which made everyone laugh. When the room settled to a silent awkwardness, I noticed my moods had been shifting in and out like an expatriate slipping between languages, incapable of keeping the friendly banter alive.

"I'm pretty knackered. Have you eaten?" I said to Henry.

He nodded.

"Okay then. I'm just going to clean up and get to bed. It was a long and extraordinary day."

J3 and I shared a meaningful glance that Henry observed, quickly jutting his head toward the canvas to underplay seeing our moment.

"See you upstairs," I said to Henry. "Good night, J3," I yelled over to him.

I deliberately refrained from thanking him for the day, making a mental note to properly address his generosity tomorrow. Perhaps in the morning after Henry left for work, since J3 kept to Pacific time.

Walking up the stairs, I couldn't help but peek inside J3's room, the door open, a blatant invitation to be looked into. I had had his room wallpapered in chamois suede, the same golden tone as the wall-to-wall sisal. He had a dark wooden Eames chair draped with a yellow and black tartan blanket. Studying the cross section of lines over boxes, I pulled my eyes in and out of focus to see the varying shapes like highways viewed from a landing plane. A vintage photograph of an American Indian wearing an elaborate headdress hung above the mahogany bed frame. A fluffy duvet was punctured in the middle like a pincushion, the top hat the button that pierced the blanket. As I stepped back from the room, the air felt crisper. I walked up the final staircase quietly, trying to conceal my steps so not to be discovered by J3 and have Henry question why I hadn't yet reached my room.

Pursing my lips, I then smiled for my electric toothbrush so it could grope its way around my mouth, buffing my front teeth jubilantly. After washing my face, I added all of the creams the woman in Sephora sold me, probably used for the down payment on Dr. Perricone's third home. She had supple skin that gleamed like dampened soap, with a dusting of freckles outlining the contour of her cheekbone, which had the sharp, curved edge of a wishbone. Her eyes were semi-slitted. She seemed Eurasian, perhaps half Polynesian, something hybrid that gave her good skin genes.

I studied the dark circles bulging beneath my eyelids and vouched that I would give up wine, alcohol, artificial sweeteners—I retracted the artificial sweetener part—and would be vigilant in taking Dr. Perricone's nutritional recommendations so I could have skin as dewy as Sephora lady, who could sample as many overly priced products she could by working at that store.

I creaked open the bathroom door, and the unlit room gave a refracted shimmer, which could have been anything from a dwindling candle to a thunderstorm, but Henry had left the television on. I crawled into bed and turned on my bedside lamp, reading the same paragraph in a magazine six times while my thoughts reenacted the day. Henry walked in, looking at me like I had partaken in a villainous scheme, and then vanished into the bathroom where I heard the chainsaw buzz from his electric toothbrush. Slipping into his place in bed, he released the mute button from the remote, dramatically changing the mood of the room. I really had no use for a television in our bedroom.

We watched the local news, Henry apologizing for the distraction of TV with excuses of how he hadn't been able to fall asleep for the past few nights. I hadn't been able to sleep for the past six weeks.

At least he chose to watch the local news over a rerun sitcom, where you deliberately chose to listen to people moan about their coddled lives. The local news, however, appeared to be the reality version of whining. As I thought of it, the local news seemed to cover the same stories, just with different players. The court proceedings of stars accused of victimizing a misguided fan, parents who coached their children's athletic teams and made their son eat his own vomit, wife beaters, drug dealers, and today's leading item, a Sesame Street character at a children's benefit who had been punched in the stomach because a man didn't believe he was the same character as the one that appeared on the show.

They covered a tourist from Toronto. They always seemed to be from Canada, a country ashamed of its geographical connection to the U.S. but proud to claim Celine Dion and Brendan Fraser. She'd been hit with a bottle by a mugger. It came with all of the packaged drama an NBC producer will crib from—complete with bandage wrapped around her head and sobbing. In between gasps, she managed to verbalize her disgust with the city and how she just wanted to return back to Toronto.

The report then cut to a police officer as he recapped her crime, apparently too taxing for the Toronto victim to recount on camera. He said she tried to defend herself and there had been a struggle because she didn't want to give up her bag with cell phone, tickets, etc.

"Well, that's pretty silly," I said to the TV. "I mean, so you lose your license? Better that than get your head smashed with a bottle. Pretty stupid actually. Go back to maple country." My tone went from amused to bellicose.

Henry gave me that look of his, the analytical one. I loathed feeling like a specimen pickled in a jar full of formaldehyde.

The report then cut back to Toronto victim, her sobs now softened to a few sniffles. She continued to say how she felt victimized, afraid, helpless. I wanted to smash a bottle on her head. The hard part of her ordeal now over, she'd fly back to Maple Leaf Country, watch hockey games, eat bacon, wear snowshoes. She'd be far from her attackers, that stalker. There would be a definite ending to her miserable incident.

I pictured a home. A converted yellow barn with heated floors, rooms painted in electric colors, and a kitchen with a cutting board made from a slab of slate. On the vast property, there would be cabins with porches closed in with flimsy wire mesh that resisted the legs of flying insects. You could look from a second-floor window to see the tops of trees, where the grooves of branches were stuffed with leaves housing a family of squirrels.

My neighbors would have jobs at the nearby university. They'd keep me updated on the celestial cycle, and we'd have dinner parties on nights the moon was up to something. I'd ask them questions about their married children and would actually be interested in the updates.

I'd have orchards—apples and peaches—and perhaps a lake. There would be ducks, maybe even hens and pigs. The home would generate milk, eggs, fruit, and berries. I'd put up college kids in one of the cabins, and they would work the farm for a small income and free board. The produce could be purchased at neighboring markets that had corkboards pinned with flyers alerting readers about bazaars and carolers who sang in the town square. On weekends, there would be tours of the farm that ended with guests sampling the teas scooped from the tops of barrels you needed a ladder to climb up to.

I could have a dog, a yellow Lab I'd name Wilber. Perhaps I'd rescue a fawn and feed her with baby bottles. Keep her as a pet, very Audrey Hepburn. I would paint the label for "Yellow Barn," having the panache of a polo horse with the recognition of a Swoosh. Once word spread about the organic, fresh bounties that came from my farm, *W* would profile me, then the *Wall Street Journal.* To be seen drinking Yellow Barn Raspberry Clove Tea at Jean Georges will be very early 2000s.

The idea of abandoning the hard steel and gray that paved an urban existence for a more rural setting made me think about why *Green Acres* didn't get its remake—wondering who Warner Brothers would choose to play the parts.

"Emily. Have you ever considered—"

"Henry! I'm not seriously considering leaving the city."

I really was more than selling sandwich spread from a Vermont barnyard.

"Okay," he said, dragging out the word. "But I was about to say consider going to Pearl Paint over Sam Flax, since Pearl is so much closer to where we live now."

"Oh. Right. Actually I usually buy my supplies at Pearl, at least my larger orders, so not much will change there."

"Good. Well then, you seem to have that covered."

I rolled away from him into my sleeping position, hearing him flick the remote from the news to Letterman. He laughed more enthusiastically at his off-handed quips than he normally did. The rotating scales of audience laughter helped me drift to sleep. I had an out-of-focus image of myself painting my logo, stumped between a singular yellow barn or a yellow barn with Wilber wearing a purple collar—the purple collar a key statement of color.

"Fuck!" Henry yelled to the world, the bed shaking.

His cursing smacked me like an unseen wave. Henry was using both of his thumbs, poking the life out of the remote.

"Henry! What is it?"

"Damn remote needs new batteries. Completely useless. What? I'm supposed to go up to the television, manually change through over 500 channels, then go back to bed and, if I don't like the show, just go back to the television and again turn the stations?"

"Or you could just go to sleep."

30

I had now completed two noncommissioned portraits. I estimated that I needed to finish one more painting before Daniel returned from Paris so he would separate me from the starting-my-own-PR-firm/handbag company/cosmetic line type who used her vocation as party drivel—the sort of girls who dated trendy boys who wore kilts and owned castles in Scotland.

I entered the kitchen. The sun was stretching her fingers in blinding definition, Henry peeled the wrapper of his Clif bar from its center seam, while J3 sat at the bar island reading something while pouring more Frosted Flakes into a pool of milk.

"So it's almost April 30," I announced, my expectant tone somewhat at odds with morning routines performed soporifically. "Actually, that's next Friday. So we all have to be very industrious and make this party happen."

I then handed both of them copies of my "Six Months to Halloween Party To Do List," the first papers breathed from my printer since being released from its packing captivity.

Henry's Clif bar fell from his mouth. J3 studied my list.

"Are you serious, Emily?" asked Henry.

"No. I just decided to make this little To Do list because that's what I do. Make To Do lists."

My words had no effect.

"Of course I'm serious! There's been this annus horribilis tone around here. A party will be good for everyone. I also want to apologize for being such an Eeyore. I've given up Equal these past few weeks. Well, I've cut down to two packs a day, so that's part of the reason why I've been so on edge."

"I didn't know you cut back on Equal, Emily. I can't believe I didn't notice," Henry said.

I took the container of milk from the fridge, poured it into a pan, and then diluted it with water. Setting it on the stove, I turned the dial midway so it gave me enough time to assemble my mug and teabag before it bubbled over, a spillage that would stain the electric range with paramecium-shaped blobs in burnt colors. Green tea. I would start having green tea in the mornings because of the antioxidants. Something the Mayo clinic said was good, according to the packaging.

"Yeah. Really trying to take Dr. Perricone's recommendations seriously."

"Wait a sec," said Henry, reaching for a green banana. "How does Dr. Perricone figure Equal into your getting better?"

I diced him with my eyes.

"Henry, you really need to read *The Wrinkle Cure*. Are you even aware of the book on my bedside table?"

The copy in question was currently folded in the middle and placed with its jacket faced toward the ceiling, looking more like an elementary doodle of a seagull.

Henry seemed unaware of his character being under attack.

"Dr. Perricone is strictly opposed to sugar—even the artificial kinds. In some ways, artificial sweeteners are even worse. Something to do with brain neurons being zapped."

"Yeah, Henry. Get with the Perricone program," J3 said mockingly.

Feeling my patience seep to the ugly side, I steered away from what appeared to be scoffs at my health and beauty concerns. So be it if they both had no consideration for their skin; exfoliation from shaving would only get them so far.

"Now, if you both don't mind taking a moment today to look over this list, organized in job responsibilities as outlined." I swiveled around Henry to point to his bar graph (Henry in charge of music and drinks). "As you see, I'm responsible for food, invitations, and decoration. J3, you have entertainment." He looked pleased. "I thought entertainment would be appropriate for you. Being that you're in entertainment and entertaining with entertainment seems a natural extension," I said. Then I directed my attention to Henry. "And it would be great if you could both get back to me at the end of the day about your progress."

Returning to the task of monitoring my new morning routine, I watched the watered-downed milk rumble and begin its volcanic rise. As girls, Anne used to say that you should never watch cheese melt in the toaster oven, otherwise it wouldn't cook. She could be rather dense. Or perhaps this just applied to toaster ovens.

I lifted the pan from the stove before the foaming-over milk would use up needed minutes of my morning from having to clean the range. After carefully pouring it over my teabag, I dumped the excess liquid down the drain and squeezed the pungency out of the tea bag by roping the string around the spoon.

"There's also the matter of you both working out who will have the loaded task of telling the neighbors and—" Abrupt pause. They both watched me expectantly. Taking a cautious sip from my boiling tea, I then threw out my words as quickly and delicately as a Band-Aid being pulled from a child's arm. "Mrs. Hallingby."

Henry moaned, saying, "Why? Why? Why?" like Nancy Kerrigan. "Why?"

"A lot of 'whys'," said J3. "Learning a new word?"

"Why do we have to even tell her?" asked Henry.

"I don't want that cursing freak show to bark her way into the party."

Then again, the theme was "Six Months to Halloween." Henry read my expression.

"Why don't you put your name on that particular task?" offered Henry, writing something on his list.

"Look, I don't make the rules."

"Then what is it exactly that you are doing?" he said, unsuccessfully holding back a laugh behind his fist.

The weakened taste of my tea upset me. I needed a sweet fix. Giving up Equal would be more difficult than I thought. I needed to know what all the hype had been over these antioxidants. I walked over to the fridge and opened the door. Looking at the shelves of food helped clear my head.

"And get me your invite list ASAP, please," I said, reaching into the freezer to munch on ice, which only intensified my sweet urge. Searching for my private stash beneath the kitchen sink, I surreptitiously took a pack of Twizzlers from an oversized canning jar secured with a clasp like the buckle of an old ski boot.

"Unfortunately, I have to do the rather cheesy thing and send e-vites and hassle people by phone."

"You should see her with the wedding planning," Henry said to J3 with a raised brow.

I couldn't quite tell what he meant by that.

"Emily, this will be great," J3 said. I wanted to squeeze his cheeks.

"Thank you," I said, as a substitute for cheek squeezing.

"And are you sure you're up for this, considering your painting deadlines?" J3 asked.

"Absolutely. And not to be completely self-absorbed, but part of the reason for throwing this party now is to celebrate my work's progress."

"You've finished two paintings," said Henry in deadpan delivery.

"Exactly," I said, shooing him out the door. I really wanted to eat a Twizzler unobserved.

"Now you have a busy day ahead, added responsibilities to your normal work duties. Go. Go. Go!"

"Okay, okay. See you later, Em." Henry kissed me on my forehead and then said his good-byes to J3.

Returning to the task of inventorying the fridge's contents, I saw Henry's Metamucil drink had spilled, the orange sugar-water beading the shelf. I mulled this over, trying to figure if Henry's putting a glass of unfinished Metamucil drink in the fridge was weirder than his drinking Metamucil. I used a kitchen towel and soapy sponge to clean and wipe in rigorous motions, as the stain had become slightly frozen from being set under the cooling duct. I scrubbed and breathed to rower movements until the clapping closed of J3's mobile caused my head to twist in his direction.

"So how does a movie screen playing *The Texas Chainsaw Massacre, The Exorcist,* and the original *Friday the Thirteenth* work for you?"

I snapped the kitchen towel in the air, spinning it above my head like a medieval weapon.

"So I gather that's a yes?"

I nodded my head spastically.

He took a moment, seeming to have an internal debate with himself, and then said, "By the way, your timing of this gathering could not be more fortuitous. It happens to coincide with Amanda's first viewing of our living arrangement. The party will be a good event to break up her time here. Thank you for that."

A mild shock wave must have passed over my face; I did my best to control my expression with my penchant for inane babbling at awkward moments.

"Great!" was all that I could come up with.

I opened the kitchen closet, entranced by the electric blue glimmer from the bottle of Windex, the feel of the bottle like a warm cup of soup with confetti-sized stars on chilled hands.

To me, Amanda had never been something real. She was the nonexistent boyfriend you told your unavailable lover about to make him jealous, the AmEx card given to you in college "for emergencies only" (and used toward J. Crew orders and campus restaurants that made their earnings on parent weekends). The excitement I once had for this party now had the looming pressure of a deadline you wanted to pass without having to do the work that led up to it.

"Emily?" said J3, taking the Windex from my hands. "Are you okay?"

Okay? Okay! No, I was not okay.

"Sure, I'm okay. Why do you ask?"

"Because you've just Windexed my cell phone."

My face stretched into a shocked expression.

"Not to worry. I never really liked this one very much."

He broke into a smile.

"Buy J3 a new phone," I announced, while jotting it down on a new To Do list.

I then plunged my hand into my bag, blindly fingering the items to locate my phone so I could loan it to J3. Unable to find the phone, I tilted the bag against the table, widened its mouth, and renegade Tic Tacs hit the surface in a pounding hailstorm of white mints. Using the sides of my hands, I brushed the candy to form a nest, prodding each one with my finger back into its container. Exhausted by the process, I aimed the container at the trash and popped the remaining Tic Tacs in my mouth like pills. I felt J3's eyes, knowing their expression.

Handing him my cell phone with pleads that he use it till I replaced his damaged one, J3 threw up his arms in resignation, saying that he'd have his assistant attend to this. I reminded him that my phone minutes were not put to proper use, then made a mental note to tell my sole caller, Mother, not to start one of her therapeutic banters if she called my mobile, for fear of J3's having to contend with such an inquisition.

31

I distanced the financial pragmatics from pride so as not to taint the excitement I had in turning down my first paying job, the client a pseudo-acquaintance of Daphne's, one of her relationships based on involved discussions of nannies, personal trainers, and other banalities to keep the tedium of a play group interesting while giving the occasional remark on how spectacular their daughters' beaded necklaces were so as not to be discovered that they were negligent on the supervision of their skills as jewelrymakers.

The mother and daughter seemed to have a discrepancy on how her bedroom should be painted, having settled on a silhouetted Manhattan skyline with a ceiling of midnight stars. After complimenting them on this thrilling concept, I apologized for taking their time, saying that mine needed to be devoted to portraits, especially in view of my maddening workload. They then asked if I'd be able to paint their portraits, and I told them to check with my assistant, giving them Henry's cell phone number.

Considering that I had already made the exhausting trip uptown, I decided to treat myself to a pedicure at Refuge, which was really closer to my neighborhood, but my feet needed pampering and it was the only acceptable place that could fit me in.

Feeling a bit frivolous as a result of having the opportunity to decline work (income that I could really have used), I had my toenails painted in granny apple green. The woman applying the polish made comments on the importance of caring for your feet, that a good man notices a woman with good feet.

She had long dark hair pulled back in a ponytail with pieces sticking out from the band. Her features were extreme, Mediterranean, with the dark, disturbed looks of one of Picasso's sitters. She appeared older than her probable age, her given beauty lost from poor life choices, but you could tell she had been attractive at one time the way a petit four looks enticing before a child chews it up and finds the need to open his mouth and show you what part of the digestive process it has reached.

In a nearby shoe store, I changed from my Pumas and bought a pair of mod orange-colored Dr. Scholl's to keep my nails from further smudging, annoyed that Saint Patrick's Day had passed, because I had a very interesting Irish flag effect happening down there.

When I arrived home, a package was resting on the wall beneath my mailbox, the old-fashioned "brown paper package tied up with string" kind. My stomach swished its happy swish typically designated for a few of my favorite things—holidays that involve presents and a Tupperware-sized Tasti-D-Lite when the featured flavor is Reese's.

The curvy penmanship unmistakable, it was a gift without being my birthday from my friend Lisa Morris, who used to work for Nike before giving her notice to travel for a few months before she would open a home furnishings boutique.

Opening the package (madly tearing at its edges), a billowy cotton gown floated from the wreckage. The top had latticed peephole embroidery like a paper cutout, seen on the heroine of a Victorian novel with her corkscrewed hair popping beneath a cotton shower cap. I caught it before it became blemished from an archipelago of dust mites floating on a sea of parquet.

Noticing a card, only slightly ripped from my decimating the package but still readable, I jigsawed a few important pieces together and felt my face boil with shame, overcome with my disrespect in not reading the card first.

The nightgown reminds me of when we were kids. Found the most terrific flea market in a small town near Dunkirk with booths peddling antique bed linens, clothes, and other heirlooms not wanted by the families of dead people. Stocking up for the new store. Yes, I am on a working holiday.

Doesn't this bring you back to dressing for bed, staying up late, and sneaking in Fantasy Island? "De plane! De plane!"

Love, Lisa

The words were artfully written, not chosen from a list of fonts, intuitive, and received without having to log on. Lisa was our housekeeper Dorit's daughter, the result of a British tourist's vacation who came away from his Jamaican holiday with more than a tan. She had that interesting blend of Island native with refined English features, a long, graceful build, but her eyes were what drew you in. They always glimmered with jubilance and were spaced far apart like the spider from *Charlotte's Web.*

We essentially grew up together; she and Dorit lived with our family, forever bound by shared trailer-park lunches of peanut butter and marshmallow Fluff sandwiches, a Zip-loc bag of smashed Oreos, and Yoohoo wrapped in tinfoil.

Feeling cheered by my unexpected gift, something seemed amiss once I walked into the apartment. A window usually shut was cracked open; added strands of hair were magnetized to the couch. What had been added, I couldn't place.

Moving through the kitchen, opening cabinet doors and the fridge, scanning the food choices even though I knew I wouldn't eat anything—the phone's ring ended this indulgent use of time, as well as saving me from shaking a can of Redi-Whip and foaming up my mouth so I'd look like a rabies-infected animal.

"Emily, dear. You really need to return my messages."

It was Mother.

"Hi, Mom. Listen. My horoscope in this month's *Vanity Fair* said that I needed to keep from speaking to family because it would only lead to unnecessary problems."

"But Emily—"

"Sorry, Mom, you won't be hearing from me for a month." Click.

And, truthfully, the *Vanity Fair* horoscope had been for the month of May, so I just gave myself over a month of not speaking to family—as good as a written doctor's note.

I went to my bedroom to take a college pre-bar-crawl-styled nap before beginning my work. The room had come together beautifully, a place that granted humans an opportunity to visit a celestial place. Always scented of gardenia from the Mathias candles I bought more than containers of Windex, silk curtains breathed from the breasts of windows, the spindled bed was in the same honey-colored wood as the floorboards. In each corner were marble columns that I bought from an antique shop that had more home wrecking detritus than hotel bars on Tuesday nights.

Putting on my new nightgown, it funneled down mellifluously. The style called for reading a leather-bound Dickens novel under the light of a beeswax candle. The embroidery was so intricate, with the emphatic cuts of patterns from stained glass, crafted from skilled fingers as opposed to electric metal bobbins. It felt sexy. Though this made Maidenform look X-rated by comparison, there was something licentious in feeling my nakedness beneath the pitched canopy of cotton.

Downstairs, I could hear the phone ring, probably Mother to pontificate that she had a week to berate me till May. I decided to let the machine care for her. Someone picked up the phone, probably J3, since he had to be home and pack before catching the red-eye tonight, and Henry wouldn't be back from work for another few hours.

I sat on the edge of the bed and tilted backward till I hit the mattress.

"Emily." Henry knocked on the door even though this was his room. I sat up.

"Hey, what are you doing home?"

"Unproductive day, so I decided to cut my losses and try again later this evening."

"Oh," I said, half listening.

He walked over to the bed and sat next to me. My knees crept closer to my chest.

"What are you wearing?" he said, grinning. "You look like a roll of toilet paper."

He then poked and tickled me, kissing a layer of Lorac off my lips. Imagine Pepe LePew mauling his unrequited feline.

"Please don't squeeze the Charmin," I said through clenched teeth and a few swats.

"So that was Daniel West on the phone. He returned from his trip and wants to meet with you."

"Okay," I said.

"Listen. We should talk."

Anything that starts "Listen. We should to talk" does not lead to something happy and fun. I plunged back onto the bed.

"Henry, no talking," I said to the ceiling. "I'm a brewing creative disaster on par with the Venus de Milo right before her arms get chopped off."

"Emily, it's important. Concerning our sex life. Or really, lack of one as of late."

I sat back up, not prepared for this subject. I knew that we'd been going through a dry spell, but vocalizing our abstinence seemed clinical.

"Hey, look at my green toenails," I said, extending my knee and wiggling my toes. "How cute are they? Martian green is the big color right now. *Allure* says so."

"And what would *Allure* say about going three weeks without sex when we normally do it every other day?"

Every other day? That seemed a bit excessive.

"Um. Haven't seen that article, but that's more of a *Cosmo* kind of thing, and I save *Cosmo* for doctors' waiting rooms. One of those guilty pleasures."

"Guilty pleasure?" Henry looked at me carefully. "I could really use a guilty pleasure."

I felt guilty, without the pleasure.

"Henry, it's okay not to have sex for a few weeks."

"We're newly engaged, Emily. We've just bought our first home together. All of the ingredients for passion. It's not like we've just had our first kid, for God's sake."

"Yes, something that won't affect us, considering that we won't be having kids."

Henry fiddled with the strap of his bag and then placed it between us.

"I've been logging on to some of the more prurient sites hosted on the World Wide Web, which have spurred some interesting ideas."

I pictured Henry logging onto teensluts.com and suddenly felt ill.

"It got me pretty excited, actually."

I would assume so.

"Spurred the imagination about what we can do to get back into the game, so to speak. How do you like the idea of 'Tricky Tuesday'?"

" 'Tricky Tuesday'?" I asked, my tone steeped in suspicion. "Is this some kinky spin-off of *Freaky Friday* the original, another Disney classic up there with *Herbie the Love Bug*? I really hate when they turn Disney classics into something lurid."

Henry shook his body like a dog drying off water.

"Emily. Listen!"

I controlled my face from making something scary and settled for a smirk.

"Every Tuesday morning, before I leave for work, we pick from a bag containing wrappers that have the names of various toys—toys that I have recently ordered."

"What?! Don't tell me you've had packages from some smutty sex shop sent to our place of domesticity."

"Would you clam it, Beaver Cleaver? And the Eager Beaver just so happens to be one of my top choices."

Henry's face brightened to an even more sinister glow as he took a catalogue from his satchel's side pocket. J. Crew it was not. Imagine pageant models in Chelsea store window poses, hands referencing sex toys in *Price Is Right* positions.

He had more pages tabbed with Post-Its than my *Vogue* spring shopping issue. His electronic shopping cart would be spilling over with the Glow-in-the-Dark Erotic Dice, Double Helix erection ring, Jack Rabbit vibrator, Smooth Scented lubricant that was modeled after my favorite collecting pastime—Scratch 'n' Sniff stickers.

Looking through pages of items that went perfectly with black leather medieval fashions in X-rated cuts, I felt smutty, and not in the sexy way Henry probably wanted me to feel. The only thing encouraging about the catalogue was their assurance of "safe, secure ordering" and "discreet packaging and shipping." Imagining a box of various sized dildos and porn films being sent in a fruit-of-the-month box.

"Henry," I said in my easing-a-tantrum-prone-child voice, "I can get off better with my electric toothbrush."

"Well then, we can just add that to the mix!"

My eyes rolled.

"Okay then," I said, lifting up my hands and waving him toward me.

"Do what you have to. Let's have sex. And if you can, make it sort of fast because I have a lot of work to do."

I plunged back onto the bed, thinking back to when Josh Bernstein had two tickets to U2 and his final cut for the extra ticket came down to Winston Fuller, his best friend, or me. He chose me. My validating his getting to second base so I could hear U2 play "I Will Follow" was completely justifiable.

Henry threw the catalogue to the floor and got up from the bed. I schemed on when I would collect and incinerate that catalogue without Henry's knowing. We then looked at the catalogue as a vantage point, where it slightly brushed the rim of my Hermes shopping bag with my new baby blue Birkin I had just picked up from being ordered—a gift I gave myself with all of my future earnings from becoming an insanely successful artist. The wispy bag toppled to its side, empty, setting off an internal alarm. Frantic, I ran over and shifted the bag over where the receipt and assorted pamphlets scattered to the floor in feather falling motions from the light wind I had caused.

"Where's my new Birkin bag?" I screamed.

"Chill," said Henry, walking over to the closet. "You already put it in its cedar cubby hole."

He opened the door to reveal the bag shelving system I had instituted. The bags looked like an Easter assortment of Godivas, my blue Birkin safely stowed in the top corner square. I sighed.

"Well, if that's not a huge relief."

Henry looked concerned by this.

"Emily? Do you love your new bag more than me?"

"Don't be silly! Of course not."

If he had referred to my cranberry red Birkin bag, there would have been a loaded pause. I had made considerable sacrifices for that bag, bought during my struggling illustrator phase. And we'd been going through a challenging period.

J3 slid into the door's frame, appearing to be in the process of making a knock before he saw us. He was dressed in jeans and a light jacket, similar to James Dean's red *Rebel Without a Cause* coat, but khaki colored. The strap of his black nylon duffle was sealed across his chest.

"Hey, you two. Glad I got you together. I'm off. Just for a few days, flying in for a meeting, and I'll be back—definitely by the first cocktail."

"That sounds simply awful," I blurted.

"Welcome to my world."

Henry watched our volley with that annoyed smirk of his.

"So, see you Friday. With Amanda."

Henry's face calmed to its packaged expression.

"Are you sure it's okay that I can't be here earlier to help?" he asked me.

"Yeah. Yeah," I said, flicking my hand as if trying to get it to work after it went limp. "We have caterers for all of that." Which was half true. In no way had I been prepared to throw this party, nearly missing sending the e-vites. Already I received an alarming number of RSVPs saying that they would be attending, no declines or maybes. I vowed to call the caterers first thing in the morning and figure how to get candy corn and popcorn balls in April without having to microwave them myself.

"Okay then," said J3. "Call me if you need any more help. And I like the nightgown, Emily."

Henry and I waved him off, though we should have voiced our good-byes, as he had already disappeared from the doorframe.

I got up, dressed out of my toilet paper wrapping and into paint clothes, and added an unnecessary layer of lipstick so I could look pretty for my art. Staring at the canvas that had been the subject of my current struggle, I added the last strokes on the painting I entitled "Mother and Mao" and became shocked upon discovering that it was past three AM. Too tired to sleep, I went into the office and watched dating programs with the production value of above-garage studios, where women wore bathing suits as clothes and the subconsciouses of the couples were exposed by pop-up bubbles. Amazing how easily newly formed partnerships could claim love.

32

The receptionist sitting behind the desk at the Daniel West Gallery gave me a wink, reminding me about the classic gesture of winking. He'd possibly be the one responsible for its comeback, along with others on the lost-but-now-hip shelf such as the fondue maker and beanbag chair.

Daniel West saw a couple out. They were lavish, almost obsequious in their praise to him about how he handled a Slavic collector into spending more money on their painting than its worth.

Something triggered when he saw me.

"Pixie!"

It's Emily.

"Well, let's have a look. Armand," he snapped to the winker behind the big desk, "help us move these paintings into the viewing room."

We looked like ants stealing place cards, each of us prodding a large canvas against our shoulder to the "Viewing Room," which served the function of "Conference Room" at my last meeting.

Leaning the portraits against the wall, Daniel steadied one eye on the paintings and then gave me a quick look in the same manner as Mother watching me splash for help in the kiddie pool while she chatted with her friends.

Daniel asked me if I would like mineral or sparkling. I would have liked the sparkling, but shook my head, Armand's cue to leave us alone. We went over the pleasantries, chitchatted about Daniel's trip, my work, and he then prattled about metaphorically, saying something about a woman and how she has the growth of a flower. She blossoms, has that moment of pure brilliance, and then withers.

I couldn't tell if I needed to follow the subtext and, if so, it wouldn't bode well for me. So I just smiled and chose to refrain from any discussions that demanded the analysis of subtext.

We both turned our positions to the canvases and fully concentrated on my work. It's a rather awkward experience, watching someone whom you don't know quite well looking subjectively at your life's calling. I would just as soon stand naked before him. At least the disastrous determination wouldn't necessitate a reconsidering of my life's calling.

Then he did that affected finger-to-the-nose bit with his lips puckered. I never assumed that Daniel wouldn't like my paintings and did not prepare for such an outcome. They were amazing—Daphne, J3, and Henry said so.

Daniel had this reflexive habit of taking a pace forward and then a few paces back. He smelled like aromatic oils, something with jasmine, but it probably came from his French-milled soaps, considering Daniel did not appear to be the bulgur eating, peace and harmony type.

At the portrait of Coffeehouse Pete, Daniel settled his hands on his hips, his right forefinger coiled like a streamer as if prepping for the grasp of his cell phone holster as he readied himself for a telecommunication showdown against Pete. My bra strap then collapsed from its resting point. I must have had a flesh-eating disease, as none of my bras were fitting lately. Though I'd rather have a flesh-eating disease than one that inflicted pain. Flesh-eating diseases go great with couture.

I became insecurely aware of the feel of rubbery band on my skin, the limpness of my breasts, and how they would inevitably sag like those old women pushing carts in the grocery store wearing patchwork house dresses with nude bra straps falling from their exposed shoulders. But if my breasts were shrinking, then they would be less apt to sag. I preferred that choice, but knew Henry would favor larger, sagging breasts.

No longer able to bear the silence, blubbering my way through the awkwardness, I began telling Daniel everything he needed to know about little Emily and Henry, giving away details I had never even considered myself, the way you BSed your way in philosophy class without reading the chapter.

I rambled about the Steiff giraffe I had painted into the picture—how it was a nostalgia/perpetuity thing. The stem of a Dum Dum lollipop dangling from FedEx Nick's mouth, I started talking about its significance and Halloween candy. Why was it that some homes gave out Mary Janes when they must have figured no one ever ate those? Sort of masochistic—in a pleasure/pain kind of way—and what did a Mary Jane even taste like? It never made it past the dated packaging, and wasn't cool in a retro way. I then invited Daniel to the Six Months to Halloween Party as a bribe for his saying something complimentary.

I loved Fruit Stripe gum.

"Fruit—"

"Pixie! Slow down."

I stopped talking in slamming-on-the-brakes delivery.

"This crazy three-legged cat creature."

Daniel pointed to Heroine. I nodded along, happy to hear him speak.

"Very clever. Sort of like the entity. Father. Son. Holy Ghost. Reincarnation. A spirituality for every man. This sitter is a deity."

"Exactly!"

I had no idea what he was talking about.

"Not only are your pieces true mastery—your color, caricaturizing the right features—but it's your use of symbolism, capturing the trueness behind the sitter."

I never thought of myself as a symbolic painter. Symbolism was very deep, almost spiritual. I felt really cool.

"It's moments like these when I become deliriously satisfied with my work. Every once in a while, I am presented with something that stretches even my imagination. Breaking ground. Giving the art world a new direction. I see it happening."

I believed my arms had just thrust up into "Score!" position.

"I'm going to sign you on!"

This man had just given me my happiest moment. What does one give to a stranger who gives you your greatest moment of euphoria without being naked or given a luxury good? I squeezed him in my arms.

"Okay then, Pixie," he said, laughing.

I'd prefer being compared to a woodland sprite, mischievous with great clothes, and wondered if the balance of control had now adjusted to my favor and I could address this.

Following Daniel toward reception, he prattled about the contractual process, numbers and percentages being thrown about like clothes in a Barney's dressing room. I had the vague idea that this would be important, and I should really be paying attention, but my focus was more attuned to the new Vuitton bag that would be taken from its front window display and paid for with my new earnings.

He continued with these seemingly important issues, saying that he would show the paintings privately, have a press viewing, and then hold my own exhibition. I then became very alert after hearing the words "forty percent cut" and wondered if showing my work via cyberspace would be more advantageous due to the low overhead and accessibility. But I never considered myself the thrifty type and flicked off the idea like lint from a sweater.

We agreed to touch base later in the week, and I then reminded him about the party. Daniel asked if he could bring someone, and I generously said he could invite as many people as he liked, but he declined my gesture, saying how he would only bring a guest. I wondered who that would be.

Walking back to the loft, veering to a more deserted avenue out of midtown to avoid contact with pedestrians because of the sparks that sweated from my body and having no interest in dealing with a lawsuit, I replayed the amazing day. The desire to return home then lost its appeal considering the message J3 left on the machine earlier, that he and Amanda would be arriving late tonight. The prospect of seeing Amanda drained my spirits like an ice cube in a glass of champagne.

33

I awoke dry eyed, but felt as if I'd spent hours crying with the kind of tears made by a child whose mother doesn't want to gamble a pair of Chanel sunglasses for a moment of quiet. Going through my morning routine, I couldn't shake the despair. Henry's side of the bed was fresh with his imprint, the duvet wrinkled in peaks and plateaus like grooves in sand. I made up the bed, wondering if Henry's recent habit of waking minutes before me had something to do with my policy that the last one awake must make the bed. I dressed in new clothes typically saved for an evening to impress and went downstairs.

Passing J3's room I slowed my pace, taking in the smell of sex and Rigaud candles. The door, partially open, gave me the right to look in. A black duffle and one of those suitcases where the wheels pressed inside the canvas like a hideaway bed spilled over with a lot of denim and clingy tops. I noticed a pair of black Jimmy Choos. Rather basic. They looked like the kind bought for a person who didn't own a pair of Jimmy Choos, getting their first ones in standard black stiletto for practicality.

I wanted to go through her things—see what labels she preferred, products she used, if she wore thongs or panties. Did she squirt her shampoo and conditioner into those little plastic travel bottles? Would she skimp with any cheesy drugstore brands? My impulse to snoop was squelched because I could not think of a good alibi quickly enough if caught.

Looking over the banister, I heard happy activity. A feminine voice was streaming through J3's and Henry's like a flute breaking through a sea of trombones and clarinets. It felt odd, hearing another woman's voice among the brusque tones of Henry and J3. I ran back up the stairs to inspect myself in the extra bathroom. My eyes were shrunken; it really did look like I had been crying. Luckily, I had on my fitted silver Dolce & Gabbana top and had the fantastic fortune of being granted a thin day.

I lingered outside the kitchen before making my entrance in hopes of overhearing something that would otherwise not be said in my presence. I worried that I'd be caught if J3 made a sudden exit, who I gathered to be closest to the entranceway, so I kept pacing back and forth so that if I was unexpectedly discovered, it would appear that I was about to enter the room. My focus on pacing made it difficult for me to concentrate on my discriminating-information-finding mission. The few words I did overhear had something to do with a trade tariff that would hit people working in steel mills who did not look like Jennifer Beals.

Walking into the kitchen felt like arriving at a party without a date, the clumps of guests broken out in pairs—this pair being a threesome. J3's eyes looked up expectantly while Henry and this rather attractive woman moved apart once she caught sight of me. She then rested her outspread hands on J3's back, coiling around him in the manner of a snake slithering up an apple.

Everything about Amanda was tall, sharp, radiant, and explosive—like one of the praised museums she designs in cities such as Milan, Rio, or Seville. She had the height, long dark hair with slips of caramel blonde running through the front strands that glistened when caught with light, thin, and she wasn't shopping for anything over a B-cup in the lingerie section, a mark against her from Henry.

She was the kind of girl who came with music when making an entrance, probably something by Alicia Keyes. Men probably asked her out on coffee lines. I bet she ate pizza without picking off all the greasy toppings. Her features were played up with good skin and the right makeup. While I found her eyes spaced too far apart as rather peculiar, I could see boys describing her as hot. She had the

low-slung jean/trendy top look that only worked if you lived in
Santa Monica and made regular sprees to Fred Segal.

Henry's laughter sputtered out like the exhaust of a dying car
once he spotted me. He dutifully joined my side, a moonbeam shin-
ing to my movements. I made the initial contact.

"Amanda? So glad to meet you. I'm Emily Briggs." I just sounded
like my mother, stumbling from this surprise like a candidate not
understanding a question. Her wrist, cuffed with a Cartier Milanese,
had an electric power that shot through me and sapped my confidence. She smiled, but I couldn't make out what it meant.

The clamorous chatter quickly resumed, my presence not inter-
fering with the momentum. They continued on about the U.S.'s
obligation to the refugees of some African country where the ruler
wore very bright clothes, the president leveraging the unrest to
viewpoints that profited his re-election platform. Amanda then jotted notes on the white of an actor's shirt on this month's *Vanity Fair*
cover, the latest issue I was shamelessly behind on. She then asked if
I had a piece of graph paper.

Oh, for God's sake.

I pulled my sketchpad from my bag and etched in boxes with a
blue pencil, sliding it over to Amanda. I used a fresh sheet to make
drawings of fairies and woodland sprites dressed in the latest fall
trends. I glanced over to make sense of Amanda's furious writing,
filled with equations seen on M.I.T. blackboards. I creased my
paper and surreptitiously dropped it in the trash.

Amanda brought up the calendar year and its impact on world
order just as I thought to introduce the popularity of surfer dialect,
if its emergence generated from Keanu Reeves in *Bill & Ted's Excellent Adventure* or could be traced even further back to Sean Penn's
Spicoli. Rationalizing that it would be best if I didn't contribute any
new topics at this time, I occupied myself with the preparation of
my breakfast, something I knew how to do better than anyone.

Still reveling in her new control, Amanda slipped in and out of
opinions on politics to the latest updates in scientific research the
way I changed shoes. Both J3 and Henry watched her, absorbed. You
needed to have a perfect score on your math SATs, subscribe to the
Nation, or play golf with a cabinet member to participate in this

conversation. I filled in the remaining milk of my cereal bowl with more Frosted Flakes.

Then I heard her say "Islamic fundamentalism."

Oh, please.

Amanda crammed erudite thoughts into the discussion the way I stuffed sweaters in a bulging suitcase. She now spoke about Rumsfeld and how he briefly worked under Reagan as an envoy in the Middle East.

"Did you know that Cheney and Rumsfeld were the two operatives behind the installation of a new president in case Reagan was killed in a nuclear attack?" I said, having no idea where this came from. Henry looked like he was on his fourth drink.

"And how do you know this, Emily?"

I had no idea.

"My friend. In the CIA."

"And who's your friend in the CIA?" Henry said with utter amusement.

"Ronald Judd."

Ronald Judd was my fourth-grade teacher.

"And did you also know that Rumsfeld was an executive of the company that brings you Equal?"

I shook my Equal packet happily—a trivia genius when the subject centered around artificially sweetened products.

"Museums!" Amanda then shouted, inflected in the same way I said "presents!"

A lot of mumbling then occurred, PBS sitting-around-a-wooden-table style. I knew public television was on a tight budget, but surely they could afford something more than the rejects of a library reading room.

"Isn't that right, Emily?" asked Amanda, her gaze prodding me to speak.

I remembered hearing something about the El Greco exhibit. I was going up in flames like El Greco's matchstick figures.

Mumbling a confirmation, the room looked at me, startled, until J3 moved on to another subject. Suddenly, I had a great idea—Amanda should go back to L.A.

I safely assessed Amanda to be the type that read Balzac by choice.

I don't know if she went to Vassar, but wouldn't be surprised if she began a discussion with, "when I went to Vassar," "what they really teach you at Vassar," or "the great thing about going to Vassar . . ."

After an inexorable volley on how fabulous Amanda was, J3 turned to me. This seemed to flummox both Henry and Amanda.

"How was that movie you went to the other night?" he asked, intended solely to me. Daphne and I had gone to the Angelica to see a British film set in turn-of-the-century India. The real lure was the costuming. The clothes were designed by one of our friends, who began her career as an accessories designer at Ralph Lauren.

"Good. A lot of people in white playing cricket. Colonialism is bad."

J3 smiled and then looked at his watch. I looked at my wrist, still no Cartier tank. He then announced his exit and kissed Amanda on the cheek, while his flattened hand brushed her stomach, causing her shirt to lift, which probably annoyed her, considering the Krispy Kreme she just inhaled. I gave a covert look to her stomach, excited by catching her in this unappealing moment. The cracker that my mother subsists on looked bloated in comparison. She had a very flat stomach.

"Okay, Jackson, and don't forget to give me the keys."

A guy named Jackson who I lived with gave keys to a woman who could resolve the Y2K mishap while wearing Jimmy Choos.

Henry waited a moment and then made excuses about loss of time and work. Leaving me alone with Amanda seemed somewhat conspicuous. I intended to paint today, but the idea of having the graciousness of someone who wears lime green capris with an Amish bonneted apron held no appeal. Since I had recently misplaced my watch (hidden in the wallet pocket of an old Fendi bag), I drummed up a plan to go on a watch-buying mission. Unless Amanda didn't have a use for hers anymore. As I was trying to make a quick exit, Amanda put down her cup of tea.

"A woman called for you earlier," she said.

"Really? I hope the phone didn't wake you. It's so early for you."

"Oh, no. No," she said as a side note, "it's actually late for me, California time."

I looked at the stove clock. 10:24 AM. 7:24 AM in California. Freak.

"I actually felt pretty bad answering the phone, but I gave a few people this number in case my cell needed recharging. Anyway, a Mrs. Fleming called. I'm afraid she was pretty upset."

Mrs. Fleming was another client my mother had brokered. A day in the life of Mrs. Fleming, similar to Mother's, was to conduct her appointments, be unjustly treated in the process, and then start a fury strong enough to roast a pig. I still hear her complain about discourteous houseguests she had seven years ago.

"This Mrs. Fleming mentioned something about how you made her look older, heavier," Amanda said, and then lifted up her bone of a wrist to make it understood that she still owned her Cartier Milanese.

"A battalion of the best plastic surgeons couldn't make that happen. I guess my brush can be seen as a sort of wand. Just call me Ponce de Leon."

Amanda looked as if her body suddenly hosted a demon. I took this to mean that she did not find my brand of humor funny. Of course, she had to be the self-righteous, do unto others, never sell after-given-insider-information type.

I thought of her pedigree, her brilliance as an architect. Celebrities invited her to their Big Sky ranches, titans flew her on their private jets, designers gave her dresses, curators wooed her, and she probably didn't give an iota for the payback unless a check for her services would be provided. And here she was picking up the phone, being keyed in to my vocational inadequacies from Mrs. Fleming, some weathered socialite living off of her second husband's inheritance made from introducing the New Car Smell air freshener.

"I waited till everyone left to tell you. I'm all too familiar with the unrealistic demands of a client."

She spoke confidently, her face having a hostile takeover from a blazing smile. Amanda may have been going for a tête à tête moment here, and I had to approach my next words delicately—sound appreciative, intelligent, but still be the one who controlled the power.

"Cool. Thanks."

I've always been better at expressing my emotions visually.

"Okay then. Big day planned," I said, wanting to execute my evacuation plan.

"Really? What's on your agenda?"

To buy a watch I couldn't afford, whereas she probably received hers in a gift bag at the luncheon of a Hollywood producer's wife.

"Meetings. Lunch with my rep," I said, trying to act important by mentioning the man I had two meetings with in my entire career. "And how about you?"

"I did schedule some meetings as well, but all I really want to do is be indulgent. Go for a walk in the park, buy something ridiculously expensive just for the shopping bag, and eat something off a grill from a city street vendor that I'll regret later. But I'll probably just end up calling my office and doing damage control."

I was so inadequate.

"Well, let me know if you need anything. Perhaps we could meet up later to take in some of that New York activity."

I hoped she wouldn't take me up on this.

"That's very kind of you, but I'd better stick to my original plan. Jackson told me how busy you are."

Whoever this Jackson was, he had a wildly uninformed conception of my disposable time.

Amanda then put her mug in the dishwasher and picked up a few papers from the table. It seemed that she lived here and I was the visitor.

"In fact, Jackson's always talking about you. That's why I feel so comfortable around you. Kind of like we've already met."

And I had no idea what she was about, aside from the *New Yorker* profile I had read almost ten times until the omission of pictures became a situation.

"Yes, I know what you mean. I feel the same about you."

Leaving Amanda to get ready for my day, I went to the bedroom and saw Henry through the opened door of the bathroom. He studied himself in the mirror, slipping his product-laced fingers through his hair. He had changed into a purple shirt that fastened with the hooks and clasps of a bra.

"Are you wearing a Dior?"

Henry looked at his shirt and then at me through the crack of the door, pushing it open.

"I don't know," he said, surely lying.

"When did you buy a Dior?"

"Someone from the office gave it to me."

"Someone from the office gave it to you? Since when did you steal Andre Leon Talley's job at *Vogue?*"

Henry turned off the bathroom light and came into the bedroom, standing so close to me I could feel his breath.

"You didn't have your cell phone today."

"Thank you for telling me that."

"I tried calling you."

"Why would you call me on my cell phone when I never use it?"

"Because I do that sometimes. I like to hear your voice without having to listen to the millions of little details you manage to get into over something like a raspberry fat-free bar you discovered at some health food store."

"Do you know where they sell raspberry fat-free bars?"

"Why didn't you have your cell phone today?"

"Because I Windexed Jackson's cell phone."

And that ended the cell phone inquiry.

"So? What do you make of Amanda?" Henry asked, saving me from having to bring her up.

"Nice. Smart. Pretty. Shrewd. And you? What do you think of her?"

Henry took a moment, apparently to consider his next words carefully.

"Hard to tell really. Seems nice."

Silence.

"What I find funny is that she never would have struck me as the type to be with J3," he said.

This fascinated me.

"Really. In what way?"

Amanda then stepped into the doorframe. Her timing paralleling a Lenny and Squiggy entrance, and I had to speculate whether she'd been eavesdropping. How dare she.

"Hey, guys," she said, tapping on the door. "Is it okay if I set myself up in the downstair office? Make some calls and catch up on paperwork?"

As she said this, she wound her two hands in the rim of her shirt, mopping up her flat tummy stuffed with a Krispy Kreme eclair with clothed fingers. I watched Henry look at her belly as if there were two arrows pointing downward with the words "Lift Here for Amanda Details."

"No, no," he rambled. "I was going to work from home because I have a creative deadline, but I don't want to be in your way."

Henry did work from home on occasion, typically during deadlines for his drawings when his creativity could be compromised by office activity. I enjoyed when we both worked at home, as it broke the monotony of my day, and I knew never to ask him if he wanted to have a leisurely lunch or escape to a matinee.

Wondering what basis I had in offering any suggestions to Amanda's dilemma, I said, "J3's offices are on Park Avenue South. Quite circuitous from anything interesting, and getting there would really crunch into your time. I'm not painting today, so you might as well take advantage of staying here."

I walked over to my bureau and thumbed through my planner till I found some particularly ink-free weeks, settling on February 15, when we went away skiing. I then jotted down Henry's cell phone number and extended my hand while making slow paces toward Amanda till she greeted me halfway.

I'd have to use Henry's mobile, which gave me a legitimate reason to answer his phone. I could just allow the caller to ramble on, gather information, until actually cuing them that Henry wasn't available.

"Call me later if you want to go shopping, have a coffee or something," I said to Amanda, the tips of my fingers wiggling the note in the motions of throwing paint from a brush.

She took the paper, studied the writing, and folded it in half.

"Thanks for this," she said with promises of seeing us later.

Henry had moved out of his previous space and into the closet to change his shirt. He mumbled something about his career, some pivotal hire that could determine cancellations—unimportant chitchat.

"Where do they have raspberry fat-free bars?" I asked.

34

A violet haze broke through the bedroom in a funneled light the same shade as my Bergdorf bag. The halogen glow emanated from one of those glorious spring late afternoons when it's about to storm. I'd had the good timing to finish the errands of the day before nature's entertainment would grumble and then stage her big performance.

I found Henry with his knees bent, his head jutted in and out in the motion of an Egyptian dancer; the movements probably lacked the rhythm of the music that played in his headphones. He suddenly busted out into ecstatic verse, a newer tune—the Wallflowers, I believed—but Jacob Dylan he was not.

Only when he began pounding his fist into the air did he notice my scrutinizing glare. Embarrassed by my discovery, he snapped off the headphones to address my presence. I could only smile. I, too, am familiar with a private moment and its persuasive childlike playfulness, mine usually in the form of dancing to my guilty pleasure of ABBA songs.

I dropped the bags and moved to him as if being pulled by a T-bar while gliding on skis. My knees collapsed and I fell to his side. It'd been so long since I'd just sat, stared, and did nothing. Dropping my head into the hole formed by Henry's Indian-style crossed legs, I focused on the darkness. The ripples of his copper colored denim pants brushed against the darkness, looking like canyons in the night sky.

I dove into the black pool of nothingness, closing my eyes to further seal off any cracks of escaping light. I swam in a sea of black until I saw two lights. I couldn't quite tell if they came from flashlights or the glimmer of someone's eyes. It felt warm in between his legs, slightly damp and humid.

Hearing a tap, I woke up dreamily. Amanda reappeared at the door in the same clothes and position I last saw her. The band of her Cartier caught a glimmer of light, and it made Tinkerbell motions across the room. I became jealous that she had that watch, the watch I've always wanted that my parents wouldn't indulged me in for fear it would postpone my finding a suitor who should attend to this need.

"J3 wanted to know if you guys wanted to rally it up tonight. Perhaps Ciprianis or something," she said in an insouciant yet faked delivery, covering up what she may have assumed was interrupting a private moment.

I looked to Henry for guidance, wanting him to make the decision. He stroked my hair and pinched my cheek. We shared a smile. Turning to Amanda, he said, "You guys should have a night to yourselves."

"All right then," Amanda responded, not retreating from her post of supporting the doorway with her weight. I wasn't sure if she wanted to add something or was waiting till one of us addressed her. I adjusted from my lying position in an effort to do something other than spew out polite chatter.

"What's that you're reading?" asked Amanda, her head nodding to my bedside table in a final pitch to legitimize her post. I looked to the book she referred to, Proust's *Swann's Way*. Daphne couldn't soldier through it, pawning it off on me. The book had been a runway for dust since I had moved in, though I am now on to the newest Perricone health book.

"Proust's *Swann's Way*. I'm reading it for the latest translation," I said, hoping she wouldn't press me for character specifics.

"I would love to get lost in a good book."

"You can borrow it."

"No, thanks. And how sweet of you, but I typically read novels in their original language."

Of course you did.

"So, see you later then," she said, disappearing by the breath of her last word.

With the added height given from my butt resting on my legs, I stared down at Henry, who fiddled with his iPod till he seemed quite taken by my grateful smile.

"What's gotten into you?" he asked, tugging me back downward by slipping his hand around my waist.

I fell onto his lap, staring into his face. With one arm to my side, I extended the other and brushed his cheek, which had a Saturday scratch to it from his not shaving this morning. Henry rubbed my belly and focused on the bureau as if it were playing the news. This went on for quite some time. My eyes absorbed into his while he seemed entranced by smoothing my stomach. I focused on the rhythm of his strokes and tried to make out if he had been drawing something. Sometimes I did that; when my arms were around his neck, I'd scratch Henry's back and make sketches, typically in the forms of stilettos and little punches that followed the strand of a diamond necklace. But Henry just seemed to be washing away my stomach.

"What's in the bags?" he said. His voice had an alarming boom due to the long lapse of silence.

"The Bergdorf one has purple fishnets and such."

"Purple fishnets!" he said, sounding like Peter Brady going through his "Time to Change" period, only missing all of the "sha la la las," which I began to hum in my head.

"I can't quite decide what I want to be for our party," I said, walking to the bag to retrieve the fishnets and then slinking back into my previous spot.

"And so what costume would purple fishnets be for?"

He took them from my hand, studied them like they were weird goo left from a departed space ship, and then went back to patting my tummy.

"I don't know, but they are awfully cute."

Henry stopped patting my stomach to look at me. When I registered his gaze, he went back to making his circular motions.

"And what bag of tricks can be found in the gray one?"

I looked over to the Saks bag, and my eyes brightened.

"So much fun! I forgot what a bonus it is to not buy beauty products from Sephora. I got two FGPs!"

He looked concerned.

"FGP?"

"Free Gift with Purchase." He really could miss the obvious.

"Wait a second. Weren't you supposed to buy a watch?"

When Henry stopped his rubbing, I lifted my head up, returned to my knees, and then fully zigzagged myself up to standing position.

"Yes," I said despondently. "It's just that I was about ten grand short. So I made up for it by buying fishnets, thongs, lip plumper, and a bronze buffer."

"I can't wait to see what you're going to be for Six Months to Halloween! And what do you really make of Amanda?" he asked, abruptly shifting topics.

I didn't respond immediately, trying to gather my thoughts so I could sound sincere, considerate, yet not too adulating, because Amanda was not the character you rooted for on a Romance Channel movie.

"Nice. Pretty. Smart," I said, amazed at my flair with words. "Why? What's your take? Really?"

"I expected her to be cool. It's just that hanging out with her today, she acted strange."

I raised my brow in its "pray tell" position. I did wonder how their time at home today progressed.

"J3 never said anything to you about her moving in here, did he?"

I answered by shaking my head. He didn't stop looking at me until I said that I had no idea.

"Why? Did she say anything to you?"

"Not overtly. I mean she kept mentioning how great the place is. And then it got progressively weirder—how this is the perfect space to raise kids. That she never would have thought of moving to New York because it's not a place to have children, but in a place like this she could rescind her previous assessment. Don't you find that kind of weird?"

No!

"Sure. I suppose."

"And then I found her inspecting the cabinets, but not taking anything out. Heard a lot of opening and shutting of doors."

Amanda did not sound like an experienced snooper.

"I thought I should just give her the floor plan," he said, followed by his familiar jocular look.

"You may be making more out of this than you really should."

He may have really been on to something.

"Perhaps."

The room became silent. I thought how it would be a good time to look through Amanda's things now that I'd be in the clear with her out to dinner. It seemed completely justifiable, considering she presumably had taken similar liberties today.

Hmm. Did I have anything incriminating that she could have found? There were those bowed Ferragamo shoes in the hall closet that I wore to lunches with Mother, which I had to get around to tossing.

"She's smart," said Henry promisingly, from nowhere. "But not at all as pretty as you."

Did I miss something? Were we in a pageant and Henry had the clipboard?

"She's gorgeous!" I said, amazed that I now found the need to defend my greatest competitor. "Sometimes, Henry Philips, you astound me. I feel like you're in search of a Harvard MBA with the measurements of a Mud Flap girl."

Henry curled me up in his arms, smiling affectionately.

"But you're that girl!"

Nudging myself into a comfortable position within his embrace, I began to zone out to the pattering rain and thought about my costume.

"Where would I be able to find purple wings?" I asked.

Henry gave me directions to a costume store located in the Flatiron District. My mind zoomed in on the vicinity, but I suddenly became lost by the streets' fragmentary grids in that area.

"There's a small sweet shop that sells Tasti D-Lite just two blocks south."

This nugget of information pinpointed the location.

"Why don't you come with? We could find you a green leather loincloth, a little felt cap, and shoes that curl up at the toes."

Henry gave me a what-a-cute-idea-but-you-know-it's-not-happening smile. He never accompanied me shopping. The few times he did, he made me wait. We rarely even did errands together unless he needed my assistance buying Christmas presents, which are now bought after asking his family to give him lists with URLs.

"So we're good?" said Henry, his tone considerably more serious.

"We're good," I said.

We both locked into a stare. Henry lifted up my shirt without taking his eyes off me. He did this cautiously, but would not hesitate even if I gave an objectionable gaze. Massaging my breast, his focus inimitable, holding me captive in that penetrating stare of his.

35

Watching the rise and fall of Henry's chest for about 1,800 breaths, it dawned on me that I was awake despite the fact that it was after 3:00 AM. I slipped on Henry's pajama bottoms and tiptoed around the bed, trying to figure how being on your tiptoes wouldn't give you away.

I went to my canvases, flicked through them as if they were huge records stacked within alphabetical dividers, and found the painting that called off my search—Henry's and my wedding portrait. My eyes scanned the image of us like a husband hunter reading the pre-nup.

The outline was simple but workable, the two of us side by side. Studying the image intrigued me with a mix of awe and scrutiny, the way you look at photos of yourself from a past time, trying to recall the circumstances of your life when the picture had been taken.

I took a brush from its cup, began mixing paints in the primary colors of Fritz Lang Films, and painted for what seemed like hours till I decided that I needed a water break. A pint of frozen yogurt, one can of Redi-Whip and two bowls of Frosted Flakes later, I just sat in the kitchen and did nothing.

Henry had this habit of posing a challenge to me. He'd ask if I could sit still for fifteen minutes, in the manner of a parent manipulating a hyper child to simmer down during a car trip. Taking him on his dare, after two minutes I found no constructive purpose in sitting and doing nothing.

Now, sitting and doing nothing, I looked at the bulbs I planted in a steel box I bought from Smith & Hawken; the stems hatching from the peeled bulb put on a daily show. I then saw the stem slither and twitch like a stealthy snake about to inhale his furry prey.

Looking around the kitchen, saying "did you see that" to the closed cabinets, I turned back to the bulbs so they could dazzle me with an encore.

"What are you doing?" asked J3, rubbing his eye with his fist.

"Watching the stems move."

J3 took a bowl from the cabinet and poured from the opened box of Frosted Flakes, then seated himself next to me. Adding the milk, he then stared at the stems in a hypnotic trance more in tune with watching an *E! True Hollywood Story* after an exhausting day.

The stems no longer moved.

"So why are you up?" I asked.

"Can't sleep. And you?"

"Same. Then I became inspired."

J3 fed a spoonful of soggy flakes into his mouth.

"I saw the canvas. Revisiting your wedding portrait, I see."

I tried to study his face, but his mouth crammed with another spoonful of flakes.

"Oh. Right. I should really get back to that."

I started to get up from my seat, giving one last soulful look at the bulbs.

"J3," I said in a whisper.

His eyes responded with a comforting look.

"Will you give a light holler if the stems move again?"

He nodded that he would.

"J3?" I asked.

Again, he responded with a look.

"Why J3? Why not J4?"

"Because I'm the third Jack."

"Right. Clever. Got it."

I started to make my exit.

"And what exactly does that mean?"

I've never been one for card games.

"My grandfather and father are named Jack. It got confusing at family holidays, so I became J3."

I thought of a little J3 bobbing up and down like a pogo stick from the sight of all of his presents, his father and grandfather eying one another with appreciative glances.

"Cute and clever," I said, which could also be used to describe J3's girlfriend, sleeping in a bed just above this ceiling.

Returning to the portrait, nearly completed, I couldn't draw myself back in. My previous analysis was that the painting had been going along swimmingly, but now it lacked depth, beauty, and any cleverness. In fact, it was a disaster. I couldn't paint. In fact, I'd be so lucky if I could make an artistic income by gluing a bunch of stones together, shaping them into cows, pigs, and other barnyard animals, and selling them in church bazaars with the crafts of ladies who dyed their hair from kits that came with latex gloves.

I wanted to call a do-over, splash the canvas with white paint, start again—feeling that there was no use in keeping it just because I already put the time into it. I'd make a career change. People changed their lives all the time. Judges who accepted bribes get hired as advisers to television shows. Mary Jo left Joey Buttafucco. I wondered what Mary Jo was up to. The name Mary Jo seemed incongruous to Long Island, more appropriate for the Jerry Falwell belt.

36

I made late-night dinner plans as an excuse to miss Amanda's early departure for a "work thing," just another shift of drama in her direction that needed to be downplayed. Daphne's husband had the good timing of being at a health conference held on a golf course. Daphne loved being the wife of a doctor—a golf widow with three weeks off from him a year as an added perk. We did what we normally do when her husband is away, which involves a blender and tequila, which meant more for me considering Daphne couldn't drink, something to do with the liability of toe counts and having a child that stuttered.

Lifting my head from the pillow, either the insides of my head gained a few pounds, I caught a brain tumor, or experienced my first hangover in weeks. I put on Henry's pajama bottoms and started my search for their owner, finding Henry in the kitchen. He placed his tumbler-sized mug that steamed with espresso on the table so he could approach me unencumbered. Henry looked determined, suctioning a perfunctory kiss to my cheek that clued me in that he had things to discuss.

Henry did not pull through on his liquor obligation, liquor fueling the success of a party, and didn't know if he'd be able to properly attend to his sole assignment, as he had lost control of his day.

Glossing over his incomplete task with a bad joke, saying he just couldn't follow simple directions, he had the good fortune—or clever timing—to benefit from my current state of exhaustion, as I was unable to sentence the appropriate ruling of grief he deserved.

My fingers became lost within my hair. I thought of memorable drinks served to me from hotels with $500-a-night rooms. The chocolate martini, Stoli sour apple, and, my favorite, the vanilla buzz—champagne and vanilla vodka. It was just as well that Henry didn't meet his responsibilities, since now I'd get what I really wanted.

Watching J3 as he made his entrance, I prepared a mug of decaf cinnamon spurted fresh from a chromed spigot. Unlike Henry, who had his own espresso machine that could double as a mechanic's shop for small electronic appliances, and who followed his morning routine with the precision of an autistic, J3 seemed comforted by adhering to my pattern.

We all clung to the safety positions of our usual spots. I became excited from thinking of the lavish praise I would receive from guests loving my drinks, and considered inviting the publishing editor I had met at one of Anne's parties so I could effectively pitch a book idea on inventive cocktails tied to party themes.

J3 seemed more upbeat than usual. I wondered if his good spirits resulted from his recent time spent with Amanda, or because she was now gone. I decided to think it was because she was gone.

"Have you guys heard of 'A Man Against It'?" J3 asked.

I was never one for Broadway with Times Square such a migraine and the tourists—those visitors who make the annual trip to The City, dine on overpriced pasta and cappuccino, and then see The Show. Their Playbills were saved and coveted—sometimes even framed to memorialize their once a year event and added to the collection of other Playbills that hung on the wood-paneled basement wall.

"A Man Against It?" asked Henry. He looked at J3 quizzically.

"Yeah. Supposedly some cool beach town in the Hamptons."

"You mean Amagansett!" I said, with the kind of laughter you make when your granny asks a question with an answer involving a sexual position.

"Right. Amagansett. Anyway, a guy from my company has a beach house there. He's being transferred to Europe and is giving me a good deal for a summer rental. What do you think? Summer weekends at the beach?"

I began planning my outfits.

"Amagansett," huffed Henry. "Georgica is the place to be."

Henry's comment made me squirm, feeling uncomfortable in my normally happy place. He acted like the guy who jumped into party pictures with socialites with five-syllable names.

Once, in a moment of intimacy—after sex—Henry told me that the dinette set in his childhood home, which he ate his holiday dinners from, had been a prize his mom won from *The Price Is Right*. She made a trip to L.A. with some of her "girlfriends," getting tickets from calling the number given at the end of the show to be a member of their studio audience. His mother always knew her prices. An economy-sized Windex at Duane Reade cost $3.89.

"Is *The Price Is Right* still on the air, or did Bob Barker become too old and weak to spin the wheel? Or maybe he just died," I said to Henry, not looking at him.

"And Amagansett is wonderful," I added, again purposely avoiding Henry's reaction. "The real Hamptons, more beachy, and you won't see as many surfboard racks at Georgica's beach. For surfing," I said, putting down my cup and fully directing my comment to Henry.

For a moment I saw him in the light of a past time, where we both shared a secret and it drew us closer. I became hopeful. With Henry's sudden brightness, J3 seemed enticed to throw in other lures the house offered. We agreed to make a drive this weekend so we could inspect the place before making any final commitments.

J3 then reached into his wallet. I wondered if he owed me money and became excited. His fingers wiggled into a pocket made from a slit of the leather and took out a wad of business cards and a crumpled Xerox. Picking at the paper's four corners, he unfolded it and then smoothed it against the table. I walked over to look at the object of his fastidiousness, which, I assumed, was a picture of the house. This adorable clapboard came from a time when men wore hats you could serve nachos in and woman purposefully dressed in skirts that gave the illusion of floatable thighs. The wood planks were dark cedar, with a door painted in patina green like a patch of moss clinging to a log.

I felt my skin turn crispy from a day of beach activity. Smelled the fish marinating in sauces bought from markets selling their cookbooks at the checkout counter. Imagined an evening sitting over local wines and foods cooked by someone other than myself. Henry became more occupied by another piece of the detritus scattered about the table.

"When did you give this to J3?" asked Henry, sliding the business-card-sized piece of paper in my direction. I pinched its edge and dragged it to my view. It was a drawing I made during a trip to L.A. of my cartoon character Lily. Her nose was pointed to the Hollywood sign, her thoughts suspended from the day's routine to fantasies of shopping for accessories, attending parties where you give advice to celebrities based on their horoscope, and being doted on wrapped in white terry cloth.

I vaguely remember giving J3 one of my scrap sketches from that workday conducted on an office lounge chair. It must have been over a year that he had this drawing, stored in a wallet pocket typically reserved for pictures of the wife and pudgy babies.

J3 folded the Xerox of the house into tight, origami corners and laid it as the foundation where he shuffled the remaining cards into a neat square. I threw my etching into the compactor of his hands.

"The Chateau Marmot," I said. "We had just met."

He smiled while Henry drank from his empty mug.

J3 put away his dishes and gathered his things, preparing for an earlier than usual departure due to a possible trip he had to make to L.A. His cell phone then rang, and he left the room to attend to the call.

Henry made comments about the house in Amagansett, saying it looked small and dark, how perhaps we should consider renting a place upstate this summer. I thought of mosquitoes and buying milk and the paper at a gas station mart. He then said Europe. Europe? We'd travel to France, rent a villa in one of those seaside villages where Matisse and Picasso had painted.

Villa? St. Tropez. Paris! The Ritz!

I couldn't remember the last time I had been in Paris. My wardrobe could benefit from a European makeover. And to have a beach holiday where I'd wear headscarves with sunglasses and bikinis that could fall apart with a pull of a string. We'd shade ourselves under an arrangement of striped umbrellas at our usual spot at the beach. I'd daintily situate myself in sidesaddle position on the seat of a bamboo bike while Henry peddled us into town to market for our dinner bought from outdoor vendors, stuffing our produce in fishnet sacks.

I gave him an approving look, along with questions on how he could manage leaving the country with his work obligations. Henry reminded me that the entertainment industry slowed during the summer months.

"Thinking about financing a film," said J3 when he returned into the kitchen.

"An update of *Sixteen Candles,* called *Thirty-Six Candles.* The Molly Ringwald character meets up with the geeky Anthony Michael Hall character and Jake Ryan. The dilemma—who does she choose!"

After an affected laugh, I said, "That's the most ridiculous idea I ever heard."

That was the most brilliant idea I had ever heard.

"And can you please tell me who she ends up with?"

I made a point not to study J3's reaction. Henry was looking at me, baffled.

J3 made his exit after taking a green banana, which should be put at the bottom of his bag to ripen, as I instructed in a muffled voice.

Henry and I were now left in near quiet, aside from the tapping of him flossing his teeth with a fingernail. Perhaps he just poked his tooth, because shoveling out plaque buildup with his nail would be gross.

The phone rang, the signal causing Henry to remove his finger from his mouth so he could attend to the call. After saying I was available before consulting me, Henry handed me the phone. I began to worry, not having paid close enough attention to which hand he used to pick up the phone and which one had been groping the insides of his mouth, and then he left the room before I had time to ask.

"Pixie, Daniel here. Great news!"

Great news!

"So I had that crazy painting of yours with the wrinkled dog and buggy lady. Olive Harper came by for one of her shopping visits—asked me how much it was. I said 45 and she took it. No negotiations!"

"45?" I asked calmly. "Do you mean $45,000 dollars?"

"No. Rupees. Of course, dollars! What do you take me for, a dealer that shows paintings in the lobbies of Marriot Hotels? And it even gets better. She came with my editor friend from *Vanity Fair*. He's doing a profile of young hot artists and may want to consider you in the mix."

"Daniel, this is so great, but I have to call you right back."

I hung up the phone to scream. Then, floating from this hyper activity, I jumped up and down. After getting in a few effective rushes from the jumps, realizing the amount of energy I still had, I did a few leap-frog exercises from back in my field hockey pre-season training days to take advantage of this fitness spurt. Running to each side of the kitchen and touching each corner could have the makings of a feng shui exercise class. I returned Daniel's call once my breathing calmed down.

This call had less excitement than the original news. I wanted to continue the euphoric momentum and became annoyed with Daniel for turning the conversation into a discussion involving business matters that required note taking and comprehension skills.

Ending the call with an excuse about a phantom appointment I was late for, I thought of calling my mother. That idea fleeted faster than handsomely dressed shrimps on a cocktail tray, because I didn't want her ability to find the negative in something purely positive to dampen my current three-times-a-year moment.

I called J3, only to get his voice mail. Not wanting to discuss my news over the phone, I left a message, asking who they'd consider for the Molly Ringwald character and Jake Ryan part. And if they were going to cast the original actors, would it be possible to meet Michael Schoeffling?

"What was going on down here?" said Henry, returning into the kitchen. His opening of the fridge swathed him in an entering-a-spaceship glow without the vapors of smoke.

"Great news! Great, great news!" I exclaimed, folding my arms against my chest, making little jumps like a doggie about to be thrown a biscuit.

"So I gather you have some news?"

"Daniel sold the Mom and Mao painting for $45,000 and *Vanity Fair* is considering including me in a profile! Sold a painting to my first stranger—45 big ones!"

I paused. Henry was silent.

"*Vanity Fair.*"

I paused. More Henry silence.

"I never knew I'd be so thrilled to reach the 45 number so quickly and unexpectedly."

Henry put his keys in his satchel and rifled about the insides. His fists punching the canvas had the ferocity of a caffeinated ferret captured in a bag. Still looking in his sack, he said, "But I thought you hated publicity?"

"*Vanity Fair* isn't publicity—it's a career move."

Henry now stuck his head in the bag in a lion-tamer performance.

"Need some help there, Henry?"

"I can't seem to find—" He gave a dramatic pause.

Your self-esteem perhaps? Henry's reaction to my news filled me with a mix of disappointment and suspicion. His competitiveness became the extra slab of butter you unnecessarily spread on your dinner roll. I competed with prep school educated artists who interlock fingers with the Donald and say "yo, wassup," not with my fiancé.

"All right then," Henry said, studying me. "This is great news. Well done. And sorry about the liquor."

37

As I opened the door to the costume store, it made the welcoming sound of the local penny candy, playing the cowbell chime attached to a chain-link cord. The tip of my pointed flat stubbed into a missing piece of linoleum, causing me to stumble with a fall that must have looked worse than it was. Luckily, no one witnessed my blunder. Aisles of mannequins, likely salvaged from Bonwit Teller circa 1978 with their bloated heads and garish makeup applications, were dressed in costumes that had the effect of a municipal building masquerading the offices as a haunted house for the holiday. Every aisle seemed to have a banal theme—superheroes, monsters, or your favorite politician—and the only original idea would be taking the effort to buy an original costume.

Hearing the cowbell chime, my breath suspended its pattern by the entrance of the person I had just been thinking about but did not expect to see. J3. It was like pouring a prize into your bowl from a box of healthy cereal. I watched his eyes sweep the room, having fun in interpreting his look that had a mix of trying to locate me and take in the place that, in a city like New York with its many map shops, dog massage parlors, and booksellers that only sold war novels, may not have a competing costume store.

After his head stopped its rotating spin upon successfully tracking me, he stepped over the missing square of linoleum and joined my side with the elegant stride of a fedora-wearing sleuth. J3 wanted to say good-bye before he left for an unexpected meeting in L.A. This could have been interpreted as excessive, but J3's unpredictable gestures were like a city inhabitant making a fuss over the assorted lobster choices from a menu in Maine.

J3 could write a software program while waiting for a dinner table, draft business plans on a cross-country flight, and take in a museum exhibition before giving a poster-sized check to the mayor. Days moved at a different pace for him, his mind always in ascending position.

I had on the hat from a Little Red Riding Hood costume. J3 said that I looked like the Sun Maid Raisin girl. I quickly took off the hat. After agreeing that the fun of a Halloween party would be compromised by not having the opportunity to design your own costume, we left the store. Parked in front of a sign informing of the cycle of street cleaning, Edward, J3's driver, put down the *Post* once he caught sight of us. J3 took my hand and, without even rationalizing my actions, I found myself in the backseat of the car.

"Lunch. Princess Diner," he directed Edward.

"Did I miss this memo?"

He smiled at me, not taking into consideration what I had said.

"Perhaps I can offer you a Dum Dum," I said, opening my bag cushioned with Dum Dum lollipops that I'd found at a Korean deli off Houston, buying them in bulk for FedEx Nick, the party, and to replenish that 3:00 PM drop in blood sugar.

J3 shook his head, declining my offer.

"Are you sure? Fat-free!"

Edward turned his head to secure our attention. I pulled out a grape Dum Dum, thinking he wanted one, but his intent was to remind J3 of his flight times. J3 nodded, thanked Edward, and then brushed his forefinger against my hand.

"I want you to have lunch with me before I leave. This diner in Queens is just great."

That J3 had a definite lunch place, a diner in Queens no less that I'd have to jab him about later, made me think he ate there regularly. I imagined J3 in this feeding/travel ritual that I had no prior awareness of, and wanted to experience it firsthand.

After consulting my business planner that had alarmingly more

tasks assigned to organizing this party than career obligations, I
agreed to accompany him, having signed-waiver-for-field-trip anticipation. The tunnel swallowed us up with no competing commuting
traffic; even the perpetually congested ramp opened up, as if the
roadways wanted me to accompany J3.

It felt comforting to drive to a restaurant and park in an actual
parking lot, rather than visit another establishment squashed between the Starbucks and Gap that marked every city block in the
universe. A sign was lit with shrunken bulbs that advertised the
perks of having chops and seafood 24 hours; rubbery stones bulged
from the concrete, appearing to be superglued. Through the double swinging doors, we looked over a sea of banquettes upholstered
in Naugahyde, Formica tables flecked with glitter, and slips of orders taped along the cutout wall where you could watch the short-
order cook flip burgers, a diner-style attraction like Beni Hana
chefs somersaulting shrimp into the air.

The restaurant seemed to be vacant, possibly from being after
three on a Wednesday afternoon in Queens. My scan settled on two
men, both crouched in the far corner booth who seemed to be here
for the warm place to sit rather than the cuisine, though they did
strike me as not the type to choose a restaurant based on a *New York*
magazine review. Their coffee mugs were topped off by a waitress as
they discussed whatever business one discusses in Queens diners in
the middle of the afternoon.

Choosing to sit on the swivel chairs for the fun swivel factor, I
asked the waitress if they had blueberries. They did not have blueberries—everything went blank. I thought back to the weekend
breakfasts I'd had when I dated a boy who lived in a fourth floor
walk-up above the Gracie Diner. My regular order was a melon with
a scoop of cottage cheese, a box of Special K, and a black and white
milkshake. To tame my levitating morning hair, I'd wear his orange
baseball hat with a sewed-on patch of three quacking ducks, which
did not support a favorite team with a duck mascot, something I
knew not to ask. He grew up in Duxbury. Nothing bad could ever
happen to you in a place called Duxbury.

J3 asked for a Reuben and side of applesauce without having to
consult the menu. When she collected our menus, J3 seemed else-
where, so I quickly asked to add a side of fries. We both studied each

stainless steel utensil placed on a paper setting with the trimmings of a homemaker's apron. Glass dividers separated the banquettes, frosted with straight and pivot renderings that gave an art deco feel. I had that vague sense I'd been here before.

"Emily," asked J3 just before my knees clicked into full standing position. "Now, why is it that you are completely addicted to fat-free foods and yet order these black and white milkshakes?"

"Ah," I breathed out. Sitting back down, I tilted my head knowingly like a sage. "Do you ever wonder why a cluster of skiers all choose the groomed run when the soft, powdery one next to it is vacant of people? Why the partitioned line in the airport is wide open while the main one moves slowly, yet they can both take your boarding pass? The same principles apply with fat-free foods. Full-fat ice pops or fat-free? Tastes the same. Loaded popcorn or air pop? Air pop, less goopy—more satisfying. But when it comes to the black and white milkshake, it's like Universal remaking a classic. Leave it alone.

"Except for *Sixteen Candles*, of course. While that's a classic, it's not a classic classic. Are you casting Michael Schoeffling? Can I meet him?" Sounding a bit anxious, I tried to control the publicist in me. "How cool it would be to meet him!"

A flicker of a smile ignited across his lips.

"How does one go about tracking Michael Schoeffling's whereabouts?"

He completely avoided the Michael Schoeffling issue. Perhaps I wasn't being clear enough.

"I'm not convinced," he said, "You're depriving yourself."

This momentarily stumped me until I became engaged in proving my point.

"Would you buy a Chanel nail polish at Bendel's when you can get the same one at Saks for the same price and it comes with an FGP?" I then said as an aside. J3 seemed utterly confused. "FGP is the acronym for Free Gift with Purchase."

"I'd be buying lipstick?"

"You're going to a music awards show."

"I suppose that FGP would make more economic sense."

"So substitute economics for calorie count and then you get what I'm saying."

He seemed hopelessly lost.

"I really love Fruit Stripe gum. Very hard to find."

The placement of lunches on Frisbee-sized plates shifted our attention, a possible relief to J3. I tore open my cereal box while J3 picked up cinnamon in a saltshaker, which must have been set earlier, and sprinkled his platter like salt to fries. As he did this, I took in the scent of the fries and winked to the waitress, saying how I hadn't ordered them but would like to keep them in case I would still be hungry.

We both slipped into the quiet made from eating. J3's applesauce interested me; the golden pool unattended, I drifted my teaspoon into its wake. It didn't have the chunky texture of homemade, but was more flavorful than Mott's.

The waitress returned to fill our glasses with water poured from a steel pitcher. Her plastic pin was embossed with the name Jill. By the way she chewed her gum and flirted with the cook, I wanted her name to be Flo.

Flo had hair that could benefit from the consistency of a product. It was the color of chocolate cake batter when adding cream to it. I feared the reaction she'd have if she walked into a Fifty-seventh Street salon, imagining the stylists appearing busy upon sight of her the way you fall to your unoccupied seat in sleeping position when spotting a 300-pound man with a comb-over as he makes his way down the aisle of a crowded train. (Not that I'd ever do such a thing.)

Jill/Flo started chatting with J3 while I ate off his plate. A legitimate conversation, no discussions of the unseasonably cold weather or what an oaf the mayor was, but opinions with thought, linked to topics centering around food distribution and the merits of refrigerated trucks. Freely calling us "sweetie," Jill/Flo asked if she could get us anything else. J3 added a side of applesauce and black and white shake, requesting that they be delivered at the same time as mine. When she went to attend to his additions, J3 leaned into me.

"You smell wonderful," he said and then excused himself to use the men's room. I focused on the crumpled napkin he'd removed from his lap.

Feeling momentarily paralyzed, a new patron seated at the edge of the counter diverted my emotions. A dark man with the build and jovial presence of George Foreman, he wore a black tee neatly tucked into charcoal pinstriped pants. They were great looking pants. His shaved head gleamed like a bowling ball, prominently setting off his two gold earrings. If the people at Mr. Clean wanted to target another demographic, this man would be their model.

Mr. Clean gave me a penetrating smile that verged on laughter.

"I know. I know," I rattled off in my scattered way. "We probably look like such the first date."

"Actually," Mr. Clean said, clearly intrigued as evidenced by his huffs and a few questionable salivary noises, "he's in love with you."

My face lost all expression. After it worked its way from paralysis to function like after a shot of Botox, I started questioning the legitimacy of Mr. Clean's competency.

"Get out!" I squealed and then, quickly adding in a more serious tone, "And why do you think that?"

He laughed into his coffee mug. Or a coffee mug camouflaged to conceal something more potent, the way you convinced the bouncer at an R.E.M. concert that you really needed to take your spiked soda can in with you because you preferred Coke over Pepsi.

"Who are you? Obi-wan?" I snorted.

"I'm not messing with you. That boy's in love with you."

J3 would be returning to his seat soon. I had to remain focused.

"I love your pants, by the way."

Mr. Clean looked startled by the compliment, and then pleased.

"Aren't they great? I go to Hong Kong once a year and add a few things to the wardrobe. It's all about the tailoring."

I nodded, affirming the importance of good tailoring.

"You need to have a basic understanding of what your look is— have a confident style—and let the tailor do his magic and bring the finery to life. These pants here, they make me appear twenty pounds slimmer, and I'd rather that than have to eat brown bread."

Mr. Clean extended his leg as if he prepared for a penalty kick. We both looked below the bar to admire the hemming of his pants. I caught his eyes, so white and deep. When he aged, you knew those eyes would always remain clear.

"How about you? What's your relationship status?" I asked.

"Don't question my authority, girl," he then laughed. I followed his head as we returned to conversing with one another over the counter. "And leave it to me to understand these things. Been with the same woman for over thirty years."

"Who's been with what and where for thirty years?" said J3 mellifluously, not startled by what must have appeared a definite moment. Adjusting himself to the swivel of a seat that must have been recently sprayed with WD-40, he returned his napkin to his lap, greeting Mr. Clean with a semi-wave.

I was relieved to discover that he had not overheard our discussion. Perhaps Mr. Clean did have a psychic read on things. He looked more composed by J3's sudden arrival.

"No. No," I said, shooting Mr. Clean a glance that told him to play along. "This man here is some kind of Oracle. He predicts things."

"Really? And how would you like to accompany me on an all-expense-paid trip to Vegas?"

"No. It's true. Tell us about your wife."

Oracle described his relationship—his first marriage, her second. He was fifty-eight, and I asked him what beauty regimen he followed with a face so absent of lines. His gut, though broad, was so firm it could serve a tray of champagne glasses.

Flo served our milkshakes in beer mugs, and I asked for a straw. When she plopped it in my drink, it released a happy emotion. J3 and I both reached for our glasses like they would soon disappear. I then noticed that I had never added my Special K to my melon, as I squished the cellophane bag to the tune of walking on seashells.

"Sorry!" I said to J3, Oracle, and the two men still seated in the far booth.

After a moment of silence, I excused myself to investigate the ladies' room. J3 and Oracle waved in a way that said I wouldn't be missed, and I knew J3 would be given his turn for an analysis.

When I returned, the Oracle had left. I asked J3 where he had gone, saddened to learn he had an appointment to get to. J3 calmed my distress by asking if he could bring me back anything from L.A. I thought of how fun it would be to get something completely girly, trendy, and impractical from Fred Segal, or that funky little shop in Melrose with the best supply of vintage Levi's and corduroy jean jackets. From J3's immersed look, I realized I needed to say something quickly and press on that cushioned buzzer before my mustached host apologized and said my time was up.

I started rambling about Fifi and Romeo—the Bergdorf's for dogs with its Jackie O sweaters and matching carrying cases, the pink and white checked label that had the *Mod Squad* pet in mind.

J3 pointed out that I didn't have a dog, missing that rationale entirely. I would never have the kind of dog that needed a better wardrobe than me. I supposed it would be a bit impractical to have a wardrobe of clothes I couldn't use, considering my current storage space crisis. I settled on having him return without a fresh tan, because jealousy didn't suit me.

I asked J3 what important meeting he needed to attend to that required such a demanding trip. He hedged my question by attending to the bill.

J3 mentioned Henry, referred to his quizzing me this morning on the difference between Hinduism, Buddhism, and other -isms in relation to something I had said about the treatment of animals in other cultures.

"Obviously, it's the Hindus that look to their animals reverentially. That whole reincarnation thing. Right?" I blurted in an insecure tone.

J3's smile said he did have a theory about religions with followers that looked to spirituality the way girls bought the newest Dior bag.

He then said something in a whisper, and I couldn't be certain if I heard him correctly.

"What would have happened if I nabbed you when you were for the taking?"

I really must have imagined this.

38

Henry greeted me at the door like the proverbial dog with slippers stuffed in his mouth, which couldn't be very sanitary. Then again, dogs probably had a different immune system than humans.

"Good thing you're home. I was wondering where you were."

He spoke quickly, not pressing me for the details of my unusually late arrival. J3 had called a car service to take him to the airport, while I had the use of Edward for the afternoon—fun, but exhausting to insert a month's worth of errands in an afternoon's time.

"We're meeting Gil and his newest conquest at Mellons."

Mellons? Mellons, the place you accompanied your mother to when she wanted to be really crazy and order fries or reunite with friends now superfluous to your lifestyle so you could cover twenty minutes of conversation by rehashing the New York you once shared?

"Can you be ready in about fifteen or do you want to meet us there?" Henry asked as a courtesy, knowing my response. I didn't want to get ready in fifteen. I didn't want to meet them there.

"I'll be ready in fifteen."

After superficially getting ready to make my "fifteen" deadline, I found Henry on the phone. I pointed to my watch and he waved me off, evidently talking to Gil. Gil, the one we'd be seeing soon, the reason why I couldn't test out more outfits.

"But, Henry," I politely whispered, "you always keep me waiting!"

He lifted up his hand and made a peace sign that, perhaps, could have also meant that he'd be off in two seconds. I stood there for over two minutes, thinking evil Henry thoughts as he sapped up my time like an airplane layover, my minutes having the importance of a Skadden Arps lawyer working overtime.

I tried to think of how I could effectively utilize this sudden ac- cumulation of time and left the kitchen to go onto the Internet. After Googling a few words, I discovered Web sites on religion for kids. Hindus did believe in reincarnation and the reverence of ani- mals. I even picked up some useful insight about hierarchy and an- imals that may be leveraged in future debates.

Almost an hour later, I found Henry in the kitchen, readjusting the phone in its receiver.

"That was J3," he said to me. "Apparently missed his flight."

"Oh. How strange."

My words floated into the air like a runaway balloon.

"And don't you look hot."

Like Tabasco.

"Right. Thanks. Had more time than I needed to get ready."

Henry approached me, going in for a kiss.

"So we should leave J3 a note," I said, reaching for the Hello Kitty pad to scribble down our itinerary and a request for his appearance with doodles and happy faces.

"Do you find J3 . . ." Henry paused. I looked at him imploringly. His body shivered as if he was about to brush this off. "You know . . . meddling. The word scram comes to mind when he's around."

"He lives with us. Your idea, getting the roommate, need I re- mind?"

He nodded. It seemed like he wanted to add something, but then motioned for us to leave.

In the cab, we both stared ourselves into unconsciousness from the city at night that blurred from windows you manually rolled down. There were a few patches of snow, the remnants of plowing from the freak snowstorm a few weeks back, now soiled with city. They looked like dirty sheep.

I suddenly felt bad that I had the use of J3's driver earlier, but quickly brushed this off considering that he checked into the kind of hotel bungalows that movie stars live in for months while shooting a film.

We had no trouble spotting Gil and a speechless blonde. Gil would soon need to make an appointment for plugs. Gil used to make a lot of bald jokes. His bushel of cottony blond now had a balding path striped in the middle like a spoon scooped into a heaping of mashed potatoes.

Girlfriend of Gil, a Hungarian import who won't be able to segue her modeling into acting because of the indecipherable accent and a childhood of not using fluoride toothpaste, wore Gaultier and a bored scowl.

With Henry's head locked in the crook of Gil's elbow, I introduced myself to Girlfriend of Gil, who responded with a smile that seemed to be a considerable inconvenience. Either she didn't know the language or had lost the skill of conversing from too much time on the catwalk.

After some chatter establishing how well Gil was doing, further reinforced by Gil saying he was "making piles of dough," Henry said he'd cover the first round. For being so well off, Gil held on to a dollar so tightly that George looked anemic. To Gil, giving a host a bunch of flowers wrapped in cellophane was generous. He stayed at hotels with free HBO on trips he couldn't expense. He put groceries in his cart based on consulting a weekly flyer, giving the cashier a special bonus card after she rung up his purchases.

Henry industriously negotiated through a swaying crowd, holding the pitcher of beer high above heads until some of it swished onto a blonde who pushed her way into him. He tossed me the stack of clear plastic cups, and we commandeered a vacant booth after hovering over a matching Barbour-jacketed couple who caught on to their need to leave. As everyone adjusted to their seats, I handed out the cups, Henry filling them.

"The bachelor party!" Gil said, with unnecessary saliva-spitting delivery.

Gil had evidently been planning Henry's bachelor party. We didn't even have a date for the wedding and Henry had already wrangled Gil into this meek excuse for boys to have a fiancée-approved evening to enact closeted lewd behavior over a platter of cubed Cracker Barrel cheeses, imported beer, and girls that cashed in their earnings made from a Saturday night.

"So? You think our love for each other can survive the big night?" asked Henry with a fiendish grin.

This annoyed me. Henry felt the sizzle of my stare and quickly turned away.

"First off, we didn't fall in love over a series of fantasy dates with hot tubs, private movie screenings, and horseback riding on the beach to a dinner served in a sandcastle. I'm not worried," I said dryly. The table looked unconvinced.

"Honestly," I began, until Henry interrupted me saying, "As opposed to dishonestly."

Lately Henry had been in the habit of correcting my grammar, which I normally accepted as one of those inconveniences you brush off the way you do Auntie Peg's custom of saying "as long as you like it dear, that's what matters," but this was the first time he had done this in public.

"Honestly," I said again, in the same tone, "do you think I'm worried about a few strippers? I can't really say I consider girls with boob jobs from doctors with practices in Flushing who buy clothes with tags that have slashed-out prices a threat."

I watched their faces twist into contemplative expressions, trying to make a visual from what I'd just described.

"Have you ever known a groom to leave his fiancée because he fell in love with the stripper he met at his bachelor party?"

No one pressed the matter. After a round of silence and forced sips from beer mugs, Henry began talking about a business trip he planned. Gil mentioned a sick uncle.

We all had to commiserate on the sadness of seeing someone's mind deteriorate to the extreme of calling everyone by the name of your childhood dog. Lots of sorrowful glances were exchanged and "taking away one's dignity" was said repeatedly. I wanted to turn to the subject of Gil's head of disappearing pubic hair.

I excused myself to use the ladies' room that I didn't need to use. Walking outside to escape the humid air of a congested bar, "you smell great" kept sounding in my head like an overplayed song.

* * *

When I returned to the table, thankfully, the conversation had veered from the inhumanity of aging to the cold winter we were coming off; otherwise it would have been time to enact my excuse and say my farewells.

"What would you rather die of—being burned to death or frozen?" said Henry, bringing me back into a conversation of infinitesimal improvement over the one I had left.

I gave Henry a look.

"So? Which is it?"

"I am not dignifying that question with an answer."

"And why not?"

"Because I will not die of either; therefore there's no point in imagining a scenario that will aggrieve me."

"Right. Emily is going for immortality," Henry said to Gil.

"That's not true."

Perhaps it was true.

"I do want my funeral to be held on a nice spring day. None of this rainy-day business with mourners dressed in black."

A girl walked by with a pixie cut, very mod sixties. It worked for her, and I became annoyed thinking of the dates she'd lose because men don't typically go for women with short hair. I then thought of pixies and woodland sprites. Woodland sprites. I would braid my hair and dance wildly with woodland sprites that would go perfectly with that lilac Prada dress I had my eye on.

"And it's just rhetorical," said Henry weakly.

"So what's the big interest in how I want to check out? What—are you thinking of murdering me?"

I started to get up from the table, worried by my abrasive tone. I needed a time-out.

"Cocktails anyone?" I said sweetly.

Waify couldn't tear away from her pouted expression to form words, while Henry said he was good. Gil lifted up his full mug of beer and began to chug, but I slipped away before he could effectively put in a request.

I walked outside, wishing I smoked, because I could have had a cigarette to offset the cold. About to search for my mobile, I overheard a girl speaking on her phone, somewhat hidden from standing in the entranceway of a closed store. But you couldn't help listening to her conversation because of the insertion of "fuck" between every word. The excessive use of curse words to aptly express a point intrigued me. To no surprise, she discussed sex, the unsuitable intentions of her boyfriend and his Jerry Springer tendencies. The Jerry Springer tendencies part made me smile, as I found her conversational skills to be suited for his studio audience. She then slid into Spanish, shaking her hips in a coochie coochie Charo movement. I understood the "oh, no, no, no. Oh, no, no, no," which she repeatedly sang like a leitmotif.

This morning I found myself in a situation with someone similar to Studio Audience woman. Waiting in line for my decaf, I accidentally bumped into a woman wearing elastic-waist pants and a coat made from the scraps of a parachute, my nose pointed to the words in my magazine and not the movements of the line. The woman spun my absentmindedness into her web of gripes, considered my bump as an intentional hit. She threatened to "slap me silly—teach me a lesson," which I found a bit excessive. If I were to be "slapped silly" over an unwarranted bumping incident, I'd be afraid to think of what could happen to someone that intentionally caused her harm, which I gathered to be a large number.

Returning to the booth, my mini-break had not been restorative. I came in as Henry and Gil howled in the air, my arrival too late to gather the cause of such laughter. I'd give them one final chance. If the discussions centered around morbid topics, I'd collect my jacket with excuses of an early morning due to the organization of the party. They were now on to the capture of some war criminal that currently garnered the most play on the 24-hour news channel tickers. I wondered which network would get the rights to make the Sunday night special.

Gil had a fascination with this hole, apparently from the same people that brought you Saddam's ditch. I asked how the military found him. Girlfriend of Gil was still too important to participate in conversation, teetering her head from one side to the other in the occasional movements of a person sunning themselves, while Henry and Gil looked at me as if I had asked which states bordered Canada.

Which states do border Canada?

I didn't find my question so absurd, since the reports I watched showed only a desert with a lot of Middle Eastern farm animals, not realizing intelligence could interpret directions that described a hut with the black-bearded goat and one-humped camel. I considered loosening a stone that followed a footpath set to the interests of Henry and Gil, redirecting it to something that Girlfriend of Gil could easily follow with topics of a celebrity nature.

They then returned to an idea they always entertained when they came together socially, having something to do with opening a ski resort in the Himalayas, which would include a ski-in/ski-out prayer temple. It was time to collect my coat.

My hands, folded on my lap and hidden beneath the table, felt a light tap—a signal for me to look at Henry. He had a warm glow to his face. Henry had been enjoying himself, finding our time with Gil and Girlfriend of Gil entertaining, and this would be that moment I'd forever refer to like a ripped and saved photograph of a really great haircut.

I couldn't hold his gaze, afraid of the involuntary arrangement my face would make. Excusing myself for the bar for about the eighteen-hundredth time, I rambled how I didn't have a taste for beer.

If I wanted to order my gimlet, I'd have to be zoning for fifty months to slip into a space along the bar. After asking a very nice young man with a gap in between his front teeth and too-dark hair that I feared was the result of an at-home dye job, I succeeded in getting my drink, turning so quickly I pushed into a chest, nearly emptying half my gimlet onto my hands. The cold stickiness worked its way to my sleeve.

"Emily," said Henry with no apologies. "Gil and his girlfriend want to leave."

Henry didn't know the name of Girlfriend of Gil either. For some unknown reason this pleased me.

"They want to see a band at CBGBs that I've never heard of. Oedipus Rex and the Mother Fuckers. Ready to go?"

Ready to go home. I nodded my head.

"Does that mean a yes or no?" he asked.

I could have made an excuse that I wanted to finish my gimlet, but I already drank the little that remained, probably so I could drink rather than speak.

"I'm just going to head home."

Henry bit his bottom lip till it turned white, his fingers clenched into knobs. Never before had he expressed physical anger toward me, probably the Buddhist in him. I tried to picture Henry in a wife-beater tee. Not his look, but that's what made it sexy.

"Emily," he directed. "This is not good. You better come with us."

I scanned our area to make sure no one could overhear. I always found couples that bickered in public to be the Planter's nuts-and-wine-with-a-screw-on-cap type.

"Are you making some kind of threat? You know I won't respond to such demands," I said, sounding like the Secretary of Defense yelling on C-SPAN.

Henry then kept saying "where's your head at?" Finding the redundant turn of our squabble to be counterproductive, I wanted to be an anonymous passenger on a departing train till it faded into nothing.

"I'll see you at home," he then huffed. I watched his back get sucked into the padding of people.

Alone and standing at the bar with my empty drink, discomforted from my hand being coated in a film of stickiness, I suddenly regretted the decision I'd made like a tired skier choosing the double diamond run but it was too late to go back uphill.

I did want to go with Henry. I wanted to go back to being the couple who considered themselves a little bit county, a little bit rock 'n' roll. We fashioned ourselves as one of the interesting ones. I could have cried, but my tears seemed to have dried up, perhaps from the extremity of the situation, the way you are when you are so exhausted you can't sleep.

"Got tied up on the phone, but thanks for the note. I always wondered, does Hello Kitty speak Japanese or English?" J3 entered my frame as he said this to me, and suddenly order had been restored.

"Bilingual," I said.

"Right. Thanks."

"And, I know it's been a while since I've put that high school French to use, but what's the Moi Moi?"

"Big Kiss. Big Kiss."

After he asked where Henry was, I wondered if I should pull J3 into the weight of my distress. I also feared he might shoulder some of the blame. J3 thought this way.

I told him that they went to see Oedipus Rex and the Mother Fuckers and, after saying this, realizing that my being left behind could have appeared as odd, quickly redirected the conversation back to Hello Kitty and if there was a video game somewhere in that.

J3 needed more details, his polite way of considering a never-to-be-realized idea. Elaborating on Hello Kitty's style, her adventures, and the friends that supported her, I realized that the stories behind cartoon characters were as fascinating as the bio of a celebrity.

The Cartoon Network should start their version of biographies of famous cartoon characters. They could even have a "Where Are They Now" special profiling Fat Albert, Mr. Magoo, and Underdog. I kept from saying this to J3, not wanting to overload him with too many sketched-on-napkin ideas.

"Do you want to see Oedipus Rex and the Mother Fuckers?" J3 asked.

"Do you?" I said, as unenthused as possible.

"Sounds a bit," pause, "Oedipal."

"I agree."

"Let's go home."

A bidding for vacant cabs erupted, jockeying on our street corner, when J3 lifted his hand. Heading downtown, I saw a diner I've always wanted to try, the real mobile-home kind underneath a bridge that hosted a flea market on Sundays. I gave J3 a look and he asked the driver to stop.

We slunk into a booth and took in our surroundings like kids inspecting Dad's new car. The waitress handed us menus, and J3 asked if I needed mine. I shook my head, ordering a grilled cheese and bacon, French fries, lightly toasted sesame bagel, and black and white milkshake, while J3 asked what the soup of the day was and then ordered a cinnamon bagel and a black and white milkshake.

When the waitress set down our food, I inhaled the aroma of the grilled cheese and French fries and then asked if she'd wrap it up so I could have it for later. I computed a host of options on how to respond if J3 pressed me on this, until he began some discussion about Madeline cookies, cinnamon, and Orson Welles' sled.

39

I awoke with the panic of hosting responsibilities, moving my fingers to count the hours, and at 5:00 AM, I would never be ready in time. Henry wasn't in bed. He'd never made it home, or possibly was still out for the night—something I'd have to shuffle in a To Do box and contend with later.

The fridge, abandoned of any food, was cleared out as if we were going on a holiday, not even a container of Ben & Jerry's in my secret hiding place. I forgot that we had to make room for the platters and beverages the caterers would be supplying. I stared blankly, feeling the chill from the open door, just hoping that something would mysteriously appear. In one of the grooves in a back compartment, I found an egg. I loved this egg. I thought of 101 ways you could have an egg. Considering Dr. Perricone, I boiled it, watching the water bring on an epileptic attack, but it never cracked.

Henry entered the kitchen smelling of smoke and the city at night. I wanted to tiptoe around the issue of Henry and me, shielding him by looking in the refrigerator. Closing the door, Henry pressed his nose in my face. It was a psychopathic moment.

"You scared the Bee Gees out of me, Henry."

This sounded all wrong. Henry's expression matched my thoughts of three longhaired Aussies howling under a disco ball.

"So. Emily. Whatever happened to you last night?"

Henry played the offense-is-the-best-defense game.

"We went out. We had a disagreement. You left me at a bar."

Just then, a confetti of egg exploded from the pan, giving our ceiling a stucco effect. Henry retreated from the shock.

"What the hell, Emily? You scared the Bee Gees out of me!"

I started to laugh. Henry began laughing, humming the bars of "You're the Only Woman for Me." I went to the closet so I could get a mop and attend to the egg mess, but Henry grabbed me, pulling me into his chest, suffocating me with his smoky smell. He had burnt egg on his face.

Releasing me so I could breathe again, he just stared at me, which made me feel uneasy. I couldn't get past the scab of egg on his face. I really should have wiped it off, but for whatever reason that's as strange as ponchos and braids worn by women over thirty who aren't part of a tribe, I didn't say anything. Henry would soon discover how foolish he looked without my assistance.

"The mover guys are coming soon," I said. "They're going to put all of the bulky furniture in the downstairs office so we can have room for a dance floor."

Where could I get a disco ball?

"Emily," he said, sounding the way a teacher did when addressing the issue of my continually disrupting class, "I was really upset last night."

"Well, so was I."

"Have you ever considered what it's like to be in someone else's shoes?"

I looked at Henry's shoes—some kind of sneakers you bought at a store that sells skateboards and rollerblades. I would never be in Henry's shoes.

"You can be pretty selfish," he said.

Selfish? Selfish! I was not. Well, perhaps a little.

"I have never sold a fish in my life," I said with I-did-not-have-improper-relations delivery.

The little kitchen television played the morning news. I didn't remember turning on the TV, thinking of last night's stupor, which I became reminded of this morning once I noticed my arms encumbered by a sweater that never made it off.

The reporter did an exposé on low-fat ice cream, showing some of my preferred brands. I felt the way I did on those mornings you should have never woken up, only to lose your job or get into a car crash. Apparently my low-fat ice cream really had been full of fat. I did a mental calculation of the numbers we were talking about. It's hard to carry the ones on mental scrap paper.

This was a tragedy of the ultimate deceit, as if I were raised under false pretenses, my parents casually announcing one evening over mushroom quiche and a Caesar's salad that I was adopted. Could I have been adopted? How great would that be, not to inherit my mother's crazy genes. I'd hire a private investigator, chosen because of the fedora hat and a dreary office with a door with chicken wire entombed in its glass. He'd discover that my mother was this amazing, beautiful woman who made ceramic jugs on a kiln in the backyard of her Santa Fe ranch.

I loved low-fat ice cream.

"Emily! Are you even listening to what I have to say?"

"Of course. Still trying to figure how you could possibly think I'm selfish. I mean, really, of all things. Me. Selfish!"

"So you haven't a clue as to why I'm mad at you?"

I am transported to a classroom, standing in front of a chalkboard with Columbus's boats written in cursive writing, feeling the illumination of a cone of light. Repeatedly, I am asked a question I know the answer to. If I say it, my time in front of the chalkboard is gone.

The buzzer from the lobby rang, another time I am saved by the bell. I spoke into the phone and granted the movers access. One had a crooked nose, out of shape from what must have been a painful break. I felt the pain that must have caused the accident. The other had a shaped nose, but his entire face could use some work. They were both movers; their navy blue shirts saying "Mover" made this clear.

A small woman trailed behind Broken Nose. She held a composition notebook that she seemed to be very proud of. She asked if I was Emily Briggs. I am Emily Briggs, I said. She wore a navy blue jacket and pants made out of rayon. She looked ready to be embalmed.

I asked Henry if he had any suggestions on how we should assemble the room. He left it up to me, trusting my instincts on these things.

After $750 for moving two couches and a metal table, I wondered if dressing for an embalming while holding a notebook I had doodled in to make the fifth grade go by faster would be a more lucrative option.

40

We mobilized. The preparations were going along smoothly, the Hello Kitty on the tip of my pen shaking about like a martini. Lots of checks were being made.

Henry slammed my pen down on my planner. I suppose he found it to be distracting. I lifted up my Smythson planner.

"Party planner," I said, reading the book's label. "And so much more effective than dealing with the whiny-voiced kind."

He didn't seem to be in a joking mood.

"Okay! Moving right along. Guests will be here in—oh!" I pulled up Henry's wrist to look at his watch. Guests would begin arriving in an hour. "Where did the time go? Do you know where the time went?"

Henry didn't know where the time went.

"We need to get all of the miniature candy, caramel apples, Halloween favors, and the array of things and put them in various bowls," I said, dumping bags of candy on the table. "Oh, my!"

"What is it!" Henry said, mirroring my panic.

"Someone removed the Snickers and Milky Way bags from the freezer." I squeezed the moistened bags in question. "I wanted to cut them up, stick toothpicks in them, and serve them from a frosted platter. Who took the chocolate bars from the freezer?" I said, with toe stomping delivery.

"I guess the caterers did." Henry opened the freezer, crammed with bags of ice.

"But what about my idea of serving cut-up frozen Snickers and Milky Way bars?"

"Were you really going to slice all of that chocolate? You know how you are with chopping, always saying chopping is a complete waste of good time."

I have said that.

"And the added effort to slice something frozen? You really should slice them first and then freeze them."

This made some sense.

Henry began to close the freezer door, but was suddenly struck by something he seemed to find compelling. He pulled out my special ice cube tray.

"Emily. What's this?"

"Iced champagne."

"I see. Korbel, I hope?"

It was Veuve Cliquot.

"Of course."

J3 walked in asking where our living room had gone. I said that for $750 you could have your living room disappear. J3 didn't get my joke. I had to stop trying to be funny.

Henry stacked the little candies into a Lincoln Log village. We had no time to be making candied cabins and forts, though it did have an artistic effect.

"What are you doing?" I asked, sounding like the authoritative figure I never was.

"Arranging your *array* of things," said Henry.

"Right, *arranging*, not constructing a miniature village made from candy."

How fun would it be to have a miniature village made from candy? I then excused myself to get ready, hoping that Henry would ignore my instructions and make a miniature village from candy.

Of course, on the night of the Six Months to Halloween party, the weather had to be more appropriate to three months to Halloween. The news said something about the city experiencing a clash of jet streams that had something to do with Canadian storms and a Southern warm front. I was just annoyed that these historic conditions made my Tyrolean Viking Vixen idea as obsolete as couture Mizrahi.

I resorted to being a geisha, which gave me the excuse to wear my favorite Pearl River black Mandarin nightgown with red Chinese motifs to a party.

Twisting my hair into an egg-in-nest bun à la "Katherine Hepburn: The Later Years," I considered powdering my face, but opted against the pale Madame Butterfly look. Anemia never flattered me. I still wore my coyote insulated boots, because I've always felt that when you were comfortable and felt good, you looked good.

The geisha look wasn't working. I must have gained weight or put on muscle around my quads. My legs were suddenly bloated to soufflé proportions. If only I could shut the oven door and have them burst and shrivel. Without having time to indulge on the immensity of my thighs, I put on Henry's pajama top and stared into the closet. I didn't have a backup. Not having a backup plan was a bad idea.

My legs looked like the Campbell's Soup boy's.

With a tap on the door, I remembered that I had told Daphne to come by earlier. Even though she couldn't drink, something about pregnancy and babies missing toes, she agreed to drink beside me with an active imagination. She entered the bedroom like a movable neon sign. Dressed in a yellow Pulitzer maternity dress, blinding in contrast to her flamingo pink lipstick, her neck was strangled by baubles of pearls in homage to Wilma and Betty.

"I like it," we both said to one another.

"Oh. I'm not dressed yet. In a bit of a panic with the damn weather," I said.

"But how clever you look. I thought you were Tom Cruise in *Risky Business*."

She thought my legs were huge.

"What a doable idea. I can still wear pajamas despite my Campbell's Soup boy legs!"

I cautiously lift the rim of my shirt to see if my legs had lost any weight since the last time I checked, disgusted by the appearance, like Mother peeking under her sandwich bread to find her turkey slathered in mayo.

"Do I look fat?" The question one doesn't ask a boyfriend if one wants to keep a boyfriend or a pregnant best friend if one wants to keep a pregnant best friend. Daphne patted her stomach, starting to show. I was a mean, mean friend—but happy to see someone else in the room fatter than me. "Okay, but you're pregnant. You're allowed to be fat. Maybe I should just shut up."

Daphne laughed.

"I actually thought you looked great. Maybe even too thin."

We were distorted, images seen through the hall of mirrors in our minds.

Daphne at four months had just a little bump in her stomach, hardly noticeable, like the diamond on my engagement ring. She smiled to her reflection so she could add her eighteen-thousandth coat of lipstick.

"Do you think neon lips are cheesy?" she asked, puckering her lips.

"Kind of like white aluminum Christmas trees, cheesy or outrageously chic, depending on who has the style to pull it off."

She smiled to herself in the mirror, evidently pleased with my answer. Daphne loves white aluminum Christmas trees. She has three.

"Ethel Kennedy?" I asked.

Daphne nodded to my reflection, fluffing her hair with her expertly tipped fingers.

I realized that if I needed to pull off my *Risky Business* costume, I was missing the essential *Risky Business* accessory—sunglasses. Opening and shutting drawers, lingering longer when searching through Henry's things, I became annoyed with the fashion industry for not bringing back the Wayfarer for my party.

"Damn sunglasses," I groaned.

"Just wear Andy's. He actually brought them with him because he has to use them when driving, and we happened to drive over. We just got the Volvo SUV—much better than the Lexus or BMW, and we shopped them all. And it's so great—if I'm cold and Andy's warm, we have air climate control that heats just my section!"

Ever heard of rolling down the window?

"And you know how cold I've always been lately."

It did seem that Daphne had a fixation with controlling the air.

"So how does all of this apply to your sunglasses?" she asked. I must have been pulling a face.

"Well. Yes." Meaning, back to me and I'd rather listen to NPR than hear the details of your new SUV.

"Andy has those glasses. He's currently into the JFK-dealing-with-the-Cuban-missile-crisis-while-sailing look."

Apparently Daphne and Andy had an obsession with the Kennedys.

"What's wrong?" asked Daphne.

I massaged my temples, feeling a migraine come on.

"My head aches," I said. "Do you have anything?"

"The strongest thing I've been taking is folic acid. Wait a sec. Hold on."

Daphne opened a bag, too large to make it as a carry-on—notebooks, bottles, wipes, the entire Dr. Perricone line. Daphne needed to employ a better method of organizing her bag. She used to be good at such things, perhaps a syndrome of kid #3.

I took the lip plumper from her pyramid of beauty products.

"Do men really like wife-beaten lips?" I said, making fish lips in the mirror.

"Who knows what they're into these days. I lost track after the Britney Spears python thing. Here it is!" Daphne cried, lifting her wallet into the air like it was the golden ticket.

"Your wallet?"

Could you bribe a migraine?

She reached into her billfold and pulled out marijuana in the kind of shrunken baggie used for earrings bought from a street vendor.

"You pothead!"

"Please, I haven't smoked since Judd Nelson made great movies. Only kept as a reminder of how cool I once was. Like a beauty queen's tiara memorialized in Lucite above the mantle."

I followed the bag as she held it up to the light.

"It looks older than my nylon Prada bag."

Daphne gave this some thought, then shrugged her shoulders.

"I don't think so. Here," she said, wiggling the baggie like a packet of Equal. I missed Equal.

"I'm sure it must still work. And pot is the best thing for a migraine."

I took the bag from her, looking at it suspiciously.

"Go on, shoo," she said, waving me off. "Smoke it in the bathroom so I won't be contaminated."

Daphne left me so she could attend to her husband and help with any last-minute preparations. I asked if she needed my assistance in my most unhelpful tone, but she had a handle on things, saying that this was what she did.

I took a pipe I found in Henry's sock drawer, curved and wooden like Sherlock's in travel size. Stuffing the pipe with Daphne's pot, the leaves were as dry as autumn, crumbling to the touch. I undressed and went into the bathroom.

Twisting the valve to release a torrent of steam, I then poured the remainder of the pot in the terracotta jar I used for eucalyptus, rosemary, or peppermint, depending on what chapter I was reading in one of my health books. I lay flat on the gray slate floor, stretched out my arms as if I were posing for Goya. Overhead, a storm cloud of mist had no place to drift to. I remained still, looking like a woodland sprite trapped in ice. I wanted to be a woodland sprite, one of the mischievous ones that mess with the heads of stupid hairy ogres.

The temperature of my pot den rose while the floor kept me cool, lying on the kind of gray slates that feel the pounding of garden party soles. Rinsing off, I redressed, dried my hair, pulled it into a low ponytail and twisted it into a bun.

Henry came in, admiring my costume. "Are you—"

"Stoned? Pretty much."

"I meant to ask if you were going as Bill Clinton."

He thought my legs were huge. I looked at myself in the mirror, wearing Henry's broadcloth blue shirt and a pair of athletic socks. I supposed I could change the socks to loafers, add some blush to my nose, look for a blue Gap dress and pour some rubber cement on it. I didn't own anything from the Gap. I needed to add something expensive, but the ideas were limiting. I put on Givenchy, from a bottle.

"Tom Cruise. *Risky Business?*"

"Oh right, makes sense. Daphne's downstairs, trying to wrangle a pair of glasses from her husband. He made a point to say that he just had them tightened."

Apparently I had a big head.

Looking at my head in the mirror, "Do I have a big head?" I asked.

Henry walked behind me, folding his hands around me. We stared at our reflection.

"You do not have a big head. It's beautiful. It's the head of Emily."

Head of Emily? I liked that concept, imagining a special club with trendy T-shirts and a Web site.

"Am I being too stoned?"

Henry laughed. I joined him, laughing at nothing.

"Drugs don't work on you—you always act stoned. Coffee spiked with caffeine? Now there's another Emily."

I turned to him. He wore tab-front bell-bottom chinos, a ribbed turtleneck of wearing-Hugo Boss-to-get-a-pedicure proportions, and a vest with suede fringe on the pockets.

"Mike Brady! How cute. Maybe I should dress as Carol Brady?"

After I said this, the idea of styling my hair into a mullet lost its appeal. The seventies weren't a good era for my features.

"I thought you said that couples who go in couple-y themes are kind of the same as buying the matching bag and shoes," Henry said.

That would be something I'd say, but I couldn't remember ever saying it. Damn pot. I needed ginseng.

"Anyway, I was supposed to be a Wild and Crazy Guy with J3, but he couldn't get his costume together in time. So I thought I'd just be a Bay City Roller."

"Okay," I said, unconvincingly.

"Do you have something against the Bay City Rollers?"

I didn't really know what a Bay City Roller was, imagining a retro drive-through on the San Francisco marina, your shake and fries delivered by a roller-skating waiter. It had been awhile since I've visited San Francisco, feeling out of that loop. I made a mental note to check out fares to San Francisco on Expedia.

Becoming concerned about J3's costume dilemma, watching Henry pull at his suede fringe for about an hour, I tried to move. The perch on my bed felt so comfortable.

"I'd better check downstairs," I said.

Henry looked perplexed, and then said he needed to send a few e-mails before meeting up with me.

41

J3 sprinkled cinnamon on his sour apple martini. He did this elegantly and with confidence. J3 could be handed the carving knives for a turkey and know what to do with them. I watched the bristle of his eyebrows move up an inch when he spotted me.

"No costume?" I asked.

"Cleaners," he groaned. "Didn't have it ready on time. What should I be?"

Opening and closing cabinets, I momentarily settled my eyes on a bottle of Windex. But I didn't know how the Windex could make a costume and used all of my strength to control myself from not taking the bottle. After some rummaging, I found a bag of black-eyed peas, bought during my ten-minute healthy-soup-cooking phase, which ended when I found that appliances other than a microwave were involved.

"Here," I said, throwing the beans to J3, who caught the bag with one hand. He stared at the peas, needing clarification.

Anne then arrived, wearing a rug from a hunting lodge.

"Spare me the Save a Bear up-and-down, animal activism so over. And the folks at PETA could use a shower."

"Anne, J3. J3, Anne," I said, making the quick introduction, concerned about distancing these two in the manner of divorcés needing to be separated at their child's wedding.

I poured Anne a glass of water. Anne does not indulge calories on beverages. She looked at me with her low-density scowl.

"What are you wearing?" she asked, her voice horrified.

"Henry's shirt."

She still looked horrified.

"It's by that new designer. Bagley Brothers. Dior really wants to sign him on."

"Oh yes, I've heard of him."

"Do you have any eyeliner?" I asked her.

Looking very inconvenienced, she reached into her Fendi fur clutch. She altered the population of luxury-pelted animals like a developer building condos on a wildlife preserve. She handed me a Lancome dark brown pencil.

"Keep it. Diseases and such."

"Right. Thanks."

I walked over to J3 and drew a circle around his eye, smudged it in with my forefinger, and then retraced one final circle. He remained stoic, allowing me to have my way with him.

"You're a black-eyed pea," I said. "Carry that bean bag and you are one hot-looking pea."

He smiled, bouncing the package of beans in the air with thanks. Situating his drink and the bag of beans in one hand, he made his departure from the room, lingering momentarily until I gave him the look to move along, and quickly.

"What is that on your breath," she huffed. "Were you smoking—" Anne paused, sniffing me like a guard dog. I must have been a sachet of pot. "Marijuana!" she screeched.

Anne's the type programmed to "Say No to Drugs."

"So? What is it? Or are you too doped up to speak?"

Doped up?

"I need to smoke on occasion."

Her face grew into something scarier.

"For medicinal purposes," I said, my tone uncontrollably defensive.

Anne carefully scanned the room, lips puckered to her index finger, as she shamelessly evaluated my home.

"This is where you live. Square footage?"

I didn't have a tape measure.

"Henry knows all of that."

She nodded, almost looking impressed, until she addressed the issue of her lateness.

"You gave me the wrong floor, you know."

This was intentional. I gave Anne Mrs. Hallingby's apartment number, thinking it would be funny.

"You do have a lovely neighbor. This Mrs. Hal—" Pause. "Hallingby. Of course, how could I be so daft? I asked if she had any relation to Queen Noor and she said no, but she was a lovely woman, however. Apparently her former husband—a Texan—you know that type, some prominent oil guy that has to do business and makes trips to those Midwest places."

Middle East.

Anne's scope of geography fit into the triangular points of New York, Palm Beach, and Aspen.

"I didn't want to pry, as he probably worked in that overtly acceptable but disreputable line of business. Innocuously but *ocuously* funding those groups you occasionally read about. You know the ones. 'I'll Cater' or something like that—those turbaned men who add even more inconveniences to traveling. She's quite an interesting lady. Actually surprised you live in a community with such types."

Suddenly a patch of Reade Street had the association of a Greenwich, Connecticut, zip code.

"And she has the most wonderful apartment—a tad whimsical for my taste, but lovely no less. I couldn't keep myself from taking her offer to have a look around."

"You mean you had a conversation with Mrs. Hallingby?"

"Conversation?" she huffed. "More than that. In fact, I wanted to accept her act of graciousness for some ginger tea, but Jason and I were already running late. Even to a family gathering, you know I hate being late."

Either the Medusa snakes of Mrs. Hallingby's head were on Xanax, or you could liken Anne's rapport to a den of wolves, good to their own kind.

"We wouldn't have arrived this late if Jason hadn't insist on watching this tiresome miniseries about some political cover-up called Floodgate. Or perhaps it was Watergate."

"Anne, that's not a miniseries. Watergate? Nixon's resignation?"

"Nixon?"

"President Nixon. Late sixties."

"And is there ash floating in my glass?" Anne held up her glass to the light, giving her most horrified look of victimization.

I stared at the glass. Something dubious was floating in there.

"That's just Sea Monkeys."

She gave the glass to a passing guest. Her face making that disapproving glare, the face she seemed to always be making with me.

"So where do we stand on the wedding planning?"

"Yes. That."

"Yes," she demanded. Poking a nail, or X-acto blade, on her dead bear.

"Well, that's been put temporarily on hold."

"Oh, really!"

I did not like the way Anne said "oh, really."

"So Auntie Peg did get through to you."

"Excuse me?" I queried, my tone matching my expression.

"Well, of course you knew that Auntie has no intention of your marrying an artist. It's very well that you take up an artistic trade, but to marry someone of such means is just not acceptable. Auntie Peg will write you right out of that will. But I am telling you all of this why? Not in my best interest at all. Just means more for me with you pulled from the takings."

"Since when have I become a heroine in a Henry James novel and why wasn't I notified?"

Silence.

"And about how much money are we talking about?"

"A dog hair!" she shrieked, pinching a microscopic thread from her coat. That she had the vision to distinguish the dog fluff from the animal draping her made me wonder if she ate carrots, which were not approved by Dr. Perricone.

"And Emily, this should be a reminder to you of why you should never have a pet," Anne said, the incriminating hair pinched between her nails, partially visible due to the back glow from the track lights.

"When did you get a dog?"

"Jason gave in to their demands."

Since when did the ASPCA employ terrorist tactics?

"The boys wanted a dog. These boys ask for such outlandish things."

With Anne's habit of referring to her children as the "boys" or "twins," I had completely forgotten their names.

"Apparently when the boys want something, we have to actually consider giving it to them."

Motherhood was a new concept to Anne, having given birth to twin boys. I'd like to see how the "sharing" concept is taught by an only child who makes Eloise look like she grew up on a farm, made pretzels, and sold them at outdoor markets.

"What kind of dog?" I asked, fighting back the laughter from imagining Anne's expression when discovering that city dogs must be cleaned up after.

"A Sharpee."

"That's a Magic Marker," said Jason in a whisper, approaching his wife from behind.

"He has premature wrinkles," Anne marveled. "Fabulous concept, they actually grow into their wrinkles with age."

"Shar-peis are so cute! What's his name?"

"Wrinkles," she said nonchalantly.

"One of the twins named him," added Jason.

An example of why you should never have preschoolers name your pets, for the likelihood of a Chihuahua called Teensy, Pomeranians Fluffy and St. Bernards the strange Pervy Guy who seemed to be looking up my shirt all evening.

42

Two blondes came into the room. The first blonde said to the second blonde . . .

I felt like a live participant in a joke told on the trading desk. But taking in the bubbly heads and voices to match, it would be easier to hear fast-forwarded messages than decipher a language with origins from a barnyard pen. And I couldn't possibly make out what they were wearing. In fact, they weren't dressed at all. Costumed as mermaids, they had scales painted on their legs in blue and green disco shades of creamy eye shadow. The only substantive clothing was blue thongs and pink shells fastened with suede twine that barely covered their nipples.

I wanted to be a mermaid.

"There's nothing here," said Blonde #1 to Blonde #2.

"I think you mean there's nothing there," said Anne, motioning to their made-up bodies with her perpetual scowl.

A brunette ran over to the two blondes, giving this a very *Charlie's Angels,* the Spelling TV version, moment.

"Did you see my monkey?" the brunette screeched to the world.

"What kind of monkey?" I calmly asked.

Her panicked face morphed into annoyance.

"Was it a baboon, orangutan, or one of those little monkeys wearing a shrunken bellboy hat while banging tambourines on the shoulder of an organ grinder?"

"A stuffed purple monkey!" she shouted, a bit hostile, especially considering that I hosted this party. People really needed to brush up on their etiquette.

"Purple monkey? Do you really mean a gorilla? Remember," I said to Anne, singing the bars of "Magilla Gorilla."

Anne shrugged her shoulders and shifted her body, unabashedly ditching this randomly formed cluster. A shame really, it probably had been Anne's most intellectual exposure in her post-collegiate life.

"And who are you all here with?" I asked.

"My sister invited us," said Blonde #1 in an accent, something Latin and forbidden. "She's with IMG. Trying to get me signed, but I'd rather focus on my music."

Great, Henry had been mass e-mailing IMG Models again. I really had to erase those numbers from his BlackBerry.

"That's her, over there," she said, pointing to Henry, who was pushing up invisible breasts on Blonde #3. Blonde #3 wore my coral suit.

"You're. Out. Of. Control," I heard Blonde #3 say repeatedly, her words stretched like the pink Bazooka she pulled from the clench of her teeth.

Henry smiled to Blonde #3 in between drags of a cigarette he must have bummed, emitting two thin streams of smoke from his nostrils like a low-voltage dragon.

He studied me, trying to gather if I was truly paying attention. The blonde moved in closer to him, her expertly bobbed hair shimmering on her face like ruffles against chiffon.

To avoid causing a scene of throwing-a-glass-in-your-face proportions, I excused myself and retreated to the bedroom so I could simmer down. Spotting the computer, I began to access the Web, Googling the harm of smoking, and made printouts while draining my third glass of champagne.

Collecting my research, I returned to the party, inserting myself in front of Blonde #3. I looked at Henry.

"Who the hell is she and why is she wearing my suit?" I asked Henry.

He dropped his cigarette in his cocktail with no reply. I followed his downward stare into his glass, such an unattractive look, the waterlogged cigarette floating in a sea of hard alcohol.

"So you started smoking again?"

He looked like a Duh.

"Here," I said, handing him the stack of sheets, topped with a natural herbal remedy to help quit smoking that also advertised its effective rate on cutting the habit.

"Think of the money you'll save!" Henry said, reading from the paper and laughing.

"And I didn't even give you the ones describing smoking and the damaging effects to your skin. Dr. Perricone says you can tell a smoker by the decades of aging it adds to your skin."

He sifted through the papers with an amused smile. I made a mental printout of Henry from when I caught him Googling his name. This made me smile.

I evaluated Blonde #3, a stewardess type, the look effectively projected by the handle of a wheeled bag that rested on her hip. She wore a hat in the shape of a tuna can, the type you'd see on those Russian dancers with smocked shirts tucked into billowy *I Dream of Jeannie* pants while thrusting their feet in muscle-tearing kicks. The turquoise color was coordinated to her neck scarf, and she had on Delta wings pinned into the boucle of her coat. I never understood pins. The accessory did nothing to enhance your features while pricking expensive materials.

"Pixie!"

Puckered lips swallowed my face. When I regained focus, I saw Daniel West with a woman who had the hair of an eighties rock star.

"Listen, can I talk to you for a moment?"

These words are never good. Daniel pulled me aside. Eighties-hair-woman flapped her arms by her side like a fish.

"Loved your latest work, but there's a problem."

"Problem?"

"One big problem. We're missing the anchor piece. The piece of meat. The queen bee."

"I'm sorry?"

"You need that one painting that centers the show. You know, that Cartier worn with a pair of Levi's."

I stared at my bare wrist, ashamed.

"Until then we don't have a show, baby. But you'll be all right, Pixies always land on their feet."

Daniel then left me to go about his socializing. At my party. The man practically fired me at my own party. Weren't there rules about this?

Having that feeling of being stared at, I noticed a man, boy really, holding a skateboard and dressed in baggy jeans, a headscarf, and shirt promoting some brand that would be blurred if he appeared on reality TV. His eyes undressed me, which must have taken all of two seconds considering I only had on Henry's shirt.

There seemed to be something familiar about him, but I became more intrigued by being a blatant sexual object. I believed he even tongued his upper lip, though this could be cribbed from my day-dreaming. The former slut in me (summer of '96 being rather pro-miscuous) wanted to take his hand, pull him into a closet, and see what would happen. If I'd had on a mask, I might have acted on my errant temptation.

I batted my stubby eyelashes, fully reveling in this moment with headscarf-wearing-skateboarder. Coral suit, headscarf-wearing-skateboarder, my mugging incident—it all came together like thousands of pixels forming into one explosive image.

Turning to Blonde #3, she had left; all that remained was a dust of "poof."

"Henry! That's the guy that mugged me," I said, pointing to headscarf-skateboarder, who then got on his skateboard. Not the most effective getaway car in a crowded party held in a loft. Henry dodged after him. J3, across the room, ran over and assisted Henry.

"It's okay, people," said J3 to quell the shock of the room as they both moved headscarf-skateboarder toward the kitchen.

Headscarf-skateboarder looked like a drenched poodle—shak-ing with wide, miserable eyes. Henry entrapped him in the side banquette, where headscarf-skateboarder appeared even more vulnerable. He was so young, and small, like a child with legs that dangled from a grown-up chair.

Henry had a water pistol suctioned to his arm, which he must have swiped from the guy costumed as William Burrows, his date wearing a Lulu Guinness hat with an apple on it.

"Nice gun," I said to Henry, and he looked perplexed, probably annoyed that I weakened his reality TV *Law & Order* moment.

"What do you want to do, Emily?" Henry said with authority, J3 guarding the interrogation from above.

"I really don't know. Never would I anticipate my mugger to have the audacity to pick me up at my own party."

Henry and J3 shared confused glances. No one needed to know of my Romance Channel fantasy, suddenly ignited to a tumultuous notch.

"What are you doing here? Who are you?" I said to headscarf-skateboarder, no longer with skateboard.

He looked scared. The do-gooder in me that donated to causes by attending tax-deductible benefit parties wanted to reach out to him, going for one of those change-one-life-to-make-a-difference moments.

"Don't worry. I am not interested in getting the police involved. But that's only if you clearly explain to me what's going on here."

His fingers became drumsticks, pounding the table, something Eminem. I gave him a glass of champagne that had been left on a forgotten server tray as a way to soften him up. He took a sip. He seemed more relaxed and ready to talk. Interrogators should give all their captives champagne.

"I had no idea you lived here," he said.

"I wouldn't think so."

"I mean, I was here because of someone else. That girl you were talking to."

"Blonde #3? Cheesy stewardess girl? Yes, I was hoping you'd make that connection for me."

Henry dropped the gun.

"I worked for her. I came to collect funds owed to me."

"So she's the one who told you to mug me." I was so Jennifer Hart. Silence.

"And you," my finger waved dramatically, instructing my miniature orchestra. "You lacked the courage-of-a-son-of-a-soybean-farmer-
to-become-leader-of-the-free-world senses—you thought that some
good money could be made by scaring a girl like me?"

"But that's before—" Headscarf-skateboarder abruptly paused. "I
just felt really bad."

Felt really bad?

"Feeling bad? Feeling bad is for blowing me off at the last minute
for the party you promised to attend with me. Calling me with some
lame excuse about an important e-mail you had to deal with."

True story. I gave Henry a look.

"I would never do such a thing," said headscarf-skateboarder.

"Feeling bad does not involve scaring the Bee Gees out of a girl
and then showing up to her party in a shroud of mystery. What's
your name, anyway?"

"Winthrop."

Somehow I doubted his name was Winthrop. Winthrop was the
guy who played backgammon in a tux, Winthrop knew how much
triple sec to add to a Long Island Iced Tea, Winthrop had a Nan-
tucket road named after him. Winthrop was not the guy who attacks, threatens, and solicits his prey at her own party.

"Your name is so not Winthrop. Let me see some ID."

I wiggled my fingers in a come-hither way. He tried to reach for
his back pocket, looking to Henry for clearance. Henry shimmied
to make room so he could take out his wallet and pull his license,
apparently being old enough to drive.

His name was Winthrop.

"Okay," I said, reading his name. "Winthrop Hawkins. You live at
151 East Sixth Street."

Fleur, my favorite florist, was on East Sixth Street. No one can
mix sunflowers, daisies, and irises with fat winged lady and wand results as well as Fleur. I was comforted to know that my assailant had
some level of sophistication by living near a clever florist, over the
target-range-type who aims at bottles on tree stumps. I wanted to
ask Winthrop what flowers were in the storefront's current display,
but he seemed preoccupied.

I took my Hello Kitty pad and pen, scribbling down his ID number and information.

"And now we have the matter of Blonde #3. Henry, who is she? Where is she?"

Both Winthrop and Henry said "Carmenia."

Carmenia? *Carmenia.*

"Carmenia butt-mole model? Henry, what the hell is going on here?"

43

We were all assigned people as if covering dodgeball opponents. Henry was on Winthrop, and J3 and I took Carmenia. J3 asked if I was okay, focusing on this one thing, if I was okay, and I wasn't. The odd thing was that Daniel West's concern about my piece of meat, the missing Cartier, shook me the most.

J3 said it would all work out, that people would pay money to public institutions to see my work, and then mumbled something about settling the current quandary.

It looked like a fun party. I took in the glassy cocktail sounds as I walked up the staircase. The roar of laughter, clashing of flutes, flirtatious maneuvers were all captured from above as I watched tray after tray of glasses, hors d'oeuvres, and party favors pave the way through small colonies of elaborately colored costumes, like from a helicopter flying above Central Park in its Technicolor glory of fall.

We searched the party for Carmenia, her friends, and sister, guessing she leveraged her buzz and outfit for an interesting night necessitating international travel.

Henry located me after his attending to Winthrop, the unfinished matter that would be dealt with as probably as the administration dealing with the polar ice caps.

Our bedroom door, slightly opened, bristled with light through its crack. I thought I had locked the door after making the print-outs on the harms of cigarette smoking. The room smelled of champagne and Jo Malone bath oil. Our eyes scanned the disarray, then connected the clues of a mess made from rifling. A spilled-over bottle of Cristal—the bottle I hid in the crisper drawer of the fridge—and a trail of my boa feathers led to the other side of the bed where my feathered Manolos were attached to someone's feet. Carmenia's feet. Then leading to her skirt, bunched up to reveal that damn mole on her butt.

She wore my shoes, ruined my boa, drank my champagne, and used my bath oil. The three bears had nothing on Goldilocks compared to this, but I wasn't about to share such annoyances with Henry, as he might have interpreted this as callous and materialistic.

Peering over the perpetrator of this crime scene, I saw one of her arms was stretched in front of her while her other was tucked beneath her stomach. The revealed wrist had the marking of a score-card, either the latest trend in body art or a few botched suicide attempts. I disturbingly rationalized it was the latter. To see the markings of someone so dissatisfied with life sent a black shudder through me, even more disturbing than seeing a slip of a girl with the sunken face of Edvard Munch's screamer or a man too large to fit through a standard-sized doorway. Her scars were literal. Focusing on the shiny bruised lines, you could visualize the cold, mirrored blade breaking flesh, picture a once-clean room splattered with blood in a moment. And the mess it would cause, and what kind of product could clean such stains.

"Carmenia," I whispered, so not to startle her if she was napping. Henry took a different approach.

"Carmenia!" he shouted, slapping her face, folding her body forward and then commanding me to help move her to the bathroom. Henry attempted to bring life back into her wilted body by plopping her rag-doll frame over the toilet.

"Call 911," he demanded.

Thrilled to be assigned a task that didn't involve watching an induced sick episode, which always made me feel nauseous, I picked up the phone, but it was engaged.

"Hello?" I said into the receiver.

"Some woman is looking for Emily Philips," said an unknown voice.

"Emily Philips—the woman who lives there?" demanded my mother.

"Hi. I have it," I said. "Mom. My name is still Briggs, I've got the bills to prove it, and this really isn't the best time."

"Emily love, you really can't keep that name. I'll soon have to charge you for that entitlement. Sort of like those club fees that kick in after a few trial months. Well, you're way past due with using the Briggs name for free this long."

My mother wanted me to pay for the use of my name. Now they're charging for rights given to you at birth.

"Now Emsy," she said, as if trying to jam strained carrots down my mouth.

"Mom, I have to go—" Click.

Anne suddenly appeared. She had ditched her coat, wearing a fur cropped sweater as if she just came from an Edith Head costuming. The woman could scare a ravenous grizzly up a tree.

"You do throw the most peculiar parties," said Anne, peeking into the bathroom.

44

Carmenia had combined champagne with enough birth control pills to make Ethel Kennedy in her rabbit-bearing years infertile. Henry and Carmenia's sister, Sylvia, got to ride in the ambulance to St. Vincent's. I didn't find it appropriate to go with them, and didn't really want to drive in the ambulance.

Even with the arrival of the paramedics, the party wouldn't come to an end, like Jason not getting the point to just die, while I watched *Friday the Thirteenth Part 2* playing from the movie screen, seating myself on a linen-covered card table. Apparently the guests thought that a body being wheeled on a stretcher made for some interesting reality-style entertainment, which was why all parties should have a Daphne.

Her ability to put an end to a party rivaled a tapped-out keg at Lambda Chi. Glasses never reached lips as she plucked them from thirsty hands, instructing servers to take away platters as anxious hands rappelled to the ground.

"Fun party," she said, once the guests were cleared. Andy's hand fiddled with the doorknob.

"Yeah. Will be a hard one to forget."

J3 walked over, a faint circle around his eye. I forgot that we were in costume. I looked down at myself, now that the party was over, and I spoke to my friends without any pants on.

"Oh, wait," I said, pulling Andy's glasses from my shirt pocket. "Thanks for these. Unfortunately, I didn't really get to use them."

Andy walked over, taking the glasses from me, unsuccessfully suppressing his relief in his determined collection. Daphne gave him a disapproving look. You knew that this would be addressed in the Volvo en route home.

The end of a party always had a moribund sadness, like a vacated fairground or finished bowl of low-fat ice cream. Taking in the tipped-over glasses and the floor smudged with the imprints of shoes, the obsessive cleaner in me wanted to tidy up so not to awake and be reminded of what was once great and was now over, which should only be destined for actors who appear in high-budget sequels.

The cleaners would be coming in the morning. I couldn't find a service that would work after 3:00 AM. With no place to sit, I unlocked the office, burrowing my way through the stored furniture with the same maneuvers of navigating a crowded bar.

I made my way around chairs and a lamp stacked on the desk, like unsightly outdoor sculptures made from salvaged trash, and to the corner of the couch. I sat and stared, trying to draw a tabloid-reading blank from anything substantive.

J3 entered the doorframe, knocking on the panel to tap me out of my zone.

"Mind if I join you?"

I nodded. Seeing him, energy had been summoned from a reserve supply, now running on battery.

"Great night," he joked.

"I'll say."

"Should we move all of this stuff back into the living room?"

No.

"I guess so."

"Or we can get the moving people to do it tomorrow," he said. J3 was smart that way. "It will only cost us another $750."

"You mean cost Henry another $750."

He looked pleased, industriously pushing his way around obstructing furniture to facilitate his sitting next to me without having to make all of the awkward shimmies I did. The circle around his eye was still visible. I traced my finger along the contour of the line.

"Don't forget to wash that off or you may awake to a stained pillowcase."

"You know what I can't understand?" J3 asked. I gave him an I-have-no-idea shrug.

"It just seemed so impolite for Carmenia to drink the good champagne. Wear all of your stuff. The girl has nerve."

"Exactly! So thought the same thing. Damn Brazilians."

"I thought she came from Argentina."

And the difference was?

"I guess there's no real difference—like Ohio over Kentucky. Or something like that," he said.

My fingers slipped from their lock around my knees, causing my legs to plummet from the grasp of my hug. A good thing, considering that I had become numb to the fact that I still only wore Henry's shirt. Putting my hand against the couch to mold myself into a new comfortable yet tasteful position, I noticed its crease spitting up something purple. I dug my hand into its cavity, my finger catching the band of a purple thong. Reeling it in, I pointed my finger into the air, the desk lamp spotlighting the object of focus.

"These yours?" I asked J3.

"Not really my style. Don't really find comfort in having a shoelace wedged up my butt."

I shot my hand back and flung the panties across the room in surfcasting motion. The thong caught on the desk lamp, the shimmer of lace creating latticed shadows on our faces.

"Well, then who the hell do they belong to?"

J3 shrugged.

"The door was locked for the party, so no one could sneak in here for a quick one. And they're not mine."

I wanted to ask if they belonged to Amanda, but that would be weird.

We heard the front door open and close, followed by voices and a crack of laughter. Then Henry said that J3 and I must be asleep.

"We're in here, the office," I yelled. J3 quickly got up from the couch and tried to make his exit, but was blocked by Henry. Sylvia shadowed him.

"Hi," said J3. Henry looked at him cautiously.

I walked over to the panties and pinched the band, holding them like a dead animal for fear of catching some backcountry disease.

"Whose are these?" I asked Henry, my voice marinated with accusation.

"How the hell should I know?" he stammered. "We just had a party where alcoholic beverages were consumed, illicit behavior an inevitable byproduct. I'm sure it's just a couple of people finding the couch a comfortable and private place to hook up."

"The door was locked. How did you know they were in the couch?"

"I didn't. I mean, I naturally assumed. Emily, what are you getting at?" Henry again employed his offence-is-the-best-defense tone.

"And how's Carmenia?" said J3.

"Fine, she just needs to spend the night in the hospital—just a little scare. I told Sylvia she could stay with us tonight, since she's visiting from Argentina and it would be a shame for her to go home to Carmenia's vacant apartment."

No, it wouldn't.

"Ez eet okie weet you?" she asked.

No, absolutely not.

"Sure. I suppose."

"Here," said J3, patting his hand on Sylvia's collapsible back. I thought she'd disintegrate like an ashen vase, she looked so frail.

J3 and Sylvia disappeared. I wondered where J3 would take her, considering the disarray of the party and no extra bedrooms. Perhaps I should have attended to her.

As I began to exit the panty-contaminated room, Henry pushed me back in, brimming with conflict.

"Emily, we need to talk."

No one must ever say "Emily, we need to talk." I needed to include this on a list of requirements that make me operate, like directions that come with a new phone.

"They belong to Carmenia, don't they?" I said, snipping the side of the thong with my pinched fingers and then slingshot them in his face.

Henry caught them, making a glass-thrown-in-face expression.

"Yes. Or I assume so. Carmenia has been here before."

That was harsh.

"And so what are we going to do about your extra-curricular sexual activities?"

"Would you stop trying to find ways to recite lines from your favorite brat pack movies—especially when it involves us?"

He busted me. I've always wanted to base my life around *St. Elmo's Fire*, but I didn't apply to Georgetown because of the fragmented social life.

"I think the issue here is you and Carmenia, and that I am handling this with remarkable alacrity and poise. You should be kissing my tasteful little butt, which would never be harnessed by a piece of purple sateen that she got free from wearing it in a catalogue shoot."

Henry looked to me sadly, disappointed. The luminosity spawned from his eyes adjusted to their brightest level, like two lit bedroom windows seen from outside.

"I am admitting to a past offense. You may recall your postponing our wedding preparations for this fear of becoming a 'Bridezilla,' which I took as rejection. Your timing came when I was being relentlessly pursued."

I felt myself fall into the couch, my body twitching. I slammed my hands against my ears. I wanted to sing nursery rhymes like a fitful child shutting out the reprimands of a parent, but thought this may appear melodramatic.

"It meant nothing. And, as you could probably gather, it became quickly evident that Carmenia is a freak. I don't know what really happened with the Winthrop/mugging episode—she's denied any wrongdoing to me—but I know the girl has severe issues and needs help."

"You had an affair with a butt model. She gets her hair done, minions dress her in lingerie you can buy in malls, she pouts in front of a camera, and then gets a paycheck."

"I have a case too, Emily. Your relationship with J3? I consider that far more damaging than anything I'm guilty of."

My face went into eighteen-hundred different directions, like erratic strokes of paint before they collided into a complete picture.

"Since he's lived here, I've had to watch the woman I am madly in love with fall in love with someone else. It's been the most difficult thing I've ever had to experience."

I became miffed by Henry's calling me a "woman." I didn't think I was a woman. I mean I'm not a girl, but definitely not yet a woman.

"Where's your engagement ring, Emily?"

My hand suddenly grabbed my naked engagement finger. I lost the ring that Henry's grandfather gave to his grandmother.

"Naturally, I'd be a lot more assured if I saw it on your finger rather than in your lingerie drawer."

The ring was in my lingerie drawer. I've never gotten around to having it resized.

How did Henry know that it was in my lingerie drawer? My brows tilted into confused flecks. Had he been snooping? How dare he.

Now we were both silent. I considered bringing up the issue of his snooping, but there may have been other issues that trumped that one.

"So what should we do now?" Henry asked.

"I want you to leave."

45

I heard Henry's voice, then the mumblings of J3 and Sylvia in the kitchen. I stood at the edge of the door, my ear like a glass suctioned to a wall. I wondered if a glass suctioned to a wall really had stethoscope-to-chest results.

On my tiptoes, I moved through the sullied living room, standing outside the kitchen door.

"I want you out of here!" yelled Henry. That came in clearly. "You are a damn manipulator. A thief. Coming in here and blatantly stealing my fiancée away from me. Get out!"

I heard J3 get up. It was too late for me to run.

Walking through the kitchen doorway, he froze at the sight of me. I couldn't believe I'd been wearing Henry's damn shirt all of this time. Surely I could have run up and put some pants on at some point in this never-ending night.

J3 just stared at me intently—that moment a couple has, wondering if it's okay to take that first kiss. J3 did have access to a roped-off place in my heart.

He then brushed passed me and went in the direction of his room.

"What are you doing?" I said, walking into the kitchen. Sylvia watched me in surprised animation. Sylvia had had a full night. "J3 lives here too."

"Right. Well, now no one has rights to this place. If I can't be here with you, J3 sure as hell can't. I'm calling Barb first thing. Back on the market."

Did he mean that he was back on the market or our fabulous home was? As everything pummeled to a loss-of-appetite-without-the-desire-to-lose-pounds end, I would have preferred for Henry to be back on the market.

"Okay," I said weakly.

J3 walked through the kitchen carrying a body bag packed with clothes, his hand nervously tugging the strap of his satchel.

"Have the rest of my stuff shipped to L.A., like we said," he said to Henry. And then J3 walked out.

"Ready, Sylvia?" Henry said

Sylvia had a sudden look of relief, pushing herself out of her chair. When they left, I took control of Sylvia's chair, my butt cushioning her fresh imprints, and downed a glass of flat champagne.

46

The morning light touched my nose with the brush of a wind. I had forgotten where I was or how I got there, like a hotel bed slept in after a late-night arrival. I lay on top of J3's duvet, which smelled like the spices baby Jesus received on his birthday, the makings of the best holiday ever. Still wearing Henry's shirt, which would be used to wipe the dust bunnies off my luggage, I smelled of cigarettes and perfume. My body was spinning with conflict. I needed a bowl of Frosted Flakes and decaf hazelnut.

It rained that morning and didn't stop for six days. I know this because I made a pact with myself that I'd deal with the current situation when the rain passed, which was six days later. The only things I did in those six days were stare out the window, move around a few things in my closet, and sleep on top of J3's duvet.

I had fallen into the habit of saying good morning when answering the phone around 4:00 PM, so Daphne took on rescue mission. I feel she was still serving penance from the time she ran over a pregnant duck while driving with her learner's permit. I heard the phone ring before 4:00 PM, but the ringing stopped before its allotted time; Daphne had let herself in and industriously began her crusade.

"Emily," she said, walking into J3's room with the cordless, "it's the movers."

"What do they want?"

"To move you."

"Okay."

"Okay?"

"They can move me."

"Emily will call you back."

She took out a small black leather pad that opened up to sheets of ecru paper and jotted something down, presenting me with the paper. I looked at it. It was beautiful, could be framed.

"I love this," I said. "Thank you."

"It's just the number for the movers."

"But you put such creativity into it."

"I'm getting a little worried."

"Worried?"

"Worried."

"Why worried?"

"Because we haven't seemed to get past the swallowing oatmeal with apple juice, dropping medication phase of this little retreat."

"Do you have any apple juice?"

Daphne took a juice box from her bag. Loving young moms, I poked the straw into the container and sipped around the sides so as not to dribble any on J3's duvet. I really needed to get J3's duvet cleaned before the movers came.

"This whole episode is so sad," said Daphne, rather melodramatically.

"Sad? How sad? Sad featherless bird that needs to be fed with an eyedropper? Or sad girl who wears slouchy boots and a pashmina with a cocktail dress?"

"It's always difficult to see people break apart."

"I found a thong," I began. "It's purple. Victoria's Secret. I've never bought undergarments from Victoria Secret. Well, unless you count college, but that was because the campus had no shops, not even a Saks in a neighboring town. And we didn't have the Internet then so I had to resort to catalogues, but you know how limited that is. And then you're walking around campus with students who are all wearing the same sweater bought from page 38 in J. Crew. I remember how every mailbox would be stuffed with a J. Crew catalogue during their bimonthly mailing. So, the last time I bought—"

"Emily!"

"Well, the thong is not mine."

I suddenly realized that this wasn't a joke. Henry had an affair.

"And I even changed my diet for him!"

"You gave up Equal."

Equal was my diet.

"And didn't you do that for your skin thing?"

Daphne could get unnecessarily bogged down with details.

"I'm so stupid. I'm so stupid. I'm so stupid!" Slamming my face into my hands, "Stupid! Stupid! Stupid!"

And then I released the flush of wetness that bulged behind my eyes. There was no control. Noises of dying birds squawked from my mouth. Polluted streams ran from my nose. It got messy. I felt like the drooled-over toy shaken in a dog's mouth.

"Stupid! And she's not even a real model, just one of those girls who take jobs with spray-on sweat in their cleavage. I even bought the same damn coral suit because of her."

"Oh," said Daphne, "the Marc Jacobs?"

Nodding my head was an effort.

"I love that dress. Don't get rid of it for emotional reasons. A complete waste."

I laughed. And Daphne was right, disposing of the coral suit would prove nothing. You could even say that Carmenia won if I discarded the suit.

"You need to move out of here. Start fresh. You're good that way, Emily."

I gave out fake sobs.

"Emily," Daphne demanded, "just think of how Jackie would handle this."

Jackie? Who did we know named Jackie?

"Jackie Kennedy."

I never met Jackie Kennedy.

"And remember, this Carmenia isn't a bright girl."

"And how is this good?"

"Oh, I'll tell you how this is good. Boys like Henry can't tolerate girls like Carmenia. They're whining their list of demands all the time. Ultimately, you were Henry's greatest prize."

"I was?"

I didn't mean to fish here, have Daphne give me the I'm-the-girl-they-intercept-at-the-airport speech, but I didn't oppose hearing her say it.

"Don't be a fool. You never asked him if you looked fat."

"That's true."

"And Carmenia did stalk you."

"Actually, she intended for me to be the shallot in a wok."

"And she wasn't one with common sense."

"I guess the mixing birth control pills with Cristal gave that away?"

We laughed.

"You'll be fine."

I would be.

"Henry had been annoying me for the past year, anyway."

"Then why did you keep this going?"

"For the same reason you don't donate your Fendi baguette to Goodwill."

Daphne nodded, completely getting it.

"I am strong. I can do anything. Except maybe drive off a cliff without wearing a seatbelt. And I can take a trip! Some expedition where I'll identify wildlife by their Latin names. I'll act responsibly. Be a woman of means and independence. I'll buy mutual funds!"

Whatever mutual funds were. Henry and I had mutual funds; that, I'd miss.

"I suppose I've been through this all before. You've had your doubts about Henry, I know that, and I understand why you've never said anything."

A mild shock wave passed over Daphne's face.

"It's okay. Really."

Daphne hugged me. I felt bad because I hadn't taken a shower and my lips were moist from nose drool. But she did have two children and had on maternity clothes.

"I always worry about you and these standards of yours."

"Pray tell?"

"I sometimes think you're holding out for Brad, thinking he'll dump Jennifer."

"No!"

Perhaps.

"So? Who's the ideal composite of this week?"

Daphne did have this intuitive read on me. I sometimes wondered if we had a soulful connection, like if she came down with a stomach illness, I'd feel the pain, like those weird identical twins.

The other night, I watched a nature program on PBS, featuring a millionaire businessman who now dedicated himself to saving the Amazon macaw from the threat of extinction. I had a crush on him. I don't know how I'd meet him and really had no time to book a trip to the Amazon right now. I supposed the real issue was that I needed to stop breathing in the sparkly dust from chasing this elusive unicorn—a hard thing, as I've always wanted to ride bareback on a unicorn, wearing a chiffony skirt that had a big show on the runways.

"Just a few specifics are needed. He'd have to be smart, passionate, and have sex appeal."

"And you're describing everyone from Justin Timberlake to John Edwards—the politician, not that weird séance guy—so let's narrow down the pool based on intensive taste tests. Which is it? Henry or J3?"

"You say this as if we were deciding outfits."

She looked at me as if this was precisely what she meant.

"Come on. Which one?"

I thought about Henry. His humor, all man, and how he got me. I thought of J3.

"And you can't deliberate. Make a choice," she quipped.

"Sure you can."

"This is not *The Bachelor*, Emily."

"Obviously, Henry and I have had our issues. He's that fun houseguest who doesn't get the second invite. Exciting at first, makes a mess, and doesn't clean up after himself. But J3? First off, he's so smart. Has these Rhodes and Fellowship distinctions without being a hobbit."

Daphne approved. She had been grading me all along.

47

Barb had no difficulties in selling the loft. I had to delete about a dozen of her congratulatory e-mails and voice mails about how fantastic a realtor she was. We did make a considerable profit, aside from this capital gains tax that made me reassess my choice in choosing a presidential candidate based on who looked best in a red Hermes tie.

Mother arranged for J3's and my things to be moved. All I had to do was put purple tabs on my belongings and green tabs on J3's. Much deliberation had been given between the purple and green tabs, settling on purple for me since the color green did not reflect my current mood. I looked over the disassembled battleground, a field of varying builds of boxes and a few cords sprouting from the floor's creases.

A few essentials were packed in a liquor box, and I sat on it, staring at the door where Mother would soon appear. Precisely fifteen minutes before her scheduled time, she made her entrance wearing all black with cordovan leather accessories. Her designer bob was pulled in a headband with the same ridges and tassels as her spectator shoes, and she wore driving gloves so tight she could operate a cell phone the size of a Franciscan monk's nose. I called this Mom's Moving Outfit.

"Okay now," she said, clapping her hands. "I handled the movers.

Did you put the tabs on your things?" I nodded, looking at the tips of my shoes; underneath, my green nail polish stubbornly clung to my cuticles, reinforcing the importance of a good pedicure.

"What color?" asked Mom.

"Green."

"So the green boxes will be sent to your Aunt Peg's and the purple ones sent to J3."

"No. The purple ones are mine."

"Then why did you say green?"

"Because my toes are green."

"Why for God's sakes are your toes green? I've told you to wear thongs in your gym's shower."

"No, they're painted green."

"How strange."

"Not really. Green is the new cranberry. *Allure* says so."

Her brows collapsed, which caused her head to shake.

"You look sour," she said.

"Thanks."

"Now, don't get yourself into a tether."

I tried to understand how one gets into a tether.

"And I saw Daphne at the New York Hospital benefit—handsome husband of hers. But she is looking rather fat."

"Mom. She's pregnant!"

"I said fat. Not pregnant—there's a difference."

Oh, good lord.

"She thinks you'll come out of this on top. Really make something from your situation and be better for it in the long term."

Daphne. A *People* magazine subscriber.

"Now, don't keep that pretty head of yours in the clouds," she directed.

I loved the idea of being so tall, like a mystical giant, that my head could be lost in the clouds.

"And your cousin Anne was at this benefit."

"I went to a benefit the other week. Rick Springfield was there!"

Mother looked confused. My singing "Jessie's Girl" was apparently of no help.

"And Anne would be a good person for you to speak to. She'd

give excellent relationship advice. So good-natured, with all of that charity work she does."

Anne, who I've witnessed taking a drag from her cigarette and blowing it into the household help's face, until her facialist told her smoking prematurely aged skin.

"She was with that boy she's always around. What's his name?"

"Jason Whitten. Her husband. You gave a speech at their wedding."

"Right. Thought that was him, by the way she kept telling him how horribly he dressed until she took control."

Anne's husband is now called "You're-Wearing-That?"

"So, the car is waiting downstairs. The movers will be here at three and know to deliver your things tomorrow at noon so it won't disrupt your Auntie Peg. They have keys, and Auntie Peg said there is a small vacant room in the basement that can be used to store everything."

"Thanks. You really took control."

"I do have an ability for this sort of thing."

I crouched down to lift up the box, dropping it on my toe.

"Oh, shit!"

Mother did not look pleased.

"Emily? Watch it."

"You know," I said, bouncing on one foot, "sometimes that word just meets the requirements of the action."

"And are you sure you want to stay at Auntie Peg's? You can always stay with us for a little bit."

My Aunt Peg would be leaving for Palm Beach tomorrow—permanently relocating for health reasons, something about avoiding the pollution, erratic weather patterns, and disagreeable people. She lived in a townhouse on East Seventy-second Street and liked the idea of her childhood home being inhabited by a Briggs.

"I sometimes wonder about Auntie Peg," said Mom. "The other day she said that I was fussy. Me? Fussy? Do you think I am fussy?"

Yes.

"No."

"She does have definite opinions, that one. Why don't you just spend the night with us? Before she leaves at least."

"No, it will be fine. And this is all temporary, you remember. Until I find my own place."

"You are becoming quite the little feminist."

This was the second time I've been called a feminist. I'd have to watch this.

"Auntie Peg's should be fine," I said, trying to soften her funny looks.

I imagined Auntie Peg's house, a.k.a. The Preppy Handbook Memorial—a basement with lots of sporting equipment made from wood, first-edition books, missing keys in the piano, creaky steps covered with tattered Orientals, and doorknobs that took a certain level of skill to open. Living there would be less than ideal.

"Every time I open something, it seems to break," I said weakly.

Mother looked petrified. I should have never said this; now I'd be subjected to regular check-ins.

We drove uptown to the hum that large limousines make. Outside Auntie Peg's, my mother, in her most unhelpful of tones, asked if she needed to accompany me inside. When I declined her offer, she had a striking resemblance to Mao after being thrown a treat.

"You know, Emily, it's a good idea that you refrain from contacting Henry. It's the dignified way to act."

I walked into Auntie Peg's, dialing Henry from the hall phone.

48

Calling Henry needed to be done, regardless. It said so beneath "Don't remind Henry to take my name off his checking account," on my To Do list.

"Emily!"

If I wasn't speaking on a phone, I'd be dodging the flecks of spit I knew were shooting from Henry's mouth.

"I was about to call you."

Then why didn't you call?

"How are you? Where are you? I miss you. What are you doing right now?"

"Hi, Henry," I said.

"Hi," he said.

"You had sex with a girl who wears purple rayon/cotton blend underwear."

"Emily. Don't do this."

"Do what?" I asked, admiring the crescent shapes of my cuticles.

"We can't speak this way. Can we meet up?"

I shook my head.

"Emily?"

"I said that we could. And probably just as well, we have business to discuss, and you know how I feel about lawyers."

"How do you feel about lawyers?"

"Don't like them."

"So, I have to go to the loft to check on things—can you meet me there in about an hour?"

"How about tonight?"

"The president is speaking tonight."

And this was important why?

"You knew the president was speaking tonight?"

Meaning, you're not so shallow and apathetic as to not listen to the leader of the free world?

"Can't you just TiVo him?"

"You can't TiVo the president."

What? Government agents will go after you?

"We don't TiVo anyway, Emily."

This was true. Henry and me, we weren't TiVo people. Considering the importance of time and feeding your mind with substance, we rarely watched television, except for WB. And tonight my shows were on, which I wouldn't be able to watch because the president decided he must rally the American people's support because it's a crucial time for his approval rating. If this president had any consideration about the improvement of this taxpayer's concerns, he would not be cutting into my WB.

"I can meet you there in about two hours," I allowed, and I didn't tack on the hour to be coy. I truly intended to use it.

"Okay. See you at 4:30 PM?"

I nodded.

"Okay, Em?"

"I said it was okay." And then I hung up the phone, immediately calling Daphne.

"Daphne. Do you have any pot?"

Daphne always had a baggie of pot hidden in her freezer the way I had low-fat Ben & Jerry's.

"Hi, Emily and, no, I had to dump it in case I had any second doubts about carrying this baby. Why, do you need some? You never smoke."

"Because I have to meet up with Henry and I really can't chance the cocktail calories, pills are too trendy, and I have to be on something."

"Do you have a pen?"

I nodded.

"555-9266."

I loved that Daphne could read my expressions while telecommunicating.

"Ask for Pippa."

Pippa?

"Pippa?"

"Pippa."

"Who's Pippa?"

"A friend from Princeton who always has pot to sell."

Silence.

"Emily?"

"Yes."

"What's wrong?"

"Well, I've never bought drugs before. I am a retail drug virgin. Kind of hoping that there would be this system of coded dialogue and secret drop-offs."

"I can ask Pippa to do that if you want."

I wanted Daphne to do that.

"That's okay."

Silence.

"Daphne?" I asked, my voice breaking into its insecure tone. "Do I look okay?"

We're speaking on the phone.

"You look fabulous, having a thin day, and I love your coat."

"Can you live with me?"

"Yes. I was hoping we could get engaged soon. I mean, who are we kidding? It's been a long time, and we're meant to be together."

This made me smile. Though I did feel a bit Camilla Parker Bowles—breaking up Daphne's marriage with Andy—and kids were involved.

After saying our "I love you's," feeling one part lesbian, I called Pippa, who lived in the same Park Avenue building as John Corzine.

I snapped closed my cell. I had been conducting all of this business in the marble-entombed hallway of Auntie Peg's. I punched the alarm, pushed the door quickly before it changed its mind, getting in a potent whiff of wet pugs and Elton John candles, and kicked my box into the entranceway, shouting "Hi, Auntie Peg! Bye,

Auntie Peg!" then tiptoed out the door mischievously and hailed a
cab so I could have my first drug deal.

Riding in passenger mode, I completely forgot the issue of my
primping for the breakup conversation. I wondered if the act of
thinking about getting stoned perpetuated symptoms.

I dropped my chin, checking out my figure. Even though I've
spent the past week subsisting on Fig Newtons and dropped exercise, I still fit into my AG's bought the week after my Ashram trip,
and my skin had the "After" picture effect of Dr. Perricone. Daphne
said this had something to do with tricking your hormones. I wondered how I could trick my hormones every day.

I asked the cab if he could wait while I went to the ATM—drug
money—but he refused, complaining about the mayor.

I paid my fare, felt very *Less Than Zero* for depleting my funds for
drug money, and bought illegal drugs from a woman with a personal
trainer, chef, two nannies, and at-home brow shaping by Eliza.

Pippa had a round face and two pen-marked eyes with a strawberry blond Dutch-boy cut. Think James from *James and the Giant
Peach* as a girl. Pippa—saying her name brought on the same happy
delirium as ordering a pint of Tasti D-Lite—Pippa, sweet enough to
offer me her bong and take a few hits with me, also gave me a quick
makeover, which involved little metal tools. I gave Pippa the low-
down on my need for drugs while she twirled my hair and created a
loose chignon, offered the use of her driver, which I declined, worried about the hidden costs. She then rearranged the collar of my
trench by folding it down and smoothing the lapels. Outside Pippa's
range of surveillance, I pulled the collar back up, appreciating the
Catherine Deneuve YSL look.

During the cab ride, Daphne and I rehearsed the impending
Henry conversation over the mobile I borrowed from the driver. He
seemed annoyed by this. She'd act out Henry's part, actually sucking in her stomach to hit the masculine chords, and I played myself—continually reminded that this would be a live taping and I
couldn't screw this one up.

Daphne asked if I was stoned. I was stoned. Perhaps the cab driver wasn't annoyed that I borrowed his phone, basing this on possible drug-induced paranoia.

"Are you sure it's a good idea that you're so stoned?" she asked. "I'm actually a bit worried about this. Why did you get stoned?"

It would be funny.

"And what are you wearing?"

I still had on the Emily moving outfit from earlier, a move that involved kicking a box into Auntie Peg's foyer, necessitating low-slung corduroys, flats, and a layering of pastel cashmere. Though I did have on the trench and the benefit of a Pippa makeover, I knew that my appearance would not pass Daphne's approval, making excuses about the phone breaking up by going through a nonexistent tunnel.

49

Riding up in the elevator, with its nice faux paneling, it felt strange to be a visitor to my residence. The doors opened as I was abusing myself for pressing the wrong floor.

"Hello, love," said Mrs. Hallingby.

She stepped into the elevator, her feet tipped in shiny loafers, dressed conservatively with a bit of an edge from the heavy purple-rimmed glasses. She resembled one of those chic older ladies they feature on computer ads to try and attract her market.

"I lost my frog," she said. "He hopped away somewhere, and I am going to find him."

"What does he look like?" I asked.

"Well, he's green," she began. "But not a Kermit green, more like *The Wind and the Willows* chap—sort of a grassy green."

I nodded along, trying to make a visual.

"Does he have any distinguishing spots or features?"

"Actually he does—a little crown perched on his head."

"But couldn't that fall off?"

"I doubt it. Krazy Glue is pretty secure."

I nodded and then said, "I see. Well, I'll be sure to keep an eye out for any crowned frogs."

"You are so kind. I'm sure he's close by. He may even hop on home without my noticing."

The elevator opened to the lobby. Mrs. Hallingby stepped out and waved good-bye while I pressed the right floor. I waved my hand, wishing her luck in the search effort for her frog right as the door closed.

Riding back up in the elevator, I wondered if faux paneling was retro cool or just cheap? The apartment was unlocked. I walked into an opera hall.

Henry walked into the room humming.

"Oh, I didn't know you were here."

"I just arrived. What the hell is with this music? The soundtrack of suicide's greatest hits?"

Henry fed a portable stereo with another CD. *Turandot,* I gathered, which made me suspect that he set this moment to music.

"I tried calling you before, but your phone must have been off."

"Didn't I say that you could never call me again?"

"No."

"Oh. Okay then. So what is that you wanted?"

"I didn't know if you had my Stanford sweatshirt."

I shook my head and shrugged.

"Well, then I must have misplaced it."

"Right. Misplaced. And Mrs. Hallingby lost her frog. Did you happen to see a frog with a crown?"

"Are you stoned?"

"No."

I couldn't chance any liability that anything I said may be used against me from Henry's knowing I may not be completely sound.

He walked over to me, kissed my cheek. I could tell he wanted to do more, but I think that my bending over to tie my ballet flat may have clued him in that I wasn't in the mood.

"So where are you staying?" he asked.

"With family."

Henry nodded, a nod that said that this made complete sense.

"I see. I'm thinking about moving back to L.A. There's no spirituality in New York."

Yes. L.A. A real Mecca.

"You should know I am staying with Sylvia. It's only temporary."

"Who the hell is Sylvia?"

"Carmenia's sister. You know her—she was there, the night of the party."

"The one that's so young she has no idea how to make a Shrinky Dink?"

Henry looked up to the ceiling, as if it were labeled with the proper response.

"Weebles Wobble but they don't fall down," I sang. I then reached for the phone pad and began making a drawing of Mrs. Hallingby's lost frog.

"Emily? What are you talking about?"

"Are you now sleeping with Sylvia?"

He started to twist pieces of hair around his finger, creating little dreads. I took this to mean yes, he was sleeping with Sylvia. The boy needed to be fixed.

"You are so Bachelor #2. She is the kind of girl who would go on television to meet a husband. Buying her prom dress is a recent memory for this girl."

"Don't be so hard on Sylvia. She's really talented—just cut a CD."
Great!

"But you're right, she is rather young. That not remembering, or even knowing that the space shuttle Columbia blew up because she wasn't alive kind of thing can be weird."

"You are so Donald Trump. You keep getting older, but your woman don't age. You are so—" I paused, exhausted from trying to drum up more comparisons. "You are so that guy who is annoying. And you're completely wrong for me. Everything with you is about money and sex."

"Emily? What on God's earth are you talking about?"

I didn't really know, but liked saying money and sex for the dramatic effect.

"I want us to work things out," he said.

Now my jaw dropped and I began to laugh, a hysterical, villainous laugh.

"Emily. Life is too short and we need to be together."

"For you—maybe—but I had my palm read. I'll be around for quite a bit."

I studied my palm, wondering which was my life line. Henry also stared at his palm.

"Where's my love line?" he asked, serving me the palm of his hand.

"That one," I said, pointing to his most frayed line, having no idea what it was. "Doesn't look good."

"So. Let's just move on. Continue where we left off before room-mates and stalkers."

"Not if you were the last man on earth. And that would never happen, because if you were, I would shoot you."

"You must really hate me. Enough to want to kill me."

I looked at Henry, wondering what I'd have for dinner that night. I'd have to research different takeout places, considering I wasn't versed in the East side's selection. Maybe I'd go out, or invite myself over to Daphne's. I'd invite myself over to Daphne's, and she could fill me in on the area's better takeout places. Perhaps she'd even give me some menus.

"No. I don't hate you. It's so beneath me and not worth a Scott Peterson. I'm also squeamish, as you know, and the mess of a body . . . Basically, I'm indifferent toward you."

Henry opened a cabinet. His box of Clif Bars remained. He took one, unwrapped its foil, and proceeded to take a bite. It looked really good.

"You're eating a Clif Bar!"

He looked at the Clif Bar as if it could plead its defense.

"I can't believe you can eat a Clif Bar now!"

Henry put down the Clif Bar. We both looked at it forlornly. A waste of beautiful food, like your hot nice gay friend, that you could never have.

"Are you seeing someone?" he asked, his voice breaking into an insecure tone, which pleased me. I considered pulling a George Glass, but didn't care enough to addle him. I settled by giving him a look.

"Emily, you and me." He smiled into the air. I had to act fast and swiped the Clif Bar. "No you and the world would be a confusing place."

I wondered if Henry would notice the missing Clif Bar.

"I see how this helps you, but how exactly does my being with you help me? You need help."

"You are so baked," he said.

"I have to give you your ring back."

"You already did."

I did?

"So we're not together?" Henry asked.

When did I give him back that ring? I became impressed with my responsibility and dignified actions, which seemed uncharacteristic in my current climate.

"We're not together. Besides. We can't be together. You're a Pisces."

"And this means?"

"Something about your emotions and my fiery nature. I called Giselle."

"You have supermodels telling you your horoscope?"

"No! So typical. Assuming that the only Giselle is—" I made a sudden pause. I was quite baked. "Sorry. I'm just sorry," I said, making a quick, deliberate turn. Walking out the door, I looked back one last time and gave an impromptu wave. Henry looked pale, attempted to raise his hand but it seemed lifeless.

Riding down in the elevator—what horrendous faux paneling— I inserted my picture of Mrs. Hallingby's lost frog into a frame that displayed some unimportant fire hazard precautions. Reflecting on what had just happened, I realized that Henry did not try to win me over with gifts, unless you counted a half-eaten Clif Bar that tasted better than taboo desserts on a Jean Georges menu. Henry did not try to win me back with material goods. Possibly I could have been convinced with a Cartier tank.

50

I do not want to date again. I look at the *Vogue* party pages, and there's a picture of J3 with Amanda. I needed to date again. Amanda wore a Gucci dress made from the scraps of paper cutout dolls, something that fit the trend of the *Vogue* style page. Kirsten Dunst had on the same dress. It looked better on Kirsten Dunst.

The room I've chosen to escape life in was solely for the purpose of television watching, The Television Room. You'd expect Hope Lange and Suzy Parker to drop by. The valances, sectional, and two slipper chairs were patterned in an antique floral print by Brunswig & Fils I've seen on the skirts of fat girls at garden parties, complimenting the borders of a Le Lac chintz carpeting, a purchase that probably came with a decorator. Picasso lithographs and fashion illustrations from fifties issues of *Vogue* were framed in olive wood with thick matting. There were ceramic monkeys that held trays, humped over, and one with a raised hand holding a light bulb. I thought of the dead monkey in the tree joke, wishing I still had on a buzz. I never knew Auntie Peg to be the monkey type and assumed she needed a pug break.

Auntie Peg probably had no idea what a plasma or flat-screen television was, the house hardly being state of the art. I'd have to chip my Ben & Jerry's from a prison of ice in the freezer that may be one of the first models. The television was large, set in its own nook in an olive-colored wall unit that had many coffee-table books on royal families, Europe, and museum art exhibitions. I thumbed through a book about Calder and considered making mobiles of people and woodland sprites.

Another shelf had souvenirs from Auntie Peg's ripe stage. I was particularly drawn to a picture of her wearing dolphin blue capris and smoking a cigarette at Les Deux Magots. Her hair was styled in a shag, the ends frayed from being cut with a razor the way you shear gift ribbons so they bounce into ringlets. Auntie Peg's hairstyles were virtual timepieces—dating back to waves made from tourniquets of ripped sheets, curlers worn under a headscarf, and at-home permanents, to her present style of turbans and feathered hats that mask the days she can't make it to the beauty parlor.

My lifting the picture's frame caused a tumble, disrupting its alternate function as a bookend to a gathering of Russians—Gogol, Chekhov, and Turgenev, each copy soaked in dust and heavily underlined. Auntie Peg was a product from when culture marked the white leather studded accessory donned by today's rap star.

I turned on the television, and an ad for Lancome's new perfume appeared. I knew this was their new perfume having its blitz of publicity, as I just saw the print ad in *W.* Normally I'd flick off a commercial as quick as a price tag for something not worth what I'd paid, but perfume commercials were different, almost poetic— beautiful creatures in exotic locations with music from progressive bands who cash in for a hefty check made after an afternoon in the recording studio.

The woman looked at her what I assumed to be lover—noted by the FCC-approved bare-shoulder insinuation of nudity—and then began to cry. I started to cry. I cried at a Lancome perfume ad that didn't show the product it peddled. The bottle made an appearance, but television had yet to master smell.

I could hear the sounds of Auntie Peg from the creaking of her walker over the old floorboards sounding like sex on a motel mattress, and the nasal infected breathing of her five dozen pugs (three, to be precise).

"Emily, darling," she muffled.

Auntie Peg was dressed as brightly as Florida produce in tangerine shantung pants, bolero, green velvet slippers, and a turban with a topaz brooch pinned to the crease. If a Matisse portrait could age on its canvas, Auntie Peg would be the sitter.

"I like your turban," I said unconvincingly. She bounced her invisible coif with the palm of her hand.

"Yes. They are quite effective when I go to the beauty parlor."

I'd recently learned that Auntie Peg referred to the salon as the beauty parlor, a place she went to almost every day.

"Are you okay, dear?"

I had forgotten that Lancome's marketing people had successfully suckered me, and I might have appeared out of sorts.

"Sure. Great."

"Well, I called your cousin Anne, as I couldn't bear the thought of you being alone while I was at my appointments."

Her appointments that would take less than two hours? I was now on suicide watch. I did cry at a Lancome perfume ad.

"Really. You shouldn't have," I said in the form of an order.

"Anne loves you."

???

"But you two girls are so different. It's as if you aren't really related."

Perhaps Auntie Peg had some insight into the matter of the man that delivered our mail in the early seventies.

"I am worried about you living here on your own. I just had an idea."

I waited for Auntie Peg to say what her idea was, but that privilege only comes by asking, "What's your idea, Auntie Peg?"

"Why don't you stay with me in Palm Beach! Lots of lovely boys."

I felt like the pretty but stupid little girl in a Brontë novel being sent away with her rich auntie so she could be appropriately matched.

"Tempting," I said.

"You know everyone wants to stay with me in Palm Beach right now because they think I'm going to die. They all want dibs on my money."

Okay, this was weird.

"What I can't understand is why they think I'd fiddle with the will now. It's not like I'm married to some bimbo like that Texan man and that Anna Nicole Simpson tart."

Auntie Peg got her tabloid stories a bit mixed.

"I mean, who else would I leave my money to?"

The pugs, considering they all received silver-framed-picture placement on the never-used piano.

"Can I ask you something, Emily?"

No.

"Sure."

"Why can't you use a cell phone on a plane? Will the plane suddenly need to make a crash landing if someone uses their cell phone?"

"Do you even have a cell phone?"

"Yes. It's very effective in the car to call my appointment if I'm running late."

The woman spends fifty dollars a month to announce her thirty-second lateness.

"I would leave your cell phone use to doing just that."

"And then there are all these disruptive requirements you need to do at the airport. These "terror" people have become quite, excuse me for saying, the pain in the ass. The airport people would think I have weapons of mass destruction hidden in my wheelchair from all of the added precautions they take. As if a little old woman in a wheelchair would be a threat?"

"I guess that's how they think the terrorists would think."

"But I've gotten around the shoe thing." Auntie Peg then began to laugh. The pugs wagged their tails and pawed her until she calmed their spastic heads with fluttered pats. "I wear slippers!"

Crazy.

"And all of the packing, only to be mussed up by these people who wash their hands with communal liquid soap. The key is to pack items in clear plastic bags. I believe they're called 'baggies.' "

Baggies, also effective for preserving marijuana in the freezer, but I didn't think Auntie Peg would care for the added uses.

"And then there's the matter of snacks."

No, not the snacks.

"I never really cared for plane food. So I just have a big breakfast and take cut vegetables and butter cookies, which I also pack in those baggies."

This conversation drove my respect-your-elder-graciousness into traffic driving delirium without having the curb to drive up on.

"So are you excited to be leaving for Florida?" I asked, saying anything to turn the conversation.

"Oh, I do love my old house. But all of my friends are doing the strangest thing."

I needed to say, "What strange thing is that?" to prompt a response.

"They're buying these condo properties on this swampy golf course. Emily, you wouldn't believe what you can see there."

I imagined two geriatric men dressed in plaid pants with neon yellow cardigans, fencing each other with golf clubs.

"There are real live alligators!"

As opposed to the mechanical ones.

"And the alligators swallow up baby ducks. Who wants to watch such a horrific thing like that?"

Actually that sounded quite interesting—very reality Discovery Channel live.

"And do you know what Mrs. Reinhardt did?"

"What did Mrs. Reinhardt do?"

"She propped open her door so the air conditioning from the hallway would filter into her condo!"

The woman stole air.

"She even had to be spoken to by the board. What an embarrassment!"

"How cheesy."

"You want some cheese, dear?"

Anne walked in, jingling to Cartier bangles as she unzipped a laptop from its case and began her presentation. She instructed Auntie Peg in kidnapper delivery that she must be reachable online, adding that the p.c. included a game of bridge as a lure.

Auntie Peg huffed, mumbling about the world's ending with electronic robots, like the ones from that Ronald Reagan movie where his eyes lit with red.

"Okay, girls, time to retire," said Auntie Peg, teetering off. "I'll see if there's anything cheesy, Emily, and have Miguel bring out some butter cookies and juice."

"She has got to be kidding," Anne scoffed as Auntie Peg took another eighteen years to wobble out of the room. When she made it to the doorway, she rang a bell set on a Limoges dish.

Miguel, otherwise referred to by Auntie Peg as "Miguel, my but-
ler of twenty-three years," entered carrying a tray. Now this was curious on many levels. That someone other than schoolchildren or
herd animals would answer to the sound of a bell. That someone
used a bell to get service from a human being. That Miguel had
been asked on his interview twenty-three years ago if he'd object to
being called upon in the manner of indentured servants.

On the coffee-table, he arranged the tea, juice, and butter cookies with oversized sugar granules that came stacked in pastry cups
from a round tin with a Danish flag.

Anne took in the setting, making mental calorie counts of each
item.

"You look terrible. Thin—but terrible."

Thanks. Glad to see you too.

"And are those Rogan?" she then said, analyzing my butt.

I nodded insouciantly, afraid that this would turn into an involved conversation, as Anne and I have been know to discuss designer low-slung jeans for over an hour. Between Auntie Peg and
Anne, my IQ dropped to monkey-pointing-at-ink-blot percentages.

"All of my low-slungs were donated to Goodwill because of the
things I gave Jason," she said.

I didn't know Jason to be the type who would give his wife butt
implants.

"Try to find a man that won't insist that you have these children—absolutely atrocious on the ass. I'm even considering having
a nip and tuck down there."

Ever hear of a Stairmaster?

"You have a great butt."

I was definitely one part lesbian—now the incestuous kind.

"And it's not as if these jeans are so great. It's actually pretty uncomfortable trying to veil your crack when you sit down," Anne
said.

"Hey!" I shrieked. Tired of tiptoeing around Anne's personality
disorder, I felt compelled to take a jab at her for all the aggrieved
years she gave me. "You were a Sassoon jean girl!"

"We never discuss my Sassoon jean period."

"Ooo. La la. Sassoon," I hummed.

Anne looked at me as if I were the only person in the room, which was partly true.

"I think I even have pictures from my birthday party at the roller rink."

I needed to find those pictures, which could have future leverage.

"Enough with the jeans. The real problem is my enormous butt," she said.

Please. Calling her butt enormous would be like calling an airplane pillow cushioned.

"But why don't you try adding an extra twenty minutes to your workout?" I offered blithely.

I was under the laser of death.

"You find twenty minutes in my day. Where? Where do I have twenty minutes?"

Start with the inane lunches, conversations on trends and shopping, tormenting the household help.

"I think Dr. Perricone just came out with a new cellulite cream."

"Tried it. Tried them all. None of them work."

I wondered how many thousands of dollars worth of bills Jason had to pay off for cellulite cream.

"And what's your obsession with that Perricone man?" she said, looking around the room as if it smelled like knock-off Tresor. "And we don't need to invite any of our mutual friends to this place."

"And here I already sent out invitations to the party I'd be throwing to celebrate my new single status."

"Right. You need to be dating again," Anne said, all business.

"I don't need to date. I have three Birkin bags and delivery service."

"Why don't you go for Gilbert Fenwick Grier? He asked about you at that party I threw six years ago at Bungalow number 8."

And you're telling me this now?

I winced. "No thanks." Sarcasm crept into my voice.

The idea of dating again held about as much appeal as going on a trip where you needed to pack a roll of toilet paper, especially dating boys named Gilbert Fenwick Grier who used Anne as a conduit to express their interest in me.

We sat down. Anne assembled the tea strainer over a cup and poured the kettle over it cautiously, repeating the process on a fresh cup.

"Or what about John Forrester?" Anne's eyes brightened. "Someone awfully rich just died in his family. And he is still keeping his job at Goldman."

"John Forrester looks like a pedophile."

"Bradley Glickman?"

Bradley Glickman was the type who covered his test paper as I attempted to cheat from it. Was this what would become of me? I'd have to end up with the guy who didn't let me coast through junior year physics with all of that wasted time I had to put in by doing the assigned reading.

I took a cautionary sip of my tea. It was strong and hot.

"Could you please pass the honey?" I asked.

"Honey is very high on the glycemic index. I'm surprised. Surely you should know that honey is not Dr. Perricone approved."

"Could you please pass the honey?"

"Daphne made an odd suggestion about your choices."

"You two are discussing me?"

"She's worried about you. Saying that you seemed dangerously close to having feelings with that J person. Never, never get your emotions involved."

Right. How could I forget—bagging a husband was a profession.

"How about that Preston doctor person who showed interest in you?"

Preston was one of my past setups. Good over cocktails. The extent of his purpose.

"And then there's all the other ones you've let slip away that you should reconsider."

Anne spoke with an affected accent, as if she spent the past day watching Grace Kelly movies. This became grating, and I considered telling her before realizing the harm that would come.

"I don't need closure on past relationships."

"You do. Rally, you do. What would you think of yourself if you let one of them slip away? Rally, Emily, be sensible."

Rally? Apparently Grace Kelly didn't copyright her voice.

"That Preston, pretty successful I hear. He started a plastic sur-gery animal practice in Aspen."

That was the stupidest idea I'd ever heard. I thought of Heroine receiving a prosthetic leg. That was the most fantastic idea I'd ever heard.

"You should visit him. I read this article in the Styles section about destination boyfriends—very hip right now."

"I'll leave my trends to shoes."

I did envision a trendy Web site—professionalhusbandhunting .com. You scrolled down a bar to "Destination Boyfriends"—the L.A. film producer, Miami music mogul, British media heir. In fact, this was-n't a bad idea. It would give Anne a career, possibly enlightening her with more perspective. You could even say it could save her pro-fessional marriage. I could help design the site and be a private backer, cashing in on her tawdry earnings, where she'd be the brand image. Her suddenly chic Grace Kelly accent would squeeze out Catherine Zeta-Jones, earning her more cash as the voice of T-Mobile. She'd host parties and singles gatherings in various cities. Perhaps I would even meet someone interesting at one of these events. But not an actual client—an investor or potential buyer, as this thing would be hotter than Starbucks. We could host our events at a Starbucks, create new flavors to their limited selection, also use coffee beans with less acidity. I looked for my pad to write all of this down, noticing Anne watching me, looking entirely inconvenienced. Fine. So be it. She'll now be out billions.

"Well, I didn't rally want to say this."

Cousin Anne seemed to spend time with Auntie Peg, as I had to say, "Say what?"

"That J person has been buying tickets for all my benefits."

Panic spread through my body; I feared that Anne would pick up on my thirst for the essentials: "How many tickets did he ask for? Did he call directly or have his secretary make the call? Did he leave a forwarding address? Do I really look thin?"

Anne scanned me, relishing her control.

"Well, why would he want tickets for one of your events?" I blurted.

"Duh! You've basically been unreachable since your episode."

She said "episode" like it was "nervous breakdown." I knew that my cancelled engagement must have been a blow to Anne for the association to scandal factor.

"You've been this sort of recluse, like those bygone actresses who rescue animals and buy beauty products from the Home Shopping Network. It would be a complete waste if you turn out to be some street vagrant that you knew had a proper upbringing from the orthodontia smile."

I never had braces.

"And living here will be of no help." She took in the room with that sour face of hers. "All Auntie Peg has is one dial-up phone, for God's sake. Whatever happened to your cell?"

Good question. J3 must have still had it from the time I loaned it to him. But that wouldn't make sense.

"Actually, can I borrow your cell? I really need to check my messages."

Again, Anne looked extremely inconvenienced. She fished through her bag and procured a phone not yet available to the general consumer, but she'd managed to get on Motorola's special product lists with the same efficiency she had in securing the special-edition LV bags.

Her phone rang as soon as she turned it on, which I imagined to be typical for her, as her expression was another version of looking extremely inconvenienced.

"Hello!" she snapped.

"Well, then why the hell do I even have a nanny if my son needs to speak to me?" Anne said to the woman who raised her children.

She paused, drumming her finger on her arm.

"Jeffrey! Do what Gretchen says. Now put her back on the phone. So, I basically handled that one, Gretchen. Now you know not to disturb me again on this phone unless it's an emergency."

Anne snapped the phone shut.

"Do you still want to use my phone?"

Uh.

"So? What is it, Emily?"

Considering all of the inconveniences Anne had been through, I decided that checking two weeks of messages pertaining to work and potential romance could wait. I nodded that I was okay.

"So why is J3 making the social rounds? He hates those things," I said as lightheartedly as possible to diffuse Anne's rancid mood.

"He probably wants to see you."

!!!

"But J3 knows I wouldn't attend any of your parties."

I didn't mean to say that.

"I found that odd as well. I mean, my parties really aren't your level."

Yes, of course Anne would see it this way.

"As much of an improvement as he is from that what's-his-name-with-the-dark-hair person." She snapped her fingers. "The last one you were with."

Henry Philips was his name. But Anne had only met him at social gatherings.

"So glad you ended it with that artist freak."

And what did she really think of the man I intended to marry?

"I mean, cavorting with some hussy type who grew up drinking powdered fruit drinks."

I loved Hi-C.

"He's actually with someone new," I said. "An aspiring pop star. Apparently she cut a CD."

"And this means what? Any kid can just cut a CD. It's as easy as burning a disc."

That sounded hard.

"So what label is she with? Who's her manager? When will she start touring? Jason works with Sony on a lot of deals. I can get the update, but need details."

"Right. I'll just send Henry an e-mail, asking him to furnish me with those facts you need."

Anne shook her head and in loud, articulate mumblings complained how inept I was. She did show extreme reason and control here, making me reassess her aptitude as more than a pretty package that didn't work like those fake television sets they display on furniture at Gracious Home.

"I'd just as soon move away from this disaster and work on the next one. This J something or the other—you need to play this one according to my terms. None of this head in the clouds, kindred spirits nonsense."

She'd been speaking with Daphne and Mother. I welcomed that idea as much as a community of ants conducting their town meeting on my kitchen table. They viewed the events of my life as entertainment, recapped like one of our favorite shows.

Anne started making her ramblings, otherwise known as The Girl's Guide to Husband Hunting—she really could make billions with the added book deal—saying things about balls in courts and unavailability.

"So my next party is Olde New York at the Frick. You will be on the list. And try not to wear one of your riskier outfits. Save such liabilities for a weekend outing in the Catskills or somewhere."

She paused, thinking loudly.

"Perhaps I'll just have something sent to you."

51

Anne wasn't kidding about the one dial-up phone. Auntie Peg had one dial-up phone mounted to the kitchen wall and a hall phone with a coily wire. Not having a cordless was as inane as changing television stations without a remote. Though I did hold Auntie Peg in a new regard in not subjecting herself to the self-inflicted brutality of depending on automated services—possibly the secret of how she's lasted this long. Considering life without e-mail and touchtone pads, I became frantic.

The phone mounted on the wall rang, a school-bell kind of toll from back when children clambered to class carrying milk pails filled with books and pencils sharpened by a pocketknife. I answered, "Hello."

"Er, hello?"

"It's Emily, Dad."

"Right. Emily," he said, repeating my name so he'd commit it to memory.

I opened and shut drawers lined with slippery paper in floral patterns resembling one of Mrs. Hallingby's dresses. Inside a cabinet hung a rack of spices, probably last used on a Betty Crocker recipe. The scent of old spice should be designated to the first boy you kissed.

Dad then mumbled with cross-bearing effort, "So your mother says you are temporarily residing at your Aunt Peg's."

Meaning my mother had forced my still-need-to-take-a-paternity-test father to call me, otherwise he'd as soon hold out till the next holiday for the one-on-one.

"Yeah. Breaking it off with your fiancé because he has a thing for brain-deficient Latinas can hamper your living arrangement."

Silence.

"So I'm actually thinking of buying a place," I said, just entertaining the idea, as it would be easier to get my own place rather than update Auntie Peg's to this century.

"Really!"

He said this as if he discovered a new tax break, which, I discovered, would be a benefit if I bought my own residence. Dad now spoke to me with his professional voice, having more clarity and ease.

After he asked for my e-mail, I quickly gathered my things so I could make a stop at Gracious Home. I noticed a note in my bag with Auntie Peg's distinctive flared handwriting. Evidently she had slipped this message into my bag. I couldn't help but wonder if the old woman had the boldness to snoop.

On a square Carroll & Dempsey card embossed with her initials, it read that there was something for me in the attic. I read it twice while my back straightened into an exclamation point. I then sprinted upstairs with images of Hermes bags, Cartier watches, and a vintage Mercedes roadster, disappointed to find an easel artfully placed in one of the window's alcoves. From outside, these windows distinguished this house from the other two that sandwiched it, popping like Marge Simpson eyes. On the window's ledge sat an ashtray, the blameless surface stained from the stubs of cigarettes, and what seemed destined to be a vase or jug settled into a squat plate, like a misguided biology major who changes bedpans.

A piece of vellum paper was clipped to the easel; a box of watercolors sat on a side table with brushes and charcoal pencils arranged in a vase like flowers. I used oils. I supposed I had to cheer myself with sentiments on thoughts that counted. I could really use a Cartier tank.

The attic wasn't your festooned with cobwebs kind, fractured with shadows over a range of sheets draping sewing machines, popcorn makers, and other unwanted Christmas gifts that would be rejected by the Salvation Army. In New York, a painted-in square for your car, a kitchen that can fit a cocktail table and stools, a closet strictly to hang your winter coats—these spaces denote extravagance.

Black watch plaid carpeted the floor, and the hunter green that dominated the plaid coordinated with the couch and two wing-back leather chairs. A mahogany side table had a green lamp with a shade as big as an *Allure* editor's beach hat and a plaid Hermes candy dish with a matchbook from Trader Vics. I took a match and lit it, watching the flame bulge and wane. Not knowing what to do with the spent match, I opened the closet to find a trash can that no one would think to dispose. Boxes shelved one wall, which I briefly considered snooping in but rationalized nothing compelling could be found among Auntie Peg's things. I also figured her to be the mothball type. Just a whiff and I'd suffer food poisoning consequences. Mom used cedar blocks after my mothball incident. I'd mistaken them for sugar cubes (I was young and addicted to sugar).

I scanned the closet a final time. She had an entire wall devoted to pug coats with labels more impressive than Princess Raina's. Next to a row of pink taffeta-covered hatboxes was a rectangular box. I thought of jewels stacked in velvet cases and a Cartier Milanese that Auntie Peg probably had no memory of. Holding my balance on a stepladder, I quickly flipped off the lid. Tearing through real estate transactions, certificates, financial documents, and deeds of no importance, my disappointment washed away upon finding a fan of cockatoo feathers, something I've never seen or would think to buy. I carefully spread out each perforation until it fully opened. The puffs resembled cones of cotton candy, which would go perfectly with a new dress.

52

Browsing through the same rack as another shopper does not entitle you to be friends by associative tastes and size label. My hand came disturbingly close to a girl in a red macramé hat the shape of a Hershey's Kiss, which had its final wear before it reached its trend expiration date. When I shot her my stare of death, she flashed me the smile I used to get free drinks, as if this entire rumination on my dilemma between Henry and J3 had crystallized into my lesbianism.

I dropped my competitive nature and moved to another rack.

"How great is this?" screamed Girl-who-lusted-for-me, holding up the most divine silver drop-waisted dress secured with two gilded straps. "It's so Nicole Kidman!"

Here's why we'd never make it to the second date. Firstly, Nicole Kidman's complexion would be washed out from such a dress. And it didn't take anyone who understood the value of reading Fitzgerald as opposed to seeing the hip-hop film adaptation to know that the dress's designer had Zelda in mind.

She then looked at the price tag and became quite hysterical, her body frenetic as if she jumped to an invisible rope.

"And it's my size and on sale!"

After sufficiently burning a thousand calories, Girl-who-lusted-for-me looked at the rack and then at me.

"Oh. It's the last one. Did you see a salesperson?"

I did. In the lingerie section.

"No."

"Well, then would you mind just keeping an eye on it for me while I get someone to assist? It can be rather Winona-ish moving from different departments while holding merchandise."

"Sure," I said sweetly.

Girl-who-lusted-for-me handed me the dress. Feeling it. Admiring it. It was the kind of desire I knew only from my first out of three hundred viewings of seeing Michael Schoeffling seated behind a school desk during homeroom. Not that I had homeroom period with Michael Schoeffling, which would have sufficiently completed the requirements of a fulfilled life.

The dress, seemingly made for my feathered fan, was reduced from numbers that could buy a compact car to the price of a knock-off dog carrier. The dress had turned me into something that would make the touch of my fingers burn pages of The Good Book. I vowed that I'd go to church next Christmas.

Through the partition glass, my eyes followed Girl-who-lusted-for-me as she absently looked about. As soon as she disappeared, I shook my head, effectively displaying the effects of shea butter hair products. After my inner thermostat went from hot to cold, deliberating if I should enact my sordid act, I stealthily darted to the section where the saleshelp filled in her slow day by assisting a lady who matched her cherry lipstick to her shoes and bag.

"I need to get this fast," I said, draping the dress on the counter.

"I will be with you in just a moment," she said in salesperson training day delivery.

A moment?

How long was a moment in actual time—like a crime mystery solved in CSI time or helping this woman color-coordinate her lingerie drawer?

"Please. I'll pay cash."

I had taken out considerably more money than needed to buy illegal drugs, also rationalizing that it would be more prudent to pay with cash, fearing that Girl-who-lusted-for-me may attempt to track me down, perhaps even stalk me—something I've been a victim of in recent history.

The saleswoman, with the unspoiled hands of someone who actually uses the moisturizer gloves you get in a beauty gift basket, looked at the lady that really did need assisting. She seemed to be giving serious consideration to a brassiere with enough padding to give Anne's butt some depth. I gave them my most artistic Emily doleful look—one usually designated for boys doing tedious assembly-required tasks that involved reading the directions.

The saleswoman took the dress and rang it up, paying me with occasional disapproving looks like a teacher changing the score of a failing test paper after hearing dead relative pleas.

Mine. Mine. Mine! I screeched to myself, all villainous.

"Thanks! Bye!" I said, and then took my change and stuffed it into my bag. The shopping bag rattling against my thigh, I became a current of determination to remove myself from Bergdorf's premises in blinding time.

Outside, I gulped in breaths of polluted air, looking down to the lilac of my bag, and my exhilaration quickly channeled to pragmatics. Apparently my efforts to not be so pragmatic had not taken hold, becoming concerned about not trying the dress on.

I called Mom.

"Who is your tailor again?" I asked.

After scolding me on proper phone announcement, she said, "Sonya. Amazing woman. But I can't quite figure why she has her business in an apartment in the corridor adjacent to the front lobby along with a few doctors' offices. And she smokes like a chimney. But no longer around the clothes—I addressed that."

"And Sonya's date of birth, SAT scores, and views on changing the interest rates?"

"I'm sorry, dear?"

"Her number? I just bought this truly amazing dress. I even had to resort to some underhanded measures in order to obtain it. But it will probably need to be fitted."

"A new dress! For Anne's party, I assume! I'd love to see it on you. Are you going to get it fitted now? I can call and see if she can squeeze you in. It is pretty difficult to secure an appointment with Sonya, you know. It's not the taking-in-a-straggler-off-the-street kind of establishment. No. Walk-ins are not her line of work. And did you buy the proper undergarments for this fitting?"

Not the undergarments conversation.

Every girlhood morning I'd be pushed off to school along with warnings from my mother to "wear good underwear" in case I was hit by the drunk Mac truck driver who went for such targets. As if the paramedics would stop treating me because I wore objectionable undergarments.

"You could have told me to look both ways before crossing the street."

"Whatever are you talking about, Emily?"

"Nothing that we have to get into now."

"So you have to get proper undergarments. Perhaps just pick something up at Bergdorf's. Aren't you right there?"

I would not be going to the lingerie section of Bergdorf's for at least another month, envisioning my picture taped on the wall of shame.

53

After shopping at Gracious Home, I had that feeling I'd been had, happy but had, like eating Chinese food or taking in giant gulps of fumes when pumping gas. I spent $484.92 on things I didn't think I needed—the marketing brilliance of an establishment that sells needlepoint pillows, ceramic toothbrush holders and rattan storage boxes in aisles near the lamps with dimmers and the special bulbs they require. In the same process as filling a grocery cart or Sephora basket, I picked phones, plastic Lego-ish pieces, things with different colored wires, and stationery hand-colored with pugs for Auntie Peg. I stood on line with Carolina Herrera, who looked dressed for the opera. (Carolina bought four oatmeal-colored hand towels with stitching that looked like the footprints of Easter chicks.)

Returning home, opening the boxes, ready to plug everything in and be in working order, I found that setting up my purchases demanded more education than an MBA. I seemed to spend more time looking at the torn boxes of electronic goods than it could have taken to assemble this home into something ticking to a twenty-first-century beat.

I started with my laptop, figuring this simply entailed plugging it in and adding a cord to a double adapter. The room brightened to a space-age light. Feeling very smart and technologically savvy, I logged online via dial-up. This took about 1,800 minutes as I listened to the sound of sinus-infected aliens.

The laptop had dirty smudges of gray like the trudging tracks of an army of dust mites. Cross-examining the plate beneath the keys, I wanted a new computer, fresh with its new-toy smell. My accountant would describe me as being in "economic unreality," something he told me every year.

The electric blue of the Windex gleamed. I had nothing to do as I waited another 1,800 minutes, give or take a minute, for Internet access. Spraying the computer, clearing the screen before the dissolving cleanser would leave an amoeba-shaped residue, I had a rush from seeing the bright difference. The smudges were still beneath my keyboard, like globs of makeup in the corners of a club girl's eyes, and I yearned for that new computer. I sprayed the keyboard, sliding a thin cloth along the ridged columns.

With access to my e-mail, I had the little girl excitement of opening presents at a birthday party with farm animals, or on my birthday being given a Cartier bag. There were about 1,800 messages from my father with subject lines on realtors, taxes, and mortgage rates that I systematically checked and deleted without reading. I decided that I no longer wanted to buy an apartment.

Then I saw his name:

J3 Hopper. Subject: Where Are You?

I screamed, looking around in case I was noticed.

My Emily:

Either you've eloped with Michael Schoeffling, are doing an Agatha Christie disappearing act to further your career, or, which I dread, intentionally trying to avoid me. You couldn't possibly be trying to avoid me?

I've been in London on business for the past few weeks. It reminds me of Prague during the revolution. Did Czechoslovakia even have a revolution?

After resting my arms from cheerleader position, I began to type. Nothing typed. The keys of my keyboard betrayed me. I broke my keyboard. There were residual smudges left from the gloppy cleaner between the letters. I could only use the arrow, effectively forwarding Daphne his e-mail.

Shutting off the computer, I decided to contend with this later. I had to put my immediate desire to connect with J3 at rest, sketching out sentiments that positioned me as the no-man-can-live-without type. This required some effort, and I searched for a distraction. Looking to the other packages, my eyes darted to the Ford Thunderbird of freezers. Behind door #1 awaited a pint of Ben & Jerry's. Packages. Freezer. Packages. Freezer. A deliberation was put on hold by that mustard yellow dial-up phone mounted on the kitchen wall ringing its dated ring, which rattled my hollow body that had the stillness of this house without its yapping pugs.

"Emily?"

It was Dash, my once-best-friend then fling-that-should-have-never-happened. That Dash could have the role of main supporter in my life was something I never considered now that he's spoken for. I thought about this sometimes. Now a husband who offers his wife's opinions on world issues in casual conversations and keeps an entire livelihood robust with his devotion to gingham and khaki, Dash and Katrina moved to Fairfield County by choice. Dash and I have not kept in regular touch.

"Hi, Dash. How did you get my number?"

"I work in television."

Right. Of course.

"Track Osama yet?"

"Er?"

"Anyway, I love your timing. First, you saved me from Ben & Jerry."

"I've been known to save you from them before. Wouldn't it be better if I just had those guys assassinated?"

"More importantly, I sprayed my computer screen with Windex."

"You shouldn't do that."

And you're telling me this now?

"The keys don't work. I can't send e-mails!"

"Did you spray your keyboard?"

"No!"

Of course I did.

Hearing the hum of a refrigerator silence, I tapped the phone to make certain it still worked, activating Dash.

"I logged on to the Apple site. They recommend turning off your computer, draining the board of any spillage. Do you have a computer fan?"

Silence, followed by funny stares at the receiver.

"Right, forgot who I was dealing with."

"Should I use a hairdryer?"

"Not a wise move. The heat could be damaging."

"Just like the sun."

"Er. I guess."

I then said in a panic, "But Dash, this is horrendous. I really need to send an e-mail, and I'm trying to get all of these phone things and caller IDs installed. I really am not in my element on this one."

More silence.

"Dash?"

"It's just that I am all too familiar with the scenario and can't get past an Emily image—you plugging an adapter, the room going dark, and your frame bounced into the air as a fluorescent skeletal figure. Do you have the packages right there?"

"Yes!"

I walked over to the boxes with the phone nestled between my chin and shoulder until it slipped and ricocheted around the room like an exploding can as I dodged it with Charlie's Angels dexterity. The phone wasn't cordless.

Picking it up, "Dash!"

"Ow," he said, not too happily.

"Sorry!"

"What's your Aunt Peg's address?"

I could hear Dash's scribbling as I told him this.

"You'll see me in fifteen."

Hanging up, I hair-dried the keyboard.

54

"Dash!" I screeched, swatting my throat to shoo away the demon that had stolen my voice.

He wore a blue gingham shirt under a slate-gray cashmere sweater. The khakis were new, fitted to his new life that had transferred his gym membership to a Metro-North commuter pass. His hair was slicked back, a consistent style that made him look like he traveled with an invisible wind fan.

He leaned in and kissed me on the cheek. Very polite.

"Thank you!"

Dash became flushed. I needed to get him some water. Ringing for the bell, testing out my hostess skills, I realized that Miguel no longer came attached to it unless he could beam *Star Trek* from Palm Beach.

"And how's Darien?"

"New Canaan."

Same thing.

"Katrina and I would love to have you up."

And that will happen, never.

"So where's the damage?"

I led Dash to the kitchen. Stealing a glance, he looked about as if he were in the vestibule of an aquarium.

Pointing to the boxes, I poured two glasses of water, handing Dash a glass as he looked through the madly torn packaging.

"Emily?"

"Oh. Would you prefer a drink? Glass of wine perhaps?"

"Please don't tell me you threw away the directions?"

I had.

"There were no directions."

"Emily," he scolded, giving me looks like I was a child with a green monster in her closet.

"You always were so anal," I said, having to retrieve the directions from a pile luckily not yet recycled.

"Need help?" I asked, unhelpfully.

"Screwdriver?"

"If you don't mind Stoli and OJ from a carton?"

"Phillips screwdriver."

"Right! I can do this."

I remembered seeing a basket of tools in the attic and excused myself while Dash plugged in the machine and set in some codes.

I returned to the kitchen. Dash had tidied up the mess. He's always been good that way. I handed him the Phillips screwdriver and remarkably passed that test.

He looked at the wall phone and became agitated.

"I'd remove this for you, but perhaps you'd rather call a curator from the Met. This thing may have some historic value."

"Maybe I should just call a guy," I offered.

"That would be a good idea."

"How does one call a guy that doesn't come dressed in gingham and Burberry?"

Dash dismounted the phone, very talented that way, assembled the new phone, and conducted a series of tests.

"So, do you want a lesson?"

No.

"Okay," I said, unhelpfully.

He started going over numbers and buttons. I wanted to make Screwdrivers.

"Emily? Are you even paying attention?"

I felt like I was being explained something by a teacher after class when I really wanted to trade sheets of puffy stickers with my friends.

"Why don't you just figure it out after the phone charges and call me if you have any questions."

"Okay!"

He smiled. I smiled back.

"And the reason I phoned you earlier."

Right. Dash had called me and, I gathered, not to pay me a visit to assist with all of my projects.

"I just wanted you to know how proud I am of you."

"Well, thanks, Dad. I mean the comprehensive essay part was rather difficult, but that private tutor really did help."

"About you and Henry."

"Right! Henry and me. Or the Henry and me of Emily past."

"Are you okay with this?"

Couldn't be better.

"Sort of. I mean I would feel a lot better if I had a Cartier Milanese."

Dash smiled. It didn't seem like he would be giving me a Cartier Milanese.

"I also feel really bad that we've been out of each other's loop." He paused. "Probably because . . ."

You married a woman who has a matching coat for shopping at Stew Leonard's.

"Well, I've never been a big fan of Henry's."

I had many questions.

"Stop looking at me like that."

"Like what?"

"In that Emily way of yours."

"Which Emily way?"

"Right. There are so many Emily ways."

"Yes. There are."

"So what's with the stare?"

"What's the real reason you never liked Henry?"

"Don't go there."

I wanted to go there.

"Quit staring at me."

"Not until you tell me what's up."

"It's just that every time I was around that guy he made me feel like I was a participant in the latest celebrity scandal."

"There's a celebrity scandal?"

"Who knows—there's always one. You pick."

I found this assignment difficult. Scandals had more substance in the days of Burton and Taylor.

"Dash," I marveled. "Always the expert."

"I do have standards and good judgment."

"When are you running?"

"I don't think I could. My policy on death to superhero villains may appear too radical in the celebrity age."

We both looked at the new phone, out of place in Auntie Peg's marigold and palace blue tiled kitchen.

"Maybe I just never got you two?" Dash said. The secretiveness of his tone made me move in closer. My head hurt from all of the work I've had to do.

"Perhaps you guys were a raging couple proportioned to that rock-star-married-to-supermodel period. I mean look at the success of Yasmin and Simon LeBon, Paulina and Rick Okasek, the hot red-headed chick and the Whitesnake guy."

"You listened to Whitesnake? A guy I dated listened to White-snake?"

In bringing up that we dated, I just touched the gorilla in the living room. We both looked at each other curiously and then the gorilla assumed its normal resting position.

"You're much better off without him."

After making future plans that we would never keep, I tried to picture the children Dash and Katrina would produce, looking like the tow-headed models wearing personalized roll-neck sweaters in those business-card-sized ads in *Town and Country*.

"Remember J3?" I asked.

"Of course I do. Now there's a guy who scores high points."

"What do you think—"

"You're not involved with J3 Hopper?"

"No. He's with someone, anyway."

"Emily and J3—that adds up to something."

I felt like part of a calculus equation.

"So there's this party at the Frick that J3 will be at. I hate doing this," I said.

"Hate having to go to these things or hate having to ask me for something? You did have an interesting way of getting me to agree to projects I didn't know I'd agreed to."

We looked at the new phone.

"Do you need an escort, Emily?"

I nodded.

"When is it?"

"Tomorrow night."

"I need to run it past Katrina."

"Should I write you a note?"

"No. You are one of the Katrina-approved girlfriends. And she has to leave for Europe this weekend for some family business."

Of course she did.

"Look at the time!" said Dash, looking at his watch.

I didn't have a watch.

"I'll pick you up tomorrow at 8:00 PM."

And I realized how easy it was to slip into old habits.

55

After watching the phone charge in the time it took to finish *Paradise Lost*, I called my mobile's number to check my messages, having to do this three times from punching too fast.

One was a click, which may have been from me, considering it gave the current time. The next message was from J3.

"The things that I will do to you the next time I get that chance" was all that he had said.

After I screamed, fully exorcising the house of Auntie Peg's dead husbands, I considered my next move. I needed to be very Bush deferring to Cheney, and called Daphne to give her the briefing. She was unreachable due to some doctor's appointment. I entertained myself by playing with my new phone and eating old lady cookies in the manner of Americans who buy their clothes from stores that sell lawn mowers and sue fast-food companies for their obesity.

I called Daphne on the hour her appointment ended.

"He called, left a message on the mobile VM."

"And how many times did you replay that message?"

"Three."

Thirty-four and counting.

"When are you going to erase the message?"

Considering that I had the tone of his voice and exact placement of his words committed to memory as clearly as the most quoted lines from *Sixteen Candles,* I supposed it was time to delete this message now stored in the database of my head. I'd delete it later.

56

Dash called me from his car. Through the window, I saw a Lincoln alongside the curb that had a hydrant. He motioned from the driver's window to verify his position. As I crossed the street before the flow of traffic would no longer be in my favor, Dash reached to push open the passenger door, and I asked him if he now moonlit as a chauffeur.

"Company car," he said defensively.

Of course.

"Right. Perks of moving to Greenwich."

"New Canaan."

"Same thing."

"I just got a Hummer. It's at home."

Silence.

"There are so many ways I could respond to this. But where should I begin?"

Dash said, "Ha, ha," waited for a cab to pass, and made a swift entry onto Seventy-second. He then commented on how nice I looked and I returned the favor. I pulled down the visor to check my appearance, but the mirror was entirely too small. I twisted the rearview. Dash adjusted its position after I applied a soft coating of lipstick. The only available parking garage was located six blocks from the museum, while my Auntie Peg lived seven blocks away. I decided not to point this out.

A smoky mist breathed into the night sky, and two globules fastened to my hand. Dash left me under the care of a bus stop and darted back to the garage. Returning, he opened up an umbrella— or party tent. We were then protected from a few isolated drops under this white dome with logos commemorating the partnership of a finance company and golf event.

Walking into the reception, I hid behind the curtain in a pink tutu anxiety, hoping we could bypass the Anne check-in. She had a patent curly wire plastered in her ear and was dressed in a sliver of the night sky with a black gown frosted with diamonds and a tiara. I wondered how the tiara reflected Old New York and attributed it to Anne's interpretation of historical facts. Anne moved the guests about in the manner of women and children being directed onto lifeboats attached to a sinking ship.

While I was looking for a fire exit or an Elroy Jetson knapsack with a helicopter propeller, she approached Dash and me. Dash was subjected to a snarl that a box of Bacon Bits couldn't subside. I'd now have to make a trip to Westport in order to repay him for his evening's services.

"He's here," Anne snapped.

I couldn't breathe, discovering that the waving of a fan does not generate oxygen tank effects.

"Dressed in tails, a silk duster, and top hat. Looking like a guy with a milk stool taming a food-deprived lion or that Monopoly board character."

I felt nude under the scan of Anne's judgmental gaze.

"Yes. You two will go perfectly together."

I didn't know what she meant by this but—considering this was Anne—something not good.

A cleared-out exhibition room contained New York's most elegant talisman, a big band orchestra playing Supertramp. Anne most likely farmed out the music responsibility to one of her minions, and I felt for the party planner in training who had failed at her task, as she would arrive at work on Monday to find her desk cleared and packed into a box.

Dash and I evaluated the dancing. The dresses began to stripe with perspiration, a lot of moves that relied too much on the shaking of one's head. Watching people dance at benefit events, I had to reconsider the talents of Britney Spears. I looked at Dash. The shimmer of the event lit onto his lapels.

"Drinks?"

I nodded.

"The usual?"

Another nod.

"I know, with vodka," he said in response to my expression.

He then left me, so I could do a more comprehensive search for the person I traveled to see with the anticipation of hobbits approaching their last leg of a quest. Just when I spotted the brim of a top hat, the back of J3's dark hair, Dash pressed the perspiring glass on my naked shoulder, which made me twitch. He muffled a few apologies.

"Dash!" said a girl in the voice of a vinyl record on the wrong speed. After flippant introductions and the city-is-a-small-world chatter, she began interrogating him on Katrina's whereabouts. I excused myself.

Again seeing the black shimmer of a top hat, I felt a tap to my shoulder.

"You!"

It was Bergdorf's girl-who-lusted-for-me, no longer lusting for me.

"You're wearing my dress!"

"Well, technically—"

I stopped myself, realizing that the timing of this confrontation needed to be postponed, or to never happen, and I excused myself. The brim of the top hat disappeared. I darted my eyes in desperation, scanning every silhouette. The swelter from dancing and the mustiness of the museum began to entrap me. My drink finished, I took a glass of champagne from a passing server and escaped outside.

The steps had the polish of a downpour and refreshing smell of a post-winter rain. There were a few other party truants who shifted about uncomfortably or sadly approached a spent cigarette, all men who came here for a moment not to be seen that gave me the faint notion of cutting class. I drank from my champagne in between flirty smiles, loving the shape of a flute and how the drink easily funneled into your body's stream.

Following a boy that looked about as ready to face a coliseum of lions, I morphed into party mode, drumming up excuses if the target of another Bergdorf's girl attack. Dash, towering above a moat of blond and black, waved uncomfortably. I waved back, planning my next move, and then felt the frisson of a light tap on my shoulder.

Ready to face the cool spray of Bergdorf's girl's sticky drink, I turned around.

It was J3.

57

He didn't say anything, just pressed his two forefingers against my shoulder and slightly maneuvered me toward the exit. I tried to stay focused on my posture, but the giggles inside me made it difficult to multitask.

"Do you have a coat?" he asked at the check-in. I pinched my ticket from the sewed-in pocket of my bag and gave it to J3. He returned, draping my goose-bumped shoulders while his fingers massaged me under the secrecy of the shawl. His hand slid down my arm, sending a current down to my wrist, and then led me outside.

This part hazy from being removed from formal surroundings. My eyes shut slightly. I felt him kissing me, pressing the hold button on my cool-as-Ingrid-Bergman strategy. This kiss had the potentially liable combination to mess with your head or be that kiss that began it all.

After another 1,800 minutes of this, I stepped away, wondering if this was real or fake. J3 did not appear to be leaving.

"It can be this easy," he instructed.

And, easy enough, there were no waits for cars or taxis. Edward pulled into view, ready to take us to wherever we wanted to go.

Driving through the city at night, we fumbled about. I found a distraction in tinkering with my fan. J3 chose this moment to drum his lapels and certify the whereabouts of his electronics. I supposed the absence of dialogue was appropriate for right now, considering we had to take in what we were experiencing.

This was awkward. This was awkward. This was awkward.

"Hey," I said, disrupting the car noise. "And what's with you and the picture of Amanda in *Vogue?* Are you working us both? Going to send me home in the limo crying?"

"That picture was taken about five years ago. Amanda and I have been off for quite some time. We actually broke up over the phone."

I quickly looked outside the window to offset my glow.

"You are so one of those guys," I said, keeping my eye on a man walking a fluffy dog.

"I am so not."

"So are."

"I did try to see her. Actually, it was that night I met you at Mellons. The trip to L.A. was to end things, but then she had to leave for Milan for three weeks and it couldn't wait."

"Oh!" That meant to be an "oh" of disappointment and concern.

"Oh," I repeated, more somber. "But you two seemed so simpatico. Had this whole voting-based-on-the-issues-rather-than-the-candidate-who-would-look-better-on-currency kind of relationship."

"And you and Henry seemed to have that ability to find humor in a package of cookies called Bananaramas."

That was pretty funny actually.

"So? What went wrong? Her calling you Jackson, I suppose."

"She always made this great effort to be serious. And I think the L.A. air had been getting to her. She's even been getting Botox injections! She's only 28!"

He sounded outraged.

"Actually, that's not so uncommon."

And why did I feel compelled to defend Amanda?

"You'd get Botox?" J3 sounded worried.

"God no! I have enough pricks poking me based on what I do for a living. But basically, I'm in the minority. And every celebrity gets Botox treatments the way I have a mani/pedi. They do it very discreetly, just a few annually, so it's not as noticeable."

J3 had on his curious expression.

"You can always pick something up while standing on the grocery line."

"It's for the best. Amanda already has a plan—to stay in Italy and perfect her Italian, travel, and take in the world's geography, languages, and cultures firsthand."

"Great. She'll make a man very happy some day. He'll never have to log on."

He smiled and quickly leaned into me, causing my head to bob, and we both laughed.

"Can we discuss how cute you are?" J3 asked.

"Okay!"

He took my hand. This seemed important to him, his taking my hand to underline something serious. A proposal!

"Cute you are. But not cute in a bad way."

"Cute in a bad way?"

"I mean, as a leather-clad dominatrix, perhaps you wouldn't look so cute."

"I don't mind looking cute."

"Really?"

"Yawning lion cubs are cute. I've been called worse."

A pixie.

"And do you mind wearing leather dominatrix swimwear?"

This didn't feel strange—J3 speaking to me in a mid-eighties miniseries kind of way.

"I'd dress up for you." This I said in a velvety voice. "Just be sure to get something from the new YSL collection. Not some Chelsea sex-shop pleather kind of place."

J3 bowed his head and then spoke.

"And how has this time been for you. Since the move? Things with Henry?"

"Weird, naturally. I mean, I did buy furniture with the boy."

"You haven't been in contact with me."

"Yes, about that. Well, I've been at my Auntie Peg's, and the last time her house had a new appliance, the pet rock was all the rage."

"Yet you still managed to send Daphne my e-mail."

My lips puckered into an *O*.

"Thought you didn't intend to hit the reply to sender button."

"Whoops! So I guess I get the Left Brain in Cab award."

"Your little blunder was actually a good thing. Gave me the determination. Oh!" he said, again padding his coat packets. "That reminds me, I have something for you."

!!!

J3 pulled my phone from the pocket of his camel coat. A ruffle of shimmery gray lining came out with it.

"I was happy to see that you kept your service activated all this time."

He returned my phone. I tried to mask my disappointment by sounding blonde.

"Goody."

J3 gave me his look, the sly one.

"But I really need to reimburse you. Knowing you, you'd never accept my paying your bill, so I thought I'd just give you this."

J3 just gave me a Cartier Milanese. I have never—

"How did you ever guess!"

"Emily?"

Right.

"And I found your cell to be the most effective Emily souvenir," J3 said, taking the phone from my hand so I could effectively play with my present. I had a Cartier Milanese. My life's mission accomplished at such an early age.

"So I have a few questions about your phone log."

"You went through my phone log?"

"Naturally."

Good man.

"You do have an entertaining system, Emily."

"Thank you."

I felt proud.

"Some names made sense, my work number being the Oval Office for instance. But do you really know Madonna?"

"Madonna is Daphne."

J3 nodded his head showing that he understood.

"And considering our current situation, I'm afraid to ask who Mustang Guy is."

"Guy who services my Mustang."

"Right. How obvious." And should I worry about Fun Bob?"

"Fun Bob! I love Fun Bob."

J3 looked crestfallen.

"Of course not *love*, just love. He's a friend from college. Good for lots of laughs—though his obsession with Monty Python is why we don't speak regularly."

J3 scrolled down to Frogger.

"Oh!" I screamed, taking the phone from his hand. I pressed the dial button.

"Excuse me for a second," I whispered, and then spoke into the mobile.

"Mrs. Hallingby? Hi, it's Emily! I just wanted to know if you ever found your frog prince."

She then rambled, profane-word free. Snapping the mobile shut, I became quite excited.

"Mrs. Hallingby said he was there all along, just hiding."

He smiled. Looking slightly confused, but happy.

"And who's 203?"

"Dash and Katrina. The only people I know in Wilton."

J3 paused, and I leaned in, chomping my teeth toward his nose.

"Right. About that, why wasn't Dash with Katrina tonight?"

"She's out of town, and I needed to have an affair to take a break from all of my relationship issues."

He credited my response without another probe, seeming embarrassed for even asking.

"Truly, I just hate these silly events. When Dash and I were close friends we were always each other's plus ones. We had a system and everything. That is, until he moved to Westport."

"I thought they lived in New Canaan?"

"Same thing."

"And why are you so opposed to Fairfield County?"

I looked out the window. We headed down Park, and I had no idea where we were destined.

"It's that whole pasteurization of life factor. But I suppose I picked up a few things from a boy I dated in college who lived in one of those towns."

J3 made no comment, wanting me to continue a subject I found tiresome.

"Let's see how I've benefited—first, there's this hyped grain alcohol thing. I don't care if you use Lemonade Crystal Light or Diet Dr. Pepper. There is no fun in mixing your drinks with grain alcohol unless you want to end your evening by staring into a bowl of toilet water."

I thought back to the weekends I had spent with Boyfriend Who Hailed from Fairfield, just a lot of tossing around a lacrosse ball, games of quarters, and his pouring packets of sugar on me whenever that Def Leppard song played.

"Oh," I chirped, remembering something cute.

I then motioned my lips in a lot of fish-blowing movements, not speaking the words.

"You love me?"

"No, silly. Olive juice!"

"Well, I love you."

58

J3 curved around me, his hand performing a dual function of holding his position and sliding up my dress. He whispered things in my ear that the mind of a hopeful artist could not imagine, which involved a combination of skills. The first, most powerful climax that night began from these words spoken in the back of a car driven by a man named Edward who would likely be shuttling J3 about till he's gray and spends weekends at his urologist's Vail condo.

J3 had temporarily located to a suite in the Sherry Netherland. I also learned that suites in the Sherry Netherland are designed for the needs of white-collar house arrest criminals, and decided not to leave. With no involved, over-breakfast-table formal discussions, J3 and I lived like Eloise and boyfriend in the later years. It always smelled clean here. Ripped-from-its-packaging new. Spraying my perfume, the scented mist came under attack from the air of newness, decimating the fragrance before it could hit my neck.

I awoke on a Wednesday, knowing it was Wednesday because the radio kept promoting music to help you through the hump day, and the date on the morning paper said so. I released a sigh of desperation. This would be a bad day. I was off and had no idea why. I searched the suite's kitchen closets and then the one in the hall. Becoming happy upon finding a Dirt Devil, evaluating an apartment that gleamed from a battalion of maids who wore little aprons around oatmeal-colored dresses and folded the toilet paper with an arrow. No accomplishment would result from my Dirt Deviling.

Turning on the Dirt Devil, I pushed its snout into those crevices no maid would ever consider, as they were paid a flat rate. Turning off the machine so I could change the plug to another outlet, I heard the phone. Accidentally flicking the switch so it made its revving sound right as I answered, I yanked the chord from the wall.

"What are you doing?" asked J3, sounding mildly worried.

"Just Dirt Deviling the corners."

"Emily, you know what I said about phone sex while I'm at the office."

I smiled, too frazzled to laugh.

"I have something for you."

"J3, you have to stop spoiling me. You'll take all of the fun out of Christmas."

I didn't mean this.

"I'll just give you a Christmas that rivals your '83."

It was '82.

"And I've thought about this spoiling. I'm a pretty smart guy."

"What were your SAT scores?"

"You need to know my SAT scores to determine whether I am smart?"

I nodded.

"Okay. I received a perfect score."

"So did I!"

"Now, establishing that we are both smart, and I want to see documentation later about those SAT scores, I've noticed this pattern with you. How you start to become a bit"—the line went quiet—"how should I say this, well, you treat your boyfriends rather wickedly when they fall out of sorts with you."

This was true.

"So, I won't ever allow that to happen with me. First off, I will put you in line when you act up."

"Like a dog on a choker?"

"I'm not giving you a diamond choker, Emily. But I will spoil you."

"That sounds like a good plan."

"So how am I doing so far?"

"Great. Wait. Do you ski? Please tell me you ski!"

"Don't worry, you can check that one off your list of points."

I made a check.

"So, can you be ready for me to take you to this surprise?"

J3 arranged to leave work early. He told me to pack enough things for a long weekend. Repeatedly saying that this meant four days' worth of clothes. My duffle was roomy, but had the appearance of being compact.

I then went to a European coffee bar and bought sandwiches of prosciutto, basil, and tomatoes on sourdough bread and bottles of their own iced green tea. Walking back to the hotel, lost in needed thoughts that would not leave behind sunglasses and toothbrushes, I saw J3 talking to a doorman dressed as a cavalry officer. He packed the car with my bags that I had left in the lobby, and complimented me on my foresight in getting sandwiches.

The late afternoon traffic already scrambled onto the conveyor belt of the Midtown Tunnel. I didn't mind. J3 had recently purchased an off-road vehicle sold to people with connections to the Department of Defense, and I had the task of programming the channels to J3's unset radio and arranging CDs. J3 poked a few buttons after I finished my task, like a parent adding a few numbers when reviewing their child's math homework. I wanted happy tunes and had rediscovered REMs earlier music, singing along, thinking I should be a rock star.

"So you just bought this car for today's secret excursion?" Our secret excursion had something to do with traveling to Long Island, noted by our driving on the LIE. I assumed that J3 had rented the house he spoke of a few months back.

"Partly. We'll need it for the summer."

"What about my Mustang?" I asked, handing J3 a sandwich. He reached for his food, made a point to look at me and smile, quickly returning to watching the car that inched its way in front of us.

"That's more of a weekend car. We also need a dependable car."

J3 was dependable.

"So. I take it you have more money than God."

J3 laughed.

"What's so funny?"

"You have iced tea on your nose."

I took a napkin from my bag, wiping off the iced tea. Olive oil dribbled from the sides of his sandwich. I gave him a fresh napkin.

"And why do we assume God has tons of money?" I asked. "Actually, I'd think God wouldn't be influenced by money and worldly possessions. They're inherently against his beliefs and values."

"Yes, but he is a man of power. Surely by osmosis and his stature as the supreme figurehead, he has wealth—an accumulative wealth, considering his age and range of power. The benefactors, donations. God has a lot of money."

He said this with such assertiveness, as if we discussed politics or the particulars of a business deal he put together.

I must have not awoken from my car nap, or J3 had a peculiar sense of humor, as I heard the breakfast cereal crackle of the drive of my Bridgehampton home.

"J3? What are we doing here?"

"You're awake," he said, pulling me from my dream.

Being especially low maintenance, my desires could never have schemed such a treat. J3 parked the car, got out, and walked in front of it, as my eyes followed him and I opened my door. He didn't help me out, but encased me so he commanded my attention.

"You may not have realized it, but I've noticed that you've been in a bit of a funk lately."

"I'm sorry. You know how I hate being an Eeyore."

"Don't apologize. I feel partly responsible."

He then started mumbling about cows and free milk.

"You haven't been painting."

I kissed his ear lobe.

"In order for you to get that piece of meat Daniel is hankering for, you need to be settled. We are here for three reasons: One. You will paint. Two. You will paint in the home I just bought."

My jaw opened, but J3 told me to shut up for once.

"The seller gave me a good deal, interesting guy. Could be on a box of popcorn. And Emily"—J3 helped me from my seat—"you will marry me."

59

Waking to a bright morning with a fresh snowfall, sitting fireside in a silk Valentino, the beams from a full moon, and the shine of a four-carat Harry Winston—J3 didn't want to chance it—there are certain glows that make your surroundings more beautiful. There's also that glow of pregnancy, but I couldn't be thinking about being pregnant at this time. Perhaps tomorrow. I began thinking about being pregnant. I'd have Marc Jacobs design me special little boxy jackets and leverage good accessories and wear stilettos.

I felt as if I had prematurely awoken from a dream of the sex-with-a-movie-legend kind, futilely attempting to fall back into sleep and return to where I had left off. Unfortunately, dreams don't have a rewind button. J3 should innovate such technology if he ever wanted to be a success destined for an *A&E Biography*.

We stared at each other till I knew the number of eyelashes he had, lying in the bed in my room because, even though this was now our house, I found it creepy to sleep in my parents' room—something J3 said I'd have to eventually get over.

"Why me?" he asked.

"Because you didn't give me a choice. Nice proposal, by the way."

"Give me another."

"Because you don't get mad when I ask your secretary to read over the famous people on your phone log."

"You do this?"

Yes.

"No."

He gave me a look.

"Perhaps once."

He gave me a look.

"I call her every afternoon at four when you do your video-conferencing thing."

"And another one."

"Because you're cute, sharp, dependable, and find my quirks irresistible."

"I find your quirks irresistible?"

"You do. And why me?"

"Because it's right."

After intense frolic behavior, we fell back to sleep. I then awoke from a dream with waterfalls and woodland sprites. I panicked, wondered if my imagination had been showing its wicked sense of humor again, like a film with subtitles that end with a sheet-covered body and you have to use your Intro to Film insight to figure out the meaning. Reassured to find J3 asleep next to me, I decided not to pinch his nose or amuse myself in other ways.

Still dressed in my pajamas, I wandered outside to my painting shed. A six-foot canvas was prepared for me next to a table with crystal knobs that displayed tubes of paints and brushes arranged in a jade-colored vase with the cloudiness of sea glass.

It poured from me, like recounting a trip moments after stepping off a Lear jet. J3 posed from behind, looking at me with that mix of mischief and admiration, while my waist was pressured in the vise of my knuckles, wearing an engagement ring absent of duct tape and a dress I've wanted to design based on a Louise Dahl photograph rubber-cemented in my inspiration book. We were the modern Phelps Stokeses, and if Sargent were alive, he'd have to take up yoga to keep in shape with the new competition.

"You did it," said J3, framed in the doorway. He walked to my side and turned his attention to me.

"Consider Daniel West your official suck-up toy."

J3 then slipped his hands around me, hugging me from behind. I turned to him and wiped my brush on his nose, making a stroke of purple. He took a brush, swished it in a bubble of white and firmed his feet in duel position, and we painted each other until our mess became dangerously close to staining Daniel's meat on the plate.

EPILOGUE

Two months later, we were married. The wedding felt like a midsummer night's dream without the woodland sprites, which are very hard to find. Barrels of fruit and flowers were illuminated from the randomly set torches in our backyard. I draped lilac shantung to create an aisle that could have been shorter, as I felt like the pews were chanting "Spaz, Spaz, Spaz," as I balanced an egg in a spoon. It led to a veranda on a stage that moonlit as the dance floor. I designed my dress to the specifications of the one I created on canvas and stuck honeysuckle in my hair like pins. We drank champagne cocktails and nibbled on bite-sized entrées.

I don't remember the photographer taking the pictures, but the simplicity is what made it novel. The most lucid moment was when J3 and I snuck away to the beach and danced under punched-in stars, the hem of my dress wet from splashing in the ocean. I asked him if he thought anyone would notice that we were missing. He assured me they wouldn't, saying it was almost four in the morning.

The sun nudged me awake. A jogger, up entirely too early for a Sunday, ran past us. J3 remained asleep on his coat jacket that we stretched out as a blanket.

"J3. J3. J3!"

"Emily, what is it?"

"Just wanted to make sure you're really here."

"I'm really here."

J3 had helped me to escape the Bridezilla.